A Girl of the Limberlost

A Girl of the Limberlost

GENE STRATTON PORTER

Illustrated

GRAMERCY BOOKS
NEW YORK

TO
ALL GIRLS OF THE LIMBERLOST
IN GENERAL
AND ONE
JEANNETTE HELEN PORTER
IN PARTICULAR

Foreword and "About the Author"
copyright © 1991 by Outlet Book Company, Inc.
All rights reserved.

This 1991 edition is published by Gramercy Books, distributed by
Outlet Book Company, Inc., a Random House Company,
225 Park Avenue South, New York, New York 10003.

Printed and bound in the United States of America

For this edition of A Girl of the Limberlost:
Cover design: Don Bender
Interior design: Helene Berinsky
Production supervision: Helen Marra
Editorial supervision: Claire Booss

Library of Congress Cataloging-in-Publication Data
Stratton-Porter, Gene, 1863-1924.
A girl of the Limberlost / by Gene Stratton Porter.
p.   cm.
Summary: Deeply wounded by her embittered mother's lack of
sympathy for her aspirations, Elnora finds comfort in the nearby
Limberlost swamp whose beauty and rich abundance provide her
with the means to better her life.
ISBN 0-517-07235-1
[1. Self-reliance—Fiction. 2. Mothers and daughters—
Fiction. 3. Forests and forestry—Fiction. 4. Interpersonal
relations—Fiction. 5. Moths—Fiction.] I. Title.
[PZ7.S9122Gi   1991]
[Fic]—dc20   91-28738   CIP   AC

8 7 6 5 4 3 2 1

Foreword

AT THE BEGINNING of the twentieth century, the American Midwest was a vast area of open plains, farmland, prairies, and fields. There were also pockets of woodlands, lakeland, marshes, and swamps. Today farmland, prairies, and plains still exist, but to a lesser extent, and most of the forests and swamplands have been cleared to make way for modern cities, larger farms, and the growing suburban sprawl which often extends from city to city.

At the turn of the century in Wabash County in northeastern Indiana, there was a vast swampland known as the Limberlost. Within its boundaries there were not only swamps and bogs, but pristine woods and meadows which reflected the beauty of the changing seasons. At the edge of this swampland, young Elnora Comstock, the girl of the Limberlost, grew from childhood to womanhood (just as her creator, Gene Stratton Porter, had done). When she was barely three years old, her father had drowned in a Limberlost swamp, and Elnora was raised by a bitter mother who mourned her husband and largely ignored her child. As a natural consequence, Elnora turns to the world around her and there finds great beauty and joy.

v

As a child, Elnora falls in love with nature—with all living things, and the Limberlost provides the antidote to her loneliness and emotional deprivation.

> Early June was rioting in fresh grasses, bright flowers, bird songs, and gay-winged creatures of the air...A turtle scrambled from a log and splashed into the water, while a red-wing shouted "O-ka-lee!" [She] paused and looked intently at the slime-covered quagmire, framed in a flower-riot and homed over by sweet-voiced birds. Then she gazed at the thing of incomparable beauty clinging to her fingers.

Elnora also turns to the people around her. Perhaps surprisingly, she gives love in such abundance that all who know her, or come to know her, cannot resist her warmth and selfless generosity. Whether it be a neglected urchin and his brother and sister begging for food by the wayside, the childless neighbors across the swamp, her snobbish classmates, the tradespeople, or her teachers, Elnora wins over everyone—except her own mother.

Elnora aspires to go to the high school in the city and then on to college. And it is the Limberlost that provides the wherewithal for her to achieve her goals. Unused to city ways, and unassisted by her mother, the naïve girl arrives at high school, on the first day inappropriately dressed in country calico and without books or equipment (having assumed that everything would be provided). She is humiliated by her ignorance and despairing. Then a sign in a shop window changes her life. Elnora discovers that the moths she collects are rare and valuable to others, to botanists, naturalists, and especially to "the Bird Woman." By selling her collections and continuing to gather more, Elnora is able to buy clothes and books, and even to reciprocate the favors of the city girls who, won over by her charm and guilelessness, have befriended her.

The story is not simplistic. The road to Elnora's maturity is littered with obstacles, and what begins as a love affair between a country girl and nature, gradually becomes a triangle—a love affair involving a girl and nature and a handsome young man from the city. The second half of the book is a true romance, complete not only with great expectations, broken hearts, noble decisions, confrontations, disappointments, and deceptions, but also journeys, balls, partings and reunions, and a most satisfactory ending.

Gene Stratton Porter's own love affair with nature is obvious on almost every page. Certainly this book will appeal to everyone involved with, or simply interested in, the environment and the natural sciences. On that basis alone, it is a timely book. But Porter is much more than a naturalist-historian. She is a writer with strong ethical values and she adeptly involves the reader by virtue of her own passion and artistry. At her best, she can be compared with Thomas Hardy, weaving an epic novel through scenes of haunting rustic beauty. Today, it is still possible to find the natural wonders that she so beautifully portrayed. But, even then, Porter could foresee the end of the Limberlost.

Men all around were clearing available land. The trees fell wherever corn would grow. The swamp was broken by several gravel roads, dotted in places around the edge with little frame houses, and the machinery of oil wells...Wherever the trees fell the moisture dried, the creeks ceased to flow, the river ran low, and at times the bed was dry. With unbroken sweep the winds of the west came, gathering force with every mile and howled and raved, threatening to tear the shingles from the roof, blowing the surface from the soil in clouds of fine dust, and rapidly changing everything.

This dramatic description of the environmental damage progress brings was written as it was happening—not after the fact.

What will never cease to exist, however, are the traits which make Elnora and her story so intensely appealing. It is impossible to read the book without empathizing with Elnora's personal victories. Her strength and uniqueness are best summed up as she speaks:

The Limberlost is life...What I like is the excitement of choosing a path carefully, in the fear that the quagmire may reach out and suck me down; to go into the swamp naked-handed and wrest from it treasures that bring me books and clothing, and I like enough of a fight for things that I always remember how I get them. I even enjoy seeing a canny old vulture eyeing me as if it were saying, "'Ware the sting of the rattler, lest I pick your bones as I did old Limbers." I like sufficient danger to put an edge on things.

A Girl of the Limberlost has a timeless appeal. The beauty of the surroundings in which the story takes place provides a literary testimonial to America's vanishing natural resources and an urgent call to preserve what remains. This, coupled with a main character of such dignity, perseverance, and strong moral values, makes this a book to treasure—a book for all ages. The Limberlost is gone, as Porter prophesied. But we can still enjoy its wonder if we listen to Elnora—

> ...Tonight we shall sing you the song of the Limberlost. You shall hear the big gold bees over the red, yellow and purple flowers, bird song, wind talk, and the whispers of Sleepy Snake Creek, as it goes past you. You will know!

PATRICIA BARRETT PERKINS

Baltimore, Maryland
1991

About the Author

GENE STRATTON PORTER was born Geneva Grace Stratton on August 17th, 1863 in Wabash County, Indiana. Her father was a farmer, and their home was near the vast swampland known as the Limberlost. As a child, she developed an interest in the wildlife of the swamp, which continued throughout her life. She collected moths, insects, and specimens of flora and fauna, and studied the birds and animals which she found near her home. Later, she turned to photography to capture her surroundings for others to enjoy. In 1886 she married Charles Porter, a local chemist, and they continued to live in the Limberlost region.

Porter's interest in nature led her to write magazine articles and to illustrate them with her photographs. In 1902, she wrote her first novel, *The Song of the Cardinal*, and in 1904, *Freckles* was published. It told the story of a young boy who lived in the Limberlost swamp and had a passion for its living creatures and air of humid mystery, and it became a bestseller of the time. *A Girl of the Limberlost* is the sequel to *Freckles*, portraying the next generation after Freckles, when he is a grown man. It, too, tells the story of a young person drawn to the richness of natural life in the swampland, and, this book, too, became an instant success.

One of the most popular and successful authors of her day, Porter was also prolific—in addition to innumerable magazine articles, and many novels, she also wrote books on natural history.

She died on December 6th, 1924 in an automobile accident in Los Angeles. She was 56 years old and at the time of her death, her books had sold in the millions. Today, there is renewed interest in her writing, as environmental consciousness grows steadily. She was a romantic with a magnificent ability to translate her passion for nature into writing.

EDITORIAL NOTE

The modern reader may be surprised to discover old-fashioned styles of punctuation and spelling, but these have been retained in order to convey the flavor of the original work.

CHAPTER 1

*Wherein Elnora Goes to High School and
Learns Many Lessons Not Found in Her Books*

"ELNORA COMSTOCK, have you lost your senses?" demanded the angry voice of Katharine Comstock as she glared at her daughter.

"Why, mother?" faltered the girl.

"Don't you 'why mother' me!" cried Mrs. Comstock. "You know very well what I mean. You've given me no peace until you've had your way about this going to school business; I've fixed you good enough, and you're ready to start. But no child of mine walks the streets of Onabasha looking like a play-actress woman. You wet your hair and comb it down modest and decent and then be off, or you'll have no time to find where you belong."

Elnora gave one despairing glance at the white face, framed in a most becoming riot of reddish-brown hair, which she saw in the little kitchen mirror. Then she untied the narrow black ribbon, wet the comb and plastered the waving curls close to her head, bound them fast, pinned on the skimpy black hat and started for the back door.

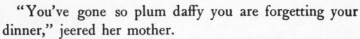

"You've gone so plum daffy you are forgetting your dinner," jeered her mother.

"I don't want anything to eat," replied Elnora without stopping.

"You'll take your dinner or you'll not go one step. Are you crazy? Walk nearly three miles and no food from six in the morning until six at night. A pretty figure you'd cut if you had your way about things! And after I've gone and bought you this nice new pail and filled it especial for the first day!"

Elnora came back with a face still whiter and picked up the lunch. "Thank you, mother! Good-bye!" she said. Mrs. Comstock did not reply. She watched the girl down the long walk to the gate and out of sight on the road in the bright sunshine of the first Monday of September.

"I bet a dollar she gets enough of it by night!" Mrs. Comstock said positively.

Elnora walked by instinct for her eyes were blinded with tears. She left the road where it turned south at the corner of the Limberlost, climbed a snake fence and entered a path worn by her own feet. Dodging under willow and scrub oak branches she at last came to the faint outline of an old trail made in the days when the precious timber of the swamp was guarded by armed men. This path she followed until she reached a thick clump of bushes. From the débris in the end of a hollow log she took a key that unlocked the padlock of a large weatherbeaten old box, inside of which lay several books, a butterfly apparatus, and an old cracked mirror. The walls were lined thickly with gaudy butterflies, dragonflies, and moths. She set up the mirror and once more pulling the ribbon from her hair, she shook the bright mass over her shoulders, tossing it dry in the sunshine. Then she straightened it, bound it loosely, and replaced her hat. She tugged vainly at the low brown calico collar and gazed despairingly at the generous length of the narrow skirt. She lifted it as she would have liked it to be cut if possible. That disclosed the heavy leather high shoes, at sight of which she looked positively ill, and hastily dropped the skirt. She opened the pail, took out the lunch, wrapped it in the napkin, and placed it in a small pasteboard box. Locking the case again she hid the key and hurried down the trail.

She followed it around the north end of the swamp and then struck into a footpath crossing a farm in the direction of the spires of the city to the northeast. Again she climbed a fence and was on the open road. For an instant she leaned against the fence staring before her, then turned and looked back. Behind her lay the land on which she had been born to drudgery and a mother who made no pretence of loving her; before her lay the city through whose schools she hoped to find means of escape and the way to reach the things for which she cared. When she thought of how she looked she leaned more heavily against the fence and groaned; when she thought of turning back and wearing such

clothing in ignorance all the days of her life, she set her teeth firmly and went hastily toward Onabasha.

At the bridge crossing a deep culvert at the suburbs she glanced around, and then kneeling she thrust the lunch box between the foundation and the flooring. This left her empty-handed as she approached the great stone high school building. She entered bravely and inquired her way to the office of the superintendent. There she learned that she should have come the week before and arranged for her classes. There were many things incident to the opening of school, and one man unable to cope with all of them.

"Where have you been attending school?" he asked, as he advised the teacher of the cooking department not to telephone for groceries until she saw how many she would have in her classes; wrote an order for chemicals for the students of science; and advised the leader of the orchestra to try to get a professional to take the place of the bass violist, reported suddenly ill.

"I finished last spring at Brushwood school, district number nine," said Elnora. "I have been studying all summer. I am quite sure I can do the first year work, if I have a few days to get started."

"Of course, of course," assented the superintendent. "Almost invariably country pupils do good work. You may enter first year, and if you don't fit, we will find it out speedily. Your teachers will tell you the list of books you must have, and if you will come with me I will show you the way to the auditorium. It is now time for opening exercises. Take any seat you find vacant." He was gone.

Elnora stood before the entrance and stared into the largest room she ever had seen. The floor sloped down to a yawning stage on which a band of musicians, grouped around a grand piano, were tuning their instruments. She had two fleeting impressions. That it was all a mistake; this was no school, but a grand display of enormous ribbon bows; and the second, that she was sinking, and had forgotten how to walk. Then a burst from the orchestra nerved her while a bevy of daintily clad, sweet-smelling things that might have been birds, or flowers, or possibly gaily dressed, happy young girls, pushed her forward. She found herself plodding across the back of the auditorium, praying for guidance, to an empty seat.

As the girls passed her, vacancies seemed to open to meet them. Their friends were moving over, beckoning and whispering invitations. Everyone else was seated, but no one paid any attention to the white-faced girl stumbling half-blindly down the aisle next the farthest wall. So she went on to the very end facing the stage. No one moved, and she could not summon courage to crowd past others to several empty seats she saw. At the end of the aisle she paused in desperation, as she stared back at the whole forest of faces most of which were now turned upon her.

In one burning flash came the full realization of her scanty dress, her pitiful little hat and ribbon, her big,

7

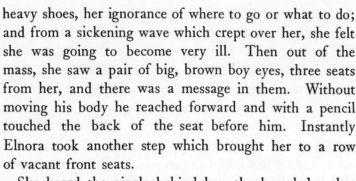

heavy shoes, her ignorance of where to go or what to do; and from a sickening wave which crept over her, she felt she was going to become very ill. Then out of the mass, she saw a pair of big, brown boy eyes, three seats from her, and there was a message in them. Without moving his body he reached forward and with a pencil touched the back of the seat before him. Instantly Elnora took another step which brought her to a row of vacant front seats.

She heard the giggle behind her, the knowledge that she wore the only hat in the room, burned her; every matter of moment, and some of none at all, cut and stung. She had no books. Where should she go when this was over? What would she give to be on the trail going home! She was shaking with a nervous chill when the music ceased, and the superintendent arose and, coming down to the front of the flower-decked platform, opened a Bible and began to read. Elnora did not know what he was reading, and she felt that she did not care. Wildly she was racking her brain to decide whether she should sit still when the rest left the room or follow, and ask some one where the Freshmen went first.

In the midst of the struggle one clean-cut sentence fell on her ear. "Hide me under the shadow of Thy wings."

Elnora began to pray frantically. "Hide me, O God, hide me, under the shadow of Thy wings."

Again and again she implored that prayer, and

before she realized what was coming, everyone had risen and the room was emptying rapidly. Elnora hurried after the nearest girl and in the press at the door touched her sleeve timidly.

"Will you please tell me where the Freshmen go?" she asked huskily.

The girl gave her one surprised glance, and drew away.

"Same place as the fresh women," she answered, and those nearest her laughed.

Elnora stopped praying suddenly and the colour swept into her face. "I'll wager you are the first person I meet when I find it," she said and stopped short. "Not that! Oh, I must not do that!" she thought in dismay. "Make an enemy the first thing I do. Oh, not that!"

She followed with her eyes as the young people separated in the hall, some climbing stairs, some disappearing down side halls, some entering doors nearby. She saw the girl overtake the brown-eyed boy and speak to him, and he glanced back at Elnora and now there was a scowl on his face. Then she stood alone in the hall.

Presently a door opened and a young woman came out and entered another room. Elnora waited until she returned, and hurried to her. "Would you tell me where the Freshmen are?" she panted.

"Straight down the hall, three doors to your left," was the answer, as the girl passed.

"One minute please, oh, please," begged Elnora. "Do I knock or just open the door?"

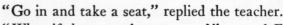

"Go in and take a seat," replied the teacher.

"What if there aren't any seats?" gasped Elnora.

"Class rooms are never half-filled, there will be plenty," was the answer.

Elnora removed her hat. There was no place to put it, so she carried it in her hand. She looked infinitely better without it. After several efforts she at last opened the door and stepping inside faced a smaller and more concentrated battery of eyes.

"The superintendent sent me. He thinks I belong here," she said to the professor in charge of the class, but she never before heard the voice with which she spoke. As she stood waiting, the girl of the hall passed on her way to the blackboard, and suppressed laughter told Elnora that her thrust had been repeated.

"Be seated," said the professor, and then because he saw Elnora was desperately embarrassed he proceeded to loan her a book and to ask her if she had studied algebra. She said she had a little, but not the same book they were using. He asked her if she felt that she could do the work they were beginning, and she said she did.

That was how it happened, that three minutes after entering the room she was compelled to take her place beside the girl who had gone last to the board, and whose flushed face and angry eyes avoided meeting Elnora's. Being compelled to concentrate on her proposition she forgot herself. When the professor asked that all pupils sign their work she firmly wrote " Elnora

Comstock" under her demonstration. Then she took her seat and waited with white lips and trembling limbs, as one after another the professor called the names on the board, while their owners arose and explained their propositions, or flunked if they had not found a correct solution. She was so eager to catch their forms of expression and prepare herself for her recitation, that she never took her eyes from the work on the board, until clearly and distinctly, "Elnora Cornstock," called the professor.

The dazed girl stared at the board. One tiny curl added to the top of the first curve of the m in her name, had transformed it from a good old English patronymic that any girl might bear proudly, to Cornstock. Elnora stared speechless. When and how did it happen? She could feel the wave of smothered laughter in the air around her. A rush of anger turned her face scarlet and her soul sick. A hot answer was on her lips. The voice of the professor addressed her straightly.

"This proposition seems to be beautifully demonstrated, Miss Cornstalk," he said. "Surely, you can tell us how you did it."

That word of praise saved her. She could do good work. They might wear their pretty clothes, have their friends and make life a greater misery than it ever before had been for her, but not one of them should do better work or be more womanly. That lay with her. She was tall, straight, and handsome as she arose.

"Of course, I can explain my work," she said in natural tones. "What I can't explain is how I happened to be so stupid as to make a mistake in writing my own name. I must have been a little nervous. Please, excuse me."

She went to the board, swept off the signature with one stroke, then without a tremor she rewrote it clearly. "My name is Comstock," she said distinctly. She returned to her seat and following the formula used by the others made her first high school recitation.

The face of Professor Henley was a study. As Elnora took her seat he looked at her steadily. "It puzzles me," he said deliberately, "how you can write as beautiful a demonstration, and explain it as clearly as ever has been done in any of my classes, and still be so disturbed as to make a mistake in your own name. Are you very sure you did that yourself, Miss Comstock?"

"It is impossible that anyone else should have done it," answered Elnora steadily.

"I am very glad you think so," said the professor. "Being Freshmen, all of you are strangers to me. I should hate to begin the year with you feeling there was one among you small enough to do a trick like that. The next proposition, please."

When the hour was gone the class filed back to the study room and Elnora followed in desperation, because she did not know where else to go. She could not study as she had no books, and when the class again left the room to go to another professor for the next recitation, she went also. At least they could put her out if she did not belong there. Noon came at last, and she kept with the others until they dispersed on the sidewalk. She was so abnormally self conscious she fancied all the hundreds of that laughing throng saw and jested at her. When she passed the brown-eyed boy walking with the girl of her encounter she knew, for she heard him say, "Did you really let that gawky piece of calico get ahead of you?" The answer was indistinct.

Elnora hurried from the city. She intended to get her lunch, eat it in the shade of the first tree, and then decide whether she would go back or go home. She knelt on the bridge and reached for her box, but it was so very light that she was prepared for the fact that it was empty before opening it. There was just one thing for which to be thankful. The boy or tramp who had seen her hide it, had left the napkin. She would not have to face her mother and account for its loss. She put it in her pocket, and threw the box into the ditch. Then she sat on the bridge and tried to think, but her brain was confused.

"Perhaps the worst is over," she said at last. "I will go back. What would mother say to me if I came home now?"

So she returned to the high school, followed some other pupils to the coat room, hung her hat, and found her way to the study where she had been in the morning. Twice that afternoon, with aching head and empty stomach, she faced strange professors, in different branches.

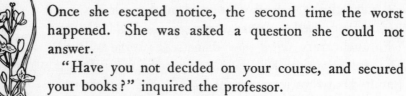

Once she escaped notice, the second time the worst happened. She was asked a question she could not answer.

"Have you not decided on your course, and secured your books?" inquired the professor.

"I have decided on my course," replied Elnora, "I do not know who to ask for my books."

"Ask?" the professor was bewildered.

"I understood the books were furnished," faltered Elnora.

"Only to those bringing an order from the township trustee," replied the Professor.

"No! Oh, no!" cried Elnora. "I will get them to-morrow," and gripped her desk for support for she knew that was not true. Four books, ranging perhaps at a dollar and a half apiece; would her mother get them? Of course she would not — could not.

Did not Elnora know the story by heart. There was enough land, but no one to do clearing and farm. Tax on all those acres, recently the new gravel road tax added, the expense of living and only the work of two women to meet all of it. She was insane to think she could come to the city to school. Her mother had been right. The girl decided that if only she lived to get home, she would stay there and lead any sort of life to avoid more of this torture. Bad as what she wished to escape had been, it was nothing like this. She never could live down the movement that went through the class when she inadvertently revealed the fact that she had expected her books to be furnished. Her mother would not get them; that settled the question.

But the end of misery is never in a hurry to come, for before the day was over the superintendent entered the room and explained that pupils from the country were charged a tuition of twenty dollars a year. That really was the end. Previously Elnora had canvassed a dozen wild plans for securing the money for books, ranging all the way from offering to wash the superintendent's dishes to breaking into the bank. This additional expense made the thing so wildly impossible, there was nothing to do but hold up her head until she was out of sight.

Down the long corridor alone among hundreds, down the long street alone among thousands, out into the country she came at last. Across the fence and field, along the old trail once trodden by a boy's bitter agony, now stumbled a white-faced girl, sick at heart. She sat on a log and began to sob in spite of her efforts at self-control. At first it was physical breakdown, later, thought came crowding.

Oh, the shame, the mortification! Why had she not known of the tuition? How did she happen to think that in the city books were furnished? Perhaps it was because she had read they were in several states. But why did she not know? Why did not her mother go with her? Other mothers — but when had her mother ever been or done anything at all like other mothers? Because she never had been it was useless to blame

her now. Elnora felt she should have gone to town the week before, called on some one and learned all these things herself. She should have remembered how her clothing would look, before she wore it in public places. Now she knew, and her dreams were over. She must go home to feed chickens, calves, and pigs, wear calico and coarse shoes, and pass a library with averted head all her life. She sobbed again.

"For pity's sake, honey, what's the matter?" asked the voice of the nearest neighbour, Wesley Sinton, as he seated himself by Elnora. "There, there," he continued, smearing tears all over her face in an effort to dry them. "Was it so bad as that, now? Maggie has been just about wild over you all day. She's got nervouser every minute. She said we were foolish to let you go. She said your clothes were not right, you ought not to carry that tin pail, and that they would laugh at you. By gum, I see they did!"

"Oh, Uncle Wesley," sobbed the girl, "why didn't she tell me?"

"Well, you see, Elnora, she didn't like to. You got such a way of holding up your head, and going through with things. She thought someway that you'd make it, till you got started, and then she begun to see a hundred things we should have done. I reckon you hadn't reached that building before she remembered that your skirt should have been pleated instead of gathered, your shoes been low, and lighter for hot September weather, and a new hat. Were your things right, Elnora?"

The girl broke into hysterical laughter. "Right!" she cried. "Right! Uncle Wesley, you should have seen me among them! I was a picture! They'll never forget me. No, they won't get the chance, for they'll see the same things to-morrow!"

"Now, that is what I call spunk, Elnora! Downright grit," said Wesley Sinton. "Don't you let them laugh you out. You've helped Margaret and me for years at harvest and busy times, what you've earned must amount to quite a sum. You can get yourself a good many clothes with it."

"Don't mention clothes, Uncle Wesley," sobbed Elnora. "I don't care now how I look. If I don't go back all of them will know it's because I am so poor I can't buy my books."

"Oh, I don't know as you are so dratted poor," said Sinton meditatively. "There are three hundred acres of good land, with fine timber as ever grew on it."

"It takes all we can earn to pay the tax, and mother wouldn't cut a tree for her life."

"Well, then, maybe, I'll be compelled to cut one for her," suggested Sinton. "Anyway, stop tearing yourself to pieces and tell me. If it isn't clothes, what is it?"

"It's books and tuition. Over twenty dollars in all."

"Humph! First time I ever knew you to be stumped by twenty dollars, Elnora," said Sinton, patting her hand.

"It's the first time you ever knew me to want money,"

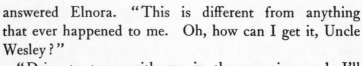

answered Elnora. "This is different from anything that ever happened to me. Oh, how can I get it, Uncle Wesley?"

"Drive to town with me in the morning and I'll draw it from the bank for you. I owe you every cent of it."

"You know you don't owe me a penny, and I wouldn't touch one from you, unless I really could earn it. For anything that's past I owe you and Aunt Margaret for all the home life and love I've ever known. I know how you work, and I'll not take your money."

"Just a loan, Elnora, just a loan for a little while until you can earn it. You can be proud with all the rest of the world, but there's no secrets between us, is there, Elnora?"

"No," said Elnora, "there are none. You and Aunt Margaret have given me all the love there has been in my life. That is the one reason above all others why you shall not give me charity. Hand me money because you find me crying for it! This isn't the first time this old trail has known tears and heartache. All of us know that story. Freckles stuck to what he undertook and won out. I stick, too. When Duncan moved away he gave me all Freckles left in the swamp, and as I have inherited his property maybe his luck will come with it. I won't touch your money, but I'll win some way. First, I'm going home and try mother. It's just possible I could find second-hand books, and perhaps all the tuition need not be paid at once. Maybe they would accept it quarterly. But, oh, Uncle Wesley, you and Aunt Margaret keep on loving me! I'm so lonely, and no one else cares!"

Wesley Sinton's jaws met with a click. He swallowed hard on bitter words and changed the thing he would have said three times before it became articulate.

"Elnora," he said at last, "if it hadn't been for one thing I'd have tried to take legal steps to make you ours when you were three years old. Maggie said then it wasn't any use, but I've always held on. You see, I was the first man there, honey, and there are things you see, that you can't ever make anybody else understand. She loved him Elnora, she just made an idol of him. There was that oozy green hole, with the thick scum broke, and two or three big bubbles slowly rising that were the breath of his body. There she was in spasms of agony, and beside her the great heavy log she'd tried to throw him. I can't ever forgive her for turning against you, and spoiling your childhood as she has, but I couldn't forgive anybody else for abusing her. Maggie has got no mercy on her, but Maggie didn't see what I did, and I've never tried to make it very clear to her. It's been a little too plain for me ever since. Whenever I look at your mother's face, I see what she saw, so I hold my tongue and say, in my heart, 'Give her a mite more time.' Some day it will come. She does love you, Elnora. Everybody does, honey. It's just that she's feeling so much, she can't express herself. You be a patient girl and wait a little longer. After all,

she's your mother, and you're all she's got, but a memory, and it might do her good to let her know that she was fooled in that."

"It would kill her!" cried the girl swiftly. "Uncle Wesley, it would kill her! What do you mean?"

"Nothing," said Wesley Sinton soothingly. "Nothing, honey. That was just one of them fool things a man says, when he is trying his best to be wise. You see, she loved him mightily, and they'd been married only a year, and what she was loving was what she thought he was. She hadn't really got acquainted with the man yet. If it had been even one more year, she could have borne it, and you'd have got justice. Having been a teacher she was better educated and smarter than the rest of us, and so she was more sensitive like. She can't understand she was loving a dream. So I say it might do her good if somebody that knew, could tell her, but I swear to gracious, I never could. I've heard her out at the edge of that quagmire calling in them wild spells of hers off and on for the last sixteen years, and imploring the swamp to give him back to her, and I've got out of bed when I was pretty tired, and come down to see she didn't go in herself, or harm you. What she feels is too deep for me. I've got to respectin' her grief, and I can't get over it. Go home and tell your ma, honey, and ask her nice and kind to help you. If she won't, then you got to swallow that little lump of pride in your neck, and come to Aunt Maggie, like you been a-coming all your life."

"I'll ask mother, but I can't take your money, Uncle Wesley, indeed I can't. I'll wait a year, and earn some, and enter next year."

"There's one thing you don't consider, Elnora," said the man earnestly. "And that's what you are to Maggie. She's a little like your ma. She hasn't given up to it, and she's struggling on brave, but when we buried our second little girl the light went out of Maggie's eyes, and it's not come back. The only time I ever see a hint of it is when she thinks she's done something that makes you happy, Elnora. Now, you go easy about refusing her anything she wants to do for you. There's times in this world when it's our bounden duty to forget ourselves, and think what will help other people. Young woman, you owe me and Maggie all the comfort we can get out of you. There's the two of our own we can't ever do anything for. Don't you get the idea into your head that a fool thing you call pride, is going to cut us out of all the pleasure we have in life beside ourselves."

"Uncle Wesley, you are a dear," said Elnora. "Just a dear! If I can't possibly get that money any way else on earth, I'll come and borrow it of you, and then I'll pay it back if I dig ferns from the swamp and sell them from door to door in the city. I'll even plant them, so that they will be sure to come up in the spring. I have been sort of panic stricken all day and couldn't think. I can gather nuts and sell them. Freckles sold moths and butterflies, and I've a lot collected.

Of course, I am going back to-morrow! I can find a way to get the books. Don't you worry about me. I am all right!"

"Now, what do you think of that?" inquired Wesley Sinton of the swamp in general. "Here's our Elnora come back to stay. Head high and right as a trivet! You've named three ways in three minutes that you could earn ten dollars, which I figure would be enough to start you. Let's go to supper and stop worrying!"

Elnora unlocked the case, took out the pail, put the napkin in it, pulled the ribbon from her hair, binding it down tight again and followed out to the road. From afar she could see her mother in the doorway. She blinked her eyes, and tried to smile as she answered Wesley Sinton, and indeed she did feel better. She knew now what she had to expect, where to go, and what to do. Get the books she must; when she got them, she would show those city girls and boys how to prepare and recite lessons, how to walk with a brave heart; and they could show her how to wear pretty clothes and have good times.

As she neared the door her mother reached for the pail. "I forgot to tell you to bring home your scraps for the chickens," she said.

Elnora entered. "There weren't any scraps, and I'm hungry again as I ever was in my life."

"I thought likely you would be," said Mrs. Comstock, "and so I got supper ready. We can eat first, and do the work afterward. What kept you so? I expected you an hour ago."

Elnora looked into her mother's face and smiled. It was a queer sort of a little smile, and would have reached the depths with any normal mother.

"I see you've been bawling," said Mrs. Comstock. "I thought you'd get your fill in a hurry. That's why I wouldn't go to any expense. If we keep out of the poorhouse we have to cut the corners close. It's likely this Brushwood road tax will eat up all we've saved in years. Where the land tax is to come from I don't know. It gets bigger every year. If they are going to dredge the swamp ditch again they'll just have to take the land to pay for it. I can't, that's all! We'll get up early in the morning and gather and hull the beans for winter, and put in the rest of the day hoeing the turnips."

Elnora again smiled that pitiful smile.

"Do you think I didn't know that I was funny and would be laughed at?" she asked.

"Funny?" cried Mrs. Comstock hotly.

"Yes, funny! A regular caricature," answered Elnora. "No one else wore calico, not even one other. No one else wore high heavy shoes, not even one. No one else had such a funny little old hat; my hair was not right, my ribbon invisible compared with the others, I did not know where to go, or what to do, and I had no books. What a spectacle I made for them!" Elnora laughed nervously at her own picture. "But there's

always two sides! The professor said in the algebra class that he never had a better solution and explanation than mine of the proposition he gave me, which scored one for me in spite of my clothes."

"Well, I wouldn't brag on myself!"

"That was poor taste," admitted Elnora. "But, you see, it is a case of whistling to keep up my courage. I honestly could see that I would have looked just as well as the rest of them if I had been dressed as they were. We can't afford that, so I have to find something else to brace me. It was pretty bad, mother!"

"Well, I'm glad you got enough of it!"

"Oh, but I haven't!" hurried in Elnora. "I just got a start. The hardest is over. To-morrow they won't be surprised. They will know what to expect. I am sorry to hear about the dredge. Is it really going through?"

"Yes. I got my notification to-day. The tax will be something enormous. I don't know as I can spare you, even if you are willing to be a laughing-stock for the town."

With every bite Elnora's courage rose, for she was a healthy young thing.

"You've heard about doing evil that good might come from it," she said. "Well, mother mine, it's a little like that with me. I'm willing to bear the hard part to pay for what I'll learn. Already I have selected the ward building in which I shall teach in about four years. I am going to ask for a room with a south ex-

CHAPTER 2

Wherein Wesley and Margaret Go Shopping, and Elnora's Wardrobe Is Replenished

WESLEY SINTON walked down the road a half-mile and turned in at the lane leading to his home. His heart was hot and filled with indignation. He had told Elnora he did not blame her mother, but he did. His wife met him at the door.

"Did you see anything of Elnora, Wesley?" she questioned.

"Most too much, Maggie," he answered. "What do you say to going to town? There's a few things has to be got right away?"

"Where did you see her, Wesley?"

"Along the old Limberlost trail, my girl, torn to pieces sobbing. Her courage always has been fine, but the thing she met to-day was too much for her. We ought to have known better than to let her go that way. It wasn't only clothes; there were books, and entrance fees for out-of-town people, that she didn't know about; while there must have been jeers, whispers, and laughing. Maggie, I feel as if I'd been a traitor to those girls of ours. I ought to have gone in and seen about this school business. I'm no man to let a fatherless

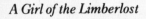

girl run into such trouble. Don't cry, Maggie. Get me some supper, and I'll hitch up and see what we can do now."

"What can we do, Wesley?"

"I don't just know. But we've got to do something. Kate Comstock will be a handful, while Elnora will be two, but between us we must see that the girl is not too hard pressed about money, and that she is dressed so she is not ridiculous. She's saved us the wages of a woman many a day, can't you make her some decent dresses, Maggie?"

"Well, I'm not just what you call expert, but I could beat Kate Comstock all to pieces. I know that skirts should be pleated to the band instead of gathered, and full enough to sit in, and short enough to walk in. I could try. There's patterns for sale. Let's go right away, Wesley."

"Well, set me a bite of supper, while I hitch up."

Margaret Sinton started for the cupboard when she remembered that Wesley had worked all day and was hungry as usual, so she built a fire, made coffee, and fried ham and eggs. She set out pie and cake and had enough for a hungry man by the time the carriage was at the door, but she had no appetite. She dressed while Wesley ate, put away the food while he dressed, and then they drove toward the city through the beautiful September evening, and as they went they planned for Elnora. The only trouble was, not whether they were generous enough to get what she needed, but whether she would accept what they got, and what her mother would say.

They went to a large dry goods store and when a clerk asked what they wanted to see neither of them knew, so they stepped to one side and held a whispered consultation.

"What had we better get, Wesley?"

"Dresses," said Wesley promptly.

"But how many dresses, and what kind?"

"Blest if I know!" exclaimed Wesley. "I thought you would manage that. I know about some things I'm going to get."

At that instant several school girls came into the store and approached them.

"There!" exclaimed Wesley breathlessly. "There, Maggie! Like them! That's what she needs! Buy like they have!"

Margaret stared. What did they wear? They were rapidly passing, they seemed to have so much, and she could not decide so quickly. Before she knew it she was among them.

"I beg your pardon, but won't you wait one minute?" she asked.

The girls stopped with wondering faces.

"It's your clothes," explained Mrs. Sinton. "You look just beautiful to me. You look exactly as I should have wanted to see my girls. They both died of diphtheria when they were little, but they had yellow hair, dark eyes and pink cheeks, and everybody thought they

were lovely. If they had lived, they'd been near your age now, and I'd want them to look like you."

There was nothing but sympathy in every girl face before Margaret Sinton.

"Why, thank you!" said one of them. "We are very sorry for you."

"Of course, you are," said Margaret. "Everybody always has been. And because I can't ever have the joy of a mother in thinking for my girls and buying pretty things for them, there is nothing left for me, but to do what I can for some one who has no mother to care for her. I know a girl, who would be just as pretty as any of you, if she had the clothes, but her mother does not think about her, so I got to mother her some myself."

"She must be a lucky girl," said another.

"Oh, she loves me," said Margaret, "and I love her. I want her to look just like you do. Please tell me about your clothes. Are these the dresses and hats you wear to school? What kind of goods are they, and where do you buy them?"

The girls began to laugh and cluster around Margaret. Wesley Sinton strode down the store with his head high in pride of her, but his heart was sore over the memory of two little faces under Brushwood sod. He inquired his way to the shoe department.

"Why, every one of us have on gingham or linen dresses," they said, "and they are our school clothes."

For a few moments there was a babel of laughing

voices explaining to the delighted Margaret that school dresses should be bright and pretty, but simple and plain, and until cold weather they should wash.

"I'll tell you," said Ellen Brownlee, "my father owns this store, I know all the clerks. I'll take you to Miss Hartley. You tell her just how much you want to spend, and what you want to buy, and she will know how to get the most for your money. I've heard papa say she was the best clerk in the store for people who didn't know precisely what they wanted."

"That's the very thing," agreed Margaret. "But before you go, tell me about your hair. Elnora's hair is bright and wavy, but yours is silky as hackled flax. How do you do it?"

"Elnora?" asked four girls in concert.

"Yes, Elnora is the name of the girl I want these things for."

"Did she come to the high school to-day?" questioned one of them.

"Was she in your classes?" demanded Margaret without reply.

Four girls stood silent and thought fast. Had there been a strange girl among them, and had she been overlooked and passed by with indifference, because she was so very shabby? If she had appeared as much better than they, as she had looked worse, would her reception have been the same?

"There was a strange girl from the country in the

Freshman class to-day," said Ellen Brownlee, "and her name was Elnora."

"That was the girl," said Margaret.

"Are her people so very poor?" questioned Ellen.

"No, not poor at all, come to think of it," answered Margaret. "It's a peculiar case. Mrs. Comstock had a great trouble and she let it change her whole life and make a different woman of her. She used to be lovely, now she is forever saving and scared to death for fear they will go to the poor-house; but there is a big farm, covered with lots of good timber. The taxes are high for women who can't manage to clear and work the land. There ought to be enough to keep two of them in good shape all their lives, if they only knew how to do it. But no one ever told Kate Comstock anything, and never will, for she won't listen. All she does is droop all day, and walk the edge of the swamp half the night, and neglect Elnora. If you girls would make life just a little easier for her, it would be the finest thing you ever did."

All of them promised they would.

"Now tell me about your hair," persisted Margaret Sinton.

So they took her to a toilet counter, and she bought the proper hair soap, also a nail file, and cold cream, for use after windy days. Then they left her with the experienced clerk, and when at last Wesley found her she was loaded with bundles and the glint of other days was in her beautiful eyes. Wesley carried some packages also.

"Did you get any stockings?" he whispered.

"No, I didn't," she said. "I was so interested in dresses and hair ribbons and a — a hat ——" she hesitated and glanced at Wesley. "Of course, a hat!" prompted Wesley. "That I forgot all about those horrible shoes. She's got to have decent shoes, Wesley."

"Sure!" said Wesley. "She's got decent shoes. But the man said some brown stockings ought to go with them. Take a peep, will you!"

Wesley opened a box and displayed a pair of thick soled, beautifully shaped brown walking shoes of low cut. Margaret cried out with pleasure.

"But, do you suppose they are the right size, Wesley? What did you get?"

"I just said for a girl of sixteen with a slender foot."

"Well, that's about as near as I could come. If they don't fit when she tries them, we will drive straight in and change them. Come on, now, let's get home."

All the way they discussed how they should give Elnora their purchases and what Mrs. Comstock would say.

"I am afraid she will be awful mad," said Margaret Sinton tremulously.

"She'll just rip!" replied Wesley graphically. "But if she wants to leave the raising of her girl to the neighbours, she needn't get fractious if they take some pride in doing a good job. From now on I calculate Elnora shall go to school; and she shall have all the clothes and books she needs, if I go around on the back of Kate Comstock's land and cut a tree, or drive off a calf to pay for

them. Why I know one tree she owns that would put
Elnora in heaven for a year. Just think of it, Margaret!
It's not fair. One-third of what is there belongs to
Elnora by law, and if Kate Comstock raises a row I'll
tell her so, and see that the girl gets it. You go to see
Kate in the morning, and I'll go with you. Tell her you
want Elnora's pattern, that you are going to make her
a dress, for helping us. And sort of hint at a few more
things. If Kate balks, I'll take a hand and settle her.
I'll go to law for Elnora's share of that land and sell
enough to educate her."

"Why, Wesley Sinton, you're perfectly wild."

"I'm not! Did you ever stop to think that such cases
are so frequent there have been laws made to provide for
them? I can bring it up in court and force Kate to
educate Elnora, and board and clothe her till she's
of age, and then she can take her share."

"Wesley, Kate would go crazy!"

"She's crazy now. The idea of any mother living
with as sweet a girl as Elnora, and letting her suffer
till I find her crying like a funeral. It makes me fighting
mad. All uncalled for. Not a grain of sense in it.
I've offered and offered to oversee clearing her land
and working her fields. Let her sell a good tree, or a few
acres. Something is going to be done, right now. Elnora's been fairly happy up to this, but to spoil the
school life she's planned, is to ruin all her life. I won't
have it! If Elnora won't take these things, so help me,
I'll tell her what she is worth, and loan her the money

and she can pay me back when she comes of age. I am going to have it out with Kate Comstock in the morning. Here we are! You open up what you got while I put away the horses, and then I'll show you."

When Wesley came from the barn Margaret had four pieces of crisp gingham, a pale blue, a pink, a gray with green stripes and a rich brown and blue plaid. On each of them lay a yard and a half of wide ribbon to match. There were handkerchiefs and a brown leather belt. In her hands she held a wide-brimmed tan straw hat, having a high crown banded with velvet strips each of which fastened with a tiny gold buckle.

"It looks kind of bare now," she explained. "It had three quills on it here."

"Did you have them taken off?" asked Wesley dubiously.

"Yes, I did. The price was two and a half for the hat, and those things were a dollar and a half apiece. I couldn't pay that."

"It does seem considerable," admitted Wesley, "but will it look right without them?"

"No, it won't!" said Margaret. "It's going to have quills on it. Do you remember those beautiful peacock wing feathers that Phœbe Simms gave me? Three of them go on just where those came off, and nobody will ever know the difference. They match the hat to a moral, and they are just a little longer and richer than the ones that I had taken off. I was wondering whether

I better sew them on to-night while I remember how they set, or wait till morning."

"Don't risk it!" exclaimed Wesley anxiously. "Don't you risk it! Sew them on right now!"

"Open your bundles, while I get the thread," said Margaret.

Wesley set out the shoes. Margaret took them up and pinched the leather and stroked them.

"My, but they are pretty!" she cried.

Wesley picked up one and slowly turned it in his big hands. He glanced at his foot and back to the shoe.

"It's a little bit of a thing, Margaret," he said softly. "Like as not I'll have to take it back. It don't look as if it could fit."

"It don't look like it dared do anything else," said Margaret. "That's a happy little shoe to get the chance to carry as fine a girl as Elnora to high school. Now, what's in the other box?"

Wesley looked at Margaret doubtfully.

"Why," he said, "you know there's going to be rainy days, and those things she has now ain't fit for anything but to drive up the cows ——"

"Wesley, did you get high shoes, too?"

"Well, she ought to have them! The man said he would make them cheaper if I took both pairs at once."

Margaret laughed aloud. "Those will do her past Christmas," she exulted. "What else did you get?"

"Well, sir," said Wesley, "I saw something to-day. You told me about Kate getting that tin pail for Elnora to carry to high school and you said you told her it was a shame. I guess Elnora was ashamed all right, for to-night she stopped at the old case Duncan gave her, and took out that pail, where it had been all day, and put a napkin inside it. Coming home she confessed she was half starved because she hid her dinner under a culvert, and a tramp took it. She hadn't had a bite to eat the whole day. But she never complained at all, she was tickled to death that she hadn't lost the napkin. So I just inquired around till I found this, and I think it's about the ticket. Decent looking and handy as you please. See here, now!"

Wesley opened the package and laid a brown leather lunch box on the table. "Might be a couple of books, or drawing tools or most anything that's neat and genteel. You see, it opens this way."

It did open, and inside was a space for sandwiches, a little porcelain box for cold meat or fried chicken, another for salad, a glass with a lid which screwed on, held by a ring in a corner, for custard or jelly, a flask for tea or milk, a beautiful little knife, fork, and spoon fastened in holders, and a place for a napkin.

Margaret was almost crying over it.

"How I'd love to fill it!" she exclaimed.

"Do it the first time, just to show Kate Comstock what love is!" said Wesley. "Get up early in the morning and make one of those dresses to-morrow. Can't you make a plain gingham dress in a day? I'll pick a chicken, and you fry it and fix a little custard

for the cup, and do it up brown. Go on, Maggie, you do it!"

"I never can," said Margaret. "I am slow as the itch about sewing, and these are not going to be plain dresses when it comes to making them. There are going to be edgings of plain green, pink, and brown to the bias strips, and tucks and pleats about the hips, fancy belts and collars, and all of it takes time."

"Then Kate Comstock's got to help," said Wesley. "Can the two of you make one, and get that lunch to-morrow?"

"Easy, but she'll never do it!"

"You see if she don't!" said Wesley. "You get up and cut it out, and soon as Elnora is gone I'll go after Kate myself. She'll take what I'll say better alone. But she'll come, and she'll help make the dress. These other things are our Christmas gifts to Elnora. She'll no doubt need them more now than she will then, and we can give them just as well. That's yours, and this is mine, or whichever way you choose."

Wesley untied a good brown umbrella and shook out the folds of a long, brown raincoat. Margaret dropped the hat, arose and took the coat. She tried it on, felt it, cooed over it and matched it with the umbrella.

"Did it look anything like rain to-night?" she inquired so anxiously that Wesley laughed.

"And this last bundle?" she said, dropping back in her chair, the coat still over her shoulders.

"I couldn't buy this much stuff for any other woman and nothing for my own," said Wesley. "It's Christmas for you, too, Margaret!" He shook out fold after fold of soft gray satiny goods that would look lovely against Margaret's pink cheeks and whitening hair.

"Oh, you old darling!" she exclaimed, and fled sobbing into his arms.

But she soon dried her eyes, raked together the coals in the cooking stove and boiled one of the dress patterns in salt water for a half-hour. Wesley held the lamp while she hung the goods on the line to dry. Then she set the irons on the stove so they would get hot the first thing in the morning.

CHAPTER 3

Wherein Elnora Visits the Bird Woman, and Opens a Bank Account

At four o'clock next morning Elnora was shelling beans. At six she fed the chickens and pigs, swept two of the rooms of the cabin, built a fire, and put on the kettle for breakfast. Then she climbed the narrow stairs to the attic she had occupied since a very small child, and dressed in the hated shoes and brown calico, plastered down her crisp curls, ate what breakfast she could, and pinning on her hat started for town.

"There is no sense in your going for an hour yet," said her mother.

"I must try to discover some way to earn those books," replied Elnora. "I am perfectly positive I shall not find them lying along the road wrapped in tissue paper, and tagged with my name."

She went toward the city as on yesterday. Her perplexity as to where tuition and books were to come from was worse but she did not feel quite so badly. She never again would have to face all of it for the first time. She had been through it once, and was yet living. There had been times yesterday when she had prayed to be hidden, or to drop dead, and neither had happened. "I guess the best way to get an answer to prayer is to work for it," muttered Elnora grimly.

Again she took the trail to the swamp, rearranged her hair and left the tin pail. This time she folded a couple of sandwiches in the napkin, and tied them in a neat light paper parcel which she carried in her hand. Then she hurried along the road to Onabasha and found a bookstore. There she asked the prices of the list of books that she needed, and learned that six dollars would not quite supply them. She anxiously inquired for second-hand books, but was told that the only way to secure them was from the last year's Freshmen. Just then Elnora felt that she positively could not approach any of those she supposed to be Sophomores and ask to buy their old books. The only balm the girl could see for the humiliation of yesterday was to appear that day with a set of new books.

"Do you wish these?" asked the clerk hurriedly, for the store was rapidly filling with school children wanting anything from a dictionary to a pen.

"Yes," gasped Elnora, "Oh, yes! But I cannot pay for them just now. Please let me take them, and I will pay for them on Friday, or return them as perfect as they are. Please trust me for them a few days."

The clerk looked at her doubtfully and took her name.

"I'll ask the proprietor," he said. When he came back Elnora knew the answer before he spoke.

"I'm sorry," he said, "but Mr. Hann doesn't recognize your name. You are not a customer of ours, and he feels

that he can't take the risk. You'll have to bring the money."

Elnora clumped out of the store, the thump of her heavy shoes beating as a hammer on her brain. She tried two other houses with the same result, and then in sick despair came into the street. What could she do? She was too frightened to think. Should she stay from school that day and canvass the homes appearing to belong to the wealthy, and try to sell beds of wild ferns, as she had suggested to Wesley Sinton? What would she dare ask for bringing in and planting a clump of ferns? How could she carry them? Would people buy them? She slowly moved past the hotel and then glanced around to see if there was a clock anywhere, for she felt sure the young people passing her constantly were on their way to school.

There it stood in a bank window in big black letters staring straight at her:

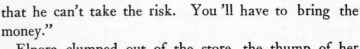

WANTED: CATERPILLARS. COCOONS. CHRYSALIDES. PUPAE CASES. BUTTERFLIES. MOTHS. INDIAN RELICS OF ALL KINDS. HIGHEST SCALE OF PRICES PAID IN CASH

Elnora caught the wicket at the cashier's desk with both hands to brace herself against disappointment.

"Who is it wants to buy cocoons, butterflies, and moths?" she panted.

"The Bird Woman," answered the cashier. "Have you some for sale?"

"I have some, I do not know if they are what she would want."

"Well, you had better see her," said the cashier. "Do you know where she lives?"

"Yes," said Elnora. "Would you tell me the time?"

"Twenty-one after eight," was the answer.

She had nine minutes to reach the auditorium or be late. Should she go to school, or to the Bird Woman? Several girls passed her walking swiftly and she remembered their faces. They were hurrying to school. Elnora caught the infection. She would see the Bird Woman at noon. Algebra came first, and that professor was kind. Perhaps she could slip to the superintendent and ask him for a book for the next lesson, and at noon — "Oh, dear Lord make it come true," prayed Elnora, at noon maybe she could sell some of those wonderful shining-winged things she had been collecting all her life around the outskirts of the Limberlost.

As she went down the long hall she noticed the professor of mathematics standing in the door of his recitation room. When she came up to him he smiled and spoke to her.

"I have been watching for you," he said, and Elnora stopped bewildered.

"For me?" she questioned.

"Yes," said Professor Henley. "Step inside."

Elnora followed him into the room and he swung the door behind them.

"At teachers' meeting last evening, one of the professors mentioned that a pupil had betrayed in class that she had

expected her books to be furnished by the city. I thought possibly it was you. Was it?"

"Yes," breathed Elnora.

"That being the case," said Professor Henley, "it just occurred to me as you had expected that, you might require a little time to secure them, and you are too fine a mathematician to fall behind for want of supplies. So I telephoned one of our Sophomores to bring her last year's books this morning. I am sorry to say they are somewhat abused, but the text is all here. You can have them for two dollars, and pay when you get ready. Would you care to take them?"

Elnora sat suddenly, because she could not stand another instant. She reached both hands for the books, and said never a word. The professor was silent also.

At last Elnora arose, hugging those books to her heart as a mother grasps a lost baby.

"One thing more," said the professor. "You can pay your tuition quarterly. You need not bother about the first instalment this month. Any time in October will do."

It seemed as if Elnora's gasp of relief must have reached the soles of her brogans.

"Did any one ever tell you how beautiful you are!" she cried.

As the professor was lank, tow-haired and so near-sighted, that he peered at his pupils through spectacles, no one ever had.

"No," said Professor Henley, "I 've waited some time

for that; for which reason I shall appreciate it all the more. Come, now, or we shall be late for opening exercises."

So Elnora entered the auditorium a second time. Her face was like the brightest dawn that ever broke over the Limberlost. No matter about the lumbering shoes and skimpy dress just now. No matter about anything, she had the books. She could take them home. In her garret she could commit them to memory, if need be. She could show that clothes were not all. If the Bird Woman did not want any of the many different kinds of specimens she had collected, she was quite sure now she could sell ferns, nuts, and a great many things. Then, too, someone moved over this morning, and several girls smiled and bowed. Elnora forgot everything save her books, and that she was where she could use them intelligently — everything except one little thing away back in her head. Her mother had known about the books and the tuition, and had not told her when she agreed to her coming.

At noon Elnora took her little parcel of lunch and started to the home of the Bird Woman. She must know about the specimens first and then she would go out to the suburbs somewhere and eat a few bites. She dropped the heavy iron knocker on the door of the big red log cabin, and her heart thumped at the resounding stroke.

"Is the Bird Woman at home?" she asked of the maid.

"She is at lunch," was the answer.

"Please ask her if she will see a girl from the Limberlost about some moths?" inquired Elnora.

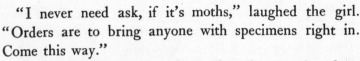

"I never need ask, if it's moths," laughed the girl. "Orders are to bring anyone with specimens right in. Come this way."

Elnora followed down the hall and entered a long room with high panelled wainscoting, old English fireplace with an overmantel and closets of peculiar china filling the corners. At a bare table of oak, yellow as gold, sat a woman Elnora often had watched and followed covertly around the Limberlost. The Bird Woman was holding out a hand of welcome.

"I heard!" she laughed. "A little pasteboard box, or just the bare word 'specimen,' passes you at my door. If it is moths I hope you have hundreds. I've been very busy all summer and unable to collect, and I need so many. Sit down and lunch with me, while we talk it over. From the Limberlost, did you say?"

"I live near the swamp," replied Elnora. "Since it's so cleared I dare go around the edge in daytime, though we are still afraid at night."

"What have you collected?" asked the Bird Woman, as she helped Elnora to sandwiches unlike any she ever before had tasted, salad that seemed to be made of many familiar things, but you were only sure of celery and apples, and a cup of hot chocolate that would have delighted any hungry schoolgirl.

Elnora said "Thank you," and set the things before her, but her eyes were on the Bird Woman's face.

"I am afraid I am bothering you for nothing, and imposing on you," she said. "That 'collected' frightens

46

me. I've only gathered. I always loved everything outdoors, and so I made friends and playmates of them. When I learned that the moths die so soon, I saved them especially, because there seemed no wickedness in it."

"I have thought the same thing," said the Bird Woman encouragingly. Then because the girl could not eat until she learned about the moths, the Bird Woman asked Elnora if she knew what kinds she had.

"Not all of them," answered Elnora. "Before Mr. Duncan moved away he often saw me near the edge of the swamp, and he showed me the box he had fixed for Freckles, and gave me the key. There were some books and things, so from that time on I studied and tried to take moths right, but I am afraid they are not what you want."

"Are they the big ones that fly mostly June nights?" asked the Bird Woman.

"Yes," said Elnora. "Great gray ones with reddish markings, pale blue-green, yellow with lavender, and red and yellow."

"What do you mean by 'red and yellow?'" asked the Bird Woman so quickly that the girl almost jumped.

"Not exactly red," explained Elnora, with tremulous voice. "A reddish, yellowish brown, with canary-coloured spots and gray lines on their wings."

"How many of them?" It was the same quick question.

"Well, I had over two hundred eggs," said Elnora, "but some of them didn't hatch, and some of the

caterpillars died, but there must be at least a hundred perfect ones."

"Perfect! How, perfect?" cried the Bird Woman.

"I mean whole wings, no down gone, and all their legs and antennæ," faltered Elnora.

"Young woman, that's the rarest moth in America," said the Bird Woman solemnly. "If you have a hundred of them, they are worth a hundred dollars according to my list. I can use all that are whole."

"What if they are not pinned right," quavered Elnora.

"If they are perfect, that does not make the slightest difference. I know how to soften them so that I can put them into any shape I choose. Where are they? When may I see them?"

"They are in Freckles's old case in the Limberlost," said Elnora. "I couldn't carry many for fear of breaking them, but I could bring a few after school."

"You come here at four," said the Bird Woman, "and we will drive out with some specimen boxes, and a price list, and see what you have to sell. Are they your very own? Are you free to part with them?"

"They are mine," said Elnora. "No one but God knows I have them. Mr. Duncan gave me the books and the box. He told Freckles about me, and Freckles told him to give me all he left. He said for me to stick to the swamp and be brave, and my hour would come, and it has! I know most of them are all right, and oh, I do need the money!"

"Could you tell me?" asked the Bird Woman softly.

"You see the swamp and all the fields around it are so full," explained Elnora. "Every day I felt smaller and smaller, and I wanted to know more and more, and pretty soon I got desperate, just as Freckles did. But I am better off than he was, for I have his books, and I have a mother; even if she don't care for me as other girls' mothers do for them, it's better than no one."

The Bird Woman's glance fell, for the girl was not conscious of how much she was revealing. Her eyes were fixed on a black pitcher filled with goldenrod in the centre of the table and she was saying what she thought.

"As long as I could go to the Brushwood school I was happy, but I couldn't go further just when things got the most interesting, so I was bound I'd come to high school and mother wouldn't consent. You see there's plenty of land, but father was drowned when I was a baby, and mother and I can't make money as men do. The taxes get bigger every year, and she said it was too expensive. I wouldn't give her any rest, until at last she got me this dress, and these shoes and I came. It was awful!"

Elnora stopped short and stared into the Bird Woman's face.

"Do you live in that beautiful cabin at the northwest end of the swamp?" asked the Bird Woman.

"Yes," said Elnora.

"I remember the place and a story about it now. You entered the high school yesterday?"

"Yes."

"It was pretty bad?"

49

"Pretty bad!" echoed Elnora.

The Bird Woman laughed.

"You can't tell me anything about that," she said. "I once entered a city school straight from the country. My dress was brown calico, and my shoes were quite heavy."

The tears began to roll down Elnora's cheeks.

"Did they ——?" she faltered.

"They did!" said the Bird Woman. "All of it. I am quite sure they did not miss one least little thing."

Then she wiped away some tears that began rolling down her cheeks, and laughed at the same time.

"Where are they now?" asked Elnora suddenly.

"Well, they are pretty widely scattered, but none of them have attained heights out of range. Some of the rich are poor, and some of the poor are rich. Some of the brightest died insane, and some of the dullest worked out high positions, some of the very worst to bear have gone out, and I frequently hear from others. Now I am here, able to remember it, and mingle laughter with what used to be all tears; for every day I have my beautiful work, and almost every day God sends some one like you to help me. What is your name, my girl?"

"Elnora Comstock," answered Elnora. "Yesterday on the board it changed to Cornstock, and for a minute I thought I'd die, but I can laugh over that already."

The Bird Woman arose and kissed her. "Finish your lunch," she said, "and I will get my price lists, and take down a memorandum of what you think you have, so I will know how many boxes to prepare. And remember this. What you are lies with you. If you are lazy, and accept your lot, you may live in it. If you are willing to work, you can write your name anywhere you choose, among the only ones who live past the grave in this world, the people who write books that help, make exquisite music, carve statues, paint pictures, and work for others. Never mind the calico dress, and the coarse shoes. Dig into the books, and before long you will hear yesterday's tormentors boasting that they were once classmates of yours. 'I could a tale unfold' ——!"

She laughingly left the room and Elnora sat thinking, until she remembered how hungry she was, so she ate the food, drank the hot chocolate and began the process of getting a grip on herself.

Then the Bird Woman came back and showed Elnora a long printed slip giving a list of graduated prices for moths, butterflies and dragon flies.

"Oh, do you want them!" exulted Elnora. "I have a few and I can get more by the thousand, with every color in the world on their wings."

"Yes," said the Bird Woman, "I will buy them, also the big moth caterpillars that are creeping everywhere now, and the cocoons that they will spin just about this time. I have a sneaking impression that the mystery, wonder, and the urge of their pure beauty, are going to force me to picture and paint our moths and put them into a book for all the world to see and know. We Limberlost people must not be selfish with the wonders God has given to us.

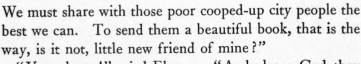

We must share with those poor cooped-up city people the best we can. To send them a beautiful book, that is the way, is it not, little new friend of mine?"

"Yes, oh yes!" cried Elnora. "And please God they find a way to earn the money to buy the books, as I have those I need so badly."

"I will pay good prices for all the moths you can find," said the Bird Woman, "because you see I exchange them with foreign collectors. I want a complete series of the moths of America to trade with a German scientist, another with a man in India, and another in Brazil. Others I can exchange with home collectors for those of California and Canada, so you see I can use all you can raise, or find. The banker will buy stone axes, arrow points, and Indian pipes. There was a teacher from the city grade schools here to-day for specimens. There is a fund to supply the ward buildings. I'll help you get in touch with that. They want leaves of different trees, flowers, grasses, moths, insects, birds' nests and anything about birds."

Elnora's eyes were blazing. "Had I best go back to school or open a bank account and begin being a millionaire? Uncle Wesley and I have a bushel of arrow points gathered, a stack of axes, pipes, skin-dressing tools, tubes and mortars. I don't know how I ever will wait three hours."

"You must go, or you will be late," said the Bird Woman. "I will be ready at four."

After school closed Elnora, seated by the Bird Woman,

drove to Freckles's old room in the Limberlost. One at a time the beautiful big moths were taken from the interior of the old black case. Not a fourth of them could be moved that night and it was almost dark when the last box was closed, the list figured, and into Elnora's trembling fingers were paid fifty-nine dollars and sixteen cents. Elnora clasped the money closely.

"Oh you beautiful stuff!" she cried. "You are going to buy the books, pay the tuition, and take me to high school."

Then because she was a woman, she sat on a log and looked at her shoes. Long after the Bird Woman drove away Elnora remained. She had her problem, and it was a big one. If she told her mother, would she take the money to pay the taxes? If she did not tell her, how could she account for the books, and things for which she would spend it. At last she counted out what she needed for the next day, placed the rest in the farthest corner of the case, and locked the door. She then filled the front of her skirt from a heap of arrow points beneath the case and started home.

CHAPTER 4

Wherein the Sintons Are Disappointed, and Mrs. Comstock Learns That She Can Laugh

With the first streak of red above the Limberlost Margaret Sinton was busy with the gingham and the intricate paper pattern she had purchased. Wesley cooked the breakfast and worked until he thought Elnora would be gone, then he started to bring her mother.

"Now you be mighty careful," cautioned Margaret. "I don't know how she will take it."

"I don't either," said Wesley philosophically, "but she's got to take it some way. That dress has to be finished by school time in the morning."

Wesley had not slept well that night. He had been so busy framing diplomatic speeches to make to Mrs. Comstock that sleep had little chance with him. Every step nearer to her he approached his position seemed less enviable. By the time he reached the front gate and started down the walk between the rows of asters and lady slippers he was perspiring, and every plausible and convincing speech had fled his brain. Mrs. Comstock helped him. She met him at the door.

"Good morning," she said. "Did Margaret send you for something?"

"Yes," said Wesley. "She sent me for you. She's got a job that's too big for her, and she wants you to help."

"Of course I will," said Mrs. Comstock. It was no one's affair how lonely the previous day had been, or how the endless hours of the present would drag. "What is she doing in such a rush?"

Now was his chance.

"She's making a dress for Elnora," answered Wesley. He saw Mrs. Comstock's form straighten, and her face harden, so he continued hastily. "You see Elnora has been helping us at harvest time, butchering, and with unexpected visitors for years. We've made out that she's saved us a considerable sum, and as she wouldn't ever touch any pay for anything, we just went to town and got a few clothes we thought would fix her up a little for the high school. We want to get a dress done to-day mighty bad, but Margaret is slow about sewing, and she never can finish alone, so I came for you."

"And it's such a simple little matter, so dead easy; and all so between old friends like, that you can't look above your boots while you explain it," sneered Mrs. Comstock. "Wesley Sinton, what put the idea into your head that Elnora would take things bought with money, when she wouldn't take the money?"

Then Sinton's eyes came up straightly.

"Finding her on the trail last night sobbing as hard as I ever saw any one at a funeral. She wasn't complaining at all, but she's come to me all her life with her little hurts,

55

and she couldn't hide how she'd been laughed at, twitted, and run face to face against the fact that there was books and tuition, unexpected, and nothing will ever make me believe you didn't know that, Kate Comstock."

"If any doubts are troubling you on that subject, sure I knew it! She was so anxious to try the world, I thought I'd just let her take a few knocks and see how she liked it."

"As if she'd ever taken anything but knocks all her life!" cried Wesley Sinton. "Kate Comstock, you are a heartless, selfish woman. You've never showed Elnora any real love in her life. If ever she finds out that thing you'll lose her, and it will serve you right."

"She knows it now," said Mrs. Comstock icily, "and she'll be home to-night just as usual."

"Well, you are a brave woman if you dared put a girl of Elnora's make through what she suffered yesterday, and will suffer again to-day, and let her know you did it on purpose. I admire your nerve. But I've watched this since Elnora was born, and I got enough. Things have come to a pass where they go better for her, or I interfere."

"As if you'd ever done anything but interfere all her life! Think I haven't watched you? Think I, with my heart raw in my breast, and too numb to resent it openly, haven't seen you and Mag Sinton trying to turn Elnora against me day after day? When did you ever tell her what her father meant to me? When did you ever try to make her see the wreck of my life, and what I've suffered? No indeed! Always it's been poor little abused Elnora, and cakes, kissing, extra clothes, and encouraging her to run to you with a pitiful mouth every time I tried to make a woman of her."

"Kate Comstock, that's unjust," cried Sinton. "Only last night I tried to show her the picture I saw the day she was born. I begged her to come to you and tell you pleasant what she needed, and ask you for what I happen to know you can well afford to give her."

"I can't!" cried Mrs. Comstock. "You know I can't!"

"Then get so you can!" said Wesley Sinton. "Any day you say the word you can sell six thousand worth of rare timber off this place easy. I'll see to clearing and working the fields cheap as dirt, for Elnora's sake. I'll buy you more cattle to fatten. All you've got to do is sign a lease, to pull thousands from the ground in oil, as the rest of us are doing all around you."

"Cut down Robert's trees!" shrieked Mrs. Comstock. "Tear up his land! Cover everything with horrid, greasy oil! I'll die first!"

"You mean you 'll let Elnora go like a beggar, and hurt and mortify her past bearing. I've got to the place where I tell you plain what I am going to do. Maggie and I went to town last night, and we got what things Elnora needs most urgent to make her look a little like the rest of the high school girls. Now here it is in plain English. You can help get these things ready, and let us give them to her as we want ——"

"She won't touch them!" cried Mrs. Comstock.

57

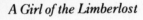

"Then you can pay us, and she can take them as her right ——"

"I won't!"

"Then I will tell Elnora just what you are worth, what you can afford, and how much of this she owns. I'll loan her the money to buy books and decent clothes, and when she is of age she can sell her share and pay me."

Mrs. Comstock gripped a chair-back and opened her lips, but no words came.

"And," Sinton continued, "if she is so much like you that she won't do that, I 'll go to the county seat and lay complaint against you as her guardian before the judge. I'll swear to what you are worth, and how you are raising her, and have you discharged, or have the judge appoint some man who will see that she is comfortable, educated and decent looking!"

"You — you wouldn't!" gasped Mrs. Comstock.

"I won't need to, Kate!" said Sinton, his heart softening the instant the hard words were said. "You won't show it, but you do love Elnora! You can't help it! You must see how she needs things; come help us fix them, and be friends. Maggie and I couldn't live without her, and you couldn't either. You've got to love such a fine girl as she is; let it show a little!"

"You can hardly expect me to love her," said Mrs. Comstock coldly. "But for her a man would stand back of me now, who would beat the breath out of your sneaking body for the cowardly thing with which you threaten me. After all I've suffered you'd drag me to court and compel me to tear up Robert's property. If I ever go they carry me. If they touch one tree, or put down one greasy old oil well, it will be over all I can shoot, before they begin. Now, see how quick you can clear out of here!"

"You won't come and help Maggie with the dress?"

For answer Mrs. Comstock looked about swiftly for some object on which to lay her hands. Knowing her temper, Wesley Sinton left with all the haste consistent with dignity. But he did not go home. He crossed a field, and in an hour brought another neighbour who was skilful with her needle. With sinking heart Margaret saw them coming.

"Kate is too busy to help to-day, she can't sew before to-morrow," said Wesley cheerfully as they entered.

That quieted Margaret's apprehension a little, though she had some doubts. Wesley prepared the lunch, and by four o'clock the pretty dress was finished as far as it possibly could be until it was fitted on Elnora. If that did not entail too much work, it could be completed in two hours.

Then the neighbour left and Margaret packed their purchases into the big market basket. Wesley took the hat, umbrella, and raincoat, and they went down to Mrs. Comstock's. As they reached the step, Margaret spoke pleasantly to Mrs. Comstock, who sat reading just inside the door, but she did not answer and deliberately turned a leaf without looking up.

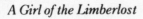

Wesley Sinton opened the door and went in followed by Margaret.

"Kate," he said, "you needn't take out your mad over our little racket on Maggie. I ain't told her a word I said to you, or you said to me. She's not so very strong, and she's sewed since four o'clock this morning to get this dress ready for to-morrow. It's done and we came down to try it on Elnora."

"Is that the truth, Mag Sinton?" demanded Mrs. Comstock.

"You heard Wesley say so," proudly affirmed Mrs. Sinton.

"I want to make you a proposition," said Wesley. "Wait till Elnora comes. Then we'll show her the things and see what she says."

"How would it do to see what she says without bribing her," sneered Mrs. Comstock.

"If she can stand what she did yesterday, and will to-day, she can bear 'most anything," said Wesley. "Put away the clothes if you want to, till we tell her."

"Well, you don't take this waist I'm working on," said Margaret, "for I have to baste in the sleeves and set the collar. Put the rest out of sight if you like."

Mrs. Comstock picked up the basket and bundles, placed them inside her room and closed the door.

Margaret threaded her needle and began to sew. Mrs. Comstock returned to her book, while Wesley fidgeted and raged inwardly. He could see that Margaret was nervous and almost in tears, but the lines in Mrs. Comstock's impassive face were set and cold. So they sat and the clock ticked off the time — one hour, two, dusk, and no Elnora. Margaret long since had taken the last stitch she could. Occasionally she and Wesley exchanged a few words. Mrs. Comstock regularly turned a leaf, and once arose and moved nearer a window. Just when Margaret and Wesley were discussing whether he had not best go to town to meet Elnora, they heard her coming up the walk. Wesley dropped his tilted chair and squared himself. Margaret gripped her sewing, and turned pleading eyes to the door. Mrs. Comstock closed her book and grimly smiled.

"Mother, please open the door," called Elnora.

Mrs. Comstock arose, and swung open the screen. Elnora stepped in beside her, bent half double, the whole front of her dress gathered into a sort of bag filled with a heavy load, and one arm stacked high with books. In the dim light she did not see the Sintons.

"Please hand me the empty bucket in the kitchen, mother," she said. "I just had to bring these arrow points home, but I'm scared for fear I've soiled my dress and will have to wash it. I'm to clean them, and take them to the banker in the morning, and oh, mother, I've sold enough stuff to pay for my books, my tuition, and maybe a dress and some lighter shoes besides. Oh, mother I'm so happy! Take the books and bring the bucket!"

Then she saw Margaret and Wesley. "Oh, glory!" she exulted. "I was just wondering how I'd ever

wait to tell you, and here you are! It's too perfectly splendid to be true!"

"Tell us, Elnora," said Sinton.

"Well, sir," said Elnora, doubling down on the floor and spreading out her skirt, "set the bucket here, mother. These points are brittle and have to be put in one at a time. If they are chipped I can't sell them. Well, sir! I've had a time! You know I just had to have books. I tried three stores, and they wouldn't trust me, not even three days, I didn't know what in this world I could do quickly enough. Just when I was about frantic I saw a sign in a bank window asking for caterpillars, cocoons, butterflies, arrow points, and everything. I went in, and it was this Bird Woman wants the insects, and the banker wants the stones. I had to go to school then, but, if you'll believe it" — Elnora beamed on all of them in turn as she talked and slipped the arrow points from her dress to the pail — "if you'll believe it — but you won't, hardly, until you look at the books — there was the mathematics teacher, waiting at his door, and he had a set of books for me that he had telephoned a Sophomore to bring."

"How did he happen to do that, Elnora?" interrupted Sinton.

Elnora blushed.

"It was a fool mistake I made yesterday in thinking books were just handed out to you. There was a teachers' meeting last night and the history teacher told about that. Professor Henley thought it was me.

You know I told you what he said about my algebra, mother. Ain't I glad I studied out some of it myself this summer! So he just telephoned and a girl brought the books. Because they are marked and abused some I get the whole outfit for two dollars. I can erase most of the marks, paste down the covers, and fix them so they look better. But I must hurry to the joy part. I didn't stop to eat, at noon, I just ran to the Bird Woman's, and I had lunch with her. It was salad, hot chocolate, and lovely things, and she wants to buy most every old scrap I ever gathered. She wants dragon flies, moths, butterflies, and he — the banker, I mean — wants everything Indian. This very night she came to the swamp with me and took away enough stuff to pay for the books and tuition, and to-morrow she is going to buy some more."

Elnora laid the last arrow point in the pail and arose, shaking leaves and bits of baked earth from her dress. She reached into her pocket and produced her money and waved it before their wondering eyes.

"And that's the joy part!" she exulted. "Put it up in the clock till morning, mother. That pays for the books and tuition and ——" Elnora hesitated, for she saw the nervous grasp with which her mother's fingers closed on the bills. Then she went on, but more slowly and thinking before she spoke.

"What I get to-morrow pays for more books and tuition, and maybe a few, just a few, things to wear. These shoes are so dreadfully heavy and hot, and they make

such a noise on the floor. There isn't another calico
dress in the whole building, not among hundreds of
us. Why, what is that? Aunt Margaret, what are you
hiding in your lap?"

She snatched the waist and shook it out, and her
face was beaming. "Have you taken to waists all
fancy and buttoned in the back? I bet you this is mine!"

"I bet you so, too," said Margaret Sinton. "You
undress right away and try it on, and if it fits, it will
be done for morning. There are some low shoes, too!"

Elnora began to dance. "Oh, you dear people!"
she cried. "I can pay for them to-morrow night! Isn't
it too splendid! I was just thinking on the way home
that I certainly would be compelled to have cooler shoes
until later, and I was wondering what I'd do when
the fall rains begin."

"I meant to get you some heavy dress skirts and a
coat then," said Mrs. Comstock.

"I know you said so!" cried Elnora. "But you
needn't now! I can get every single stitch I need
myself. Next summer I can gather up a lot more stuff,
and all winter on the way to school. I am sure I can
sell ferns, I know I can nuts, and the Bird Woman says
the grade rooms want leaves, grasses, birds' nests, and
cocoons. Oh, isn't this world lovely! I'll be helping
with the tax, next, mother!"

Elnora waved the waist and started for the bedroom.
When she opened the door she gave a little cry.

"What have you people been doing?" she demanded.

"I never saw so many interesting bundles in all my life. I'm 'skeered' to death for fear I can't pay for all of them, and will have to give up something."

"Wouldn't you take them, if you could not pay for them, Elnora?" asked her mother instantly.

"Why, not unless you did," answered Elnora. "People have no right to wear things they can't afford, have they?"

"But from such old friends as Maggie and Wesley!" Mrs. Comstock's voice was oily with triumph.

"From them least of all," cried Elnora stoutly. "From a stranger sooner than from them, to whom I owe so much more than I ever can pay now."

"Well, you don't have to," said Mrs. Comstock. "Maggie just selected these things, because she is more in touch with the world, and has got such good taste. You can pay as long as your money holds out, and if there's more necessary, maybe I can sell the butcher a calf, or if there's things too costly for us, of course, they can take them back. Anything that ain't used can be returned. They were only brought here on trial. Put on the waist now, and then you can look over the rest and see if they are suitable, and what you want."

Elnora stepped into the adjoining room and closed the door. Mrs. Comstock picked up the bucket and started for the well with it. At the bedroom she paused.

"Elnora, were you going to wash these arrow points?"

"Yes. The Bird Woman says they sell better if

they are clean, so it can be seen that there are no defects in them."

"Of course," said Mrs. Comstock. "Some of them seem quite baked. Shall I put them to soak? Do you want to take them in the morning?"

"Yes, I do," answered Elnora. "If you would just fill the pail with water."

Mrs. Comstock left the room. Wesley Sinton sat with his back to the window in the west end of the cabin which overlooked the well. A suppressed sound behind him caused him to turn quickly. Then he arose and leaned over Margaret.

"She's out there laughing like a blamed monkey!" he whispered indignantly.

"Well, she can't help it!" exclaimed Margaret.

"I'm going home!" said Wesley.

"Oh, no, you are not!" retorted Margaret. "You are missing the point. The point is not how you look, or feel. It is to get these things in Elnora's possession past dispute. You go now, and to-morrow Elnora will wear calico, and Kate Comstock will return these goods. Right here I stay until everything we bought is Elnora's."

"What are you going to do?" asked Wesley.

"You'll have to watch me," said Margaret. "I don't know yet, myself."

Then she arose and peered from the window. At the well curb stood Katharine Comstock. The strain of the day was finding reaction. Her chin was in the air, she was heaving, shaking and strangling to suppress any sound. The word that slipped between Margaret Sinton's lips shocked Wesley until he dropped on his chair, and recalled her to her senses. She was fairly composed as she turned to Elnora, and began the fitting. When she had pinched, pulled, and patted she called, "Come see if you think this fits, Kate."

Mrs. Comstock had gone around to the back door and answered from the kitchen. "You know more about it than I do. Go ahead! I'm getting supper. Don't forget to allow for what it will shrink in washing!"

"I set the colors and washed the goods last night; it can be made to fit right now," answered Margaret past the pins between her teeth.

When she could find nothing more to alter she told Elnora to see how quickly she could heat a pail of water. After she had done that the girl began opening packages.

The hat came first.

"Mother!" cried Elnora. "Mother, of course, you have seen this, but you haven't seen it on me. I must try it on."

"Don't you dare put that on your head until your hair is washed and properly combed," said Margaret.

"Oh!" cried Elnora. "Is that water to wash my hair? I thought it was to set the color in another dress."

"Well, you thought wrong," said Margaret simply. "Your hair is going to be washed and brushed until it shines like copper. While it dries you can eat your supper, and this dress will be finished. Then you can

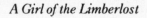

put on your new ribbon, and your hat. You can try your shoes now, and if they don't fit, you and Wesley can drive to town and change them. That little round bundle on the top of the basket is your stockings."

Margaret sat down and began sewing swiftly, and a little later opened the machine, and ran several long seams.

Elnora was back in a few minutes holding up her skirts and stepping daintily in the beautiful new shoes.

"Don't soil them, honey, else you're sure they fit," cautioned Wesley.

"They seem just a trifle large, maybe," said Elnora dubiously, and Wesley got down to feel. He and Margaret thought them a fit, and then Elnora appealed to her mother. Mrs. Comstock appeared wiping her hands on her apron. She examined the shoes critically.

"They seem to fit," she said, "but they are away too fine to walk country roads."

"I think so, too," said Elnora instantly. "We had better take these back and get a cheaper pair."

"Oh, let them go for this time," said Mrs. Comstock. "They are so pretty, I hate to part with them. You can get cheaper ones after this."

Wesley and Margaret scarcely breathed for a long time.

Then Wesley went to do the feeding. Elnora set the table. When the water was hot, Margaret pinned a big towel around Elnora's shoulders and washed and dried the lovely hair according to the instructions she had been given the previous night. As the hair began to dry it billowed out in a sparkling sheen that caught the light and gleamed and flashed.

"Now, the idea is to let it stand naturally, just as the curl will make it. Don't you do any of that nasty, untidy snarling, Elnora," cautioned Margaret. "Wash it this way every two weeks while you are in school, shake it out, and dry it. Then part it in the middle and turn a front quarter on each side from your face. You tie the back at your neck with a string — so, and the ribbon goes in a big, loose bow. I'll show you." One after another Margaret Sinton tied the ribbons, creasing each of them so they could not be returned, as she explained that she was trying to see which was most becoming. Then she produced the raincoat which carried Elnora into transports.

Mrs. Comstock objected. "That won't be warm enough for cold weather, and you can't afford it and a coat, too."

"I'll tell you what I thought," said Elnora. "I was planning on the way home. These coats are fine because they keep you dry. I thought I would get one, and a warm sweater to wear under it cold days. Then you always would be dry, and warm, too. The sweater only costs three dollars, so I could get it and the raincoat both for half the price of a heavy cloth coat."

"You are right about that," said Mrs. Comstock. "You can change more with the weather, too. Keep the raincoat, Elnora."

"Wear it until you try the hat," said Margaret. "It will have to do until the dress is finished."

Elnora picked up the hat dubiously. "Mother, may I wear my hair as it is now?" she asked.

"Let me take a good look," said Katharine Comstock.

Heaven only knows what she saw. To Wesley and to Margaret the bright young face of Elnora, with its pink tints, its heavy dark brows, its bright blue-gray eyes, and its frame of curling reddish brown hair was the sweetest sight on earth, and at that instant Elnora was radiant.

"So long as it's your own hair, and combed back as plain as it will go, I don't suppose it cuts much ice whether it's tied a little tighter or looser," conceded Mrs. Comstock. "If you stop right there, you may let it go at that."

Elnora set the hat on her head. It was just a wide tan straw with three exquisite peacock quills at one side. Margaret Sinton cried out, Wesley slapped his knee and sighed like a blast, and Mrs. Comstock stood speechless for a second.

"I wish you had asked the price before you put that on," she said impatiently. "We never can afford it."

"It's not so much as you think," said Margaret. "Don't you see what I did? I had them take off the quills, and I put on some of those Phœbe Simms gave me from her peacocks. The hat will only cost you a dollar and a half."

70

She avoided Wesley's eyes, and looked straight at Mrs. Comstock. Elnora removed the hat to examine it.

"Why, they are those reddish tan quills of yours!" she cried. "Mother, look how beautifully they are set on! I think they are fine. I'd much rather have them than those from the store."

"So would I," said Mrs. Comstock. "If Margaret wants to spare them, that will make you a beautiful hat; dirt cheap, too! You must go past Mrs. Simms and show her. She would be pleased to see them."

Elnora sank into a chair because she couldn't stand any longer and contemplated her toe. "Landy, ain't I a queen?" she murmured. "What else have I got?"

"Just a belt, some handkerchiefs, and a pair of top shoes for rainy days and colder weather," said Margaret, handing over parcels.

"About those high shoes, that was my idea," said Wesley. "Soon as it rains, low shoes won't do, and by taking two pairs at once I could get them some cheaper. The low ones are two and the high ones two fifty, together three seventy-five. Ain't that cheap?"

"That's a real bargain," said Mrs. Comstock, "if they are good shoes, and they look it."

"This," said Wesley, producing the last package, "is your Christmas present from your Aunt Maggie. I got mine, too, but it's at the house. I'll bring it up in the morning."

He handed Margaret the umbrella, and she passed it over to Elnora who opened it and sat laughing under

its shelter. Then she kissed both of them. She got a pencil and a slip of paper and set down the prices they gave her of everything they had brought except the umbrella, added the sum, and said laughingly, "Will you please wait till to-morrow for the money? I will have it then, sure."

"Elnora," said Wesley Sinton. "Wouldn't you——"

"Elnora, hustle here a minute!" called Mrs. Comstock from the kitchen. "I need you!"

"One second, mother," answered Elnora, throwing off the coat and hat, and closing the umbrella as she ran. There were several errands to do in a hurry, and then supper. Elnora chattered incessantly, Wesley and Margaret talked all they could, while Mrs. Comstock said a word now and then, which was all she ever did. But Welsey Sinton was watching her, and time and again he saw a peculiar little twist around her mouth. He knew that for the first time in sixteen years she really was laughing over something. She had all she could do to preserve her usually sober face. Wesley knew what she was thinking.

After supper the dress was finished, the plans for the next one discussed, and then the Sintons went home. Elnora gathered her treasures.

As she started for the stairs she stopped. "May I kiss you good-night, mother?" she asked lightly.

"Never mind any slobbering," said Mrs. Comstock. "I should think you'd lived with me long enough to know that I don't care for it."

72

"Well, I'd love to show you in some way how happy I am, and how I thank you?"

"I wonder what for?" said Mrs. Comstock. "Mag Sinton picked that stuff and brought it here and you pay for it."

"Yes, but you seemed willing for me to have it, and you said you would help me if I couldn't pay all," insisted Elnora.

"Maybe I did," said Mrs. Comstock. "Maybe I did. I meant to get you some heavy dress skirts about Thanksgiving, and I still can get them. Go to bed, and for any sake don't begin mooning before a mirror, and make a dunce of yourself."

Mrs. Comstock picked up several papers and blew out the kitchen light. She stood in the middle of the sitting-room floor for a time and then went into her room and closed the door. Sitting on the edge of the bed she thought for a few minutes and then suddenly buried her face in the pillow and again heaved with laughter.

Down the road plodded Margaret and Wesley Sinton. Neither of them had words to utter their united thought.

"Done!" hissed Wesley at last. "Done brown! Did you ever feel like a bloomin', confounded donkey? How did the woman do it?"

"She didn't do it!" gulped Margaret through her tears. "She didn't do anything. She just trusted to Elnora's great big soul to bring her out right, and really she was right, and so it had to bring her. She's a

darling, Wesley! But she's got a time before her. Did you see Kate Comstock grab that money? Before six months she'll be out combing the Limberlost for bugs and arrow points to help pay the tax. I know her."

"Well, I don't!" exclaimed Sinton, "She's too many for me. But there is a laugh left in her yet! I didn't s'pose there was. Bet you a dollar, if we could see her this minute, she'd be chuckling over the way we got left."

Both of them stopped in the road and looked back.

"There's Elnora's light in her room," said Margaret. "The poor child will feel those clothes, and pore over her books till morning, but she'll look decent to go to school, anyway. Nothing is too big a price to pay for that."

"Yes, if Kate lets her wear them. Ten to one, she makes her finish the week with that old stuff!"

"No, she won't," said Margaret. "She don't dare. Kate made some concessions, all right; big ones for her —if she did get her way in the main. She bent some, and if Elnora proves that she can walk out barehanded in the morning and come back with that much money in her pocket, an armful of books, and buy a turnout like that, she proves that she is of some consideration, and Kate's smart enough. She'll think twice before she'll do that. Elnora won't wear a calico dress to high school again. You watch and see if she does. She may have got the best clothes she'll get for a time, for the least money, but she won't know it until she tries to buy goods herself at the same rates. Wesley, what about those prices? Didn't they shrink considerable?"

"You began it," said Wesley. "Those prices were all right. We didn't say what the goods cost us, we said what they would cost her. Surely, she's mistaken about being able to pay all that. Can she pick up stuff of that value around the Limberlost? Didn't the Bird Woman see her trouble, and just give her the money?"

"I don't think so," said Margaret. "Seems to me I've heard of her paying, or offering to pay them that would take the money, for bugs and butterflies, and I've known people who sold that banker Indian stuff. Once I heard that his pipe collection beat that of the Government at the Philadelphia Centennial. Those things have come to have a value."

"Well, there's about a bushel of that kind of valuables piled up in the woodshed, that belongs to Elnora. At least, I picked them up because she said she wanted them. Ain't it queer that she'd take to stones, bugs, and butterflies, and save them. Now they are going to bring her the very thing she wants the worst. Lord, but this is a funny world when you get to studying! Looks like things didn't all come by accident. Looks as if there was a plan back of it, and somebody driving that knows the road, and how to handle the lines. Anyhow, Elnora's in the wagon, and when I get out in the night and the dark closes around me, and I see the stars, I don't feel so cheap. Maggie, how the nation did Kate Comstock do that?"

"You will keep on harping, Wesley. I told you she didn't do it. Elnora did it! She walked in and took things right out of our hands. All Kate had to do was to enjoy having it go her way, and she was cute enough to put in a few questions that sort of guided Elnora. But I don't know, Wesley. This thing makes me think, too. S'pose we'd got Elnora when she was a baby, and we'd heaped on her all the love we can't on our own, and we'd coddled, petted, and shielded her, would she have made the woman that living alone, learning to think for herself, and taking all the knocks Kate Comstock could give, have made of her?"

"You bet your life!" cried Wesley, warmly. "Loving anybody don't hurt them. We wouldn't have done anything but love her. You can't hurt a child loving it. She'd have learned to work, be sensible, study, and grown into a woman with us, without suffering like a poor homeless dog."

"But you don't get the point, Wesley. She would have grown into a fine woman with us; just seems as if Elnora was born to be fine, but as we would have raised her, would her heart ever have known the world as it does now? Where's the anguish, Wesley, that child can't comprehend? Seeing what she's seen of her mother hasn't hardened her. She can understand any mother's sorrow. Living life from the rough side has only broadened her. Where's the girl or boy burning with shame, or struggling to find a way, that will cross Elnora's path and not get a lift from her?

She's had the knocks, but there'll never be any of the thing you call 'false pride' in her. I guess we better keep out. Maybe Kate Comstock knows what she's doing. Sure as you live, Elnora has grown bigger on knocks than she would on love."

"I don't s'pose there ever was a very fine point to anything but I missed it," said Wesley, "because I am blunt, rough, and have no book learning to speak of. Since you put it into words I see what you mean, but it's dinged hard on Elnora, just the same. And I don't keep out. I keep watching closer than ever. I got my slap in the face, but if I don't miss my guess, Kate Comstock learned her lesson, same as I did. She learned that I was in earnest, that I would haul her to court if she didn't loosen up a bit, and she'll loosen. You see if she don't. It may come hard, and the hinges creak, but she'll fix Elnora decent after this, if Elnora don't prove that she can fix herself. As for me, I found out that what I was doing was as much for myself as for Elnora. I wanted her to take those things from us, and love us for giving them. It didn't work, and but for you, I'd messed the whole thing and stuck like a pig crossing a bridge. But you helped me out; Elnora's got the clothes, and by morning, maybe I won't grudge Kate the only laugh she's had in sixteen years. You been showing me the way quite a spell now, ain't you, Maggie?"

Then they went out of the night, and lay down together with Margaret's hand just touching Wesley's sleeve.

Up in the attic Elnora lighted two candles, set them

on her little table, stacked the books, and put away the precious clothes. How lovingly she hung the hat and umbrella, folded the raincoat, and spread the new dress over a chair. She fingered the ribbons, and tried to smooth the creases from them. She put away the hose neatly folded, touched the handkerchiefs, and tried the belt. Then she slipped into her little white nightdress, shook down her hair that it might become thoroughly dry, set a chair before the table, and reverently opened one of the books. A stiff draught swept the attic, for it stretched the length of the cabin, and had a window in each end. Elnora arose and going to the east window closed it. She stood for a minute looking at the stars, the sky, and the dark outline of the straggling trees of the rapidly dismantling Limberlost. In the region of her case a tiny point of light flashed and disappeared. Elnora straightened and wondered. Was it wise to leave her precious money there? The light flashed once more, wavered a few seconds, and died out. The girl waited. She did not see it again, and so she went back to her books.

In the Limberlost the hulking figure of a man slouched down the trail.

"The Bird Woman was at Freckles's room this evening," he muttered. "Wonder what for?"

He left the trail, entered the enclosure still distinctly outlined and approached the case. The first point of light flashed from the tiny electric lamp on his vest. He took a duplicate key from his pocket, felt for the padlock and opened it. The door swung wide. The light flashed the second time. Swiftly his glance swept the interior.

"'Bout a fourth of her moths gone. Elnora must have been with the Bird Woman and given them to her." Then he stood tense. His keen eyes discovered the roll of bills hastily thrust back in the bottom of the case. He snatched them up, shut off the light, relocked the case by touch, and swiftly went down the trail. Every few seconds he paused and listened intently. Just as he reached the road, the low hoot of a screech owl, waveringly prolonged, fell on his ears, and he stopped. An instant later a second figure approached him.

"Is it you, Pete?" came the whispered question.

"Yes," said the first man.

"I was coming down to take a peep, when I saw your flash," he said. "I heard the Bird Woman had been at the case to-day. Anything doing?"

"Not a thing," said Pete. "She just took away about a fourth of the moths. Probably had the Comstock girl getting them for her. Heard they were together. Likely she'll get the rest to-morrow. Ain't picking gettin' bare these days?"

"Well, I should say so," said the second man, turning back in disgust. "Coming home, now?"

"No, I am going down this way," answered Pete, for his eyes caught the gleam from the window of the Comstock cabin, and he had a desire to learn why Elnora's attic was lighted at that hour.

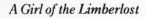

He slouched down the road, occasionally feeling the size of the roll he had not taken time to count. He chuckled frequently.

"Feels fat enough to pay," he whispered. "Bill, I beat you just about seven minutes."

The attic was too long, the light too near the other end, and the cabin stood much too far back from the road. He could see nothing although he climbed the fence and walked back opposite the window. He knew Mrs. Comstock was probably awake, and that she sometimes went to the swamp behind her home at night. At times a cry went up from that locality that paralyzed anyone near, or sent them fleeing as if for life. He did not care to cross behind the cabin. He returned to the road, passed, and again climbed the fence. Opposite the west window he could see Elnora. She sat before a small table reading from a book between two candles. Her hair fell in a bright sheen around her, and with one hand she lightly shook, and tossed it as she studied. The man stood out in the night and watched.

For a long time a leaf turned occasionally and the hair-drying went on. The man drew nearer. The picture grew more beautiful as he approached. He could not see as well as he desired, for the screen was of white mosquito netting, and it angered him. He cautiously crept closer. The elevation shut off his view. Then he remembered the great willow tree shading the well and branching across the window at the west end of the cabin. From childhood Elnora had stepped from

the sill to a limb and slid down the slanting trunk of
the tree. He reached it and noiselessly swung himself
up. Three steps out on the big limb the man shuddered.
He was within a few feet of the girl.

He could see the throb of her breast under its thin
covering and smell the fragrance of the tossing hair.
He could see the narrow bed with its pieced calico cover,
the whitewashed walls with gay lithographs, and every
crevice stuck full of twigs with dangling cocoons. There
were pegs for the few clothes, the old chest, the little
table, the two chairs, the uneven floor covered with
rag rugs, and braided corn husk. But nothing was worth
a glance save the perfect face and form within reach by
one spring through the rotten mosquito bar. He gripped
the limb above that on which he stood, licked his lips,
and breathed through his throat to be sure he was making
no sound. Elnora closed the book and laid it aside.
She picked up a towel, and turning the gathered ends
of her hair rubbed them across it, and dropping the towel
on her lap, tossed the hair again. Then she sat in deep
thought. By and by words began to come softly. Near
as he was the man could not hear at first. He bent
closer and listened intently.

"— ever could be so happy," murmured the soft voice.
"The dress is so pretty, such shoes, the coat and everything. I won't have to be ashamed again, not ever
again, for the Limberlost is full of precious moths, and
I always can collect them. The Bird Woman will buy
more to-morrow, and the next day, and the next. When

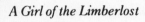

they are all gone, I can spend every minute gathering
cocoons, and hunting other things I can sell. Oh,
thank God, for my precious, precious money. Why,
I didn't pray in vain after all! I thought when I asked
the Lord to hide me, there in that big hall, that He
wasn't doing it, because I wasn't covered from sight
that instant. But I'm hidden now, I feel that." Elnora
lifted her eyes to the beams above her. "I don't know
much about praying properly," she muttered, "but I
do thank you, Lord, for hiding me in your own time and
way."

Her face was so bright that it shone with a white
radiance. Two big tears welled from her eyes, and
rolled down her smiling cheeks. "Oh, I do feel that
you have hidden me," she breathed. Then she blew
out the lights, and the little wooden bed creaked under
her weight.

Pete Corson dropped from the limb and found his
way to the road. He stood still a long time, then started
back to the Limberlost. A tiny point of light flashed in
the region of the case. He stopped with an oath.

"Another hound trying to steal from a girl," he
exclaimed. "But it's likely he thinks if he gets anything it will be from a woman who can afford it, as
I did."

He went on, but beside the fences, and very cautiously.

"Swamp seems to be alive to-night," he muttered.
"That's three of us out."

He entered a deep place at the northwest corner, sat

on the ground and taking a pencil from his pocket, he tore a leaf from a little notebook, and laboriously wrote a few lines by the light he carried. Then he went back to the region of the case and waited. Before his eyes swept the vision of the slender white creature with tossing hair. He smiled, and worshipped it, until a distant rooster faintly announced dawn.

Then he unlocked the case again, and replaced the money, laid the note upon it, and went back to concealment, where he remained until Elnora came down the trail in the morning, looking very lovely in her new dress and hat.

CHAPTER 5

Wherein Elnora Receives a Warning, and Billy Appears on the Scene

IT would be difficult to describe just how happy Elnora was that morning as she hurried through her work, bathed and put on the neat, dainty gingham dress, and the tan shoes. She had a struggle with her hair. It crinkled, billowed, and shone, and she could not avoid seeing the becoming frame it made around her face. But in deference to her mother's feelings the girl set her teeth, and bound her hair close to her head with a shoe-string. "Not to be changed at the case," she told herself.

That her mother was watching she was unaware. Just as she picked up the beautiful brown ribbon Mrs. Comstock spoke.

"You had better let me tie that. You can't reach behind yourself and do it right."

Elnora gave a little gasp. Her mother never before had proposed to do anything for the girl that by any possibility she could do herself. Her heart quaked at the thought of how her mother would arrange that bow, but Elnora dared not refuse. The offer was too precious. It might never be made again.

"Oh, thank you!" said the girl, and sitting down she held out the ribbon.

Her mother stood back and looked at her critically.

"You haven't got that like Mag Sinton had it last night," she announced. "You little idiot! You've tried to plaster it down to suit me, and you missed it. I liked it away better as Mag fixed it, after I saw it. You didn't look so peeled."

"Oh, mother, mother!" laughed Elnora, with a half sob in her voice.

"Hold still, will you?" cried Mrs. Comstock. "You'll be late, and I haven't packed your dinner yet."

She untied the string and shook out the hair. It rose with electricity and clung to her fingers and hands. Mrs. Comstock jumped back as if bitten. She knew that touch. Her face grew white, and her eyes angry.

"Tie it yourself," she said shortly, "and then I'll put on the ribbon. But roll it back loose like Mag did. It looked so pretty that way."

Almost fainting Elnora stood before the glass, divided off the front parts of her hair, and rolled them as Mrs. Sinton had done; tied it at the nape of her neck, then sat while her mother arranged the ribbon.

"If I pull it down till it comes tight in these creases where she had it, it will be just right won't it?" queried Mrs. Comstock, and the amazed Elnora stammered "Yes."

When she looked in the glass the bow was perfectly

tied, and how the gold tone of the brown did match the lustre of the shining hair! "That's awful pretty," commented Mrs. Comstock's soul, but her stiff lips had said all that could be forced from them for once. Just then Wesley Sinton came to the door.

"Good morning," he cried heartily. "Elnora, you look a picture! My, but you're sweet! If any of them city boys get sassy you tell your Uncle Wesley, and he'll horsewhip them. Here's your Christmas present from me." He handed Elnora the leather lunch box, with her name carved across the strap in artistic lettering.

"Oh, Uncle Wesley!" and that was all Elnora could say.

"Your Aunt Maggie filled it for me for a starter," he said. "Now, if you are ready, I'm going to drive past your way and you can ride almost to Onabasha with me, and save the new shoes that much."

Elnora was staring at the box. "Oh, I hope it isn't impolite to open it before you," she said. "I just feel as if I must see inside."

"Don't you stand on no formality with the neighbors," laughed Sinton. "Look at your box if you want to!"

Elnora slipped the strap and turned back the lid.

This disclosed the knife, fork, napkin, and spoon, the milk flask, and the interior packed with dainty sandwiches wrapped in tissue paper, and the little compartments for meat, salad, and the custard cup.

"Oh, mother!" cried Elnora. "Oh, mother, isn't it fine? What made you think of it, Uncle Wesley? How

86

will I ever thank you? No one will have a finer lunch box than I. Oh, I do thank you! That's the nicest gift I ever had. How I love Christmas in September!"

"It's a mighty handy thing," assented Mrs. Comstock, taking in every detail with sharp eyes. "I guess you are glad now you went and helped Mag and Wesley when you could, Elnora?"

"Deedy, yes," laughed Elnora, "and I'm going again first time they have a big day if I stay out of school to do it."

"You'll do no such thing!" said the delighted Sinton. "Come now, if you're going!"

"If I ride, can you spare me time to run into the swamp to my box just a minute?" asked Elnora.

The light she had seen the previous night troubled her.

"Sure," said Wesley largely. He was having such a good time nothing could hurry him. So they drove away and left a white-faced woman watching them from the door, her heart just a little sorer than usual.

"I'd give a pretty to hear what he'll say to her!" she said bitterly. "Always sticking in, always doing things I can't ever afford. Where on earth did he get that thing and what did it cost?"

Then she entered the cabin and began the day's work, but mingled with the brooding bitterness of her soul was the vision of a sweet young face, glad with a gladness never before seen on it, and over and over she repeated, "I wonder what he'll say to her!"

What he said was that she looked as fresh and sweet

as a posy, and to be careful not to step in the mud or scratch her shoe when she went to the case.

Elnora found her key and opened the door. Not where she had placed it, but conspicuously in front lay her little heap of bills, and a crude scrawl of writing beside it. Elnora picked up the note in astonishment.

DERE ELNORY,

the lord amighty is hiding you all right done you ever dout it this money of yourn was took for some time las nite but it is returned with intres for god sake done ever come to the swamp at nite or late evnin or mornin or far in any time sompin worse an you know could git you

A FREND.

Elnora began to tremble. She hastily glanced about. The damp earth before the case had been trodden by large, roughly shod feet. She caught up the money and the note, thrust them into her guimpe, locked the case, and ran for the road.

She was so breathless and her face so white Sinton noticed it.

"What in the world's the matter, Elnora?" he asked as he helped her into the carriage.

"I am half afraid!" she panted.

"Tut, tut, child!" said Wesley Sinton. "Nothing in the world to be afraid of. What happened?"

"Uncle Wesley," said Elnora, "I had more money than I brought home last night, and I put it in my case. Someone has been there. The ground is all trampled, and they left this note."

"And took your money, I'll wager," said Sinton angrily.

"No," answered Elnora. "Read the note and, oh, Uncle Wesley, tell me what it means!"

Sinton's face was a study. "I don't know what it means," he said. "Only one thing is clear. It means some beast who doesn't really want to harm you, has got his eye on you, and he is telling you plain as he can, not to give him a chance. You got to keep along the roads, in the open, and not let the biggest moth that ever flew toll you out of hearing of us, or your mother. It means that, plain and distinct."

"Just when I can sell them! Just when everything is so lovely on account of them! I can't! I can't stay away from the swamp. The Limberlost is going to buy the books, the clothes, pay the tuition, and even start a college fund. I just can't!"

"You've got to," said Sinton. "This is plain enough. You go far in the swamp at your own risk, even in day-time."

"Uncle Wesley," said the girl in a whisper, "last night before I went to bed, I was so happy I tried to pray, and I thanked God for hiding me 'under the shadow of His wing.' But how in the world could anyone know it?"

Wesley Sinton's heart gave one great leap in his breast. His face was whiter than the girl's now.

"Was you praying out loud, honey?" he almost whispered.

"I might have said words," answered Elnora. "I know I do sometimes. I've never had anyone to talk

to, and I've played with and talked to myself all my life. You've caught me at it often, but it always makes mother angry when she does. She says it's silly. I forget and do it, when I'm alone. But, Uncle Wesley, if I said anything last night, you know it was the merest whisper, because I'd have been so afraid of waking mother. Don't you see? I sat up late, and did two lessons."

Sinton was steadying himself. "I'll stop and examine the case as I come back," he said. "Maybe I can find some clue. That other — that was just accidental. It's a common expression. All the preachers use it. If I was going to pray, that would be the very first thing I'd say."

The colour came back to Elnora's face.

"Did you tell your mother about this money, Elnora?" he asked.

"No, I didn't," said Elnora. "It's dreadful not to, but I was afraid. You see they are clearing the swamp so fast. Every year it grows harder to find things, and Indian stuff gets scarcer. I want to graduate, and that's four years unless I can double on the course. That means twenty dollars tuition each year, and new books, and clothes. There won't ever be so much at one time again, that I know. I just got to hang to my money. I was afraid to tell her, for fear she would want it for taxes, and she really must sell a tree or some cattle for that, mustn't she, Uncle Wesley?"

"On your life, she must!" said Wesley. "You put your little wad in the bank all safe, and never mention it to a living soul. It don't seem right, but your case is peculiar. Every word you say is a true word. Each year you will get less from the swamp, and things everywhere will be scarcer. If you ever get a few dollars ahead, that can start your college fund. You know you are going to college, Elnora!"

"Of course I am," said Elnora. "I settled that as soon as I knew what a college was. I will put all my money in the bank, except what I owe you. I'll pay that now."

"If your arrows are heavy," said Wesley, "I'll drive on to Onabasha with you."

"But they are not. Half of them were nicked, and this little box held all the good ones. It's so surprising how many are spoiled when you wash them."

"What does he pay?"

"Ten cents for any common perfect one, fifty for revolvers, a dollar for obsidian, and whatever is right for enormous big ones."

"Well, that sounds fair," said Sinton. "It's more than I would want to give for the things. You can come down Saturday and wash up the stuff at our house, and I'll take it in when we go marketing in the afternoon."

Elnora jumped from the carriage. She soon found that with her books, her lunch box, and the points she had a heavy load. She was almost to the bridge crossing the culvert when she heard the distressed screams of a child. Across an orchard of the suburbs came a small

boy, after him a big dog, urged by a man in the background. Elnora's heart was with the small flying figure in
any event whatever. She dropped her load on the bridge,
and with practised hand caught up a stone and flung
it at the dog. The beast curled double with a howl.
The boy reached the fence, and Elnora was there to
help him over. As he touched the top she swung
him to the ground, but he clung to her, clasping
her tightly, sobbing and shivering with fear. Elnora
carried him to the bridge, and sat with him in her
arms. For a time his replies to her questions were
indistinct, but at last he became quieter and she could
understand.

He was a mite of a boy, nothing but skin-covered
bones, his burned, freckled face in a mortar of tears
and dust, his clothing unspeakably dirty, one great toe
in a festering mass from a broken nail, and sores all
over the visible portions of the small body.

"You won't let the mean old thing make his dog get
me!" he wailed.

"Indeed no," said Elnora, hugging him closely

"You wouldn't set a dog on a boy for just taking a
few old apples when you fed 'em to pigs with a shovel
every day, would you?"

"No, I would not," said Elnora hotly.

"You'd give a boy all the apples he wanted, if he
hadn't any breakfast, and was so hungry he was all
twisty inside, wouldn't you?"

"Yes, I would," said Elnora.

"If you had anything to eat you would give me something right now, wouldn't you?"

"Yes," said Elnora. "There's nothing but just stones in the package. But my dinner is in that case. I'll gladly divide."

She opened the box. The famished child gave a little cry and reached both hands. Elnora caught them back.

"Did you have any supper?"

"No."

"Any dinner yesterday?"

"An apple and some grapes I stole."

"Whose boy are you?"

"Old Tom Billings's."

"Why don't your father get you something to eat?"

"He does most days, but he's drunk now."

"Hush, you must not!" said Elnora. "He's your father!"

"He's spent all the money to get drunk, too," said the boy, "and Jimmy and Belle are both crying for breakfast. I'd a got out all right with an apple for myself, but I tried to get some for them, and the dog got too close. Say, you can just throw, can't you?"

"Yes," admitted Elnora. She poured half the milk into the cup. "Drink this," she said, holding it to him.

The boy gulped the milk and swore joyously, gripping the cup with shaking fingers.

"Hush!" cried Elnora. "That's dreadful!"

"What's dreadful?"

"To say such awful words."

93

"Huh! pa says worser 'an that every breath he draws."

Elnora stared into the quaint little face, and saw that the child was older than she had thought. He might have been forty by his hard, unchildish expression.

"Do you want to be like your father?"

"No, I want to be like you. Couldn't a angel be prettier 'an you. Can I have more milk?"

Elnora emptied the flask. The boy drained the cup. He drew a breath of satisfaction as he gazed into her face.

"You wouldn't go off and leave your little boy, would you?" he asked.

"Did someone go away and leave you?" questioned Elnora in return.

"Yes, my mother went off and left me, and left Jimmy and Belle, too," said the boy. "You wouldn't leave your little boy, would you?"

"No."

The boy looked eagerly at the box. Elnora lifted a sandwich and uncovered the fried chicken. The boy gasped with delight.

"Say, I could eat the stuff in the glass, and the other box and carry the bread and the chicken to Jimmy and Belle," he offered.

Elnora silently uncovered the custard with preserved cherries on top and handed it and the spoon to the child. Never did food disappear faster. The salad went next, and a sandwich and half a chicken breast followed.

"I better leave the rest for Jimmy and Belle," he said, "they're 'ist fightin' hungry."

Elnora gave him the remainder of the carefully prepared lunch. The boy clutched it and ran with a sidewise hop like a wild thing.

Elnora covered the dishes and cup, polished the spoon, replaced it, and closed the beautiful case. She caught her breath in a tremulous laugh.

"If Aunt Margaret knew that, she'd never forgive me," she said. "It seems as if secrecy is literally forced upon me, and I hate it. What will I do for lunch? I'll have to go sell my arrows and keep enough money for a restaurant sandwich."

So she walked hurriedly into town, sold her points at a good price, deposited her funds, and went away with a neat little bank book and the note from the Limberlost carefully folded inside. Elnora passed down the great hall that morning, and no one paid the slightest attention to her. The truth was she looked so like everyone else that she was perfectly inconspicuous. But in the coat room there were members of her class. Surely no one intended it, but the whisper was too loud.

"Look at the girl from the Limberlost in the clothes that woman gave her!"

Elnora turned on them. "I beg your pardon," she said unsteadily, "I couldn't help hearing that! No one gave me these clothes. I paid for them myself."

Some one muttered, "Pardon me," but incredulous faces greeted her.

Elnora felt driven. "Aunt Margaret selected them, and she meant to give them to me," she explained, " but I

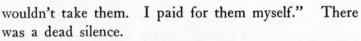

wouldn't take them. I paid for them myself." There was a dead silence.

"Don't you believe me?" panted Elnora.

"Really, it is none of our affair," said another girl. "Come on, let's go."

Elnora stepped before the girl who had spoken. "You have made this your affair," she said, "because you told a thing which was not true. No one gave me what I am wearing. I paid for my clothes myself with money I earned selling moths to the Bird Woman. I just came from the bank where I deposited what I did not use. Here is my credit." Elnora drew out and offered the little red book. "Surely you will believe that," she said.

"Why, of course," said the girl who first had spoken. "We met such a lovely woman in Brownlee's store, and she said she wanted our help to buy some things for a girl, and that's how we came to know."

"Dear Aunt Margaret," said Elnora, "it was like her to ask you. Isn't she splendid?"

"She is indeed," chorused the girls. Elnora set down her lunch box and books, unpinned her hat, hanging it beside the others, and taking up the books she reached to set the box in its place and dropped it. With a little cry she snatched at it and caught the strap on top. That pulled from the fastening, the cover unrolled, the box fell away as far as it could, two porcelain lids rattled on the floor, and the one sandwich rolled like a cartwheel across the room. Elnora lifted a ghastly face. For once no one laughed. She stood an instant staring.

"It seems to be my luck to be crucified at every point of the compass," she said at last. "First two days you thought I was a pauper, now you will think I'm a fraud. All of you will believe I bought an expensive box, and then was too poor to put anything but a restaurant sandwich in it. You must stop till I prove to you that I'm not."

Elnora gathered up the lids, and kicked the sandwich into a corner.

"I had milk in that bottle, see! And custard in the cup. There was salad in the little box, fried chicken in the large one, and nut sandwiches in the tray. You can see the crumbs of all of them. A man set a dog on a child who was so starved he was stealing apples. I talked with him, and I thought I could bear hunger better, he was such a little boy, so I gave him my lunch, and got the sandwich at the restaurant."

Elnora held out the box. The girls were laughing by that time. "You goose," said one, "why didn't you give him the money, and save your lunch?"

"He was such a little fellow, and he really was hungry," said Elnora. "I often go without anything to eat at noon in the fields and woods, and never think of it."

She closed the box and set it beside the lunches of other country pupils. While her back was turned, into the room came the girl of her encounter on the first day, walked to the rack, and with an exclamation of approval took down Elnora's hat.

"Just the thing I have been wanting!" she said. "I

never saw such beautiful quills in all my life. They match my new broadcloth to perfection. I've got to have that kind of quills for my hat. I never saw the like! Whose is it, and where did it come from?"

No one said a word, for Elnora's question, the reply, and her answer, had gone the rounds of the high school. Everyone knew that the Limberlost girl had come out ahead and Sadie Reed had not felt amiable, when the little flourish had been added to Elnora's name in the algebra class. Elnora's swift glance was pathetic, but no one helped her. Sadie Reed glanced from the hat to the faces around her and wondered.

"Why, this is the Freshman section, whose hat is it?" she asked again, this time impatiently.

"That's the tassel of the cornstock," said Elnora with a forced laugh.

The response was genuine. Everyone shouted. Sadie Reed blushed, but she laughed also.

"Well, it's beautiful," she said, "especially the quills. They are exactly what I want. I know I don't deserve any kindness from you, but I do wish you would tell me at whose store you got those quills."

"Gladly!" said Elnora. "You can't get quills like those at a store. They are from a living bird. Phœbe Simms gathers them in her orchard as her peacocks shed them. They are wing quills from the males."

Then there was a perfect silence. How was Elnora to know that not a girl there would have told that?

"I haven't a doubt but I can get you some," she

offered. "She gave Aunt Margaret a great bunch, and those are part of them. I am quite sure she has more, and would spare some."

Sadie Reed laughed shortly. "You needn't trouble," she said, "I was fooled. I thought they were expensive quills. I wanted them for a twenty-dollar velvet toque to match my new suit. If they are picked off the ground, really, I couldn't use them."

"Only in spots!" said Elnora. "They don't just cover the earth. Phœbe Simms's peacocks are the only ones within miles of Onabasha, and they moult but once a year. If your hat only cost twenty dollars, it's hardly good enough for those quills. You see, the Almighty made and coloured those Himself; and He puts the same kind on Phœbe Simms's peacocks, that He put on the head of the family in the forests of Ceylon, away back in the beginning. Any old manufactured quill from New York or Chicago will do for your little twenty-dollar hat. You ought to have something infinitely better than that to be worthy of quills that are made by the Creator."

How those girls did laugh! One of them walked by Elnora to the auditorium, sat with her during exercises, and tried to talk whenever she dared, to keep Elnora from seeing the curious and admiring looks bent upon her. For the brown-eyed boy whistled, and there was pantomime of all sorts going on behind Elnora's back that day. Happy with her books, no one knew how much she saw, and from her absorption in her studies

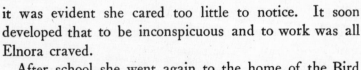

it was evident she cared too little to notice. It soon developed that to be inconspicuous and to work was all Elnora craved.

After school she went again to the home of the Bird Woman, and together they visited the swamp and took away more specimens. This time Elnora asked the Bird Woman to keep the money until noon of the next day, when she would call for it and have it added to her bank account. She slowly walked home, for the visit to the swamp had brought back full force the experience of the morning. Again and again she examined the crude little note, for she did not know what it meant, yet it bred vague fear. The only thing on earth of which Elnora knew herself afraid was her mother; when with wild eyes and ears deaf to childish pleading, she sometimes lost control of herself in the night and visited the pool where her husband had sunk before her, calling his name in unearthly tones and begging of the swamp to give back its dead.

CHAPTER 6

Wherein Mrs. Comstock Indulges in "Frills," and Billy Reappears

It was Wesley Sinton who really wrestled with the problem as he drove about his business. He did not have to ask himself what it meant; he knew. The old Corson gang was still holding together. Elder members who had escaped the law had been joined by a younger brother of Jack's, and they met in the thickest of the few remaining fast places of the swamp to drink, gamble, and loaf. Then, suddenly, there would be a robbery in some country house where a farmer that day had sold his wheat or corn and not paid a visit to the bank; or in some neighbouring village.

The home of Mrs. Comstock and Elnora adjoined the swamp. Sinton's land lay next, and not another residence or man easy to reach in case of trouble. Whoever wrote that note had some human kindness in his breast, but the fact stood revealed that he feared his strength if Elnora was delivered into his hands. Where had he been the previous night when he heard that prayer? Was that the first time he had been in such proximity? Sinton drove fast, for he wished to reach the swamp

before Elnora and the Bird Woman would go there for more moths.

At almost four he came to the case, and dropping on his knees studied the ground, every sense alert. He found two or three little heel prints. Those were made by Elnora or the Bird Woman. What Sinton wanted to learn was whether all the rest were the footprints of one man. It was easily seen, they were not. There were deep, even tracks made by fairly new shoes, and others where a well-worn heel cut deeper on the inside of the print than at the outer edge. Undoubtedly some of Corson's old gang were watching the case, and the visits of the women to it. There was no danger that anyone would attack the Bird Woman. She never went to the swamp at night, and on her trips in the daytime, every one knew that she carried a revolver, understood how to use it, and pursued her work in a fearless manner.

Elnora, prowling around the swamp and lured into the interior by the flight of moths and butterflies; Elnora, without father, money, or friends save himself, to defend her — Elnora was a different proposition. For the thing to happen just when the Limberlost was bringing light, hope, and the very desire of her heart to the girl, it was too bad.

Sinton was afraid for her, yet he did not want to add the burden of fear to Katharine Comstock's trouble, or to disturb the joy of Elnora in her work. He stopped at the cabin and slowly went up the walk. Mrs. Com-

stock was sitting on the front step with some sewing.
The work looked to Sinton as if she might be engaged
in putting a tuck in a petticoat. He thought of how
Margaret had shortened Elnora's dress to the accepted
length for girls of her age, and made a mental note of
Mrs. Comstock's occupation.

Mrs. Comstock dropped her work on her lap, laid
her hands on it and looked into his face with a sneer.

"You didn't let any grass grow under your feet,"
she said.

Sinton saw her white, drawn face and comprehended.

"I went to pay a debt and see about this opening of
the ditch, Kate."

"You said you were going to prosecute me."

"Good gracious, Kate!" cried Sinton. "Is that
what you have been thinking all day? I told you before
I left yesterday that I would not need do that. And I
won't! We can't afford to quarrel over Elnora. She's
all we've got. Now that she has proved that if you
don't do just what I think you ought by way of clothes
and schooling, she can take care of herself, I put that
out of my head. What I came to see you about is a
kind of scare I've had to-day. I want to ask you if
you ever see anything about the swamp that makes
you think the old Corson gang is still alive?"

"Can't say that I do," said Mrs. Comstock. "There's
kind of dancing lights there sometimes, but I supposed
it was just people passing along the road with lanterns.
Folks hereabout are none too fond of the swamp. I

hate it like death. I've never stayed here a night in my life without Robert's revolver, clean and loaded, under my pillow, and the shotgun, same condition, by the bed. I can't say that I'm afraid here at home. I'm not. I can take care of myself. But none of the swamp for me!"

"Well, I'm glad you are not afraid, Kate, because I got to tell you something. Elnora stopped at the case this morning, and somebody had been into it in the night."

"Broke the lock?"

"No. Used a duplicate key. To-day I heard there was a man here last night. I want to nose around a little."

Sinton went to the east end of the cabin and looked up at the window. There was no way anyone could have reached it without a ladder, for the logs were hewed and mortar filled the cracks even. Then he went to the west end, the willow faced him as he turned the corner. He examined the trunk carefully. There was no mistake about small particles of black swamp muck adhering to the sides of the tree. He reached the low branches and climbed the willow. There was earth on the large limb crossing Elnora's window. He stood on it, holding the branch as had been done the night before, and looked into the room. He could see very little, but he knew that if it had been dark outside and sufficiently light for Elnora to study inside he could have seen vividly. He brought his face close to the netting, and he could see the bed with its head to the east, at its foot the table with the candles and the chair before it, and then he knew where the man had been who had heard Elnora's prayer.

Mrs. Comstock had followed around the corner and stood watching him. "Do you think some slinking hulk was up there peekin' in at Elnora?" she demanded indignantly.

"There is muck on the trunk, and plenty on the limb," said Sinton. "Hadn't you better get a saw and let me take this branch off?"

"No, I hadn't," said Mrs. Comstock. "First place, Elnora's climbed from that window on that limb all her life, and it's hers. Second place, no one gets ahead of me after I've had warning. Any crow that perches on that roost again, will get its feathers somewhat scattered. Look along the fence, there, and see if you can find where he came in."

The place was easy to find as was a trail leading for some distance west of the cabin.

"You just go home, and don't fret yourself," said Mrs. Comstock. "I'll take care of this. If you should hear the dinner bell at any time in the night you come down. But I wouldn't say anything to Elnora. She best keep her mind on her studies, if she's going to school."

When the work was finished that night Elnora took her books and went to her room to prepare some lessons, but every few minutes she looked toward the swamp to see if there were lights near the case. Mrs. Comstock raked together the coals in the cooking stove, got out

the lunch box, and sitting down she studied it grimly. At last she arose.

"Wonder how it would do to show Mag Sinton a frill or two," she murmured.

She went to her room, knelt by a big black-walnut chest and hunted through its contents until she found an old-fashioned cook book. She tended the fire as she read and presently was in action. She first sawed an end from a fragrant, juicy, sugar-cured ham and put it to cook. Then she set a couple of eggs boiling, and after long hesitation began creaming butter and sugar in a crock. An hour later the odour of the ham, mingled with some of the richest spices of "happy Araby," in a combination that could mean nothing save spice cake, crept up to Elnora so strongly that she lifted her head and sniffed amazedly. She would have given all her precious money to go down and throw her arms around her mother's neck, but she did not dare move, even to open the door for a better smell.

Mrs. Comstock was up early, and without a word handed Elnora the case as she left the next morning.

"Thank you, mother," said Elnora, and went on her way.

She walked down the road looking straight ahead until she came to the corner, where she usually entered the swamp. She paused, glanced that way and smiled. Then she turned and looked back. There was no one coming in any direction. She kept to the road until well around the corner, then she stopped and sat on a grassy spot, laid her books beside her and opened the lunch box. Last night's odours had in a measure prepared her for what she would see, but not quite. She scarcely could believe her senses. Half the bread compartment was filled with dainty sandwiches of bread and butter sprinkled with the yolk of egg and the rest with three large slices of the most fragrant spice cake imaginable. The meat dish contained shaved cold ham, of which she knew the quality, the salad was tomatoes and celery, and the cup held preserved pear, clear as amber. There was milk in the bottle, two tissue-wrapped cucumber pickles in the folding drinking-cup, and a fresh napkin in the ring. No lunch was ever daintier or more palatable; of that Elnora was perfectly sure. And her mother had prepared it for her!

She glanced around her and then to her old refuge, the sky. "She does love me!" cried the happy girl. "Sure as you're born she loves me; she just hasn't found it out yet!"

She touched the papers daintily, and smiled at the box as if it were a living thing. As she began closing it a breath of air swept by, lifting the covering of the cake. It was like an invitation, and breakfast was several hours away. Elnora picked up a piece and ate it. That cake tasted even better than it looked. Then she tried a sandwich. How did her mother come to think of making them that way. They never had any at home. She slipped out the fork, sampled the salad, and one-quarter of pear. Then she closed the box

107

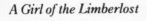

and started down the road nibbling one of the pickles
and trying to decide exactly how happy she was,
but just then she could find no standard high enough
for a measure.

She was to go to the Bird Woman's after school for
the last load from the case. Saturday she would take
the arrow points and specimens to the bank. That
would exhaust her present supplies and give her enough
money ahead to pay for books, tuition, and clothes for
at least two years. She would work early and late
gathering nuts. In October she would sell all the ferns
she could find. She must collect specimens of all tree
leaves before they fell, gather nests and cocoons later,
and keep her eyes wide open for anything the grades
could use. She would see the superintendent that night
about selling specimens to the ward buildings. She
must be ahead of anyone else if she wanted to furnish
these things. So she approached the bridge.

That it was occupied could be seen from a distance.
As she came up she found the small boy of yesterday
awaiting her with a confident smile.

"We brought you something!" he announced without
greeting. "This is Jimmy and Belle — and we brought
you a present."

He offered a parcel wrapped in brown paper.

"Why, how lovely of you!" said Elnora. "I supposed
you had forgotten me when you ran away so fast yesterday."

"Naw, I didn't forget you," said the boy. "I wouldn't

forget you, not ever! Why, I was ist a-hurrying to take them things to Jimmy and Belle. My, they was glad!"

Elnora glanced at the children. They sat on the edge of the bridge, obviously clad in a garment each, very dirty and unkept, a little boy and a girl of about seven and nine. Elnora's heart began to ache.

"Say," said the boy. "Ain't you going to look what we have gave you?"

"I thought it wasn't polite to look before people," answered Elnora. "Of course, I will, if you would like to have me."

Elnora opened the package. She had been presented with a quarter of a stale loaf of baker's bread, and a big piece of ancient bologna."

"But don't you want this yourselves?" she asked in surprise.

"Gosh, no! I mean ist plain no," said the boy. "We always have it. We got stacks this morning. Pa's come out of it now, and he's so sorry he got more 'an ever we can eat. Have you had any before?"

"No," said Elnora, "I never did!"

The boy's eyes brightened and the girl moved restlessly.

"We thought maybe you hadn't," said the boy. "First you ever have, you like it real well; but when you don't have anything else for a long time, years an' years, you git so tired."

He hitched at the string which held his trousers and eyed Elnora speculatively.

"I don't s'pose you'd trade what you got in that box for ist old bread and bologna now, would you? Mebby you'd like it! And I know, I ist know, what you got would taste like heaven to Jimmy and Belle. They never had nothing like that! Not even Belle, and she's most ten! No, sir-ee, they never tasted things like you got!"

It was in Elnora's heart to be thankful that she had got even a taste in time, as she knelt on the bridge, opened the box and divided her lunch into three equal parts, the smaller boy getting most of the milk. Then she told them it was school time and she must go.

"Why don't you put your bread and bologna in the nice box?" asked the boy.

"Of course," said Elnora. "I didn't think."

When the box was arranged to the children's satisfaction all of them accompanied Elnora to the corner where she turned toward the high school. Elnora and Billy led the way, Jimmy and Belle followed.

"Billy," said Elnora, "I would like you much better if you were cleaner. Surely, you have water! Can't you children get some soap and wash yourselves? Gentlemen are never dirty. You want to be a gentleman, don't you?"

"Is being clean all you have to do to be a gentleman?"

"No," said Elnora. "You must not say bad words, and you must be kind and polite to your sister."

"Must Belle be kind and polite to me, else she ain't a lady?"

"Yes."

"Then Belle's no lady!" said Billy succinctly.

Elnora could say nothing more just then, and she bade them good-bye and started them home.

"The poor little souls!" she mused. "I think the Almighty put them in my way to show me real trouble. I won't be likely to spend much time pitying myself while I can see them." She glanced at the lunch box. "What on earth do I carry this for? I never had anything that was so strictly ornamental! One sure thing! I can't take this stuff to the high school. You never seem to know just what is going to happen to you while you are there."

As if to provide a way out of her difficulty a big dog arose from a lawn, and came toward the gate wagging his tail. "If those children ate the stuff, it can't possibly kill him!" thought Elnora, so she offered the bologna. The dog accepted it graciously, and being a pedigreed beast he trotted around to a side porch and laid the bologna before his mistress. The woman snatched it, screaming, "Come, quick! Someone is trying to poison Pedro!" Her daughter came running from the house. "Go see who is on the street. Hurry!" cried the excited mother.

Ellen Brownlee ran and looked. Elnora was a half block away, and no one nearer. Ellen called loudly, and Elnora stopped. Ellen came running toward her.

"Did you see anyone give our dog something?" she cried as she approached.

Elnora saw no escape.

"I gave it a piece of bologna myself," she said. "It was fit to eat. It wouldn't hurt the dog."

Ellen stood and looked at her. "Of course, I didn't know it was your dog," explained Elnora. "I just had something I wanted to throw to some dog, and that one looked big enough to manage it."

Ellen had arrived at her conclusions. "Pass over that lunch box," she demanded.

"I will not!" said Elnora.

"Then I will have you arrested for trying to poison our dog," laughed the girl as she took the box.

"One chunk of stale bread, one half mile of antique bologna contributed for dog feed; the remains of cake, salad and preserves in an otherwise empty lunch box. One ham sandwich yesterday. I think it's lovely you have the box. Who got your lunch?"

"Same," confessed Elnora, "but there were three of them to-day."

"Wait, until I run back and tell mother about the dog, and get my books."

Elnora waited, and that morning she walked down the hall and into the auditorium beside one of the very nicest girls in Onabasha, and it was the fourth day. But the surprise came at noon when Ellen insisted upon Elnora lunching at the Brownlee home, and convulsed her parents and family, and overwhelmed Elnora by a greatly magnified, but moderately accurate history of her lunch box.

"Gee! but it's a box, daddy!" cried the laughing

girl. "It's carved leather and fastens with a strap
that's got her name on it. Inside are trays for things
all complete, and it bears evidence of having enclosed
delicious food, but Elnora never gets any. She's carried
it two days now, and both times it has been empty before
she reached school. Isn't that killing?"

"It is, Ellen, in more ways than one. No girl is going
to eat breakfast at six o'clock, walk three miles, and do
good work with no lunch. You can't tell me anything
about that box. I sold it last Monday night to Wesley
Sinton, one of my good country customers. He told
me it was a present for a girl who was worthy of it, and I
see he was right."

"He's so good to me," said Elnora. "Sometimes
I look at him and wonder if a neighbour can be so kind
to one, what a real father would be like. I envy a girl
with a father unspeakably."

"You have cause," said Ellen Brownlee. "A father
is the very nicest thing in the whole round world, except
a mother, who is just as nice." The girl, starting to
pay tribute to her father, saw that she must include
her mother, and said the thing before she remembered
what Mrs. Sinton had told the girls in the store. She
stopped in dismay. Elnora's face paled a trifle, but she
smiled bravely.

"Then I'm fortunate in having a mother," she said.

Mr. Brownlee lingered at the table after the girls
had excused themselves and returned to school.

"There's a girl Ellen can't see too much of, in my

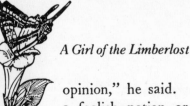

opinion," he said. "She is every inch a lady, and not a foolish notion or action about her. I can't understand just what combination of circumstances produced her in this day."

"It has been an unusual case of repression, for one thing. She waits on her elders and thinks before she speaks," said Mrs. Brownlee.

"She's mighty pretty. She looks so sound and wholesome, and she's neatly dressed."

"Ellen says she was a fright the first two days. Long brown calico dress almost touching the floor, and big, lumbering shoes. Those Sinton people bought her clothes. Ellen was in the store, and the woman stopped her crowd and asked them about their dresses. She said the girl was not poor, but her mother was selfish and didn't care for her. But Elnora showed a bankbook the next day, and declared that she paid for the things herself, so the Sinton people must just have selected them. There's something peculiar about it, but nothing wrong I am sure. I'll encourage Ellen to ask her again."

"Well, I should say so, especially if she is going to keep on giving away her lunch."

"She lunched with the Bird Woman one day this week."

"She did!"

"Yes, she lives out by the Limberlost. You know the Bird Woman works there a great deal, and probably knows her that way. I think the girl gathers specimens for her. Ellen says she knows more than the teachers about any nature question that comes up, and she is going to lead all of them in mathematics, and make them work in any branch."

When Elnora entered the coat room after having had luncheon with Ellen Brownlce there was such a difference in the atmosphere that she could feel it.

"I am almost sorry I have these clothes," she said to Ellen.

"In the name of sense, why?" cried the astonished girl.

"Everyone is so nice to me in them, it just sets me to wondering if in time I could have made them be equally friendly in the others."

Ellen looked at her introspectively.

"Well, sir, I believe you could," she announced at last. "But it would have taken time and heartache, and your mind would have been less free to work on your studies. No one is happy without friends, and I just simply can't study when I am unhappy."

That night the Bird Woman made the last trip to the swamp. Every specimen she possibly could use had been purchased at a fair price, and three additions had been made to the bank-book, carrying the total a little past two hundred dollars. There remained the Indian relics to sell on Saturday, and Elnora had secured the order to furnish material for nature work for the grades. Life suddenly grew very full. There was the most excitingly interesting work for every hour, and that work was to pay high-school expenses and

start the college fund. There was just one little rift in her joy. All of it would have been so much better if she could have told her mother, and given the money into her keeping. But the struggle to get a start had been so terrible, Elnora was afraid to take the risk.

When she reached home, she only told her mother that the last of the things had been sold that evening.

"I think," said Mrs. Comstock, "that we will get Wesley to move that box over here back of the garden for you. There you are apt to get tolled farther into the swamp than you intend to go, and you might mire or something. There ought to be just the same things in our woods, and along our swampy places, as there are in the Limberlost. Can't you hunt your stuff here?"

"I can try," said Elnora. "I don't know what I can find until I do. Our woods are undisturbed, and there is a possibility they might be even better hunting than the swamp. But I wouldn't have Freckles's case moved for the world. He might come back some day, and not like it. I've tried to keep his room the best I could, and taking out the box would make a great hole in one side of it. Store boxes don't cost much. I will have Uncle Wesley buy me one, and set it up wherever hunting looks the best, early in the spring. I would feel safer at home."

"Shall we do the work or have supper first?"

"Let's do the work," said Elnora. "I can't say that I'm hungry now. Don't seem as if I ever could

be hungry again with such a lunch. I am quite sure
no one carried more delicious things to eat than I."

Mrs. Comstock was pleased. "I put in a pretty good
hunk of cake," she said. "Did you divide it with anyone?"

"Why, yes, I did," admitted Elnora.

"Who?"

Things were getting uncomfortable. "I ate the biggest piece myself," said Elnora, "and gave the rest to
a couple of boys named Jimmy and Billy and a girl
named Belle. They said it was very best cake they ever
tasted in all their lives."

Mrs. Comstock sat straight. "I used to be a master
hand at spice cake," she boasted. "But I'm a little
out of practice. I must get to work again. With the
very weeds growing higher than our heads, we should
get plenty of good stuff to eat off this land, if we can't
afford anything else but taxes."

Elnora laughed and hurried up stairs to change her
dress.

Margaret Sinton came that night bringing a beautiful
blue one in its stead, and carried away the other to
launder.

"Do you mean to say those dresses are to be washed
every two days?" questioned Mrs. Comstock.

"They have to be, to look fresh," replied Margaret.
"We want our girl sweet as a rose."

"Well, of all things!" cried Mrs. Comstock. "Every
two days! Any girl who can't keep a dress clean longer

than that is a dirty girl. You'll wear the goods out
and fade the colours with so much washing."

"We 'll have a clean girl, anyway."

"Well, if you like the job you can have it," said Mrs.
Comstock. "I don't mind the washing, but I'm so
inconvenient with an iron."

Elnora sat late that night working hard over her lessons.
The next morning she put on her blue dress and ribbon
and in those she was a picture. Mrs. Comstock caught
her breath with a queer stirring around her heart, and
looked twice to be sure of what she saw. As Elnora
gathered her books her mother silently gave her the
lunch box.

"Feels heavy," said Elnora gaily. "And smelly!
Like as not I 'll be called upon to divide again."

"Then you divide!" said Mrs. Comstock. "Eating
is the one thing we don't have to economize on, Elnora.
Spite of all I can do food goes to waste in this soil every
day. If you can give some of those city children a taste
of the real thing, why, don't be selfish."

Elnora went down the road thinking of the city children with whom she probably would divide. Of course,
the bridge would be occupied again. So she stopped and
opened the box. Undoubtedly Mrs. Comstock was
showing Margaret Sinton the "frills." The cake was
still fresh, and there were four slices. The sandwiches
had to be tasted twice before Elnora discovered that
beechnuts had been used in a peanut recipe, and they
were a great improvement. There were preserved

strawberries in the cup, potato salad with mint and cucumber in the dish, and a beautifully browned squab from the stable loft.

"I don't want to be selfish," murmured Elnora, "but it just seems as if I can't give away this lunch. If mother did not put love into it, she's substituted something that's likely to fool me."

She almost felt her steps lagging as she approached the bridge. A very hungry dog had been added to the trio of children. Elnora loved all dogs, and, as usual, this one came to her in friendliness. The children said "Good morning!" with alacrity, and another paper parcel lay conspicuous.

"How are you this morning?" inquired Elnora.

"All right!" cried the three, while the dog sniffed ravenously at the lunch box, and beat a perfect tattoo with his tail.

"How did you like the bologna?" questioned Billy eagerly.

"One of the girls took me to lunch at her home yesterday," answered Elnora.

Dawn broke beautifully over Billy's streaked face. He caught the package and thrust it toward Elnora.

"Then maybe you'd like to try the bologna to-day!"

The dog leaped in glad apprehension of something, and Belle scrambled to her feet and took a step forward. The look of famished greed in her eyes was more than Elnora could bear. It was not that she cared for the food so much. Good things to eat had been in abundance

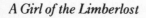

all her life. She wanted with this lunch to try to absorb what she felt must be an expression of some sort from her mother, and if it was not a manifestation of love, she did not know what to think it. But it was her mother who had said "be generous." She knelt on the bridge. "Keep back the dog!" she warned the elder boy.

She opened the box and divided the milk between Billy and the girl. She gave each a piece of cake leaving one and a sandwich. Billy pressed forward eagerly, bitter disappointment on his face, and the elder boy forgot his charge.

"Aw, I thought they'd be meat!" lamented Billy.

Elnora gave way.

"There is!" she said gladly. "There is a little pigeon bird. I want just a teeny piece of the breast, for a sort of keepsake, just one bite, and you can have the rest among you."

Elnora drew the knife from its holder and cut off the wishbone. Then she held the bird toward the girl.

"You can divide it," she said. The dog made a bound and seizing the squab sprang from the bridge and ran for life. The girl and boy hurried after him. With awful eyes Billy stared and swore tempestuously. Elnora caught him and clapped her hand over the little mouth. A delivery wagon came tearing down the street, the horse running full speed, passed the fleeing dog with the girl and boy in pursuit, and stopped at the bridge. High school girls began to roll from all sides of it.

"A rescue! A rescue!" they shouted.

It was Ellen Brownlee and her crowd, and every girl of them carried a big parcel. They took in the scene as they approached. The fleeing dog with something in its mouth, the half-naked girl and boy chasing it told the story. Those girls screamed with laughter as they watched the pursuit.

"Thank goodness, I saved the wishbone!" said Elnora. "As usual, I can prove that there was a bird." She turned toward the box. Billy had improved the time. He had the last piece of cake in one hand, and the last bite of salad disappeared in one great gulp. Then the girls shouted again.

"Let's have a sample ourselves," suggested one. She caught up the box and handed out the remaining sandwich. Another girl divided it into bites each little over an inch square, and then she lifted the cup lid and deposited a preserved strawberry on each bite. "One, two, three, altogether now!" she cried.

Billy let out a roar. "You old mean things!" he screamed.

In an instant he was down in the road and handfuls of dust began to fly among them. The girls scattered before him.

"Billy!" cried Elnora. "Billy! I'll never give you another bite as long as I live, if you throw dust on any-one!"

Then Billy dropped the dust, bored both fists into his eyes, and fled sobbing into Elnora's new blue skirt. She stooped to meet him and consolation began. Those

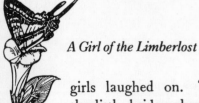

girls laughed on. They screamed and shouted until the little bridge shook.

"To-morrow might as well be a clear day," said Ellen, passing around and feeding the remaining berries to the girls as they could compose themselves enough to take them. "Billy, I admire your taste more than your temper."

Elnora looked up. "The little soul is nothing but skin and bones," she said. "I never was really hungry myself; were any of you?"

"Well, I should say so," cried a plump, rosy girl. "I'm famished right now. Let's have breakfast immediate!"

"We got to refill this box first!" said Ellen Brownlee. "Who's got the butter?" A girl advanced with a wooden tray.

"Put it in the preserve cup, a little strawberry flavour won't hurt it. Next!" called Ellen.

A loaf of bread was produced and Ellen cut off a piece which filled the sandwich box.

"Next!" A bottle of olives was unwrapped. The grocer's boy who was waiting opened that, and Ellen filled the salad dish.

"Next!"

A bag of macaroons was produced and the cake compartment filled.

"Next!"

"I don't suppose this will make quite as good dog feed as a bird," laughed a girl holding open a bag of sliced ham while Ellen filled the meat dish.

"Next!"

A box of candy was handed her and she stuffed every corner of the lunch box with chocolates and nougat. Then it was closed and formally presented to Elnora. The girls each helped themselves to candy and olives, and gave Billy the remainder of the food. Billy took one bite of ham, and approved. Belle and Jimmy had given up chasing the dog and, angry and ashamed, stood waiting a half block away.

"Come back!" screamed Billy. "You great big dunces, come back! They's a new kind of meat, and cake and candy."

The boy delayed, but the girl joined Billy. Ellen wiped her fingers, stepped to the cement abutment and began reciting "Horatio at the Bridge!" substituting Elnora wherever the hero appeared in the lines.

Elnora gathered up the sacks, and gave them to Belle telling her to take the food home, cut and spread the bread, set things on the table, and eat nicely.

Then Elnora was hustled into the wagon with the girls, and driven on the run to the high school. They sang a song beginning—

> "Elnora please give me a sandwich.
> I'm ashamed to ask for cake"

as they went. Elnora did not know it, but that was her initiation. She belonged to "the crowd." She only knew that she was happy, and vaguely wondered what her mother and Aunt Margaret would have said about the proceedings.

CHAPTER 7

Wherein Mrs. Comstock Manipulates Margaret and Billy Acquires a Residence

SATURDAY morning Elnora helped her mother with the work. When she had finished Mrs. Comstock told her to go to Sinton's and wash her Indian relics, so that she would be ready to accompany Wesley to town in the afternoon. Elnora hurried down the road and was soon at the cistern with a tub busily washing arrow points, stone axes, tubes, pipes, and skin-cleaning implements. There were not so many points as she had supposed, and some she had thought the finest were chipped and broken, still there was quite a large box of perfect pieces to carry to the city.

Then Elnora hurried home, dressed and was waiting when the carriage reached the gate. She stopped at the bank with the box, and Sinton went to do his marketing and a little shopping for his wife.

At the dry goods store Mr. Brownlee called to him, "Hello, Sinton!" how do you like the fate of your lunch box?" Then he began to laugh.

"I always hate to see a man laughing alone," said Sinton. "It looks so selfish! Tell me the fun, and let me help you."

Brownlee wiped his eyes.

"I supposed you knew, but I see she hasn't told."

Then the three days' history of the lunch box was repeated with particulars which included the dog.

"Now laugh!" concluded Brownlee.

"Blest if I see anything funny!" replied Sinton. "And if you had bought that box and furnished one of those lunches yourself, you wouldn't either. I call such a work a shame! I'll have it stopped."

"Some one must see to that, all right. They are little leeches. Their father earns enough to support them, but they have no mother, and they run wild. I suppose they are crazy for cooked food. But it is funny, and when you think it over you will see it, if you don't now."

"About where would a body find that father?" inquired Sinton grimly. Mr. Brownlee told him and he started, locating the house with little difficulty. House was the proper word, for of home there was no sign. Just a small empty house with three unkept little children racing through and around it. The girl and the elder boy hung back, but dirty little Billy greeted Sinton with, "What you want here?"

"I want to see your father," said Sinton.

"Well, he's asleep," said Billy.

"Where?" asked Sinton.

"In the house," answered Billy, "and you can't wake him."

"Well, I'll try," said Wesley.

Billy led the way. "There he is!" he said. "He is drunk again."

On a dirty mattress in a corner lay a sleeping man who appeared to be strong and well.

Billy was right. You could not awake him. He had gone the limit, and a little beyond. He was now facing eternity.

Sinton went out and closed the door.

"Your father is sick and needs help," he said. "You stay here, and I will send a man to see him."

"If you just let him 'lone, he'll sleep it off," volunteered Billy. "He's that way all the time, but he wakes up and gets us something to eat after awhile. Only waitin' twists you up inside pretty bad."

The boy wore no air of complaint. He was merely stating facts.

Wesley Sinton looked hard at Billy. "Are you twisted up inside now?" he asked.

Billy laid a grimy hand on the region of his stomach and the filthy little waist sank close to the backbone. "Bet yer life, boss," he said cheerfully.

"How long have you been twisted?" asked Sinton.

Billy appealed to the others. "When was it we had the stuff on the bridge?"

"Yesterday morning," said the girl.

"Is that all gone?" asked Sinton.

"She went and told us to take it home," said Billy ruefully, "and 'cause she said to, we took it. Pa had come back, he was drinking some more, and he ate a lot of it —'most the whole thing, and it made him sick as a dog, and he went and wasted all of it. Then he got drunk some more, and now he's asleep again. We didn't get hardly none."

"You children sit on the steps until the man comes," said Sinton. "I'll send you some things to eat with him. What's your name, sonny?"

"Billy," said the boy.

"Well, Billy, I guess you better come with me. I'll take care of him," Sinton promised the others. He reached a hand to Billy.

"I ain't no baby, I 'm a boy!" said Billy, as he shuffled along beside Sinton, taking a kick at every movable object without regard to his battered toes.

Once they passed a great Dane dog lolling after its master, and Billy ascended Sinton as if he was a tree, and clung to him with trembling hot hands.

"I ain't afraid of that dog," scoffed Billy, as he was again placed on the walk, "but onc't he took me for a rat or somepin' and his teeth cut into my back. If I'd a done right, I 'd a took the law on him."

Sinton looked down into the indignant little face. The child was bright enough, he had a good head, but, oh, such a body!

"I 'bout got enough of dogs," said Billy. "I used to like 'em, but I 'm getting pretty tired. You ought to seen the lickin' Jimmy and Belle and me give our dog when we caught him, for taking the little bird she gave us. We waited 'till he was asleep 'nen laid a board on him and all of us jumped on it to onc't. You could a heard him yell a mile. Belle said mebbe we could

squeeze the bird out of him. But, squeeze nothing!
He was holler as us, and that bird was lost long
'fore it got to his stummick. It was ist a little one,
anyway. Belle said it wouldn't 'a' made a bite apiece
for three of us nohow, and the dog got one good
swaller. We didn't get much of the meat, either.
Pa took most of that. Seems like pas and dogs gets
everything."

Billy laughed ruefully. Involuntarily Wesley Sinton
reached his hand. They were coming into the business
part of Onabasha and the streets were crowded. Billy
understood it to mean that he might lose his companion
and took a grip. That little hot hand clinging tight to
his, the sore feet recklessly scouring the walk, the
hungry child panting for breath as he tried to keep even,
the brave soul jesting in the face of hard luck, caught
Sinton in a tender, empty spot.

"Say, son," he said. "How would you like to be
washed clean, and have all the supper your skin could
hold, and sleep in a good bed?"

"Aw, gee!" said Billy. "I ain't dead yet! Them
things is in heaven! Poor folks can't have them. Pa
said so."

"Well, you can have them if you want to go with me
and get them," promised Sinton.

"Honest!"

"Yes, honest."

"Crost yer heart?"

"Yes," said Sinton.

"Kin I take some to Jimmy and Belle?"

"If you 'll come with me and be my boy, I 'll see that they have plenty."

"What will pa say?"

"Your pa is in that kind of sleep now where he won't wake up, Billy," said Sinton. "I am pretty sure the law will give you to me, if you want to come."

"When people don't ever wake up they're dead," announced Billy. "Is my pa dead?"

"Yes, he is," answered Sinton.

"And you 'll take care of Jimmy and Belle, too?"

"I can't adopt all three of you," said Sinton. "I'll take you, and see that they are well provided for. Will you come?"

"Yep, I 'll come," said Billy. "Let 's eat, first thing we do."

"All right," agreed Sinton. "Come into this restaurant." He lifted Billy to the lunch counter and ordered the clerk to give him as many glasses of milk as he wanted, and a biscuit. "I think there's going to be fried chicken when we get home, Billy," he said, "so you just take the edge off now, and fill up later."

While Billy lunched Sinton called up the different departments and notified the proper authorities ending with the Women's Relief Association. He sent a basket of food to Belle and Jimmy, bought Billy a pair of trousers, and a shirt, and went to bring Elnora.

"Why, Uncle Wesley!" cried the girl. "Where did you find Billy?"

"I've adopted him for the time being, if not longer," replied Sinton.

"Where did you get him?" queried the astonished Elnora.

"Well, young woman," said Sinton, "Mr. Brownlee told me the history of your lunch box. It didn't seem so funny to me as it does to the rest of them; so I went to look up the father of Billy's family, and make him take care of them, or allow the law to do it for him. It will have to be the law."

"He's deader than anything!" broke in Billy. "He can't ever take all the meat any more."

"Billy!" gasped Elnora.

"Never you mind!" said Sinton. "A child don't say such things about a father who loved and raised him right. When it happens, the father alone is to blame. You won't hear Billy talk like that about me when I cross over."

"You don't mean you are going to take him to keep!"

"I'll soon need help," said Sinton. "Billy will come in just about right ten years from now, and if I raise him I'll have him the way I want him."

"But Aunt Margaret don't like boys," objected Elnora.

"Well, she likes me, and I used to be a boy. Anyway, as I remember she has had her way about everything at our house ever since we were married. I am going to please myself about Billy. Hasn't she always done just as she chose so far as you know? Honest, Elnora!"

"Honest!" replied Elnora. "You are beautiful to all of us, Uncle Wesley; but Aunt Margaret won't like Billy. She won't want him in her home."

"In our home," corrected Sinton.

"What makes you want him?" marvelled Elnora.

"God only knows," said Sinton. "Billy ain't so beautiful, and he ain't so smart, I guess it's because he's so human. My heart goes out to him."

"So did mine," said Elnora. "I love him. I'd rather see him eat my lunch than have it myself any time."

"What makes you like him?" asked Sinton.

"Why, I don't know," pondered Elnora. "He's so little, he needs so much, he's got such splendid grit, and he's perfectly unselfish with his brother and sister. But we must wash him before Aunt Margaret sees him. I wonder if mother ——?"

"You needn't bother. I'm going to take him home the way he is," said Sinton. "I want Maggie to see the worst of it."

"I'm afraid ——" began Elnora.

"So am I," said Sinton, "but I won't give him up. He's taken a sort of grip on my heart. I've always been crazy for a boy. Don't let him hear us."

"Don't let him get killed!" cried Elnora. During their talk Billy had wandered to the edge of the walk and barely escaped the wheels of a passing automobile in an effort to catch a stray kitten that seemed in danger.

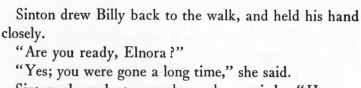

Sinton drew Billy back to the walk, and held his hand closely.

"Are you ready, Elnora?"

"Yes; you were gone a long time," she said.

Sinton glanced at a package she carried. "Have to have another book?" he asked.

"No, I got this for mother. I've had such splendid luck selling my specimens, I didn't feel right about keeping all the money for myself, so I saved enough from the Indian relics to get a few things I wanted. I would have liked to have gotten her a dress, but I didn't dare, so I compromised on a book."

"What did you select, Elnora?" asked Sinton wonderingly.

"Well," said she, "I have noticed mother always seemed interested in anything Mark Twain wrote in the newspapers, and I thought it would cheer her up a little, so I just got his 'Innocents Abroad.' I haven't read it myself, but I've seen mention made of it all my life, and the critics say it's genuine fun."

"Good!" cried Sinton. "Good! You've made a splendid choice. It will take her mind off herself a lot. But she will scold you."

"Of course," assented Elnora. "But possibly she will read it, and feel better. I'm going to serve her a trick. I am going to hide it until Monday, and set it on her little shelf of books the last thing before I go away. She must have all of them by heart. When she sees a new one she can't help being glad, for she loves to read, and if she has all day to get interested, maybe she'll like it so she won't scold so much."

"We are both in for it, but I guess we are prepared. I don't know what Margaret will say, but I'm going to take Billy home and see. Maybe he can win with her, as he did with us."

Elnora had her doubts, but she did not say anything more.

When they started home Billy sat on the front seat. He drove with the hitching strap tied to the railing of the dashboard, flourished the whip, and yelled with delight. At first Sinton laughed with him, but by the time he left Elnora with several packages at her gate, he was looking serious enough.

Margaret was at the door as they drove up the lane. Sinton left Billy in the carriage, hitched the horses and went to explain to her. He had not reached her before she cried, "Look, Wesley, that child! You'll have a runaway!"

Wesley looked and ran. Billy was standing in the carriage slashing the mettlesome horses with the whip.

"See me make 'em go!" he shouted as the whip fell a second time.

He did make them go. They took the hitching post and a few fence palings, which scraped the paint from a wheel. Sinton missed the lines at the first effort, but the dragging post impeded the horses, and he soon caught them. He led them to the barn,

and ordered Billy to remain in the carriage while he unhitched. Then leading Billy and carrying his packages he entered the yard.

"You run play a few minutes, Billy," he said. "I want to talk to the nice lady."

The nice lady was looking rather stupefied as Sinton approached her.

"Where in the name of sense did you get that awful child?" she demanded.

"He is a young gentleman who has been stopping Elnora and eating her lunch every day, part of the time with the assistance of his brother and sister, while our girl went hungry. Brownlee told me about it at the store. It's happened three days running. The first time she did without anything, the second time Brownlee's girl took her to lunch, and the third a crowd of high school girls bought a lot of stuff and met them at the bridge. The youngsters seemed to think they could rob her every day, so I went to see their father about having it stopped."

"Well, I should think so!" cried Margaret.

"There were three of them, Margaret," said Sinton, "that little fellow ——"

"Hyena, you mean," interpolated Margaret.

"'Hyena'," corrected Sinton gravely, "and another boy and a girl, all equally dirty and hungry. The man was dead. They thought he was in a drunken sleep, but he was stone dead. I brought the little boy with me, and sent the officers and other help to the house.

He's half starved. I want to wash him, and put clean clothes on him, and give him some supper."

"Have you got anything to put on him?"

"Yes,"

"Where did you get it?"

"Bought it. It ain't much. All I got didn't cost a dollar."

"A dollar is a good deal when you work and save for it the way we do."

"Well, I don't know a better place to put it. Have you got any hot water? I'll use this tub at the cistern. Please give me some soap and towels."

Instead Margaret pushed by him with a shriek. Billy had played by producing a cord from his pocket, and having tied the tails of Margaret's white kittens together, he had climbed on a box and hung them across the clothes line. Wild with fright the kittens were clawing each other to death, and the air was white with fur. The string had twisted and the frightened creatures could not recognize friends. Margaret stepped back with bleeding hands. Sinton cut the cord with his knife and the poor little cats raced under the house bleeding and disfigured. Margaret white with wrath faced Sinton.

"If you don't hitch up and take that animal back to town," she said, "I will."

Billy threw himself on the grass and began to scream.

"You said I could have fried chicken for supper," he wailed. "You said she was a nice lady!"

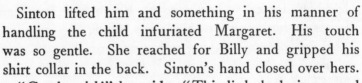

Sinton lifted him and something in his manner of handling the child infuriated Margaret. His touch was so gentle. She reached for Billy and gripped his shirt collar in the back. Sinton's hand closed over hers.

"Gently, girl!" he said. "This little body is covered with sores."

"Sores!" she ejaculated. "Sores? What kind of sores?"

"Oh, they might be from bruises made by fists or boot toes, or they might be bad blood, from wrong eating, or they might be pure filth. Will you hand me some towels?"

"No, I won't!" said Margaret.

"Well, give me some rags, then,"

Margaret compromised on pieces of old tablecloth.

Sinton led Billy to the cistern, pumped cold water into the tub, poured in a kettle of hot, and beginning at the head scoured him. The boy shut his little teeth, and said never a word though he twisted occasionally when the soap struck a raw spot. Margaret watched the process from the window in amazed, and ever-increasing anger. Where did Wesley learn it? How could his big hands be so gentle? Sinton came to the door.

"Have you got any peroxide?" he asked.

"A little," she answered stiffly.

"Well, I need about a pint, but I'll begin on what you have."

Margaret handed him the bottle. Wesley took a

cup weakened the drug and said to Billy. "Man, these sores on you must be healed. Then you must eat the kind of food that's fit for little men. I am going to put some medicine on you, and it is going to sting like fire. If it just runs off, I won't use any more. If it boils, there is poison in these places, and they must be tied up, dosed every day, and you must be washed, and kept mighty clean. Now, hold still, because I am going to put it on."

"I think the one on my leg is the worst," said the undaunted Billy, holding out a raw place. Sinton poured on the drug. Billy's body twisted and writhed, but he did not run.

"Gee, look at it boil!" he cried. "I guess they's poison. You'll have to do it to all of them."

Sinton's teeth were set, as he watched the boy's face. He poured the drug, strong enough to do effective work, on a dozen places over that little body and bandaged all he could. Billy's lips quivered at times, and his chin jumped, but he did not shed a tear or utter a sound other than to take a deep interest in the boiling. As Sinton put the small shirt on the boy, and fastened the trousers, he was ready to reset the hitching post and mend the fence without a word.

"Now am I clean?" asked Billy.

"Yes, you are clean outside," said Sinton. "There is some dirty blood in your body, and some bad words in your mouth, that we have to get out, but that takes time. If we put right things to eat into your stomach

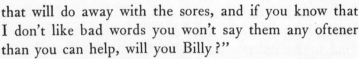

that will do away with the sores, and if you know that
I don't like bad words you won't say them any oftener
than you can help, will you Billy?"

Billy leaned against Sinton in apparent indifference.

"I want to see me!" he demanded.

Sinton led the boy into the house, and lifted him to
a mirror.

"My, I'm purty good-looking, ain't I?" bragged
Billy. Then as Sinton stooped to set him on the floor
Billy's lips passed close to the big man's ear and hastily
whispered a vehement "No!" as he ran for the door.

"How long until supper, Margaret?" asked Sinton
as he followed.

"You are going to keep him for supper?" she asked.

"Sure!" said Sinton. "That's what I brought him
for. It's likely he never had a good square meal of
decent food in his life. He's starved to the bone."

Margaret arose deliberately, removed the white cloth
from the supper table and substituted an old red one
she used to wrap the bread. She put away the pretty
dishes they commonly used and set the table with old
plates for pies and kitchen utensils. But she fried the
chicken, and was generous with milk and honey, snowy
bread, gravy, potatoes, and fruit.

Sinton repainted the scratched wheel. He mended
the fence, with Billy holding the nails and handing the
pickets. Then he filled the old hole, digged a new one
and set the hitching post.

Billy hopped on one foot at his task of holding the

post steady as the earth was packed around it. There was not the shadow of a trouble on his little freckled face. Sinton threw in stones and pounded the earth solid around the post. The sound of a gulping sob attracted him to Billy. The tears were rolling down his cheeks. "If I'd a knowed you'd have to get down in a hole, and work so hard I wouldn't 'a' hit the horses," he said.

"Never you mind, Billy," said Sinton. "You will know next time, so you can think over it, and make up your mind whether you really want to before you strike."

Sinton went to the barn to put away the tools. He thought Billy at his heels, but the boy lagged on the way. A big snowy turkey gobbler resented the small intruder in his especial preserves, and with spread tail and dragging wings came at him threateningly. If that turkey gobbler had known the sort of things with which Billy was accustomed to holding his own, he never would have issued that challenge. Billy accepted instantly. He danced around with stiff arms at his sides and imitated the gobbler. Then came his opportunity, and he jumped on the big turkey's back. Wesley heard Margaret's scream in time to see the flying leap and admire its dexterity. The turkey tucked its tail and scampered. Billy slid from its back and as he fell he clutched wildly, caught the folded tail, and instinctively hung on for life. The turkey gave one scream and relaxed its muscles. Then it fled in disfigured defeat to the haystack. Billy scrambled to his feet holding the tail, and his eyes were bulging.

"Why, the blasted old thing came off!" he said to Sinton, holding out the tail in amazed wonder.

Sinton, caught suddenly, forgot everything and roared. Seeing which, Billy thought a turkey tail of no account and flung that one high above him shouting in wild childish laughter, as the feathers scattered and fell.

Margaret, watching, burst into tears. Wesley had gone mad. For the first time in her married life she wanted to tell her mother. When Wesley had waited until he was so hungry he could wait no longer he invaded the kitchen to find a cooked supper baking on the back of the stove, while Margaret with red eyes nursed a pair of demoralized white kittens.

"Is supper ready?" he asked.

"It has been for an hour," answered Margaret.

"Why didn't you call us?"

That "us" had too much comradeship in it. It irritated Margaret.

"I supposed it would take you even longer than that to fix things decent again. As for my turkey, and my poor little kittens, they don't matter."

"I am mighty sorry about them, Margaret, you know that. Billy is very bright, and he will soon learn ——"

"Soon learn!" cried Margaret. "Wesley Sinton, you don't mean to say that you think of keeping that creature here for some time?"

"No, I think of keeping a decent, well-behaved little boy."

Margaret set the supper on the table. Seeing the

old red cloth Wesley stared in amazement. Then he understood. Billy capered around in delight.

"Ain't that pretty?" he exulted. "I wish Jimmy and Belle could see. We, why we ist eat out of our hands or off a old drygoods box, and when we fix up a lot, we have newspaper. We ain't ever had a nice red cloth like this."

Wesley looked straight at Margaret, so intently that she turned away, her face flushing. He stacked the dictionary and the geography of the world on a chair, and lifted Billy beside him. He heaped a plate generously, cut the food, put a fork into Billy's little fist, and made him eat slowly and properly. Billy did his best. Occasionally greed overcame him, and he used his left hand to pop a bite into his mouth with his fingers. These lapses Wesley patiently overlooked, and went on with his general instructions. Luckily Billy did not spill anything on his clothing or the cloth. After supper Wesley took him to the barn until he finished the night work. Then he went and sat by Margaret on the front porch. Billy appropriated the hammock, and swung by pulling a rope tied around a tree. The very energy with which he went at the work of swinging himself appealed to Wesley.

"Mercy, but he's an active little body," he said. "There isn't a lazy bone in him. See how he works to pay for his fun."

"There goes his foot through it!" cried Margaret. "Wesley, he shall not ruin my hammock."

"Of course he shan't!" said Wesley. "Wait, Billy, let me show you."

Thereupon he explained to Billy that ladies wearing beautiful white dresses sat in hammocks, so little boys must not put their dusty feet in them. They must just sit in them, and let their feet hang down. Billy immediately sat, and allowed his feet to swing.

"Margaret," said Sinton after a long silence on the porch, "isn't it true that if Billy had been a half-starved sore cat, dog, or animal of any sort, that you would have pitied, and helped care for it, and been glad to see me get any pleasure out of it I could?"

"Yes," said Margaret coldly.

"But because I brought a child with an immortal soul, there is no welcome."

"That isn't a child, it's an animal."

"You just said you would have welcomed an animal."

"Not a wild one. I meant a tame beast."

"Billy is not a beast!" said Wesley hotly. "He is a very dear little boy. Margaret, you've always done the church-going and Bible reading for this family. How do you reconcile that 'Suffer little children to come unto Me' with the way you are treating Billy?"

Margaret arose. "I haven't treated that child. I have only let him alone. I can barely hold myself. He needs the hide tanned about off him!"

"If you'd cared to look at his body, you'd know that you couldn't find a place to strike without cutting into a raw spot," said Sinton. "Besides, Billy has not done a thing for which a child should be punished. He is only full of life, no training, and with a boy's love of mischief. He did abuse your kittens, but an hour before I saw him risk his life to save one from being run over. He minds what you tell him, and doesn't do anything he is told not to. He thinks of his brother and sister right away when anything pleases him. He took that stinging medicine with the grit of a bulldog. He is just a bully little chap, and I love him."

"Oh, good heavens!" cried Margaret, going into the house as she spoke.

Sinton sat still. At last Billy tired of the swing, came to him and leaned his slight body against the big knee.

"Am I going to sleep here?" he asked.

"Sure you are!" said Sinton.

Billy swung his feet as he laid across Wesley's knee. "Come on," said Sinton, "I must clean you up for bed."

"You have to be just awful clean here," announced Billy. "I like to be clean, you feel so good, after the hurt is over."

Sinton registered that remark, and worked with especial tenderness as he redressed the ailing places and washed the dust from Billy's feet and hands.

"Where can he sleep?" he asked Margaret.

"I'm sure I don't know," she answered.

"Oh, I can sleep ist any place," said Billy. "On the floor or anywhere. Home, I sleep on pa's coat on a storebox, and Jimmy and Belle they sleep on the storebox, too. I sleep between them, so's I don't roll

off and crack my head. Ain't you got a storebox and a old coat?"

Sinton arose and opened a folding lounge. Then he brought an armload of clean horse blankets from a closet.

"These don't look like the nice white bed a little boy should have, Billy," he said, "but we'll make them do. This will beat a storebox all hollow."

Billy took a long leap for the lounge. When he found it bounced, he proceeded to bounce, until he was tired. By that time the blankets had to be refolded. Wesley had Billy take one end and help, while both of them seemed to enjoy the job. Then Billy lay down and curled up in his clothes like a little dog. But sleep would not come. Finally he sat up. He stared around restlessly. Then he arose, went to Sinton, and leaned against his knee. Sinton picked up the boy and folded his arms around him. Billy sighed in rapturous content.

"That bed feels so lost like," he said. "Jimmy always jabbed me on one side, and Belle on the other, and so I knew I was there."

Sinton laughed the best he could.

"Do you know where they are?" asked Billy.

"They are with kind people who gave them a fine supper, a clean bed, and will always take good care of them."

"I wisht I was" — Billy hesitated and looked earnestly at Sinton. "I mean, I wish they was here."

"You are about all I can manage, Billy," said Sinton.

Billy sat up. "Can't she manage anything?" he asked, waving toward Margaret.

"Indeed, yes," said Sinton. "She has managed me for twenty years."

"My, but she made you nice!" said Billy. "I just love you. I wisht she'd take Jimmy and Belle and make them nice as you."

"She isn't strong enough to do that, Billy. They will grow into a good boy and girl where they are."

Billy slid from Sinton's arms and walked toward Margaret until he reached the middle of the room. Then he stopped, and at last sat on the floor. Finally he lay down and closed his eyes. "This feels more like my bed; if only Jimmy and Belle was here to crowd up a little, so it wasn't so alone like."

"Won't I do, Billy?" asked Sinton in a husky voice.

Billy moved restlessly. "Seems like — seems like — towards night as if a body got kind o' lonesome for a woman person — like her."

Billy indicated Margaret and then closed his eyes so tight his small face wrinkled.

Soon he was up again. "'Wisht I had Snap," he said. "Oh, I ist wisht I had Snap!"

"I thought you laid a board on Snap and jumped on it," said Sinton.

"We did!" cried Billy — "oh, you ought to heard him squeal!" Billy laughed loudly, then his face clouded. "But I want Snap to lay beside me so bad now — that

if he was here I'd give him a piece of my chicken, 'fore I ate any. Do you like dogs?"

"Yes, I do," said Sinton.

Billy was up instantly. "Would you like Snap?"

"I am sure I would," said Sinton.

"Would she?" Billy indicated Margaret. And then he answered his own question. "But of course, she wouldn't, cos she likes cats, and dogs chases cats. Oh, dear, I thought for a minute maybe Snap could come here." Billy lay down and closed his eyes resolutely.

Suddenly they flew open. "Does it hurt to be dead?" he demanded.

"Nothing hurts you after you are dead, Billy," said Sinton.

"Yes, but I mean does it hurt getting to be dead?"

"Sometimes it does. It did not hurt your father, Billy. It came softly while he was asleep."

"It ist came softly?"

"Yes,"

"I kind o' wisht he wasn't dead!" said Billy. "'Course I like to stay with you, and the fried chicken, and the nice soft bed, and — and everything, and I like to be clean, but he took us to the show, and he got us gum, and he never hurt us when he wasn't drunk."

Billy drew a deep breath, and tightly closed his eyes. But very soon they opened. Then he sat up. He looked at Sinton pitifully, and then he glanced at Margaret. "You don't like boys, do you?" he questioned.

"I like good boys," said Margaret.

Billy was at her knee instantly. "Well, say, I'm a good boy!" he announced joyously.

"I do not think boys who hurt helpless kittens and pull out turkeys' tails are good boys."

"Yes, but I didn't hurt the kittens," explained Billy. "They got mad 'bout ist a little fun and scratched each other. I didn't s'pose they'd act like that. And I didn't pull the turkey's tail. I ist held on to the first thing I grabbed, and the turkey pulled. Honest, it was the turkey pulled." He turned to Sinton. "You tell her! Didn't the turkey pull? I didn't know its tail was loose, did I?"

"I don't think you did, Billy," said Sinton.

Billy stared into Margaret's cold face. "Sometimes at night, Belle sits on the floor, and I lay my head in her lap. I could pull up a chair and lay my head in your lap. Like this, I mean." Billy pulled up a chair, climbed on it and laid his head on Margaret's lap. Then he shut his eyes again. Margaret could have looked little more repulsed if he had been a snake.

Billy was soon up.

"My, but your lap is hard," he said. "And you are a good deal fatter 'an Belle, too!" He slid from the chair and came back to the middle of the room.

"Oh, but I wisht he wasn't dead!" he cried. The flood broke and Billy screamed in desperation.

Out of the night a soft, warm young figure flashed through the door and with a swoop caught him in her

arms. She dropped into a chair, nestled him closely, and drooped her fragrant brown head over his little bullet-eyed red one, and rocked softly as she crooned over him—

"Billy, boy, where have you been?
　　Oh, I have been to seek a wife,
　　She 's the joy of my life,
But then she 's a young thing and she can't leave her mammy!"

Billy gripped her with a death grip. Elnora wiped his eyes, kissed his face, swayed and sang.

"Why aren't you asleep?" she asked at last.

"I don't know," said Billy. "I tried. I tried awful hard 'cos I thought he wanted me to, but it ist wouldn't come. Please tell her I tried." He appealed to Margaret.

"He did try to go to sleep," admitted Margaret.

"Maybe he can't sleep in his clothes," suggested Elnora. "Haven't you an old dressing sacque? I could roll the sleeves."

Margaret got an old sacque, and Elnora put it on Billy. Then she brought a basin of water and bathed his face and head. She gathered him up and began to rock again.

"Have you got a pa?" asked Billy.

"No," said Elnora.

"Is he dead like mine?"

"Yes."

"Did it hurt him to die?"

"I don't know."

Billy was wide awake again. "It didn't hurt my

148

pa," he boasted; "he ist died while he was asleep. He didn't even know it was coming."

"I am glad of that," said Elnora, pressing the little head against her breast again.

Billy escaped her hand and sat up. "I guess I won't go to sleep," he said. "It might 'come softly' and get me."

"It won't get you, Billy," said Elnora, rocking and singing between sentences. "It don't get little boys. It just takes big people who are sick."

"Was my pa sick?"

"Yes," said Elnora. "He had a dreadful sickness inside him that burned, and made him drink things. That was why he would forget his little boys and girl. If he had been well, he would have gotten you good things to eat, clean clothes, and had the most fun with you."

Billy leaned against her and closed his eyes, and Elnora rocked hopefully.

"If I was dead would you cry?" he was up again.

"Yes, I would," said Elnora gripping him closer until Billy almost squealed with the embrace.

"Do you love me tight as that?" he questioned blissfully.

"Yes, bushels and bushels," said Elnora. "Better than any little boy in the whole world."

Billy looked at Margaret. "She don't!" he said. "She 'd be glad if it would get me 'softly,' right now. She don't want me here 't all."

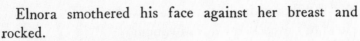

Elnora smothered his face against her breast and rocked.

"You love me, don't you?"

"I will, if you will go to sleep."

"Every single day you will give me your dinner for the bologna, won't you," said Billy.

"Yes, I will," replied Elnora. "But you will have as good lunch as I do after this. You will have milk, eggs, chicken, all kinds of good things, little pies, and cakes, maybe."

Billy shook his head. "I am going back home soon as it is light," he said, "she don't want me. She thinks I'm a bad boy. She's going to whip me — if he lets her. She said so. I heard her. Oh, I wish he hadn't died! I want to go home." Billy shrieked again.

Mrs. Comstock had started to walk slowly and meet Elnora. The girl had been so late that her mother reached the Sinton gate and came up the path until the picture inside became visible. Elnora had told her about Sinton taking Billy home. Mrs. Comstock had some curiosity to see how Margaret bore the unexpected addition to her family. Billy's voice raised with excitement, was plainly audible. She could see Elnora holding him, and hear his excited wail. Sinton's face was drawn and haggard, and Margaret's set and defiant. A very imp of perversity entered the breast of Mrs. Comstock and danced there.

"Hoity, toity!" she said as she suddenly appeared

in the door. "Blest if I ever heard a man making sounds like that before!"

Billy ceased suddenly. Mrs. Comstock was tall, angular, and her hair was prematurely white, for she was only thirty-six, though she looked fifty. But there was an expression on her usually cold face that was attractive just then, and Billy was in search of attractions.

"Have I stayed too late, mother?" asked Elnora anxiously. "I truly intended to come straight back, but I thought I could get Billy to sleep first. Everything is strange, and he's so nervous."

"Is that your ma?" demanded Billy.

"Yes."

"Does she love you?"

"Of course!"

"My mother didn't love me," said Billy. "She went away and left me, and never came back. She don't care what happens to me. You wouldn't go away and leave your little girl, would you?" questioned Billy of Mrs. Comstock.

"No," said Katharine Comstock, "and I wouldn't leave a little boy, either."

Billy was half off Elnora's knees.

"Do you like boys?" he questioned.

"If there is anything I love it is a boy," said Mrs. Comstock assuringly. Billy was on the floor.

"Do you like dogs?"

"Yes. Almost as well as boys. I am going to buy a dog just as soon as I can find a good one."

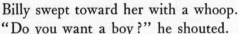

Billy swept toward her with a whoop.

"Do you want a boy?" he shouted.

Katharine Comstock stretched out her arms, and gathered him in.

"Of course, I want a boy!" she rejoiced.

"Maybe you'd like to have me?" offered Billy.

"Sure I would," triumphed Mrs. Comstock. "Anyone would like to have you. You are just a real boy, Billy."

"Will you take Snap?"

"I'd like to have Snap almost as well as you."

"Mother!" breathed Elnora imploringly. "Don't! Oh, don't! He thinks you mean it!"

"And so I do mean it," said Mrs. Comstock. "I'll take him in a jiffy. I throw away enough to feed a little tyke like him every day. His chatter would be great company while you are gone. Blood soon can be purified with right food and baths, and as for Snap, I meant to get a bulldog, but possibly Snap will serve just as well. All I ask of a dog is to bark at the right time. I'll do the rest. Would you like to come and be my boy, Billy?"

Billy leaned against Mrs. Comstock, reached his arms around her neck and gripped her with all his puny might. "You can whip me all you want to," he said. "I won't make a sound."

Mrs. Comstock held him closely and her hard face was softening, of that there could not be a doubt.

"Now, why would anyone whip a nice little boy like you?" she asked wonderingly.

"She" — Billy from his refuge waved toward Margaret — "she was going to whip me 'cause her cats fought, when I tied their tails together and hung them over the line to dry. How did I know her old cats would fight?"

Mrs. Comstock began to laugh suddenly, and try as she would she could not stop as soon as she desired. Billy studied her.

"Have you got turkeys?" he demanded.

"Yes, flocks of them," said Mrs. Comstock, vainly struggling to suppress her mirth, and settle her face in its accustomed lines.

"Are their tails fast?" demanded Billy.

"Why, I think so," marvelled Mrs. Comstock.

"Hers ain't!" said Billy with the wave toward Margaret that was becoming familiar. "Her turkey pulled, and its tail comed right off. She's going to whip me if he lets her. I didn't know the turkey would pull. I didn't know its tail would come off. I won't ever touch one again, will I?"

"Of course, you won't," said Mrs. Comstock. "And what's more, I don't care if you do! I'd rather have a fine little man like you than all the turkeys in the country. Let them lose their old tails if they want to, and let the cats fight. Cats and turkeys don't compare with boys, who are going to be fine big men some of these days."

Then Billy and Mrs. Comstock hugged each other rapturously, and their audience stared in silent amazement.

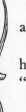

"You like boys!" exulted Billy, and his head dropped against Mrs. Comstock in unspeakable content.

"Yes, and if I don't have to carry you the whole way home, we must start right now," said Mrs. Comstock. "You are going to be asleep before you know it."

Billy opened his eyes and braced himself. "I can walk," he said proudly.

"All right, we must start. Come, Elnora! Good night, folks!" Mrs. Comstock set Billy on the floor, and arose gripping his hand. "You take the other side, Elnora, and we will help him as much as we can," she said.

Elnora stared piteously at Margaret, then at Wesley, and arose in white-faced bewilderment.

"Billy, are you going to leave without even saying good-bye to me?" asked Sinton, with a great gulp in his throat.

Billy held tight to Mrs. Comstock and Elnora.

"Good-bye!" he said casually. "I'll come and see you some time."

Wesley Sinton gave a smothered sob, and strode from the room.

Mrs. Comstock started for the door, dragging at Billy as Elnora pulled back, but Mrs. Sinton was before them, her eyes flashing.

"Kate Comstock, you think you are mighty smart, don't you?" she cried.

"I ain't in the lunatic asylum, where you belong, anyway," said Mrs. Comstock. "I am smart enough to tell a dandy boy when I see him, and I'm good and glad to get him. I'll love to have him!"

"Well, you won't have him!" exclaimed Margaret Sinton. "That boy is Wesley's! He got him, and brought him here. You can't come in and take him like that! Let go of him!"

"Not much, I won't!" cried Mrs. Comstock. "Leave the poor sick little soul here for you to beat, because he didn't know just how to handle things! Of course, he'll make mistakes. He's got to have a lot of teaching, but not the kind he'll get from you! Clear out of my way!"

"You let go of our boy," ordered Margaret.

"Why? Do you want to whip him, before he can go to sleep?" jeered Mrs. Comstock.

"No, I don't!" said Margaret. "He's Wesley's, and nobody shall touch him. Wesley!"

Wesley Sinton appeared behind Margaret in the doorway, and she turned to him. "Make Kate Comstock let go of our boy!" she demanded.

"Billy, she wants you now," said Wesley Sinton. "She won't whip you, and she won't let anyone else. You can have stacks of good things to eat, ride in the carriage, and have a great time Won't you stay with us?"

Billy drew away from Mrs. Comstock and Elnora.

He faced Margaret, his eyes shrewd with unchildish wisdom. Necessity had taught him to strike the hot iron, to drive the hard bargain.

"Can I have Snap to live here always?" he demanded.

155

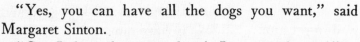

"Yes, you can have all the dogs you want," said Margaret Sinton.

"Can I sleep close enough so's I can touch you?"

"Yes, you can move your lounge up so that you can hold my hand," said Margaret.

"Do you love me now?" questioned Billy.

"I'll try to love you if you are a good boy," said Margaret.

"Then I guess I'll stay," said Billy walking over to her.

Out in the night Elnora and her mother went down the road in the moonlight, and every few rods Mrs. Comstock laughed aloud.

"Mother, I don't understand you," sobbed Elnora.

"Well, maybe when you have gone to high school longer you will," said Mrs. Comstock. "Anyway, you saw me bring Mag Sinton to her senses, didn't you?"

"Yes, I did," answered Elnora, "but I thought you were in earnest. So did Billy, and Uncle Wesley, and Aunt Margaret."

"Well, wasn't I?" inquired Mrs. Comstock.

"But you just said you brought Aunt Margaret to!"

"Well, didn't I?"

"I don't understand you."

"That's the reason I am recommending more schooling!"

Elnora took her candle and went to bed. Mrs. Comstock was feeling too good to sleep. Twice of late she really had enjoyed herself for the first in sixteen years, and a sort of greediness for more of the same feeling crept into her blood like intoxication. As she sat brooding alone she knew the truth. She would have loved to take Billy. She would not have minded his mischief, his chatter, or his dog. He would have meant a sort of salvation from herself that she greatly needed, she was even sincere about the dog. She meant to tell Sinton to buy her one at the very first opportunity. Her last thought was of Billy. She chuckled softly, for she was not saintly, and now she knew what she could do that would fill her soul with grim satisfaction.

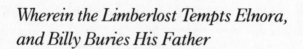

Wherein the Limberlost Tempts Elnora, and Billy Buries His Father

IMMEDIATELY after dinner on Sunday Wesley Sinton stopped at the Comstock gate to ask if Elnora wanted to go to town with them. Billy sat beside him and he did not look as if he were on his way to a funeral. Elnora said she had to study and could not go, but she suggested that her mother take her place. Mrs. Comstock put on her hat and went at once, which surprised Elnora. She did not know that her mother was anxious for an opportunity to speak with Sinton alone. Elnora knew why she was repeatedly cautioned not to leave their land, if she went specimen hunting, to remain along the roads, or at least not to enter the swamp.

She studied two hours and was several lessons ahead of her classes. There was no use to go further. She would take a walk and see if she could gather any caterpillars or find any freshly spun cocoons. She searched the bushes and low trees behind the garden and all about the edge of the woods on their land, and having little success, at last came out to the road. Almost the first thorn bush she examined yielded a Polyphemus

158

cocoon. Elnora lifted her head with the instinct of
a hunter on the chase, and began work. She reached
the swamp before she knew it, carrying five fine cocoons
of different species as her reward. She pushed back
her hair and gazed around longingly. A few rods
inside she thought she saw cocoons on a bush, to which
she went, and found several. Sense of caution was
rapidly vanishing, she was in a fair way to forget everything and plunge into the swamp when she thought she
heard footsteps coming down the trail. She went back,
and came out almost facing Pete Corson.

That ended her difficulty. She had known him since
childhood. When she sat on the front bench of the
Brushwood schoolhouse, Pete had been one of the big
boys at the back of the room. He had been rough and
wild, but she never had been afraid of him, and often he
had given her pretty things from the swamp.

"What luck!" she cried. "I promised mother I
would not go inside the swamp alone, and will you look
at the cocoons I've found! There are more just screaming for me to come get them, because the leaves will fall
with the first frost, and then the jays and crows will begin
to tear them open. I haven't much time, since I'm
going to school. You will go with me, Pete! Please
say yes! Just a little way!"

"What are those things?" asked the man, his keen
black eyes fast upon her.

"They are the cases these big caterpillars spin for
winter, and in the spring they come out great night

moths, and I can sell them. Oh, Pete, I can sell them for enough to take me through high school and dress me so like the rest that I don't look different, and if I have very good luck I can save some for college. Pete, please go with me?"

"Why don't you go like you always have?"

"Well, the truth is, I had a little scare," said Elnora. "I never did mean to go alone; sometimes I sort of wandered inside farther than I intended, chasing things. You know Duncan gave me Freckles's books, and I have been gathering moths like he did. Lately I found I could sell them. If I can make a complete collection, I can get three hundred dollars for it. Three such collections would take me almost through college, and I've four years in the high school yet. That's a long time. I might get them."

"Can every kind there is be found here?"

"No, not all of them, but when I get more than I need of one kind, I can trade them with collectors farther north and west, so I can complete sets. It's the only way I see to earn the money. Look what I have already. Big gray Cecropias come from this kind; brown Polyphemus from that, and green Lunas from these. You aren't working on Sunday. Go with me just an hour, Pete!"

The man looked at her narrowly. She was young, wholesome, and beautiful. She was innocent, intensely in earnest, and she needed the money, he knew that.

"You didn't tell me what scared you," he said.

"Oh, I thought I did! Why, you know, I had Freckles's box packed full of moths and specimens, and one evening I sold some to the Bird Woman. Next morning I found a note telling me it wasn't safe to go inside the swamp. That sort of scared me. I think I'll go alone, rather than miss the chance, but I'd be so happy if you would take care of me. Then I could go anywhere I chose, because if I mired you could pull me out. You will take care of me, Pete?"

That was the finishing stroke.

"Yes, I'll take care of you," promised Pete Corson.

"Goody!" said Elnora. "Let's start quick! And Pete, you look at these closely, and when you are hunting or going along the road, if one dangles under your nose, you cut off the little twig and save it for me, will you?"

"Yes, I'll save you all I see," promised Pete. He pushed back his hat and followed Elnora. She plunged fearlessly through bushes, over underbrush, and across dead logs. One minute she was crying wildly, that here was a big one, the next she was reaching for a limb above her head or on her knees overturning dead leaves under a hickory or oak tree, or pushing aside black muck with her bare hands as she searched for buried pupæ cases. For the first hour Pete bent back bushes and followed, carrying what Elnora discovered. Then he found one.

"Is this the kind of thing you are looking for?" he asked, bashfully, as he presented a wild cherry twig.

"Oh, Pete, that's a Promethea! I didn't even hope to find one."

"What's the bird like?" asked Pete.

"Almost black wings," said Elnora, "with clay-coloured edges, and the most wonderful wine-coloured flush over the under side if it's a male, and stronger wine above and below if it's a female. Oh, aren't I happy!"

"How would it do to make what you have into a bunch that we could leave here, and come back for them?"

"That would be all right."

Relieved of his load Pete began work. First, he narrowly examined the cocoons Elnora had found. He questioned her as to what other kinds would be like. He began to use the eyes of a trained woodman and hunter in her behalf. He saw several so easily, and moved through the forest so softly, that Elnora forgot the moths in watching him. Presently she was carrying the specimens, and he was making the trips of investigation to see which was a cocoon and which a curled leaf, or he was down on his knees digging around stumps. As he worked he kept asking questions. What kind of logs were best to look beside, what trees were pupæ cases most likely to be under; on what bushes did caterpillars spin most frequently? Time passed, as it always does when one's occupation is absorbing.

When the Sintons had taken Mrs. Comstock home, they stopped to see if Elnora was safe. She was not at home, and they had not seen her along the way. Mrs. Comstock called about the edge of her woods and received no reply. Then Sinton turned and drove back to the Limberlost. He left Margaret and Mrs. Comstock holding the team and entertaining Billy, and entered the swamp.

Elnora and Pete had left a wide trail behind them. Before Sinton had thought of calling, he heard voices and approached with some caution. Soon he saw Elnora, her flushed face beaming as she bent with an armload of twigs and branches and talked to a kneeling man.

"Now go cautiously!" she was saying. "I am just sure we will find an Imperialis here. It's their very kind of a place. There! What did I tell you! Isn't that splendid? Oh, I am so glad you came with me!"

Sinton stood and stared in speechless astonishment, for the man had risen, brushed the dirt from his hands, and held out to Elnora a small shining dark pupa case. As his face swung into view Sinton almost cried out, for he was the one man of all others Wesley knew with whom he most feared for Elnora's safety. She had him on his knees digging pupa cases for her from the loose swamp loam.

"Elnora!" called Sinton. "Elnora!"

"Oh, Uncle Wesley!" cried the girl. "See what luck we've had! I know we have a dozen and a half cocoons and we have three pupa cases. It's much harder to get the cases because you have to dig for them, and you can't see where to look. But Pete is fine at it! He's found three, and he says he will keep watch along

the roads, and through the woods as he hunts. Isn't that splendid of him? Uncle Wesley, there is a college over there on the western edge of the swamp. Look closely, and you can see the great dome up among the clouds."

"I should say you have had luck," said Sinton striving to make his voice natural. "But I thought you were not coming to the swamp?"

"Well, I wasn't," said Elnora, "but I couldn't find many anywhere else, honest, I couldn't, and just as soon as I came to the edge I began to see them here. I kept my promise. I didn't come in alone. Pete came with me. He's so strong, he isn't afraid of anything, and he's perfectly splendid to locate cocoons! He's found half of these. Come on, Pete, it's getting dark now, and we must go."

They started for the trail, Pete carrying the cocoons. He left them at the case, while Elnora and Sinton went on to the carriage together.

"Elnora Comstock, what does this mean?" demanded her mother.

"It's all right, one of the neighbours was with her, and she got several dollars' worth of stuff," interposed Sinton.

"You oughter seen my pa," shouted Billy. "He was 'ist all whited out, and he laid as still as anything. They put him away deep in the ground."

"Billy!" breathed Margaret in a prolonged groan.

"Jimmy and Belle are going to be together in a nice

place. They are coming to see me, and Snap is right down here by the wheel. Here, Snap! My, but he'll be tickled to get something to eat! He's 'most twisted as me. They got new clothes, and all they want to eat, too, but they'll miss me. They couldn't have got along without me. I took care of them. I had a lot of things give to me 'cause I was the littlest, and I always divided with them. But they won't need me now."

When she left the carriage Mrs. Comstock gravely shook hands with Billy. "Remember," she said to him, "I love boys, and I love dogs. Whenever you don't have a good time up there, take your dog and come right down and be my little boy. We will just have loads of fun. You should hear the whistles I can make. If you aren't treated right you come straight to me."

Billy wagged his head sagely. "You 'ist bet I will!" he said.

"Mother, how could you?" asked Elnora as they walked up the path.

"How could I, missy? You better ask how couldn't I? I just couldn't! Not for enough to pay my road tax! Not for enough to pay the road tax, and the dredge tax, too!"

"Aunt Margaret always has been lovely to me, and I don't think it's fair to worry her."

"I choose to be lovely to Billy, and let her sweat out her own worries just as she has me, these sixteen years. There is nothing in all this world so good for people as getting a dose of their own medicine. The difference is

that I am honest. I just say in plain English, 'if they don't treat you right, come to me.' They have only said it in actions and inferences. I want to teach Mag Sinton how her own doses taste, but she begins to sputter before I fairly get the spoon to her lips. Just you wait!"

"When I think what I owe her ——" began Elnora.

"Well, thank goodness, I don't owe her anything, and so I'm perfectly free to do what I choose. Come on, and help me get supper. I'm hungry as Billy!"

Margaret Sinton rocked slowly back and forth in her chair. On her breast lay Billy's red head, one hand clutched her dress front with spasmodic grip, even after he was unconscious.

"You mustn't begin that, Margaret," said Sinton. "He's too heavy. And it's bad for him. He's better off to lie down and go to sleep alone."

"He's very light, Wesley. He jumps and quivers so. He has to be stronger than he is now, before he will sleep soundly."

CHAPTER 9

Wherein Elnora Discovers a Violin, and
Billy Disciplines Margaret

ELNORA missed the little figure at the bridge the next
morning. She slowly walked up the street and turned in
at the wide entrance to the school grounds. She scarcely
could comprehend that only a week ago she had gone
there friendless, alone, and so sick at heart that she was
physically ill. To-day she had decent clothing, books,
friends, and her mind was at ease to work on her studies.

As she approached home that night the girl paused
in amazement. Her mother had company, and she was
laughing. Elnora entered the kitchen softly and peeped
into the sitting room. Mrs. Comstock sat in her chair
holding a book and every few seconds a soft chuckle
broke into a real laugh. Mark Twain was doing his
work; while Mrs. Comstock was not lacking in a sense of
humour. Elnora entered the room before her mother
saw her. Mrs. Comstock looked up with flushed face.

"Where did you get this?" she demanded.

"I bought it," said Elnora.

"Bought it! With all the taxes due!"

"I paid for it out of my Indian money, mother," said
Elnora. "I couldn't bear to spend so much on myself

167

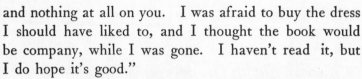

and nothing at all on you. I was afraid to buy the dress I should have liked to, and I thought the book would be company, while I was gone. I haven't read it, but I do hope it's good."

"Good! It's the biggest piece of foolishness I have read in all my life. I've laughed all day, ever since I found it. I had a notion to go out and read some of it to the cows and see if they wouldn't laugh."

"If it made you laugh, it's a wise book," said Elnora.

"Wise!" cried Mrs. Comstock. "You can stake your life it's a wise book. It takes the smartest man there is to do this kind of fooling," and she began laughing again.

Elnora, highly satisfied with her purchase, went to her room and put on her working clothes. Thereafter she made a point of getting a book that she thought would interest her mother, from the library every week, and leaving it on the sitting-room table. Every night she carried home at least two school books and studied until she had mastered the points of each lesson. She did her share of the work faithfully, and every available minute she was in the fields searching for cocoons, for the moths promised to become her best source of income.

She gathered large baskets of nests, flowers, mosses, insects, and all sorts of natural history specimens and sold them to the grade teachers. At first she tried to tell these instructors what to teach their pupils about the specimens; but recognizing how much more she knew than they, one after another begged her to study at home, and use her spare hours in school to exhibit and explain nature subjects to their pupils. Elnora loved the work, and she needed the money, for every few days some matter of expense arose that she had not expected.

From the first week she had been received and invited with the crowd of girls in her class, and it was their custom in passing through the business part of the city to stop at the confectioners' and take turns in treating to expensive candies, ice cream sodas, hot chocolate, or whatever they fancied. When first Elnora was asked she accepted without understanding. The second time she went because she seldom had tasted these things, and they were so delicious she could not resist. After that she went because she knew all about it, and had decided to go.

She had spent a half-hour on the log by the trail in deep thought and had arrived at her conclusions. She worked harder than usual for the next week, but she seemed to thrive on work. It was October and the red leaves were falling when her first time came to treat. As the crowd flocked down the broad walk that night Elnora called "Girls, it's my treat to-night! Come on!"

She led the way through the city to the grocery they patronized when they had a small spread, and entering came out with a basket, which she carried to the bridge on her home road. There she arranged the girls in two rows on the cement abutments and opening her basket she gravely offered each girl an exquisite little basket of bark, lined with red leaves, in one end of which

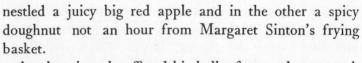

nestled a juicy big red apple and in the other a spicy doughnut not an hour from Margaret Sinton's frying basket.

Another time she offered big balls of popped corn stuck together with maple sugar, and liberally sprinkled with beechnut kernels. Again it was hickory nut kernels glazed with sugar, another time maple candy, and once a basket of warm pumpkin pies. She never made any apology, or offered any excuse. She simply gave what she could afford, and the change was as welcome to those city girls, accustomed to sodas and French candy as were these same things to Elnora surfeited on pop-corn and pie. In her room was a little slip containing a record of the number of weeks in the school year, the times it would be her turn to treat and the dates on which such occasions would fall, with a number of suggestions by each. Once the girls almost fought over a basket lined with yellow leaves, and filled with fat, very ripe red haws. In late October there was a riot over one which was lined with red leaves and contained big fragrant pawpaws frost-bitten to a perfect degree. Then hazel nuts were ripe, and once they served. One day Elnora at her wits' end, explained to her mother that the girls had given her things and she wanted to treat them. Mrs. Comstock, with characteristic stubbornness, had said she would leave a basket at the grocery for her, but firmly declined to say what would be in it. All day Elnora struggled to keep her mind on her books. For hours she wavered in tense uncertainty.

What would her mother do? Should she take the girls to the confectioner's that night or risk the basket? Mrs. Comstock could make delicious things to eat, but would she?

As they left the building Elnora made a final rapid mental calculation. She could not see her way clear to a decent treat for ten people for less than two dollars. and if the basket was nice, then the money would be wasted. She decided to risk it. As they went to the bridge the girls were betting on what the treat would be, and crowding near Elnora like spoiled small children. Elnora set down the basket.

"Girls," she said, "I don't know what this is myself, so all of us are going to be surprised. Here goes!"

She lifted the cover and perfumes from the land of spices rolled up. In one end of the basket lay ten enormous sugar cakes the tops of which had been liberally dotted with circles cut from stick candy. The candy had melted in baking and made small transparent wells of waxy sweetness and in the centre of each cake was a fat turtle made from a raisin with cloves for head and feet. The remainder of the basket was filled with big spiced pears that could be held by their stems while they were eaten. The girls shrieked and attacked the cookies, and of all the treats Elnora offered perhaps none was quite so long remembered as that.

When Elnora took her basket, placed her books in it, and started home, all the girls went with her as far as the fence where she crossed the field to the swamp. When

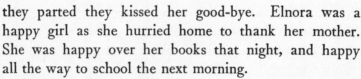

they parted they kissed her good-bye. Elnora was a happy girl as she hurried home to thank her mother. She was happy over her books that night, and happy all the way to school the next morning.

When the music swelled from the orchestra her heart almost broke with throbbing joy. For music always had affected her strangely, and since she had been comfortable enough in her surroundings to notice things, she had listened to every note to find what it was that literally hurt her heart and at last she knew. It was the talking of the violins. They were human voices, and they spoke a language Elnora understood. It seemed to her that she must climb up on the stage, take the instruments from the fingers of the players and make them speak what was in her heart. She fairly prayed to get hold of one, if only for a second.

That night she said to her mother, "I am perfectly crazy for a violin. I am sure I could play one, sure as I live. Did anyone ——" Elnora never completed that sentence.

"Hush!" thundered Mrs. Comstock. "Be quiet! Never mention those things before me again — never as long as you live! I loath them! They are a snare of the very devil himself! They were made to lure men and women from their homes and their honour. If ever I see you with one in your fingers I will smash it in pieces."

Naturally Elnora hushed, but she thought of nothing else after she had done justice to her lessons. At last there came a day when for some reason the leader of the orchestra left his violin on the grand piano. That morning Elnora made her first mistake in algebra. At noon, as soon as the great building was empty, she slipped into the auditorium, found the side door which led to the stage, and going through the musicians' entrance she took the violin. She carried it back into the little side room where the orchestra assembled, closed all the doors, opened the case and lifted out the instrument.

She laid it on her breast, dropped her chin on it and drew the bow softly across the strings. One after another she tested the open notes. They reminded her of things. Gradually her stroke ceased to tremble and she drew the bow firmly. Then her fingers began to fall and softly, slowly she searched up and down those strings for sounds she knew. Standing in the middle of the floor, she tried over and over. It seemed scarcely a minute before the hall was filled with the sounds of hurrying feet, and she was forced to put away the violin and go to her classes. Of food she never thought until she noticed how heavy her lunch box was on the way home, so she sat on the log by the swamp and remedied that. The next day she prayed that the violin would be left again, but her petition was not answered.

That night when she returned from school she made an excuse to go down to see Billy. He was engaged in hulling walnuts by driving them through holes in a board. His hands were protected by a pair of Margaret's

old gloves, but he had speckled his face generously. He looked well, and greeted Elnora hilariously.

"Me an' the squirrels are laying up our winter stores," he shouted. "'Cos the cold is coming, an' the snow an' if we have any nuts we have to fix 'em now. But I'm ahead, 'cos Uncle Wesley made me this board, and I can hull a big pile while the old squirrel does only 'ist one with his teeth."

Elnora picked him up and kissed him. "Billy, are you happy?" she asked.

"Yes, and so's Snap," answered Billy. "You ought to see him make the dirt fly when he gets after a chipmunk. I bet you he could dig up pa, if anybody wanted him to."

"Billy!" gasped Margaret as she came out to them.

"Well, me and Snap don't want him up, and I bet you Jimmy and Belle don't, either. I ain't been twisty inside once since I been here, and I don't want to go away, and Snap don't, either. He told me so."

"Billy! That is not true. Dogs can't talk," cautioned Margaret.

"Then what makes you open the door when he asks you to?" demanded Billy.

"Scratching and whining isn't talking."

"Anyway, it's the best Snap can talk, and you get up and do things he wants done. Chipmunks can talk too. You ought to hear them dam things holler when Snap gets them!"

"Billy! When you want a cooky for supper and I

don't give it to you it is because you said a wrong word."

"Well, for——" Billy clapped his hand over his mouth and stained his face in swipes. "Well, for — anything! Did I go an' forget again! The cookies will get all hard, won't they? I bet you ten dollars I don't say that any more."

He espied Wesley and ran to show him a walnut too big to go through the holes, and Elnora and Margaret went into the house.

They talked of many things for a time and then Elnora said suddenly, "Aunt Margaret, I like music."

"I've noticed that in you all your life," answered Margaret.

"If dogs can't talk, I can make a violin talk," announced Elnora, and then in amazement watched the face of Margaret Sinton grow pale.

"A violin!" she wavered. "Where did you get a violin?"

"They fairly seemed to speak to me in the orchestra. One day the conductor left his in the auditorium, and I took it, and, Aunt Margaret, I can make it do the wind in the swamp, the birds, and the animals. I can make any sound I ever heard on it. If I had a chance to practise a little, I could make it do the orchestra music, too. I don't know how I know, but I do."

"Did — did you ever mention it to your mother?" faltered Margaret.

"Yes, and she seems prejudiced against them. But,

oh, Aunt Margaret, I never felt so about anything, not even going to school. I just feel as if I'd die if I didn't have one. I could keep it at school, and practise at noon a whole hour. Soon they'd ask me to play in the orchestra. I could keep it in the case and practise in the woods in summer. You'd let me play here over Sunday. Oh, Aunt Margaret, what does one cost? Would it be wicked for me to take of my money and buy a very cheap one? I could play on the least expensive one made."

"Oh, no you couldn't! A cheap machine makes cheap music. You got to have a fine fiddle to make it sing. But there's no sense in your buying one. There isn't a decent reason on earth why you shouldn't have your fa ——"

"My father's!" cried Elnora. She caught Margaret Sinton by the arm. "My father had a violin! He played it. That's why I can! Where is it! Is it in our house? Is it in mother's room?"

"Elnora!" panted Margaret. "Your mother will kill me! She always hated it."

"Mother dearly loves music," said Elnora.

"Not when it took the man she loved away from her to make it!"

"Where is my father's violin?"

"Elnora!"

"I've never seen a picture of my father. I've never heard his name mentioned. I've never had a scrap that belonged to him. Was he my father, or am I a charity child like Billy, and so she hates me?"

176

"She's got good pictures of him. Seems she just can't bear to hear him talked about. Of course, he was your father. They lived right there when you were born. She don't dislike you, she just tries to make herself think she does. There's no sense in the world in you not having his violin. I've a great notion ——"

"Has she got it?"

"No. I've never heard her mention it. It was not at home when he — when he died."

"Do you know where it is?"

"Yes. I'm the only person on earth who does, except the one who has it."

"Who is that?"

"I can't tell you, but I will see if they have it yet, and get it if I can. But, if your mother finds it out she will never forgive me."

"I can't help it," said Elnora. "I want that violin. I want it now."

"I'll go to-morrow, and get it if it has not been destroyed."

"Destroyed! Oh, Aunt Margaret! Would anyone dare?"

"I hardly think so. It was a good instrument. He played it like a master."

"Tell me!" breathed Elnora.

"His hair was red and curled more than yours, and his eyes were blue. He was tall, slim, and the very imp of mischief. He joked and teased all day until he picked

up that violin. Then his head bent over it, and his eyes got big and earnest. He seemed to listen as if he first heard the notes, and then copied them. Sometimes he drew the bow trembly, like he wasn't sure it was right, and he might have to try again. He could almost drive you crazy when he wanted to, and no man that ever lived could make you dance as he could. He made it all up as he went. He seemed to listen for his dancing music, too. It appeared to come to him; he'd begin to play and you had to keep time or die. You couldn't be still; he loved to sweep a crowd around with that bow of his. I think it was the thing you call inspiration. I can see him now, his handsome head bent, his cheeks red, his eyes snapping, and that bow going across the strings, and driving us like sheep. He always kept his body swinging, and he loved to play. He often slighted his work shamefully, and sometimes her a little; that is why she hated it — Elnora, what are you making me do?"

The tears were rolling down Elnora's cheeks. "Oh, Aunt Margaret," she sobbed. "Why haven't you told me about him sooner? I feel as if you had given my father to me living, so that I could touch him. I can see him, too! Why didn't you ever tell me before? Go on! Go on!"

"I can't, Elnora! I'm scared to death! I never meant to say anything. If I hadn't promised her not to talk of him to you she wouldn't have let you come here. She made me swear it."

"But why? Why? Was he a shame? Was he disgraced?"

"Maybe it was that unjust feeling that took possession of her when she couldn't help him from the swamp. She had to blame some one, or go crazy, so she took it out on you. At times, those first ten years, if I had talked to you, and you had repeated anything to her, she might have struck you too hard. She was not master of herself. You must be patient with her, Elnora. God only knows what she has gone through, but I think she is a little better lately."

"So do I," said Elnora. "She seems more interested in my clothes, and she fixes me such delicious lunches that the girls bring fine candies and cake and beg to trade. I gave half my lunch for a box of candy one day, brought it home to her, and told her. Since, she has wanted me to carry a market basket and treat the crowd every day, she was so pleased. Life has been too monotonous for her. I think she enjoys even the little change made by my going and coming. She sits up half the night to read the library books I bring, but she is so stubborn she won't even admit that she touches them. Tell me more about my father."

"Wait until I see if I can get the violin."

So Elnora went home in suspense, and that night she added to her prayers, "Dear Lord, be merciful to my father, and, oh, do help Aunt Margaret to get his violin."

Wesley and Billy came in to supper tired and hungry. Billy ate heartily, but his eyes often rested on a plate of

tempting cookies, and when Wesley offered them to the boy he reached for one. Margaret was compelled to explain that cookies were forbidden that night.

"What!" said Wesley. "Wrong words been coming again. Oh, Billy, I do wish you could remember! I can't sit and eat cookies before a little boy who has none. I'll have to put mine back, too."

Billy's face was a puzzle. It twisted in despair.

"Aw, go on!" he said gruffly, but his chin was jumping, for Wesley was his idol.

"Can't do it," said Wesley. "It would choke me."

Billy turned to Margaret. "You make him," he appealed.

"He can't, Billy," said Margaret. "I know how he feels. You see, I can't myself."

Then Billy slid from his chair, ran to the couch, buried his face in the pillow and cried heart-brokenly. Wesley hurried to the barn, and Margaret to the kitchen. When the dishes were almost washed Billy slipped from the back door.

Wesley piling hay into the mangers heard a sound behind him and inquired, "That you, Billy?"

"Yes," answered Billy, "and it's all so dark you can't see me now, isn't it?"

"Well, mighty near," answered Wesley.

"Then you stoop down and open your mouth."

Sinton had shared bites of apple and nuts for weeks, for Billy had not learned how to eat anything without dividing with Jimmy and Belle. Since he was separated

from them, he shared with Wesley and Margaret. So
he bent over the small figure and received an instalment
of cooky that almost choked him.

"Now you can eat it!" shouted Billy in delight.
"It's all dark! I can't see what you're doing 't all!"

Wesley picked up the small figure and set the boy
on the back of a horse to bring his face level so that they
could talk as men. He never towered from his height
above Billy, but always lifted the little soul when important matters were to be discussed.

"Now what a dandy scheme," he commented. "Did
you and Aunt Margaret fix it up?"

"No. She ain't had hers yet. But I got one for
her. Ist as soon as you eat yours, I am going to take
hers, and feed her first time I find her in the dark."

"But, Billy, where did you get the cookies? You
know Aunt Margaret said you were not to have any."

"I ist took them," said Billy, "I didn't take them for
me. I ist took them for you and her."

Wesley swallowed hard and thought fast. In the warm
darkness of the barn the horses crunched their corn, a
rat gnawed at a corner of the granary, and among the
rafters the white pigeon cooed a soft sleepy note to his
dusky mate.

"Did — did — I steal?" wavered Billy through the
darkness.

Wesley's big hands closed until he almost hurt the boy.

"No!" he said vehemently. "That is too big a word.
You just made a mistake. You were trying to be a fine

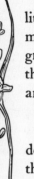

little man, but you went at it the wrong way. You only made a mistake. All of us do that, Billy. The world grows that way. When we make mistakes we can see them; that teaches us to be more careful the next time, and so we learn."

"How wouldn't it be a mistake?"

"If you had told Aunt Margaret what you wanted to do, and asked her for the cookies she would have given them to you."

"But I was 'fraid she wouldn't, and you ist had to have it."

"Not if it was wrong for me to have it, Billy. I don't want it that much."

"Must I take it back?"

"You think hard, and decide yourself," suggested Wesley.

"Lift me down," said Billy, after a silence. "I got to put this in the jar, and tell her."

Wesley set the boy on the floor, but as he did so he paused one second and strained him close to his breast.

Margaret sat in her chair sewing, Billy slipped in and crept up beside her. The little face was lined with tragedy.

"Why, Billy, whatever is the matter?" she cried as she dropped her sewing and held out her arms. Billy stood back. He gripped his little fists tight and squared his shoulders. "I got to be shut up in the closet," he said.

"Oh, Billy! What an unlucky day! What have you done now?"

"I stold!" gulped Billy. "He said it was ist a mistake, but it was worser 'an that. I took something you told me I wasn't to have."

"Stole!" Margaret was in despair. "What, Billy?"

"Cookies!" answered Billy in equal trouble.

"Billy!" wailed Margaret. "How could you?"

"It was for him and you," sobbed Billy. "He said he couldn't eat it 'fore me, but out in the barn it's all dark and I couldn't see. I thought maybe he could there. Then we might put out the light and you could have yours. He said I only made it worse, 'cos I mustn't take things, and I know I mustn't, so I got to go in the closet."

Margaret gazed at him helplessly.

"Will you hold me tight a little bit first? He did."

Margaret opened her arms and Billy rushed in and clung to her a few seconds, with all the force of his being, then he slipped to the floor and marched to the closet. Margaret opened the door. Billy gave one glance at the light, clinched his fists and walking inside climbed on a box. Margaret shut her eyes and closed the door.

Then she sat and listened. Was the air pure enough? Possibly he might smother. She had read something once. Was it very dark? What if there should be a mouse in the closet and it should run across his foot and frighten him into spasms. Somewhere she had heard —— Margaret leaned forward with tense face and listened. Something dreadful

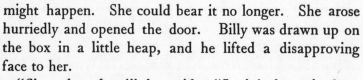

might happen. She could bear it no longer. She arose hurriedly and opened the door. Billy was drawn up on the box in a little heap, and he lifted a disapproving face to her.

"Shut that door!" he said. "I ain't been in here near long enough yet!"

CHAPTER 10

*Wherein Elnora Has More Financial
Troubles, and Mrs. Comstock Again
Hears the Song of the Limberlost*

THE next night Elnora hurried to Sinton's. She
threw open the back door and searched Margaret's face
with anxious eyes.

"You got it!" panted Elnora. "You got it! I can
see by your face that you did. Oh, give it to me!"

"Yes, I got it, honey, I got it all right, but don't be so
fast. You can't have it before Saturday. It had been
kept in such a damp place it needed glueing, it had to
have strings, and a key was gone. I knew how much
you wanted it, so I sent Wesley right to town with it.
They said they could fix it good as new, but it should be
varnished, and that it would take several days for the
glue to set. You can have it Saturday."

"You found it where you thought it was? You know
it's his?"

"Yes, it was just where I thought, and it's the
same violin I've seen him play hundreds of times. It's
all right, only laying so long it needs fixing."

"Oh, Aunt Margaret! Can I ever wait?"

"It does seem a long time, but how could I help it?

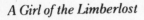

You couldn't do anything with it as it was. You see, it had been hidden away in a garret, and it needed cleaning and drying to make it fit to play again. You can have it Saturday sure."

"Saturday morning?"

"He just said Saturday. But Elnora, you've got to promise me that you will leave it here, or in town, and not let your mother get a hint of it. I don't know what she'd do."

"Uncle Wesley can bring it here until Monday. Then I will take it to school so that I can practise at noon. Oh, I don't know how to thank you. And there's more than the violin for which to be thankful. You've given me my father. Last night I saw him plain as life."

"Elnora you were dreaming! You couldn't have seen him."

"I know I was dreaming, but I saw him. I saw him so closely that a tiny white scar at the corner of his eyebrow showed. I was just reaching out to touch him when he disappeared."

"Who told you there was a scar on his forehead?"

"No one ever did in all my life. I saw it last night just as he went down. And, oh, Aunt Margaret! I saw what she did, and I heard his cries! No matter what she does, I don't believe I ever can be angry with her again. Her heart is broken, and she can't help it. Oh, it was terrible, but I am glad I saw it. Now, I will always understand."

"I don't know what to make of that," said Margaret.

"I don't believe in such stuff at all, but you couldn't make it up, for you didn't know."

"I only know that I played the violin last night, as he played it, and while I played he came through the woods from the direction of Carney's. It was summer and all the flowers were in bloom. He wore gray trousers and a blue shirt, his head was bare, and his face was beautiful. I could almost touch him when he sank."

Margaret Sinton stood perplexed. "Well, I don't know what to think of that!" she ejaculated. "I was next to the last person who saw him before he was drowned. It was late on a June afternoon, and he was dressed as you describe. He was bareheaded because he had found a quail's nest before the bird began to brood, and he gathered the eggs in his hat and left it in a fence corner to get on his way home; they found it afterward."

"Was he coming from Carney's?"

"He was on that side of the quagmire. Why he ever skirted it so close as to get caught is a mystery you will have to dream out. I never could understand it."

"Was he doing something he didn't want my mother to know?"

"Why?"

"Because if he was, he might have cut close the swamp so he couldn't be seen from the garden. You know, the whole path straight to the pool where he sank can be seen from our back door. It's firm on our side. The danger is on the north and east. If he didn't want

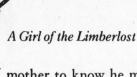

mother to know he might have tried to pass on either of those sides and gone too close. Was he in a hurry?"

"Yes, he was," said Margaret. "He had been away longer than he expected, and he almost ran when he started home."

"And he'd left his violin somewhere that you knew, and you went and got it. I'll wager he was going to play, and didn't want mother to find it out!"

"It wouldn't make any difference to you if you knew every little thing, so quit thinking about it, and just be glad you are to have what he loved best of anything."

"That's true, and I must hurry home, or I'll have to be cutting too close the swamp myself. I am dreadfully late."

Elnora sprang up and ran down the road, but when she was near the cabin she climbed the fence, crossed the open woods pasture diagonally and entered at the back garden gate. As she often came that way when she had been looking for cocoons her mother asked no questions.

Elnora lived by the minute until Saturday, when, contrary to his usual custom, Sinton went to town in the forenoon, taking her along to buy some groceries. Sinton drove straight to the music store, and asked for the violin he had left to be mended.

In its new coat of varnish, with new keys and strings, it looked greatly like any other violin to Sinton, but to Elnora it was the most beautiful instrument ever made, and a priceless treasure. She held it in her arms, touched the strings softly and then she drew the bow across them in whispering measure. She had no time to think what a remarkably good bow it was for sixteen years' disuse. The tan leather case might have impressed her as being in fine condition also, had she been in a state to question anything. She did remember to ask for the bill and she was gravely presented with a slip calling for four strings, one key, and a coat of varnish, total, one dollar fifty. It seemed to Elnora she never could put the precious instrument in the case and start home. Wesley left her in the music store where the proprietor showed her all he could about tuning, and gave her several beginners' sheets of notes and scales. She carried the violin in her arms as far as the crossroads at the corner of their land, then reluctantly put it under the carriage seat.

As soon as her work was done she ran down to Sintons' and began to play, and on Monday the violin went to school with her. She made arrangements with the superintendent to leave it in his office and scarcely took time for her food at noon, she was so eager to practise. Often one of the girls asked her to stay in town all night for some lecture or entertainment. She could take the violin with her, practise, and secure help. Her skill was so great that the leader of the orchestra offered to give her lessons if she would play to pay for them, so her progress was rapid in technical work. But from the first day the instrument became hers, with perfect faith that she could play as her father did, she spent half her practice

189

time in imitating the sounds of all outdoors and im-
provising the songs her happy heart sang in those days.

So the first year went, and the second and third were
a repetition; but the fourth was different, for that was
the close of the course, ending with graduation and all
its attendant ceremonies and expenses. To Elnora
these appeared mountain high. She had hoarded every
cent, thinking twice before she parted with a penny,
but teaching natural history in the grades had taken
time from her studies in school which must be made up
outside. She was a conscientious student, ranking first
in most of her classes, and standing high in all branches.
Her interest in her violin had grown with the years.
She went to school early and practised a half-hour in
the little room off the stage, while the orchestra gathered.
She put in a full hour at noon, and remained another
half hour at night. She carried the violin to Sinton's
on Saturday and practised all the time she could there,
while Margaret watched the road to see that Mrs. Comstock was not coming. She had become so skilful that
it was a delight to hear her play the music of any com-
poser, but when she played her own, that was joy inex-
pressible, for then the wind blew, the water rippled,
the Limberlost sang her songs of sunshine, shadow,
black storm, and white night.

Since her dream Elnora had regarded her mother with
peculiar tenderness. The girl realized, in a measure,
what had happened. She avoided anything that possibly could stir bitter memories or draw deeper a line

on the hard, white face. This cost many sacrifices, much work, and sometimes delayed progress, but the horror of that awful dream remained with Elnora. She worked her way cheerfully, doing all she could to interest her mother in things that happened in school, in the city, and by carrying books that were interesting from the public libraries.

Three years had changed Elnora from the girl of sixteen to the very verge of womanhood. She had grown tall, round, and her face had the loveliness of perfect complexion, beautiful eyes and hair and an added touch from within that might have been called comprehension. It was a compound of self-reliance, hard knocks, heart hunger, unceasing work, and generosity. There was no form of suffering with which the girl could not sympathize, no work she was afraid to attempt, no subject she had investigated she did not understand. These things combined to produce a breadth and depth of character altogether unusual. She was so absorbed in her classes and her music that she had not been able to gather specimens as usual. When she realized this and hunted assiduously, she soon found that changing natural conditions had affected such work. Men all around were clearing available land. The trees fell wherever corn would grow. The swamp was broken by several gravel roads, dotted in places around the edge with little frame houses, and the machinery of oil wells; one especially low place around the region of Freckles's room was nearly all that remained of the original.

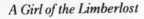

Wherever the trees fell the moisture dried, the creeks ceased to flow, the river ran low, and at times the bed was dry. With unbroken sweep the winds of the west came, gathering force with every mile and howled and raved; threatening to tear the shingles from the roof, blowing the surface from the soil in clouds of fine dust and rapidly changing everything. From coming in with two or three dozen rare moths in a day, in three years' time Elnora had grown to be delighted with finding two or three. Big pursy caterpillars could not be picked from their favourite bushes, when there were no bushes. Dragon flies would not hover over dry places, and butterflies became scarce in proportion to the flowers, while no land yields over three crops of Indian relics.

All the time the expense of books, clothing and incidentals had continued. Elnora added to her bank account whenever she could, and drew out when she was compelled, but she omitted the important feature of calling for a balance. So, one early spring morning in the last quarter of the fourth year, she almost fainted when she learned that all her funds were gone. Commencement with its extra expense was coming, she had no money, and very few cocoons to open in June, which would be too late. She had one collection for the Bird Woman complete to a pair of Imperialis moths, and that was her only asset. On the day she added these big yellow Emperors she would get a check for three hundred dollars, but she would not get it until these specimens were secured. She remembered that she never had found an Emperor before June.

Moreover, that sum was for her first year in college. Then she would be of age, and she meant to sell enough of her share of her father's land to finish. She knew her mother would oppose her bitterly in that, for Mrs. Comstock had clung to every acre and tree that belonged to her husband. Her land was almost complete forest where her neighbours owned cleared farms, dotted with wells that every hour sucked oil from beneath her holdings, but she was too absorbed in the grief she nursed to know or care. The Brushwood road and the redredging of the great Limberlost ditch had been more than she could pay from her income, and she had trembled before the wicket as she asked the banker if she had funds to pay it, and wondered why he laughed as he assured her she had. For Mrs. Comstock had spent no time on compounding interest, and never added the sums she had been depositing through nearly twenty years. Now she thought her funds were almost gone, and every day she worried over expenses. She could see no reason in going through the forms of graduation when pupils had all in their heads that was required to graduate. Elnora knew she had to have her diploma in order to enter the college she wanted to attend, but she did not dare utter the word, until high school was finished, for, instead of softening as she hoped her mother had begun to do, she seemed to remain very much the same.

When the girl reached the swamp she sat on a log and thought bitterly over the absolute expense she was compelled to meet. Every member of her particular set was having an expensive photograph taken to exchange with the others. Elnora loved these girls and boys, and to say she could not have their pictures to keep was more than she could bear. Each one would give to all the others a handsome graduation present. She knew they would prepare gifts for her whether she could make a present in return or not. Then it was the custom for each graduating class to give a great entertainment and use the funds to present the school with a statue for the entrance hall. Elnora had been cast for and was practising a part in that performance. She was expected to furnish her dress and personal necessities. She had been told that she must have a green dress, and where was it to come from?

Every girl of the class would have three beautiful new frocks for Commencement; one for the baccalaureate sermon, another, which could be plainer, for graduation exercises, and a handsome one for the banquet and ball. Elnora faced the past three years and wondered how she could have spent so much money and not kept account of it. She did not realize where it had gone. She did not know what she could do now. She thought over the photographs, and at last settled that question to her satisfaction. She studied longer over the gifts, ten handsome ones there must be, and at last decided she could arrange for them. The green dress came first.

The lights would be dim in the scene, and the setting deep woods. She could manage that. She simply could not have three dresses. She would have to get a very simple one for the sermon and do the best she could for graduation. Whatever she got for that must be made with a guimpe that could be taken out to make it a little more festive for the ball. But where could she get even two pretty dresses?

The only hope she could see was to break into the collection of the man from India, sell some moths, and try to replace them in June. But in her soul she knew that never would do. No June ever brought just the things she hoped it would. If she spent the college money she knew she could not replace it. If she did not, the only way was to try for a room in the grades and teach a year. Her work there had been so appreciated that Elnora felt with the recommendation she knew she could get from the superintendent and teachers she could secure a position. She was sure she could pass the examinations easily. She had once gone on Saturday, taken them and secured a licence for a year before she left the Brushwood school.

She wanted to start to college when the other girls were going. If she could make the first year alone, she could manage the rest. But make that first year herself, she must. Instead of selling any of her collection, she must hunt as she never before had hunted and find a yellow Emperor. She had to have it, that was all. Also, she had to have those dresses. She thought of

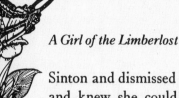

Sinton and dismissed it. She thought of the Bird Woman, and knew she could not tell her. She thought of every way in which she ever had hoped to earn money and realized that with the play, committee meetings, practising, and final examinations she scarcely had time to live, much less to do more than the work required for her pictures and gifts. Again, Elnora was in trouble, and this time it seemed the worst of all.

It was dark when she arose and went home.

"Mother," she said, "I have a piece of news that is decidedly not cheerful."

"Then keep it to yourself!" said Mrs. Comstock. "I think I have enough to bear without a great girl like you piling trouble on me."

"My money is all gone!" said Elnora.

"Well, did you think it would last forever? It's been a marvel to me that it's held out as well as it has, the way you've dressed and gone."

"I don't think I've spent any that I was not compelled to," said Elnora. "I've dressed on just as little as I possibly could to keep going. I am heartsick. I thought I had over fifty dollars to put me through Commencement, but they tell me it's all gone."

"Fifty dollars! To put you through Commencement! Well, what on earth are you proposing to do?"

"The same as the rest of them, in the very cheapest way possible."

"And what might that be?"

Elnora omitted the photographs, the gifts and the

play. She told only of the sermon, graduation exercises, and the ball.

"Well, I wouldn't trouble myself over that," sniffed Mrs. Comstock. "If you want to go to a sermon, put on the dress you always use for meeting. If you need white for the exercises wear the new dress you got last spring. As for the ball, the best thing for you to do is to stay a mile away from such folly. In my opinion you'd best bring home your books, and quit right now. You can't be fixed like the rest of them, don't be so foolish as to run into it. Just stay here and let these last few days go. You can't learn enough more to be of any account."

"But, mother," gasped Elnora. "You don't understand!"

"Oh, yes, I do!" said Mrs. Comstock. "I understand perfectly. So long as the money lasted, you held up your head, and went sailing without even explaining how you got it from the stuff you gathered. Goodness knows I couldn't see. But now it's gone, you come whining to me. What have I got? Have you forgot that the ditch and the road completely strapped me? I haven't any money. There's nothing for you to do but get out of it."

"I can't!" said Elnora desperately. "I've gone on too long. It would make a break in everything. They wouldn't let me have my diploma!"

"What's the difference? You've got the stuff in your head. I wouldn't give a rap for a scrap of paper. That don't mean anything!"

"But I've worked four years for it, and I can't enter —
I ought to have it to help me get a school, when I want
to teach. If I don't have my grades to show, people
will think I quit because I couldn't pass my examinations. I must have my diploma!"

"Then get it!" said Mrs. Comstock.

"The only way is to graduate with the rest."

"Well, graduate if you are bound to!"

"But I can't, unless I have things enough like the
others, that I don't look as I did that first day."

"Well, please remember I didn't get you into this,
and I can't get you out. You are set on having your
wn way. Go on, and have it, and see how you like
it!"

Elnora went upstairs and did not come down again
that night, which her mother called pouting.

"I've thought all night," said the girl at breakfast,
"and I can't see any way but to borrow the money of
Uncle Wesley and pay it back from some that the Bird
Woman will owe me, when I get one more specimen.
But that means that I can't go to — that I will have
to teach this winter, if I can get a city grade or a country
school."

"Just you dare go dinging after Wesley Sinton for
money," cried Mrs. Comstock. "You won't do any
such a thing !"

"I can't see any other way. I've got to have the
money!"

"Quit, I tell you!"

"I can't quit! — I've gone too far!"

"Well, then, let me get your clothes, and you can pay me back."

"But you said you had no money!"

"Maybe I can borrow some at the bank. Then you can return it when the Bird Woman pays you."

"All right," said Elnora. "I don't have to have expensive things. Just some kind of a pretty cheap white dress for the sermon, and a white one a little better than I had last summer, for Commencement and the ball. I can use the white gloves and shoes I got myself for last year, and you can get my dress made at the same place you did that one. They have my measurements, and do perfect work. Don't get expensive things. It will be warm so I can go bareheaded."

Then she started to school, but was so tired and discouraged she scarcely could walk. Four years' plans going in one day! For she felt that if she did not get started to college that fall she never would. Instead of feeling relieved at her mother's offer, she was almost too ill to go on. For the thousandth time she groaned, "Oh, why didn't I keep account of my money?"

After that the days went so swiftly she scarcely had time to think, but several trips her mother made to town, and the assurance that everything was all right, satisfied Elnora. She worked very hard to pass good final examinations and perfect herself for the play. For two days she had remained in town with the Bird Woman in order to spend more time practising and at her work.

Often Margaret had asked about her dresses for graduation, and Elnora had replied that they were with a woman in the city who had made her a white dress for last year's Commencement when she was a junior usher, and they would be all right. So Margaret, Wesley, and Billy concerned themselves over what they would get her for a present. Margaret suggested a beautiful dress. Sinton said that would look to every one as if she needed dresses. The thing was to get a handsome gift like all the rest would have. Billy wanted to present her a five-dollar gold piece to buy music for her violin. He was positive Elnora would like that best of anything.

It was toward the close of the term when they drove to town one evening to try to settle this important question. They knew Mrs. Comstock had been alone several days, so they asked her to accompany them. She had been more lonely than she would admit, filled with unusual unrest besides, and so she was glad to go. But before they had driven a mile Billy had told that they were going to buy Elnora a graduation present, and Mrs. Comstock devoutly wished that she had remained at home. She was prepared when Billy asked, "Aunt Kate, what are you going to give Elnora when she graduates?"

"Plenty to eat, a good bed to sleep in, and do all the work while she trollops," answered Mrs. Comstock dryly.

Billy reflected. "I guess all of them have got that,"

he said. "I mean a present you buy at the store, like Christmas?"

"It is only rich folks that buy presents at stores," replied Mrs. Comstock. "I can't afford it."

"Well, we ain't rich," he said, "but we are going to buy Elnora something as fine as the rest of them have if we sell a corner of the farm. Uncle Wesley said so."

"A fool and his land is soon parted," said Mrs. Comstock tersely. Wesley and Billy laughed, but Margaret did not enjoy the remark.

While they were searching the stores for something on which all of them could decide, and Margaret was holding Billy to keep him from saying anything before Mrs. Comstock about the music on which he was determined; Mr. Brownlee met Wesley and stopped to shake hands.

"I see your boy came out finely," he said.

"I don't allow any boy anywhere to be finer than Billy," said Sinton.

"I guess you don't allow any girl to surpass Elnora," said Mr. Brownlee. "She comes home with Ellen often, and my wife and I love her. Ellen says she is great in her part to-night. Best thing in the whole play! Of course, you are in to see it! If you haven't reserved seats, you'd best start pretty soon, for the high school auditorium only seats a thousand. It's always jammed at these home-talent plays. All of us want to see how our children perform."

"Why, yes, of course," said the bewildered Sinton.

Then he hurried to Margaret. "Say," he said, "there is going to be a play at the high school to-night; and Elnora is in it. Why hasn't she told us?"

"I don't know," said Margaret, "but I'm going."

"So am I," said Billy.

"Me, too!" said Wesley, "unless you think for some reason she don't want us. Looks like she would have told us if she had. I'm going to ask her mother."

"Yes, that's what's she's been staying in town for," said Mrs. Comstock. "It's some sort of a swindle to raise money for her class to buy some silly thing to stick up in the school house hall to remember them by. I don't know whether it's now or next week, but there's something of the kind to be done."

"Well, it's to-night," said Wesley, "and we are going. It's my treat, and we've got to hurry or we won't get in. There's reserved seats, and we have none, so it's the gallery for us, but I don't care so I get to take one good peep at Elnora."

"S'pose she plays?" whispered Margaret in his ear.

"Aw, tush! She couldn't!" said Wesley.

"Well, she's been doing it three years in the orchestra, and working like a slave at it."

"Oh, well that's different. She's in the play to-night. Brownlee told me so. Come on, quick! We'll drive and hitch closest place we can find to the building."

Margaret went in the excitement of the moment, but she was troubled.

When they reached the building Wesley tied the team

to a railing and Billy sprang out to help Margaret. Mrs. Comstock sat still.

"Come on, Kate," said Wesley, reaching his hand.

"I'm not going anywhere," said Mrs. Comstock, settling comfortably back against the cushions.

All of them begged and pleaded, but it was no use. Not an inch would Mrs. Comstock budge. The night was warm and the carriage comfortable, the horses were securely hitched. She did not care to see what idiotic thing a pack of school children were doing, she would wait until the Sintons returned. Wesley told her it might be two hours, and she said she did not care if it was four, so they left her.

"Did you ever see such ——?"

"Cookies!" cried Billy.

"Such blamed stubbornness in all your life?" demanded Sinton. "Won't come to see as fine a girl as Elnora in a stage performance. Why, I wouldn't miss if for fifty dollars!"

"I think it's a blessing she didn't," said Margaret placidly. "I begged unusually hard so she wouldn't. I'm scared of my life for fear Elnora will play."

They found seats near the door where they could see fairly well. Billy stood at the back of the hall and had a good view. By and by, a great volume of sound welled from the orchestra, but Elnora was not playing.

"Told you so!" said Sinton. "Got a notion to go out and see if Kate won't come now. She can take my seat, and I'll stand with Billy."

"You sit still!" said Margaret emphatically. "This is not over yet."

So Wesley remained in his seat. The play opened and went on very much like all high school plays have gone for the past fifty years. But Elnora did not appear in any of the scenes.

Out in the warm summer night a sour, grim woman nursed an aching heart and tried to justify herself. The effort irritated her intensely. She felt that she could not afford the things that were being done. The old fear of losing the land that she and Robert Comstock had purchased and began to clear, was strong upon her. She was thinking of him, how she needed him, when the orchestra music poured from the open windows near her. She leaned back, closed her eyes and tried to make her mind a blank, to shut out even the music, when the leading violin began a solo. Mrs. Comstock bore it as long as she could, and then slipped from the carriage and fled down the street.

She did not know how far she went or how long she stayed, but everything was still, save an occasional raised voice when she wandered back. She stood looking at the building. Slowly she entered the wide gates and followed up the walk. Elnora had been coming here for almost four years. When Mrs. Comstock reached the door she looked inside. The wide hall was lighted with electricity, and the statuary and the decorations of the walls did not seem like pieces of foolishness. The marble looked pure, white, and the big pictures most interesting. She walked the length of the hall and slowly read the title of the statues and the names of the pupils who had donated them. She speculated on where the piece Elnora's class would buy could be placed to advantage.

Then she wondered if they were having a large enough audience to buy marble. She liked it better than the bronze, but it looked as if it cost more. How white the broad stairway was! Elnora had been climbing those stairs for years and never told her they were marble. Of course, she thought they were wood. Probably the upper hall was even grander than this. She went over to the fountain, took a drink, climbed to the first landing and looked about her, and then without thought to the second. There she came opposite the wide open doors and the entrance to the auditorium packed with people and a crowd standing outside. When they noticed a tall woman with white face and hair and black dress, one by one they stepped a little aside, so that Mrs. Comstock could see the stage. It was covered with curtains, and no one was doing anything. Just as she turned to go a sound so faint that everyone leaned forward and listened, drifted down the auditorium. It was difficult to tell just what it was, after one instant half the audience looked toward the windows, for it seemed only a breath of wind rustling freshly opened leaves, just a hint of stirring air.

Then the curtains were swept aside swiftly. The stage had been transformed into a lovely little corner

of creation, where trees and flowers grew and moss carpeted the earth. A soft wind blew and it was the gray of dawn. Suddenly a robin began to sing, then a song sparrow joined him, and then several orioles began talking at once. The light grew stronger, the dew drops trembled, flower perfume began to creep out to the audience; the air moved the branches gently and a rooster crowed. Then all the scene was shaken with a babel of bird notes in which you could hear a cardinal whistling, and a blue finch piping. Back somewhere among the high branches a dove cooed and then a horse neighed shrilly. That set a blackbird crying, "T' check," and a whole flock answered it. The crows began to caw and a lamb bleated. Then the grosbeaks, chats, and vireos had something to say, the sun rose higher, the light grew stronger and the breeze rustled the tree-tops loudly; a cow bawled and the whole barnyard answered. The guineas were clucking, the turkey gobbler strutting, the hens calling, the chickens cheeping, the light streamed down straight overhead and the bees began to hum. The air stirred strongly, and off in an unseen field a reaper clacked and rattled through ripening wheat while the driver whistled. An uneasy mare whickered to her colt, the colt answered, and the light began to decline. Miles away a rooster crowed for twilight, and dusk was coming down. Then a catbird and a brown thrush sang against a grosbeak and a hermit thrush. The air was tremulous with heavenly notes, the lights went out in the hall, dusk swept across the stage, a cricket sang and a katydid answered, and a wood pewee wrung the heart with its lonesome cry. Then a night hawk screamed, a whip-poor-will complained, a belated killdeer swept the sky, and the night wind sang a louder song. A little screech owl tuned up in the distance, a barn owl replied, and a great horned owl drowned both their voices. The moon shone and the scene was warm with mellow light. The bird voices died and soft exquisite melody began to swell and roll. In the centre of the stage, piece by piece the grasses, mosses and leaves dropped from an embankment, the foliage softly blew away, while plainer and plainer came the outlines of a lovely girl figure draped in soft clinging green. In her shower of bright hair a few green leaves and white blossoms clung, and they fell over her robe down to her feet. Her white throat and arms were bare, she leaned forward a little and swayed with the melody, her eyes fast on the clouds above her, her lips parted, a pink tinge of exercise in her cheeks as she drew her bow. She played as only a peculiar chain of circumstances puts it in the power of a very few to play. All nature had grown still, the violin sobbed, sang, danced and quavered on alone, no voice in particular, just the soul of the melody of all nature combined in one great outpouring.

At the doorway, a white-faced woman bore it as long as she could and then fell senseless. The men nearest carried her down the hall to the fountain, revived her, and then placed her in the carriage to which she directed them.

The girl played on and never knew. When she finished, the uproar of applause sounded a block down the street, but the half-senseless woman scarcely realized what it meant. Then the girl came to the front of the stage, bowed, and lifting the violin she played her conception of an invitation to dance. Every living soul within sound of her notes strained their nerves to sit still and let only their hearts dance with her. When that began the woman ran toward the country. She never stopped until the carriage overtook her half-way to her cabin. She only said she had grown tired of sitting, and walked on ahead. That night she asked Billy to remain with her and sleep on Elnora's bed. Then she pitched headlong upon her own, and suffered agony of soul such as she never before had known. The swamp had sent back the soul of her loved dead and put it into the body of the daughter she resented, and it was almost more than she could bear and live.

CHAPTER 11

Wherein Elnora Graduates, and Freckles and the Angel Send Gifts

THAT was Friday night. Elnora came home Saturday morning and went to work. Mrs. Comstock asked no questions, and the girl only told her that the audience had been large enough to more than pay for the piece of statuary the class had selected for the hall. Then she inquired about her dresses and was told they would be ready for her. She had been invited to go to the Bird Woman's to prepare for both the sermon and Commencement exercises. Since there was so much practising to do, it had been arranged that she should remain there from the night of the sermon until after she was graduated. If Mrs. Comstock decided to attend she was to drive in with the Sintons. When Elnora begged her to come she said she thought not. She cared nothing about such silliness.

It was almost time for Wesley to come to take Elnora to the city when, fresh from her bath, with shining, crisply washed hair, and dressed to her outer garment, she stood with expectant face before her mother and cried, "Now my dress, mother!"

Mrs. Comstock was pale as she replied, "It's on my bed. Help yourself."

Elnora opened the door and stepped into her mother's room with never a misgiving. Since the night Margaret and Wesley had brought her clothing, when she first started to school, her mother had selected all of her dresses, with Mrs. Sinton's help made most of them, and Elnora had paid the bills. The white dress of the previous spring was her first made at a dressmaker's. She had worn that as junior usher at Commencement. But her mother had selected the goods, had it made, and it had fitted perfectly and had been suitable in every way. So with her heart at rest on that point, Elnora hurried to the bed to find only her last summer's white dress, freshly washed and ironed. For an instant she stared at it, then she picked up the garment, looked at the bed beneath it, and then her gaze slowly swept the room.

It was a very unfamiliar room. Perhaps this was the third time she had been in it since she was a very small child. Her eyes ranged over the beautiful walnut dresser, the tall bureau, the big chest, inside which she never had seen, and the row of masculine attire hanging above it. Somewhere a dainty lawn or mull dress simply must be hanging. But it was not. Elnora dropped on the chest because she felt too weak to stand. In less than two hours she must be in the church, at Onabasha. She could not wear a last year's washed dress. She had nothing else. She leaned against the wall and her father's overcoat brushed her face. She caught the folds and clung to it with all her might.

"Oh, father! Father!" she moaned. "I need you! I don't believe you would have done this!"

She clung to the coat in dry-eyed agony and tried to think what she could do. At last she opened the door.

"I can't find my dress," she said.

"Well, as it's the only one there I shouldn't think it would be much trouble."

"You mean for me to wear an old washed dress to-night?"

"It's a good dress. There isn't a hole in it! There's no reason on earth why you shouldn't wear it."

"Except that I will not," said Elnora. "Didn't you get me any dress for Commencement, either?"

"If you soil that to-night, I've plenty of time to wash it again."

Sinton's voice called from the gate.

"In a minute," answered Elnora.

She ran upstairs and in an incredibly short time came down wearing one of her gingham school dresses. With a cold, hard face she passed her mother and went into the night. A half hour later Margaret and Billy stopped for Mrs. Comstock with the carriage. She had determined fully that she would not go before they called. With the sound of their voices a sort of horror of being left seized her, so she put on her hat, locked the door and went out to them.

"How did Elnora look?" inquired Margaret anxiously.

"Like she always does," answered Mrs. Comstock curtly.

"I do hope her dresses are as pretty as the rest," said Margaret. "None of them will have prettier faces or nicer ways."

"They just don't have one-half as pretty faces or one-tenth as nice ways," boasted Billy, who was wrestling with fractions.

"Oh, you two make me tired!" scoffed Mrs. Comstock.

Wesley was waiting before the big church to take care of the team. As they stood watching the people enter the building, Mrs. Comstock felt herself growing ill, without knowing why. When they went inside among the lights, saw the flower-decked stage, and the masses of finely dressed people, she grew no better. She could hear Margaret and Billy softly commenting on what was being done.

"That first chair in the very front row is Elnora's," exulted Billy, "'cos she's got the highest grades, and so she gets to lead the procession to the platform."

"The first chair!" "Lead the procession!" Mrs. Comstock was dumfounded. The notes of the pipe organ began to fill the building in a slow rolling march. Would Elnora lead the procession in a gingham dress? Or would she be absent and her chair vacant on this great occasion? For now, Mrs. Comstock could see that it was a great occasion. Everyone would remember how Elnora had played a few nights before, and they would miss her and pity her. Pity? Because she had no one to care for her. Because she was worse off than if she had no mother. For the first time in her life, Mrs. Comstock began to study herself as she would appear to others. Every time a junior girl came fluttering down the aisle, leading someone to a seat, and Mrs. Comstock saw a beautiful white dress pass, a wave of positive illness swept over her. What had she done? What would become of Elnora?

As Elnora rode to the city, she answered Wesley's questions in monosyllables so that he thought she was nervous or rehearsing her speech and did not care to talk. Several times the girl tried to tell him and realized that if she said the first word it would bring a torrent of tears. The Bird Woman opened the screen and stared unbelievingly.

"Why, I thought you would be ready; you are so late!" she said. "If you have waited to dress here, we will have to hurry."

"I have nothing to put on," said Elnora.

In bewilderment the Bird Woman drew her inside.

"Did — did —" she faltered, "did you think you would wear that?"

"No. I thought I would telephone Ellen that there had been an accident and I could not come. I don't know yet how to explain. I'm too sick to think. Oh, do you suppose I can get something made by Tuesday, so that I can graduate?"

"Yes; and you'll get something on you to-night, so

that you can lead your class, as you have done for four
years. Go to my room and take off that gingham,
quickly. Anna, drop everything, and come help me."

The Bird Woman ran to the telephone and called Ellen
Brownlee.

"Elnora has had an accident. She will be a little
late," she said. "You have got to make them wait.
Have them play an extra musical number before the
march."

Then she turned to the maid. "Tell Benson to have
the carriage at the gate, just as soon as he can get it
there. Then come to my room. Bring the thread box
from the sewing room, that roll of wide white ribbon on
the cutting table, and gather all the white pins from every
dresser in the house. But first come with me a minute."

"I want that trunk with the Swamp Angel's stuff in
it, from the cedar closet," she panted as they reached
the top of the stairs.

They hurried down the hall together and dragged the
big trunk to the Bird Woman's room. She opened it
and began tossing out white stuff.

"How lucky that she left these things!" she cried.
"Here are white shoes, gloves, stockings, fans, everything!"

"I am all ready but a dress," said Elnora.

The Bird Woman began opening closets and pulling
out drawers and boxes.

"I think I can make it this way," she said.

She snatched up a creamy lace yoke with long sleeves

that recently had been made for her and held it out.
Elnora slipped into it, and the Bird Woman began smooth-
ing out wrinkles and sewing in pins. It fitted very well
with a little lapping in the back. Next, from among
the Angel's clothing she caught up a white silk waist
with low neck and elbow sleeves, and Elnora put it on.
It was large enough, but distressingly short in the waist,
for the Angel had worn it at a party when she was sixteen. The Bird Woman loosened the sleeves and pushed
them to a puff on the shoulders, catching them in places
with pins. She began on the wide draping of the yoke,
fastening it front, back and at each shoulder. She
pulled down the waist and pinned it. Next came a
soft white silk dress skirt of her own. By pinning her
waist band quite four inches above Elnora's, the Bird
Woman could secure a perfect Empire sweep, with the
clinging silk. Then she began with the wide white
ribbon that was to trim a new frock for herself, bound
it three times around the high waist effect she had managed, tied the ends in a knot and let them fall to the
floor in a beautiful sash.

"I want four white roses, each with two or three
leaves," she cried.

Anna ran for them, while the Bird Woman added pins.

"Elnora," she said, "forgive me, but tell me truly.
Is your mother so extremely poor as to make this necessary?"

"No," answered Elnora. "Next year I am heir to
my share of over three hundred acres of land covered

with almost as valuable timber as was in the Limberlost. We adjoin it. There could be dozens of oil wells drilled that would yield to us the thousands our neighbours are draining from under us, and the bare land is worth over one hundred dollars an acre for farming. She is not poor, she is — I don't know what she is. A great trouble soured and warped her. It made her peculiar. She does not in the least understand, but it is because she don't care to, instead of ignorance. She does not ——"

Elnora stopped.

"She is — is different," finished the girl.

Anna came with the roses. The Bird Woman set one on the front of the draped yoke, one on each shoulder and the last among the bright masses of brown hair. Then she turned the girl facing the tall mirror.

"Oh!" panted Elnora. "Is that me? You are a genius! Why, I will look as well as any of them."

"Well, thank goodness for that!" cried the Bird Woman. "If it wouldn't do, I should have been ill. You are lovely; altogether lovely! Ordinarily I shouldn't say that; but when I think of how you are carpentered, I'm adoring the result."

The organ began rolling out the march as they came in sight. Elnora took her place at the head of the procession, while every one wondered. Secretly they had hoped that she would be dressed well enough, that she would not appear poor and neglected. What this radiant young creature, gowned in the most recent style, her smooth skin flushed with excitement, and a rose-set coronet of red gold on her head, had to do with the girl they knew was difficult to decide. The signal was given and Elnora began the slow march across the vestry and down the aisle. The music welled softly, and Margaret began to sob without knowing why.

Mrs. Comstock gripped her hands together and shut her eyes. It seemed an eternity to the suffering woman before Margaret caught her arm and whispered, "Oh, Kate! For any sake look at her! Here! The aisle across!"

Mrs. Comstock opened her eyes and directing them where she was told, gazed intently, and slid down in her seat on the verge of collapse. She was saved by Margaret's tense grip and her command, "Here! Idiot! Stop that!"

In the blaze of light Elnora climbed the steps to the palm-embowered platform, crossed it and took her place. Sixty young men and women, each of them dressed the best possible, followed her. There were manly, fine looking men in that class which Elnora led. There were girls of beauty and grace, but not one of them was handsomer or clothed in better taste than she.

Billy thought the time never would come when Elnora would see him, but at last she caught his eye, then Margaret and Wesley got faint signs of recognition in turn, but there was no softening of the girl's face and no hint of a smile when she saw her mother.

Heartsick, Katharine Comstock gripped her seat and tried to prove to herself that she was justified in what she had done, but she could not. She tried to blame

Elnora for not saying that she was to lead a procession and sit on a platform in the sight of hundreds of people; but that was impossible for she realized that she would have scoffed and not understood if she had been told. Her heart pained until she suffered acute agony with every breath.

When at last the exercises were over she climbed into the carriage and rode home without a word. She did not hear what Margaret and Billy were saying. She scarcely heard Sinton, who drove behind, when he told her that Elnora would not be home until Wednesday. Early the next morning Mrs. Comstock was on her way to Onabasha. She was waiting when the Brownlee store opened. She examined ready-made white dresses, but they had only one of the right size, and it was marked forty dollars. Mrs. Comstock did not hesitate over the price, but whether the dress would be suitable. She would have to ask Elnora. She inquired her way to the home of the Bird Woman and knocked.

"Is Elnora Comstock here?" she asked the maid.

"Yes, but she is still in bed. I was told to let her sleep as long as she would."

"Maybe, I could sit here and wait," said Mrs. Comstock. "I want to see about getting her a dress for to-morrow. I am her mother."

"Then you don't need wait or worry," said the girl cheerfully. "There are two women up in the sewing-room at work on a dress for her right now. It will be done in time, and it will be a beauty."

Mrs. Comstock turned and trudged back to the Limberlost. The bitterness in her soul became a physical actuality, and water would not wash the taste of wormwood from her lips. She was too late! She was not needed. Another woman was mothering her girl. Another woman would prepare a beautiful dress such as Elnora had worn last night. The girl's love and gratitude would go to her. Mrs. Comstock tried the old process of blaming someone else, but she felt no better. She nursed her grief as closely as ever in the long days of the girl's absence. She brooded over Elnora's possession of the forbidden violin and her ability to play it until the performance could not have been told from her father's. She tried every refuge her mind could conjure, to quiet her heart and remove the fear that the girl never would come home again, but it persisted. Mrs. Comstock could neither eat nor sleep. She wandered about the cabin and garden. She kept far from the pool where Robert Comstock had sunk from sight for she felt that it would entomb her also if Elnora did not come home Wednesday morning. The mother told herself that she would wait, but the waiting was bitter as anything she ever had known.

When Elnora awoke Monday another dress was in the hands of a seamstress and was soon fitted. It had belonged to the Angel, and was a soft white thing that with a little alteration would serve admirably for Commencement and the ball. All that day Elnora worked, helping prepare the auditorium for the exercises,

rehearsing the march and the speech she was to make in behalf of the class. The next day was even more busy. But her mind was at rest, for the dress was a soft delicate lace, easy to change, and the marks of alteration impossible to detect.

The Bird Woman had telephoned to Grand Rapids, explained the situation and asked the Angel if she might use it. The reply had been to give the girl all the things the chest contained. When the Bird Woman told Elnora, tears filled her eyes.

"I will write at once and thank her," she said. "With all her beautiful things she does not need them, and I do. They will serve for me often, and be much finer than anything I could afford. It is lovely of her to give me the dress and of you to have it altered for me, as I never could."

The Bird Woman laughed. "I feel quite religious to-day," she said. "You know the first and greatest rock of my salvation is 'Do unto others.' I'm only doing to you what there was no one to do to me when I was a girl very like you. Anna tells me your mother was here early this morning and that she came to see about getting you a dress."

"She is too late!" said Elnora coldly. "She had over a month to prepare my dresses, and I was to pay for them, so there is no excuse."

"Nevertheless, she is your mother," said the Bird Woman, softly. "I think almost any kind of a mother must be better than none at all, and you say she has had great trouble."

"She loved my father and he died," said Elnora. "The same thing, in quite as tragic a manner, has happened to thousands of other women, and they have gone on with calm faces and found happiness in life by loving others. There was something else I am afraid I never shall forget; this I know I shall not, but talking does not help. I must deliver my presents and photographs to the crowd. I have a picture and I made a present for you, too, if you would care for them."

"I shall love anything you give me," said the Bird Woman. "I know you well enough to know that whatever you do will be beautiful."

Elnora felt good over that, and as she tried on her dress for the last fitting she was really happy. She looked lovely in the dainty gown, it would serve finely for the ball and many other like occasions, and it was her very own.

The Bird Woman's driver took Elnora in the carriage and she called on all the girls with whom she was especially intimate, and left her picture and the package containing her gift to them. By the time she returned, parcels for her were arriving. Friends seemed to spring from everywhere. Almost everyone she knew had some gift for her, while because they so loved her the members of her crowd had made her beautiful presents. There were books, vases, silver pieces, handkerchiefs, fans, boxes of flowers and candy. One big package settled the trouble at Sintons', for it contained a dainty dress from Margaret, a five-dollar gold piece, conspicuously labeled, "I earned this myself," from Billy,

with which to buy music; and a gorgeous cut glass perfume bottle, it would have cost five dollars to fill with even a moderate-priced scent, from Wesley.

In an expressed crate was a fine curly-maple dressing table, sent by Freckles. The drawers were filled with wonderful toilet articles from the Angel. The Bird Woman added an embroidered linen cover and a small silver vase for a few flowers and no girl of the class had finer gifts. Elnora laid her head on the table sobbing happily, and the Bird Woman was almost crying herself. Professor Henley sent an elegantly printed and illustrated butterfly book, the grade rooms in which Elnora had taught gave her a set of volumes covering every phase of life afield, in the woods, and water. Elnora had no time to read so she just carried one of these books around with her hugging it as she went. After she had gone to dress a queer looking package was brought by a small boy who hopped on one foot as he handed it in and said, "Tell Elnora that is from her ma."

"Who are you?" asked the Bird Woman, as she took the bundle.

"I'm Billy!" announced the boy. "I gave her the five dollars. I earned it myself dropping corn, sticking onions, and pulling weeds. My, but you got to drop, and stick, and pull a lot before it's five dollars' worth."

"Would you like to come in and see Elnora's gifts?"

"Yes, ma'm!" said Billy trying to stand quietly.

He followed into the room and gazed around.

"Gee-mentley!" he gasped. "Does Elnora get all this?"
"Yes."

"I bet you a thousand dollars I be first in my class when I graduate. Say, have the others got a lot more than Elnora?"

"I think not."

"Well, Uncle Wesley said to find out if I could, and if she didn't have as much as the rest, he'd buy till she did, if it took a hundred dollars. Say, you ought to know him! He's just scrumptious! There ain't anybody anywhere finer 'an he is. My, he's grand!"

"I'm quite sure of it!" said the Bird Woman. "I've often heard Elnora say so."

Billy strutted around the table admiringly.

"I bet you nobody can beat this!" he boasted. Then he stopped, thinking deeply. "I don't know, though," he began reflectively. "Some of them are awful rich; they got big families to give them things and wagon loads of friends, and I haven't seen what they got. Now, maybe Elnora is getting left, after all!"

He lifted an anxious little freckled face to the Bird Woman. She cleared her throat.

"Don't worry, Billy," she said. "I will watch and if I find Elnora is 'getting left' I'll buy her some more things myself. But I'm sure she is not. She has more beautiful gifts now than she will know what to do with, and others will come. Tell your Uncle Wesley his girl is bountifully remembered, very happy, and she sends her dearest love to all of you. Now you must go, so I can

help her dress. You will be there to-night to see her, of course?"

"Yes, sir-ee! She got me a seat, third row from the front, middle section, so I can see, and she's going to wink at me, after she gets her speech off her mind. She kissed me, too! She's a perfect lady, Elnora is. I'm going to marry her when I get big enough."

"Why isn't that splendid!" laughed the Bird Woman as she hurried upstairs.

"Dear!" she called. "Here is another gift for you."

Elnora was half disrobed as she took the package and, sitting on a couch, opened it. The Bird Woman bent over her and tested the fabric with her fingers.

"Why, bless my soul!" she cried. "Hand woven, hand embroidered linen, fine as silk. It's priceless! I haven't seen such things in years. My mother had garments like those when I was a child, but my sisters had them cut up for collars, belts, and fancy waists while I was small. Look at the exquisite work!"

"Where could it have come from?" cried Elnora.

She shook out a petticoat, with a hand-wrought ruffle a foot deep, then an old-fashioned chemise the neck and sleeve work of which was elaborate and perfectly wrought. On the breast was pinned a note that she hastily opened.

"I was married in these," it read, "and I had intended to be buried in them, but perhaps it would be more sensible for you to graduate and get married in them yourself, if you would like. Your mother."

"From my mother!" Wide-eyed, Elnora looked at

the Bird Woman. "I never in my life saw the like. Mother does things I think I never can forgive, and when I feel hardest, she turns around and does something that makes me think she just must love me a little bit, after all. Any of the girls would give almost anything to graduate in hand-embroidered linen like that. Money can't buy such things. And they came just when I was thinking she didn't care what became of me. Do you suppose she can be insane?"

"Yes," said the Bird Woman. "Stark, staring mad! Wildly insane, if she does not love you and care what becomes of you."

Elnora arose and held the petticoat to her. "Will you look at it?" she cried. "Only imagine her not getting my dress ready, and then turning around and sending me such a petticoat as this! Ellen would pay a hundred dollars for it and never blink. I suppose mother has had it all my life, and I never saw it before."

"Go, take your bath and put on those things," said the Bird Woman. "Forget everything and be happy. She is not insane! She is embittered. She did not understand how things would be. When she saw, she came at once to get you a dress. This is her way of saying she is sorry she did not get the other. You notice she has not spent any money, so perhaps she is quite honest in saying she has none."

"Oh, she is honest!" said Elnora. "She wouldn't care enough to tell an untruth. She'd say just how things were, no matter what happened."

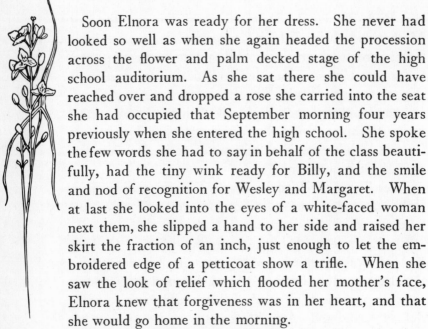

Soon Elnora was ready for her dress. She never had looked so well as when she again headed the procession across the flower and palm decked stage of the high school auditorium. As she sat there she could have reached over and dropped a rose she carried into the seat she had occupied that September morning four years previously when she entered the high school. She spoke the few words she had to say in behalf of the class beautifully, had the tiny wink ready for Billy, and the smile and nod of recognition for Wesley and Margaret. When at last she looked into the eyes of a white-faced woman next them, she slipped a hand to her side and raised her skirt the fraction of an inch, just enough to let the embroidered edge of a petticoat show a trifle. When she saw the look of relief which flooded her mother's face, Elnora knew that forgiveness was in her heart, and that she would go home in the morning.

It was late afternoon before she arrived, and a dray followed with a load of packages. Mrs. Comstock was overwhelmed. She sat half dazed and made Elnora show her each costly and beautiful or simple and useful gift, tell her carefully what it was and from where it came. She studied the faces of Elnora's particular friends intently. The gifts from them had to be selected and set in a group. Several times she started to speak and then stopped. At last, between her dry lips, came a harsh whisper.

"Elnora, what did you give back for these things?"

"I 'll show you," said Elnora cheerfully. "I got the

same thing for the Bird Woman, Aunt Margaret and you, if you care for it. But I have to run upstairs to get it."

When she returned she handed her mother an oblong frame, hand carved, enclosing Elnora's picture, taken by a schoolmate's camera. She wore her storm-coat and carried a dripping umbrella. From under it looked her bright face; her books and lunchbox were on her arm, and across the bottom of the frame was carved, "Your Country Classmate."

Then she offered another frame.

"I am strong on frames," she said. "They seemed to be the best I could do without money. I located the maple and the black walnut myself, in a little corner that had been overlooked between the river and the ditch. They didn't seem to belong to anyone so I just took them. Uncle Wesley said it was all right, and he cut and hauled them for me. I gave the mill half of each tree for sawing and curing the remainder. Then I gave the wood-carver half of that for making my frames. A photographer gave me a lot of spoiled plates, and I boiled off the emulsion, and took the specimens I framed from my stuff. The man said the white frames were worth three and a half, and the black ones five. I exchanged those little framed pictures for the photographs of the others. For presents, I gave each one of my crowd one like this, only a different moth. The Bird Woman gave me the birch bark. She got it up north last summer."

Elnora handed her mother a handsome black-walnut

frame a foot and a half wide by two long. It finished a small shallow glass-covered box of birch bark, to the botttom of which clung a big night moth with delicate pale green wings and long exquisite trailers. A more beautiful thing would have been difficult to imagine.

"So you see I did not have to be ashamed of my gifts," said Elnora. "I made them myself and raised and mounted the moths."

"Moth, you call it," said Mrs. Comstock. "I've seen a few of the things before."

"They are thick around us every June night, or at least they used to be," said Elnora. "I've sold hundreds of them, with butterflies, dragon flies, and other specimens. Now, I must put away these and get to work, for it is almost June and there are a few more I want dreadfully. When I get them I will be paid some money for which I have worked a long time."

She was afraid to say college just then. She thought it would be better to wait a few days and see if an opportunity would not come when it would work in more naturally. Besides, unless she could secure the yellow Emperor she needed to complete her collection, she could not talk college until she was of age, for she would have no money.

CHAPTER 12

*Wherein Margaret Sinton Reveals a Secret,
and Mrs. Comstock Possesses the Limberlost*

"ELNORA, bring me the towel, quick!" cried Mrs. Comstock.

"In a minute, mother," mumbled Elnora.

She was standing before the kitchen mirror, tying the back part of her hair, while the front turned over her face.

"Hurry! There's a varmint of some kind!"

Elnora ran into the sitting room and thrust the heavy kitchen towel into her mother's hand. Mrs. Comstock swung open the screen door and struck at some object. Elnora tossed the hair from her face so that she could see past her mother. The girl screamed wildly.

"Don't! Mother, don't!"

Mrs. Comstock struck again. Elnora caught her arm.

"It's the one I want! It's worth a lot of money! Don't! Oh, you shall not!"

"Shan't, missy?" blazed Mrs. Comstock. "When did you get to bossing me?"

The hand that held the screen swept a half-circle and stopped at Elnora's cheek. She staggered with the blow, and across her face, paled with excitement, a red mark

rose rapidly. The screen slammed shut, throwing the creature on the floor before them. Instantly Mrs. Comstock's foot crushed it. Elnora stepped back. Excepting the red mark, her face was very white.

"That was the last moth I needed," she said, "to complete a collection worth three hundred dollars. You've ruined it before my eyes!"

"Moth!" cried Mrs. Comstock. "You say that because you are mad. Moths have big wings. I know a moth!"

"I've kept things from you," said Elnora, "because I didn't dare confide in you. You had no sympathy with me. But you know I never told you untruths in all my life."

"It's no moth!" reiterated Mrs. Comstock.

"It is!" cried Elnora. "It's just out of a case in the ground. Its wings take two or three hours to expand and harden."

"If I had known it was a moth —" Mrs. Comstock wavered.

"You did know! I told you! I begged you to stop! It meant just three hundred dollars to me."

"Bah! Three hundred fiddlesticks!" sneered Mrs. Comstock.

"They are what have paid for books, tuition, and clothes for the last four years. They are what I could have started on to college. You've crushed the last one I needed before my face. You never have made any pretence of loving me. At last I'll be equally frank with you. I hate you! You are a selfish, wicked woman! I hate you!"

Elnora turned, went through the kitchen and out the back door. She followed the garden path to the gate and walked toward the swamp a short distance when reaction overtook her. She dropped on the ground and leaned against a big log. When a little child, desperate as now, she had tried to die by holding her breath. She had thought in that way to make her mother sorry, but she had learned that life was a thing thrust upon her and death would not come at her wish.

She was so crushed over the loss of that moth, which she had childishly named the yellow Emperor, that she scarcely remembered the blow. She had thought no luck in all the world would be so rare as to complete her collection, and she just had been forced to see a splendid Imperialis crushed to a mass before her. There was a possibility that she could find another, but now she was facing the certainty that the one she might have had and with which she undoubtedly could have attracted others, was ruined — by her mother. How long she sat there Elnora did not know or care. She simply suffered in dumb, abject misery, an occasional dry sob shaking her. Aunt Margaret was right. Elnora felt that morning that her mother never would be any different. The girl had reached the place where she realized that she could bear it no longer.

As Elnora left the room, Mrs. Comtock took one step after her.

"You little huzzy!" she gasped.

But Elnora was gone. Her mother stood staring.

"She never did lie to me," she muttered. "I guess it was a moth. And the only one she needed to get three hundred dollars, she said. I wish I hadn't been so fast! I never saw anything like it. I thought it was some deadly, stinging, biting thing. A body does have to be mighty careful here. But likely I've spilt the milk now. Pshaw! She can find another! There's no use to be foolish. Maybe moths are like snakes, where there's one, there's two."

Mrs. Comstock took the broom and swept the moth out of the door. Then she got down on her knees and carefully examined the steps, logs and the earth of the flower beds at each side. She found the place where the creature had emerged from the ground, and the hard, dark brown case which had enclosed it, still wet inside. Then she knew Elnora had been right. It was a moth. Its wings had been damp and not expanded. Mrs. Comstock never before had seen one in that state, and she did not know how they originated. She had thought all of them came from cases spun on trees or against walls or boards. She only had seen enough to know that there were such things, just as a flash of white told her that an ermine was on her premises, or a sharp "buzzzzz" warned her of a rattler.

So it was from creatures like that Elnora had gotten

232

her school money. In one sickening sweep there rushed
into the heart of the woman a full realization of the
width of the gulf which separated her from her child.
Lately many things had pointed toward it, none more
plainly than when Elnora, like a reincarnation of her
father, had stood fearlessly before a large city audience
and played with even greater skill than he, on what Mrs.
Comstock felt very certain, was his violin. But that
little crawling creature of earth, crushed by her before
its splendid yellow and lavender wings could spread
and carry it into the mystery of night, had brought a
realizing sense.

"We are nearer strangers with each other than we are
with any of the neighbours," she muttered.

So one of the Almighty's most delicate and beautiful
creations was sacrificed without fulfilling the law, yet
none of its species ever served so glorious a cause, for
at last Mrs. Comstock's inner vision had cleared. She
went through the cabin mechanically. Every few minutes
she glanced toward the back walk to see if Elnora was
coming. She knew arrangements had been made with
Margaret to go to the city some time that day, so she
grew more nervous and uneasy every moment. She
was haunted by the fear that the blow might discolour
Elnora's cheek, and that she would tell Margaret. She
went down the back walk, looking intently in all direc-
tions, left the garden and took the swamp path. Her
step was noiseless on the soft, black earth, and soon
she came near enough to see Elnora. Mrs. Comstock

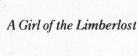

stood looking at the girl in troubled uncertainty. Not knowing what to say, at last she turned and went back to the cabin.

Noon came and she prepared dinner, calling, as she always did, when Elnora was in the garden, but she got no response, and the girl did not come. A little after one o'clock Margaret stopped at the gate.

"Elnora has changed her mind. She is not going," called Mrs. Comstock.

She felt that she hated Margaret as she hitched her horse and came up the walk instead of driving on.

"You must be mistaken," said Margaret. "I was going on purpose for her. She asked me to take her. I had no errand. Where is she?"

"I will call her," said Mrs. Comstock.

She followed the path again, and this time found Elnora sitting on the log. Her face was swollen and discoloured, and her eyes red with crying. She paid no attention to her mother.

"Mag Sinton is here," said Mrs. Comstock harshly. "I told her you had changed your mind, but she said you asked her to go with you, and she had nothing to go for herself."

Elnora arose, recklessly took a short cut through the deep swamp grasses and so reached the path ahead of her mother. Mrs. Comstock followed as far as the garden, but she could not enter the cabin. She busied herself among the vegetables, barely looking up when the back door screen slammed noisily. Margaret Sinton

approached colourless, and with such flaming eyes that
Mrs. Comstock shrank back.

"What's the matter with Elnora's face?" demanded
Margaret.

Mrs. Comstock made no reply.

"You struck her, did you?"

"I thought you wasn't blind!"

"I have been, for twenty long years now, Kate Comstock," said Margaret Sinton, "but my eyes are open
at last.   What I see is that I've done you no good
and Elnora a big wrong.   I had an idea that it would
kill you to know, but I guess you are tough enough to
stand anything.   Kill or cure, you get it now!"

"What are you frothing about?" coolly asked Mrs.
Comstock.

"You!" cried Margaret.   "You! The woman who
don't pretend to love her only child.   Who lets her
grow to a woman, as you have let Elnora, and can't be
satisfied with every sort of neglect, but must add abuse
yet; and all for a fool idea about a man who wasn't
worth his salt!"

Mrs. Comstock picked up a hoe.

"Go right on!" she said.   "Empty yourself.   It's
the last thing you'll ever do!"

"Then I'll make a tidy job of it," said Margaret.
"You'll not touch me.   You'll stand there and hear
the truth at last, and because I dare face you and tell
it, you will know in your soul it is truth.   When Robert
Comstock shaved that quagmire out there so close he

went in, he wanted to keep you from seeing where he was coming from. He'd been to see Elvira Carney. They had plans to go to a dance that night ——"

"Close your lips!" said Mrs. Comstock in a voice of deadly quiet.

"You know I wouldn't dare open them if I was not telling you the truth. I can prove what I say. I was coming from Reeds. It was hot in the woods and I stopped at Carney's as I passed for a drink. Elvira's bedridden old mother heard me, and she was so crazy for some one to talk with, I stepped in a minute. I saw Robert come down the path. Elvira saw him, too, and she ran out of the house to head him off. It looked funny, and I just deliberately moved where I could see and hear. He brought her his violin, and told her to get ready and meet him in the woods with it that night, and they would go to a dance. She took it and hid it in the little loft to the well-house and promised she'd go."

"Are you done?" demanded Mrs. Comstock.

"No. I am going to tell you the whole story. You don't spare Elnora anything. I shan't spare you. I hadn't been here that day, but I can tell you just how he was dressed, which way he went and every word they said, though they thought I was busy with her mother and wouldn't notice them. Put down your hoe, Kate. I went to Elvira, told her what I knew and made her give me Comstock's violin for Elnora over three years ago. She's been playing it ever since. I won't see her slighted and abused another day on account of a man who would have broken your heart if he had lived. Six months more would have showed you what everybody else knew. He was one of those men who couldn't trust himself, and so no woman was safe with him. Now, will you drop grieving over him, and do Elnora justice?"

Mrs. Comstock gripped the hoe tighter and turning she went down the walk, and started across the woods to the home of Elvira Carney. With averted head she passed the pool, steadily pursuing her way. Elvira Carney, hanging towels across the back fence, saw her coming and went toward the gate to meet her. Twenty years she had dreaded that visit. Since Margaret Sinton had compelled her to produce the violin she had hidden so long, because she was afraid to destroy it, she had come more near expectation than dread. The wages of sin are the hardest debts on earth to pay, and they are always collected at inconvenient times and unexpected places. Mrs. Comstock's face and hair were so white, that her dark eyes seemed burned into their setting. Silently she stared at the woman before her a long time.

"I might have saved myself the trouble of coming," she said at last, "I see you are guilty as sin!"

"What has Mag Sinton been telling you?" panted the miserable woman, gripping the fence.

"The truth!" answered Mrs. Comstock succinctly. "Guilt is in every line of your face, in your eyes, all over

your wretched body. If I'd taken a good look at you any time in all these past years, no doubt I could have seen it just as plain as I can now. No woman or man can do what you've done, and not get a mark set on them for everyone to read."

"Mercy!" gasped weak little Elvira Carney. "Have mercy!"

"Mercy?" scoffed Mrs. Comstock. "Mercy! That's a nice word from you! How much mercy did you have on me? Where's the mercy that sent Comstock to the slime of the bottomless quagmire, and left me to see it, and then struggle on in agony all these years? How about the mercy of letting me allow my baby to be neglected all the days of her life? Mercy! Do you really dare use the word to me?"

"If you knew what I've suffered!"

"Suffered?" jeered Mrs. Comstock. "That's interesting. And pray, what have you suffered?"

"All the neighbours have suspected and been down on me. I ain't had a friend. I've always felt guilty of his death! I've seen him go down a thousand times, plain as ever you did. Many's the night I've stood on the other bank of that pool and listened to you, and I tried to throw myself in to keep from hearing you, but I didn't dare. I knew God would send me to burn forever, but I'd better done it; for now, He has set the burning on my body, and every hour it is slowly eating the life out of me. The doctor says it's a cancer ——"

Mrs. Comstock exhaled a long breath. Her grip on the hoe relaxed and her stature lifted to towering height.

"I didn't know, or care, when I came here, just what I did," she said. "But my way is beginning to clear. If the guilt of your soul has come to a head, in a cancer on your body, it looks as if the Almighty didn't need any of my help in meting out His punishments. I really couldn't fix up anything to come anywhere near that. If you are going to burn until your life goes out with that sort of fire, you don't owe me anything!"

"Oh, Katherine Comstock!" groaned Elvira Carney, clinging to the fence for support.

"Looks as if the Bible is right when it says, 'The wages of sin is death,' don't it?" asked Mrs. Comstock. "Instead of doing a woman's work in life, you chose the smile of invitation, and the dress of unearned cloth. Now you tell me you are marked to burn to death with the unquenchable fire. And him! It was shorter with him, but let me tell you he got his share! He left me with an untruth on his lips, for he told me he was going to take his violin to Onabasha for a new key, when he carried it to you. Every vow of love and constancy he ever made me was a lie, after he touched your lips, so when he tried the wrong side of the quagmire, to hide from me the direction in which he was coming, it reached out for him, and it got him. It didn't hurry, either! It just sucked him down, slow, and deliberate."

"Mercy!" groaned Elvira Carney. "Mercy!"

"I don't know the word," said Mrs. Comstock. "You

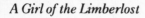

took all that out of me long ago. The last twenty years haven't been of the sort that taught mercy. I've never had any on myself and none on my child. Why, in the name of justice, should I have mercy on you, or on him? You were both older than me, both strong, sane people, you deliberately chose your course when you lured him, and he, when he was unfaithful to me. When a Loose Man and a Light Woman face the death the Almighty ordained for them, why should they shout at me for mercy? What did I have to do with it?"

Elvira Carney sobbed in panting gasps.

"You've got tears, have you?" marvelled Mrs. Comstock. "Mine all dried long ago. I've none left to shed over my wasted life, my disfigured face and hair, my years of struggle with a man's work, my wreck of land among the tilled fields of my neighbours, or the final knowledge that the man I so gladly would have died to save, wasn't worth the sacrifice of a rattlesnake. If anything yet could wring a tear from me, it would be the thought of the awful injustice I always have done my girl. If I'd lay hand on you for anything, it would be for that."

"Kill me if you want to," sobbed Elvira Carney. "I know that I deserve it, and I don't care."

"You are getting your killing fast enough to suit me," said Mrs. Comstock. "I wouldn't touch you, any more than I would him, if I could. Once is all any man or woman deceives me about the holiest things of life. I wouldn't touch you any more than I would the black plague. I am going back to my girl."

Mrs. Comstock turned and started swiftly through the woods, but she had gone only a few rods when she stopped, and leaning on the hoe, she stood thinking deeply. Then she turned back. Elvira still clung to the fence, sobbing bitterly.

"I don't know," said Mrs. Comstock, "but I left a wrong impression with you. I don't want you to think that I believe the Almighty set a cancer to burning you as a punishment for your sins. I don't! I think a lot more of the Almighty. With a whole sky-full of worlds on His hands to manage, I'm not believing that He has time to look down on ours, and pick you out of all the millions of we sinners, and set a special kind of torture to eating you. It wouldn't be a gentlemanly thing to do, and, first of all, the Almighty is bound to be a gentleman. I think likely a bruise and bad blood is what caused your trouble. Anyway, I 've got to tell you that the cleanest housekeeper I ever knew, and one of the noblest Christian women, was slowly eaten up by a cancer. She got hers from the careless work of a poor doctor. The Almighty is to forgive sin and heal disease, not to invent and spread it."

She had gone only a few steps when she again turned back.

"If you will gather a lot of red clover bloom, make a tea strong as lye of it, and drink quarts, I think likely it will help you, if you are not too far gone.

Anyway, it will cool your blood and make the burning easier to bear."

Then she swiftly walked home. Enter the lonely cabin she could not, neither could she sit outside and think. She attacked a bed of beets and hoed until the perspiration ran from her face and body, then she began on the potatoes. When she was too tired to take another stroke she bathed and put on dry clothing. In securing her dress she noticed her husband's carefully preserved clothing lining one wall. She gathered it in a great armload and carried it out to the swamp. Piece by piece she pitched into the green maw of the quagmire all those articles she had dusted carefully and fought moths from for years, and stood watching as it slowly sucked them down. She went back to her room and gathered every scrap that had in any way belonged to Robert Comstock, excepting his gun and revolver, and threw it into the swamp. Then for the first time she set her door wide open.

She was too weary now to do more, but an urging unrest drove her. She wanted Elnora. It seemed to her she never could wait until the girl came and delivered her judgment. At last in an effort to get nearer to her, Mrs. Comstock climbed the stairs and stood looking around Elnora's room. It was very unfamiliar. The pictures were strange to her. Commencement had filled it with packages and bundles. The walls were covered with cocoons; moths and dragon flies were pinned about. Under the bed she could see a half-dozen large white boxes. She did not know what they contained. She pulled out one and lifted the lid. The bottom was covered with a sheet of thin cork, and on long pins sticking in it were dozens of great, velvet-winged moths. Each one was labelled, always there were two of a kind, in many cases four, showing under and upper wings of both male and female. They were of every colour and shape.

Mrs. Comstock caught her breath sharply. When and where had Elnora gotten all of them? They were the most exquisite sight the woman ever had seen, so she opened all the boxes to feast on their beautiful contents. As she did so there came more fully a sense of the distance between her and her child. She could not understand how Elnora had gone to school, and performed all this work secretly. When it was finished, up to the very last moth, she, the mother who should have been the first confidant and helper, had been the one to bring disappointment. Small wonder Elnora had come to hate her.

Mrs. Comstock carefully closed and replaced the boxes, and again stood looking around the room. This time her eyes rested on some books she did not remember having seen before, so she picked up one and found that it was a moth book. She glanced over the first pages and was soon eagerly reading. When the text reached the classification of species, she laid it down, took up another and read its introductory chapters. Then she found some papers and studied them. By

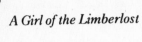

that time her brain was in a confused jumble of ideas about capturing moths with differing baits and bright lights.

She went downstairs thinking deeply. Being unable to sit still and having nothing else to do she glanced at the clock and began preparing supper. The work dragged. A chicken was snatched up and dressed hurriedly. A spice cake sprang into being in short order. Strawberries that had been intended for preserves went into shortcake. Delicious odours crept from the cabin. She put many extra touches on the table and then commenced watching the road. Everything was ready, but Elnora did not come. Then began the anxious process of trying to keep cooked food warm and not spoil it. The birds went to bed and dusk came. Mrs. Comstock gave up the fire and set the supper on the table. Then she went out and sat on the front door step watching night creep all around her. She started eagerly as the gate creaked, but it was only Wesley Sinton coming down the walk.

"Katharine, Margaret and Elnora passed where I was working this afternoon, and Margaret got out of the carriage and called me to the fence. She told me what she had done. I've come to say to you that I am sorry. She has heard me threaten to do it a good many times, but I never would have got it done. I'd give a good deal if I could undo it, but I can't, so I've come to tell you how sorry I am."

"You've got something to be sorry for," said Mrs.

Comstock, "but likely we ain't thinking of the same thing. It hurts me less to know the truth, than to live in ignorance. If Mag had the sense of a pewee, she'd told me long ago. That's what hurts me, to think that both of you knew Robert was not worth an hour of honest grief, yet you'd let me mourn him all these years and neglect Elnora while I did it. If I have anything to forgive you, that is what it is."

Sinton took off his hat and sat on a bench.

"Katharine," he said solemnly, "nobody ever knows how to take you."

"Would it be asking too much to take me for having a few grains of plain common sense?" she inquired. "You've known all this time that Comstock got what he deserved, when he undertook to sneak in an unused way across a swamp, with which he was none too familiar. Now I should have thought that you'd figure that knowing the same thing would be the best method to cure me of pining for him, and slighting my child."

"Heaven only knows we have thought of that, and talked of it often, but we were both too big cowards. We didn't dare tell you."

"So you have gone on year after year, watching me show indifference to Elnora, and yet a little horse-sense would have pointed out to you that she was my salvation. Why, look at it! Not married quite a year. All his vows of love and fidelity made to me before the Almighty forgotten in a few months, and a dance and a Light Woman so alluring he had to lie and sneak for

245

them. What kind of a prospect is that for a life? I know men and women. An honourable man is an honourable man, and a liar is a liar; both are born and not made. One cannot change to the other any more than that some old leopard can change its spots. After a man tells a woman the first untruth of that sort, the others come piling thick, fast, and mountain high. The desolation they bring in their wake overshadows anything I have suffered completely. If he had lived six months more I should have known him for what he was born to be. It was in the blood of him. His father and grandfather before him were fiddling, dancing people; but I was certain of him. I thought we could leave Ohio and come out here alone, and I could so love him and interest him in his work, that he would be a man. Of all the fool, fruitless jobs, making anything of a creature that begins by deceiving her, is the foolest a sane woman ever undertook. I am more than sorry you and Margaret didn't see your way clear to tell me long ago. I'd have found it out in a few more months if he had lived, and I wouldn't have borne it a day. The man who breaks his vows to me once, don't get the second chance. I give truth and honour. I have a right to ask it in return. I am glad I understand at last. Now, if Elnora will forgive me, we will take a new start and see what we can make out of what is left of life. If she won't, then it will be my time to learn what suffering really means."

"But she will," said Sinton. "She must! She can't

help it when things are explained. Don't you worry over her."

"I notice she isn't hurrying any about coming home. Do you know where she is or what she is doing?"

"I do not. But likely she will be along soon. I must go help Billy with the night work. Good-bye, Katharine. Thank the Lord you have come to yourself at last!"

They shook hands and Sinton went down the road while Mrs. Comstock entered the cabin. She went to the supper table, but she could not swallow food. She stood in the back door watching the sky for moths, but they did not seem to be very numerous. Her spirits sank and she breathed unevenly. Then she heard the front screen. She reached the middle door as Elnora touched the foot of the stairs.

"Hurry, and get ready, Elnora," she said. "Your supper is almost spoiled now."

Elnora closed the stair door behind her, and for the first time in her life, threw the heavy lever which barred out anyone from downstairs. Mrs. Comstock heard the thud, and knew what it meant. She reeled slightly and caught the doorpost for support. For a few minutes she clung there, then sank to the nearest chair. After a long time she arose and stumbling half blindly, she put the food in the cupboard and covered the table. She took the lamp in one hand, the butter in the other, and started for the spring house. Something brushed close by her face, and she looked just

in time to see a winged creature rise above the cabin and sail away.

"That was a night bird," she muttered. As she stooped to set the butter in the water, came another thought. "Perhaps it was a moth!" Mrs. Comstock dropped the butter and hurried out with the lamp, she held it high above her head and waited until her arms ached. Small insects of night gathered, and at last a little dusty miller, but nothing came of any size.

"I got to go where they are, if I get them," muttered Mrs. Comstock.

She hurried into the cabin, set the lamp on the table, and stood thinking deeply. She went to the barn for the pair of stout high boots she used in feeding stock in deep snow. Throwing the boots by the back door she climbed to the loft over the spring house, and hunted an old lard oil lantern and one of first manufacture for oil. Both these she cleaned and filled. She listened until everything upstairs had been still for over a half-hour. By that time it was after eleven o'clock. Then she took the good lantern from the kitchen, the two old ones, a handful of matches, a ball of twine, and went from the cabin, softly closing the door.

Sitting on the back steps, she put on the boots, and then stood gazing into the sweet June night, first in the direction of the woods on her land, then toward the Limberlost. Its outline looked so dark and forbidding she shuddered and went down the garden, taking the path toward the woods, but as she neared the pool her

knees wavered and her courage fled. The knowledge
that in her soul she was now glad Robert Comstock
was at the bottom of it made a coward of her, who
fearlessly had mourned him there, nights untold. She
could not go on. She skirted the back of the garden,
crossed a field, and came out on the road. Soon she
reached the Limberlost. She hunted until she found
the old trail, then followed it stumbling over logs and
through clinging vines and grasses. The heavy boots
clumped on her feet, overhanging branches whipped her
face and pulled her hair. But her eyes were on the sky
as she went straining into the night, hoping to find signs
of a living creature on wing.

By and by she began to see the wavering flight of
something she thought near the right size. She had no
idea where she was, but she stopped, lighted a lantern
and hung it as high as she could reach. A little distance
away she placed the second and then the third. The
objects came nearer and sick with disappointment she
saw that they were bats. Crouching in the damp swamp
grasses, without a thought of snakes or venomous insects, she waited, her eyes roving from lantern to lantern.
Once she thought a creature of high flight dropped near
the lard oil light, so she arose breathlessly waiting, but
either it passed or it was an illusion. She glanced at
the old lantern, then at the new, and was on her feet
in an instant creeping close. Something large as a small
bird was fluttering around. Mrs. Comstock began
to perspire, while her hand shook wildly. Closer she

crept and just as she reached for it, something similar swept by and both flew away together.

Mrs. Comstock set her teeth and stood shivering. For a long time the locusts rasped, the whip-poor-wills cried and a steady hum of night life throbbed in her ears. Away in the sky she saw something coming when it was no larger than a falling leaf. Straight on toward the light it came. Without in the least realizing what she was doing, Mrs. Comstock began to pray aloud.

"This way, O Lord! Make it come this way! Please! You know how I need it! O Lord, send it lower!"

The moth hesitated at the first light, then slowly, easily it came toward the second, as if following a path of air. It touched a leaf near the lantern and settled. As Mrs. Comstock reached for it a thin yellow spray wet her hand and the surrounding leaves. When its wings raised above its back, her fingers came together. She held the moth to the light. It was nearer brown than yellow, and she remembered having seen some like it in the boxes that afternoon. It was not the one needed to complete the collection, but Elnora might want it, so Mrs. Comstock held on. Just there the Almighty was kind, or nature was sufficient, as you look at it, for following the law of its being when disturbed, the moth again threw the spray by which some suppose it attracts its kind, and liberally sprinkled Mrs. Comstock's dress front and arms. From that instant, she became the best moth

bait ever invented. Every Polyphemus in range hastened
to her, and other fluttering creatures of night followed.
The influx came her way. She snatched wildly here
and there until she had one in each hand and no place
to put them. She could see more coming, and her aching
heart, swollen with the strain of long excitement, hurt
pitifully. She prayed in broken exclamations that did
not always sound reverent, but never was human soul
in more deadly earnest.

Moths were coming. She had one in each hand.
They were not yellow, and she did not know what to do.
She glanced around to try to discover some way to keep
what she had, and her throbbing heart stopped and
every muscle stiffened. There was the dim outline of
a crouching figure not two yards away, and a pair of
eyes their owner thought hidden, caught the light in a
cold stream. Her first impulse was to scream and fly
for life. Before her lips could open a big moth alighted
on her breast while she felt another walking over her
hair. All sense of caution deserted her. She did not
care to live if she could not replace the yellow moth she
had killed. She set her eyes on those among the leaves.

"Here, you!" she cried hoarsely. "I need you! Get
yourself out here, and help me. These critters are
going to get away from me, and I 've got to have them.
Hustle!"

Pete Corson parted the bushes and stepped into the
light.

"Oh, it's you!" said Mrs. Comstock. "I might have

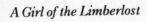

known! But you gave me a start. Here, hold these
until I make some sort of bag for them. Go easy! If you
break them I don't guarantee what will happen to you!"

"Pretty fierce, ain't you!" laughed Pete, but he advanced and held out his hands. "For Elnora, I s'pose?"

"Yes," said Mrs. Comstock. "In a mad fit, I trampled
one this morning, and by the luck of the old boy himself
it was the last moth she needed to complete a collection.
I got to get another one or die."

"Then I guess it's your funeral," said Pete. "There
ain't a chance in a dozen the right one will come. What
colour was it?"

"Yellow, and big as a bird."

"The Emperor, likely," said Pete. "You dig for
that kind, and they are not numerous, so's 'at you can
smash 'em for fun."

"Well, I can try to get one, anyway," said Mrs. Comstock. "I forgot all about bringing anything to put
them in. You take a pinch on their wings until I make
a poke."

Mrs. Comstock removed her apron, tearing off the
strings. She unfastened and stepped from the skirt of her
calico dress. With one apron string she tied shut the
band and placket. She pulled a wire pin from her hair,
stuck it through the other string, and using it as a bodkin
ran it around the hem of her skirt. Her fingers flew,
and shortly she had a large bag. She put several branches
inside to which the moths could cling, closed the mouth
partially and held it toward Pete.

"Put your hand well down and let the things go!" she ordered. "But be careful, man! Don't run into the twigs! Easy! That's one. Now the other. Is the one on my head gone? There was one on my dress, but I guess it flew. Here comes a kind of a gray-looking one."

Pete slipped several more moths into the bag.

"Now, that's five, Mrs. Comstock," he said. "I'm sorry, but you'll have to make that do. You must get out of here lively. Your lights will be taken for hurry calls, and inside the next hour a couple of men will ride here like fury. They won't be nice Sunday school men, and they won't hold bags and catch moths for you. You must go quick!"

Mrs. Comstock laid down the bag and pulled one of the lanterns lower.

"I won't budge a step," she said. "This land don't belong to you. You have no right to order me off it. Here I stay until I get a yellow Emperor, and no little petering thieves of this neighbourhood can scare me away."

"You don't understand," said Pete. "I'm willing to help Elnora, and I'd take care of you, if I could, but there will be too many for me, and they will be mad at being called out for nothing."

"Well, who's calling them out?" demanded Mrs. Comstock. "I'm catching moths. If a lot of good-for-nothings get fooled into losing some sleep, why, let them, they can't hurt me, or stop my work."

"They can, and they'll do both."

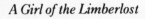

"Well, I'll see them do it!" said Mrs. Comstock. "I've got Robert's revolver in my dress, and I can shoot as straight as any man, if I'm mad enough. Anyone that interferes with me to-night will find me mad a-plenty. There goes another!"

She stepped into the light and waited until a big brown moth settled on her and was easily taken. Then in light, airy flight came a delicate pale green thing, and Mrs. Comstock started in pursuit. But the scent was not right. The moth fluttered high, then dropped lower, still lower, and sailed away. With outstretched hands Mrs. Comstock pursued it. She hurried one way and another, then ran over an object which tripped her and she fell. She regained her feet in an instant, but she had lost sight of the moth. With livid face she turned on the crouching man.

"You nasty, sneaking son of Satan!" she cried. "Why are you hiding there? You made me lose the one I wanted most of any I've had a chance at yet. Get out of here! Go this minute, or I'll fill your worthless carcass so full of holes you'll do to sift cornmeal. Go, I say! I'm using the Limberlost to-night, and I won't be stopped by the devil himself! Cut like fury, and tell the rest of them they can just go home. Pete is going to help me, and he is all of you I need. Now go!"

The man turned and went. Pete leaned against a tree, held his mouth shut and shook inwardly. Mrs. Comstock came back panting.

"The old scoundrel made me lose that!" she said.

254

"If anyone else comes snooping around here I'll just blow them up to start with. I haven't time to talk. Suppose that had been yellow! I'd have killed that man, sure! The Limberlost isn't safe to-night, and the sooner those whelps find it out, the better it will be for them."

Pete stopped laughing to look at her. He saw that she was speaking the truth. She was quite past reason, sense, or fear. The soft night air stirred the wet hair around her temples, the flickering lanterns made her face a ghastly green. She would stop at nothing, that was evident. Pete suddenly began catching moths with exemplary industry. In putting one into the bag, another escaped.

"We must not try that again," said Mrs. Comstock. "Now, what will we do?"

"We are close to the old case," said Pete. "I think I can get into it. Maybe we could slip the rest in there."

"That's a fine idea!" said Mrs. Comstock. "They'll have so much room there they won't be likely to hurt themselves, and the books say they don't fly in daytime unless they are disturbed, so they will settle when it's light, and I can come with Elnora to get them."

They captured two more, and then Pete carried them to the case.

"Here comes a big one!" he cried as he returned.

Mrs. Comstock looked up and stepped out with a prayer on her lips. She could not tell the colour at that distance, but the moth appeared different from the others.

On it came, dropping lower and darting from light to light. As it swept near her, "O Heavenly Father!" exulted Mrs. Comstock, "it's yellow! Careful, Pete! Your hat, maybe!"

Pete made a long sweep. The moth wavered above the hat and sailed away. Mrs. Comstock leaned against a tree and covered her face with her shaking hands.

"That is my punishment!" she cried. "Oh, Lord, if you will give a moth like that into my possession, I'll always be a better woman!"

The Emperor again came in sight. Pete stood tense and ready. Mrs. Comstock stepped into the light and watched the moth's course. Then a second appeared in pursuit of the first. The larger one wavered into the radius of light once more. The perspiration rolled down the man's tense face. He half lifted the hat.

"Pray, woman! Pray now!" he panted.

"I guess I best get over by that lard oil light and go to work," breathed Mrs. Comstock. "The Lord knows this is all in prayer, but it's no time for words just now. Ready, Pete! You are going to get a chance first!"

Pete made another long, steady sweep, but the moth darted beneath the hat. In its flight it came straight toward Mrs. Comstock. She snatched off the remnant of apron she had tucked into her petticoat band and held the calico before her. The moth struck full against it and clung to the goods. Pete crept up stealthily. The second moth followed the first, and the spray showered the apron.

"Wait!" gasped Mrs. Comstock. "I think they have settled. The books say they won't leave now."

The big pale yellow creature clung firmly, lowering and raising its wings. The other came nearer. Mrs. Comstock held the cloth with rigid hands, while Pete could hear her breathing in short gusts.

"Shall I try now?" he implored.

"Wait!" whispered the woman. "Something seems to say wait!"

The night breeze stiffened and gently waved the apron. Locusts rasped, mosquitoes hummed and frogs sang uninterruptedly. A musky odour slowly filled the air.

"Now shall I?" questioned Pete.

"No. Leave them alone. They are safe now. They are mine. They are my salvation. God and the Limberlost gave them to me! They won't move for hours. The books all say so. O Heavenly Father, I am thankful to You, and you, too, Pete Corson! You are a good man to help me. Now, I can go home and face my girl."

Instead, Mrs. Comstock dropped suddenly. She spread the apron across her knees. The moths were undisturbed. Then her tired white head dropped, the tears she had thought forever dried gushed forth, and she sobbed for pure joy.

"Oh, I wouldn't do that now, you know!" comforted Pete. "Think of getting two! That's more than you ever could have expected. A body would think you would cry, if you hadn't got any. Come on, now. It's almost morning. Let me help you home."

Pete took the bag and the two old lanterns. Mrs. Comstock carried her moths and the best lantern and went ahead to light the way.

Elnora had sat by her window far into the night. At last she undressed and went to bed, but sleep would not come. She had gone to the city to talk with members of the School Board about a room in the grades. There was a possibility that she might secure the moth, and so be able to start to college that fall, but if she did not, then she wanted the school. She had been given some encouragement, but she was so unhappy that nothing mattered. She could not see the way open to anything in life, while she remained with her mother, save a long series of disappointments. Yet Margaret Sinton had advised her to go home and try once more. Margaret had seemed so sure there would be a change for the better, that Elnora had consented, although she had no hope herself. So strong is the bond of blood, she could not make up her mind to seek a home elsewhere, even after the day which had passed. Unable to sleep she arose at last, and the room being warm, she sat on the floor by the window. The lights in the swamp caught her eye. She was very uneasy, for quite a hundred of her best moths were in the case. However, there was no money, and no one ever had touched a book or any of her apparatus. Watching the lights set her thinking, and before she realized it, she was in a panic or fear.

She hurried down the stairway softly calling her mother. There was no answer. She lightly stepped across the sitting room and looked in at the open door. There was no one, and the bed had not been used. Her first thought was that her mother had gone to the pool; and the Limberlost was alive with signals. Pity and fear mingled in the heart of the girl. She opened the kitchen door crossed the garden and ran back to the swamp. As she neared it she listened, but she could hear only the usual voices of night.

"Mother!" she called softly. Then louder, "Mother!"

There was not a sound. Chilled with fright she hurried back to the cabin. She did not know what to do. She understood what the lights in the Limberlost meant. Where was her mother? She was afraid to enter, while she was growing very cold and still more fearful about remaining outside. At last she went to her mother's room, picked up the gun, carried it into the kitchen, and crowding in a little corner behind the stove, she waited in trembling anxiety. The time was dreadfully long before she heard her mother's voice. Then she decided that someone had been ill and sent for her, so she took courage, and stepping swiftly across the kitchen she unbarred the door and drew back out of sight by the table.

Mrs. Comstock entered dragging her heavy feet. Her dress skirt was gone, her petticoat wet and drabbled, and the waist of her dress was almost torn from her body. Her hair hung in damp strings; her eyes were red with crying. In one hand she held the lantern, and in the other stiffly extended before her, on a wad of calico

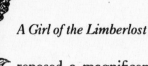

reposed a magnificent pair of yellow Emperors. Elnora stared, her lips parted.

"Shall I put these others in the kitchen?" inquired a man's voice.

The girl shrank back to the shadows.

"Yes, anywhere inside the door," replied Mrs. Comstock as she moved a few steps to make way for him. Pete's head appeared. He set down the moths and was gone.

"Thank you, Pete, more than ever woman thanked you before!" said Mrs. Comstock.

She placed the lantern on the table and barred the door. As she turned Elnora came into view. Mrs. Comstock leaned toward her, and held out the moths. In a voice vibrant with tones never before heard she said, "Elnora, my girl, mother's found you another moth!"

CHAPTER 13

Wherein Mother Love Is Bestowed on
Elnora, and She Finds an Assistant in
Moth Hunting

ELNORA awoke at dawn and lay gazing around the
unfamiliar room. She noticed that every vestige of
masculine attire and belongings was gone, and knew,
without any explanation, what that meant. For some
reason every tangible evidence of her father was banished,
and she was at last to be allowed to take his place. She
turned to look at her mother. Mrs. Comstock's face
was white and haggard, but on it rested an expression
of profound peace Elnora never before had seen. As
she studied the features on the pillow beside her, the heart
of the girl throbbed in tenderness. She realized as
fully as any one else could what her mother had suffered.
Thoughts of the night brought shuddering fear. She
softly slipped from the bed, went to her room, dressed
and entered the kitchen to attend the Emperors and
prepare breakfast. The pair had been left clinging to
the piece of calico. The calico was there and a few
pieces of beautiful wing. A mouse had eaten the moths!

"Well, of all the horrible luck!" gasped Elnora.

With the first thought of her mother, she caught up
the remnants of the moths, burying them in the ashes

of the stove. She took the bag to her room, hurriedly releasing its contents, but there was not another yellow one. Her mother had said some had been confined in the case in the Limberlost. There was still a hope that an Emperor might be among them. She peeped at her mother, who still slept soundly.

Elnora took a large piece of mosquito netting, and ran to the swamp. Throwing it over the top of the case, she unlocked the door. She reeled, faint with distress. The living moths that had been confined there in their fluttering to escape to night and the mates they sought not only had wrecked the other specimens of the case, but torn themselves to ribbons on the pins. A third of the rarest moths of the collection for the man of India were antennæless, legless, wingless, and often headless. Elnora sobbed aloud.

At last she closed the door, dropped the netting, and sank on a log, staring before her with unseeing eyes, trying to think.

"This is overwhelming," she said at last. "It is making a fatalist of me. I am beginning to think things happen as they are ordained from the beginning, this plainly indicating that there is to be no college, at least, this year, for me. My life is all mountain-top or cañon. I wish someone would lead me into a few days of 'green pastures.' Last night I went to sleep on mother's arm, the moths all secured, love and college, certainties. This morning I wake to find all my hopes wrecked. I simply don't dare let mother know that instead of helping me,

she has ruined my collection. Everything is gone! —
unless the love lasts. That actually seemed true. I
believe I will go see."

The love remained. Indeed, in the overflow of the
long hardened, pent-up heart, the girl was almost suffo-
cated with tempestuous caresses and generous offerings.
Before the day was over, Elnora realized that she never
had known her mother at all. The woman who now
busily went through the cabin, her eyes bright, eager,
alert, constantly planning, was a stranger. Her very
face was different, while it did not seem possible
that during one night the acid of twenty years
could disappear from a voice and leave it sweet and
pleasant.

For the next few days Elnora worked at mounting
the moths her mother had taken. She had to go to the
Bird Woman and tell about the disaster, but Mrs. Comstock was allowed to think that Elnora delivered the
moths when she made the trip. If she had told her
what actually happened, the chances were that Mrs.
Comstock again would have taken possession of the
Limberlost, hunting there until she replaced all the
moths that had been destroyed. But Elnora knew from
experience what it meant to collect such a list in pairs.
Valiant as she was in any good cause, this time she was
compelled to admit that she was defeated. It would
require hard work for at least two summers to replace
the lost moths. When she left the Bird Woman she went
to the president of the Onabasha schools and asked him

to do all in his power to secure her a room in one of the ward buildings.

The next morning the last moth was mounted, and the house work finished. Elnora said to her mother, "If you don't mind, I believe I will go into the woods pasture beside Sleepy Snake creek and see if I can catch some dragon flies or moths."

"Wait until I get a knife and a pail and I will go along," answered Mrs. Comstock. "The dandelions are plenty tender for greens among the deep grasses, and I might just happen to see something myself. My eyes are pretty sharp."

"I wish you could realize how young you are," said Elnora. "I know women in Onabasha who are ten years older than you, yet they look twenty years younger. So could you, if you would dress your hair becomingly, and wear appropriate clothes."

"I think my hair puts me in the old woman class permanently," said Mrs. Comstock, but there was no bitterness in her voice.

"Well, it don't!" cried Elnora. "There is a woman of twenty-eight who has hair as white as yours from sick headaches, but her face is young and beautiful. If your face would grow a little fuller and those lines would go away, you'd be lovely!"

"You little pig!" laughed Mrs. Comstock. "Anyone would think you would be satisfied with having a splinter new mother, without setting up a kick on her looks, first thing. Greedy!"

"That is a good word," said Elnora. "I admit the charge. I am greedy over every wasted year. I want you young, lovely, prettily dressed and enjoying life like the other girls' mothers."

Mrs. Comstock laughed softly as she pushed back her sunbonnet so that shrubs and bushes along the way could be scanned closely. Elnora walked ahead with a case over her shoulder, a net in her hand. Her head was bare, the rolling collar of her lavender gingham dress was cut in a V at the throat, the sleeves only reached the elbows. Every few steps she paused and examined the shrubbery carefully, while Mrs. Comstock was watching until her eyes ached, but there were no dandelions in the pail she carried.

Early June was rioting in fresh grasses, bright flowers, bird songs, and gay-winged creatures of air. Down the footpath the two went through the perfect morning, the love of God and all nature in their hearts. At last they reached the creek, following it toward the bridge. Here Mrs. Comstock found a large bed of tender dandelions and stopped to fill her pail. Then she sat on the bank, picking over the greens, while she listened to the creek softly singing its June song.

Elnora remained within calling distance, and was having good success. At last she crossed the creek, following it up to a bridge. There she began a careful examination of the under sides of the sleepers and flooring for cocoons. Mrs. Comstock could see her and the creek for several rods above. The mother sat beating the long

green leaves across her hand, carefully picking out the white buds, because Elnora liked them, when a splash up the creek attracted her attention.

Around the bend came a man. He was bareheaded, dressed in a white sweater, and waders which reached his waist. He kept on the bank, only entering the water when necessary. He had a queer basket strapped on his hip, and with a small rod he sent a long line spinning before him down the creek, deftly manipulating with it a little floating object. He was nearer Elnora than her mother, but Mrs. Comstock thought possibly by hurrying she could remain unseen and yet warn the girl that a stranger was coming. Thrusting the greens into the pail she ran down the creek bank. As she neared the bridge, she caught a sapling and leaned over the water to call Elnora. With her lips parted to speak, she hesitated a second to watch a sort of insect that flashed past on the water, when a splash from the man attracted the girl.

She was under the bridge, one knee planted in the embankment and a foot braced to support her. Her hair was tousled by wind and bushes, her face flushed, and she lifted her arms above her head, working to loosen a cocoon she had found. The call Mrs. Comstock had intended to utter never found voice, for as Elnora looked down at the sound, "Possibly I could get that for you," suggested the man.

Mrs. Comstock drew back. He was a young man with a wonderfully attractive face, although it was too white for robust health, broad shoulders, and slender upright frame.

"Oh, I do hope you can!" answered Elnora. "It's quite a find! It's one of those lovely pale red cocoons described in the books. I suspect it comes from having been in a dark place and screened from the weather."

"Is that so?" cried the man. "Wait a minute. I've never seen one. I suppose it's a Cecropia, from the location."

"Of course," said Elnora. "It's so cool here the moth hasn't emerged. The cocoon is a big, baggy one, and it is as red as fox tail."

"What luck!" he cried. "Are you making a collection?"

He reeled in his line, laid his rod across a bush and climbed the embankment to Elnora's side, produced a knife and began the work of whittling a deep groove around the cocoon.

"Yes. I paid my way through the high school in Onabasha with them. Now I am starting a collection which means college."

"Onabasha!" said the man. "That is where I am visiting." He paused to rest, for the bridge flooring was hard lumber, and the task he had set himself not easy. "Possibly you know my people — Dr. Ammon's? The doctor is my uncle. My home is in Chicago. I've been having typhoid fever, something fierce. In the hospital six weeks. Didn't gain strength right, so Uncle Doc sent for me. I am to live out of doors all summer,

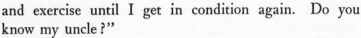

and exercise until I get in condition again. Do you know my uncle?"

"Yes. He is Aunt Margaret's doctor, and he would be ours, only we are never ill."

"Well, you look it!" said the man, appraising Elnora at a glance.

"Strangers always mention it," sighed Elnora. "I wonder how it would feel to be a pale languid lady and ride in a carriage."

"Ask me!" laughed the man. "It feels like the — dickens! I'm so proud of my feet. It's quite a trick to stand on them now. I have to keep out of the water all I can and stop to baby every half-mile. But with interesting outdoor work I'll be myself in a week."

"Do you call that work?" Elnora indicated the creek.

"I do, indeed! Nearly three miles, banks too soft to brag on and never a strike. Wouldn't you call that hard labour?"

"Yes," laughed Elnora. "Work at which you might kill yourself and never get a fish. Did anyone tell you there were trout in Sleepy Snake Creek?"

"Uncle said I could try."

"Oh, you can," said Elnora. "You can try no end, but you'll never get a trout. This is too far south and too warm for them. If you sit on the bank and use worms you might get some perch or catfish."

"But that isn't exercise."

"Well, if you only want exercise, go right on fishing. You can get a creel full of invisible results every night."

"I object," said the man emphatically. He stopped work again and studied Elnora. Even the watching mother could not blame him. Against the embankment, in the shade of the bridge Elnora's bright head, and her lavender dress made a picture worthy of much contemplation.

"I object!" repeated the man. "When I work I want to see results. I'd rather exercise sawing wood, making one pile grow little and the other big, than to cast all day and catch nothing because there is not a fish to take. Work for work's sake don't appeal to me. I work for results."

He digged the groove around the cocoon with skilled hand.

"Now there is some fun in this!" he said. "It's going to be a fair job to cut it out, but when it comes, it is not only beautiful, but worth a price; it will help you on your way. I think I'll put up that rod and hunt moths. That would be something like! Don't you want help?"

Elnora parried the question.

"Have you ever hunted moths, Mr. Ammon?"

"Enough to know the ropes in taking them, and to distinguish the commonest ones. I go wild on Catocalæ. There's too many of them, all too much alike for Philip, but I know all these fellows. One flew into my room when I was about ten years old, and we thought it a miracle. None of us ever had seen one so we took it over to the museum to Dr. Dorsey. He said they were common enough, but we didn't see them

because they flew at night. He showed me the museum collection, and I was so interested I took mine back home and started to hunt them. Every year after that we went to our cottage a month earlier, so I could find them, and all my family helped. I stuck to it until I went to college. Then, keeping the little moths out of the big ones was too much for the mater, so father advised that I donate mine to the museum. He bought a fine case for them with my name on it, which constitutes my sole contribution to science. I know enough to help you all right."

"Aren't you going north this year?"

"All depends on how this fever leaves me. Uncle says the nights are too cold and the days too hot there for me. He thinks I had better stay in an even temperature until I am strong again. I am going to stick pretty close to him until I know I am. I wouldn't admit it to anyone at home, but I was almost gone. I don't believe anything can eat up nerve much faster than the burning of a slow fever. No, thanks, I have enough. I stay with Uncle Doc, so if I feel it coming again he can do something quickly."

"I don't blame you," said Elnora. "I never have been sick, but it must be dreadful. I am afraid you are tiring yourself over that. Let me take the knife awhile."

"Oh, it isn't so bad as that! I wouldn't be wading creeks if it were. I just need a few more days to get steady on my feet again. I'll have this cut out in a minute."

"It is kind of you to get it," said Elnora. "I should have had to peel it, which would spoil the cocoon, for a specimen and ruin the moth."

"You haven't said yet whether I may help you while I am here."

Elnora hesitated.

"You better say 'yes,'" he persisted. "It would be a real kindness. It would keep me out doors all day and give an incentive to work. I'm good at it. I'll show you if I am not in a week or so. I can 'sugar,' manipulate lights, and mirrors, and all the expert methods. I'll wager moths are thick in the old swamp over there."

"They are," said Elnora. "Most I have I took there. A few nights ago my mother caught a good many, but we don't dare go alone."

"All the more reason why you need me. Where do you live? I can't get an answer from you, I'll just go tell your mother who I am and ask her if I may help you. I warn you, young lady, I have a very effective way with mothers. They almost never turn me down."

"Then it's probable you will have a new experience when you meet mine," said Elnora. "She never was known to do what anyone expected she surely would."

The cocoon came loose. Philip Ammon stepped down the embankment turning to offer his hand to Elnora. She ran down as she would have done alone, and taking the cocoon turned it end for end to learn if the imago it contained was alive. Then Ammon took back the cocoon to smooth the edges. Mrs. Comstock

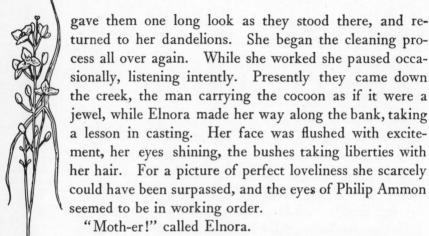

gave them one long look as they stood there, and returned to her dandelions. She began the cleaning process all over again. While she worked she paused occasionally, listening intently. Presently they came down the creek, the man carrying the cocoon as if it were a jewel, while Elnora made her way along the bank, taking a lesson in casting. Her face was flushed with excitement, her eyes shining, the bushes taking liberties with her hair. For a picture of perfect loveliness she scarcely could have been surpassed, and the eyes of Philip Ammon seemed to be in working order.

"Moth-er!" called Elnora.

There was an undulent, caressing sweetness in the girl's voice, as she sung out the call in perfect confidence that it would bring a loving answer, that struck deep in Mrs. Comstock's heart. She never had heard that word so pronounced before and a lump rose in her throat.

"Here!" she answered.

She went on examining the dandelion leaves.

"Mother, this is Mr. Philip Ammon, of Chicago," said Elnora. "He has been ill and he is staying with Dr. Ammon in Onabasha. He came fishing down the creek and cut this cocoon from under the bridge for me. He feels that it would be better to hunt moths than to fish, until he gets well. What do you think about it?"

Philip Ammon extended his hand.

"I am glad to know you," he said.

"You may take the hand-shaking for granted," replied Mrs. Comstock. "Dandelions have a way of making

the fingers sticky, and I like to know a man before I
take his hand, anyway. That introduction seems mighty
comprehensive on your part, but it still leaves me un-
classified. My name is Comstock."

Philip bowed.

"I am sorry to hear you have been sick," said Mrs.
Comstock. "But if people will live where they have
such vile water as they do in Chicago, I don't see what
else they are to expect."

Ammon studied her intently.

"I am sure I didn't have a fever on purpose," he said.

"You do seem a little wobbly on your legs," she ob-
served. "Maybe you had better sit and rest while I
finish these greens. It's late for the genuine article,
but in the shade, among long grass they are still tender."

"May I have a leaf?" asked Ammon reaching for one
as he sat on the bank, looking from the little creek at
his feet, away through the dim cool spaces of the June
forest on the opposite side. He drew a deep breath.
"Glory, but this is good after almost two months inside
hospital walls!"

He stretched on the grass and lay gazing up at the
leaves, occasionally asking the interpretation of a bird
note or the origin of an unfamiliar forest voice. Elnora
began helping with the dandelions.

"Another, please," said the young man, holding out
his hand.

"Do you suppose this is the kind of grass Nebuchad-
nezzar ate?" she asked, giving the leaf.

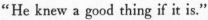

"He knew a good thing if it is."

"Oh, you should taste dandelions boiled with bacon and accompanied by mother's especial brand of corn-bread."

"Don't! My appetite is twice my size now. While it is — how far is it to Onabasha, shortest cut?"

"Three miles."

The man lay in perfect content, nibbling leaves.

"This surely is a treat," he said. "No wonder you find good hunting here. There seems to be foliage for almost every kind of caterpillar. But I suppose you have to exchange for northern species and Pacific Coast kinds?"

"Yes. And everyone wants Regalis in trade. I never saw the like. They consider a Cecropia or a Polyphemus an insult, and a Luna is barely acceptable."

"What authorities have you?"

Elnora began to name text-books which started a discussion. Mrs. Comstock listened. She cleaned dandelions with greater deliberation than they ever before were examined. In reality she was taking stock of the young man's long, well-proportioned frame, his strong hands, his smooth, fine-textured skin, his thick shock of dark hair, and making mental notes of his simple manly speech and the fact that he evidently did know a great deal about moths. It pleased her to think that if he had been a neighbour boy who had lain beside her every day of his life while she worked, he could have been no more at home. She liked the things he said, but she was proud that Elnora had a ready answer which always seemed appropriate.

At last Mrs. Comstock finished the greens.

"You are three miles from the city and less than a mile from where we live," she said. "If you will tell me what you dare eat, I suspect you had best go home with us and rest until the cool of the day before you start back. Probably some one that you can ride in with will be passing before evening."

"That is mighty kind of you," said Philip. "I think I will. It don't matter so much what I eat, the point is that I must be moderate. I am hungry all the time."

"Then we will go," said Mrs. Comstock, "and we will not allow you to make yourself sick with us."

Philip Ammon was on his feet. Picking up the pail of greens and his fishing rod he stood waiting. Elnora led the way. Mrs. Comstock motioned Philip to follow and she walked in the rear. The girl carried the cocoon and the box of moths she had taken, searching every step for more. The young man frequently set down his load to join in the pursuit of a dragon fly or moth, while Mrs. Comstock watched the proceedings with sharp eyes. Every time Philip picked up the pail of greens she struggled to suppress a smile.

Elnora proceeded slowly chattering about everything along the trail. Philip was interested in all the objects she pointed out, noticing several things which escaped her. He carried the greens just as casually when they took a short cut down the roadway as along the trail.

When Elnora turned toward the gate of her home Philip Ammon stopped, took a long look at the big hewed log cabin, the vines which clambered over it, the flower garden ablaze with beds of bright bloom interspersed with strawberries and tomatoes, the trees of the forest rising north and west like a green wall and exclaimed, "How beautiful!"

Mrs. Comstock was pleased. "If you think that," she said, "perhaps you will understand, how in all this present-day rush to be modern, I have preferred to remain as I began. My husband and I took up this land, and enough trees to build the cabin, stable, and out buildings are about all we ever cut. Of course, if he had lived, I suppose we should have kept with our neighbours. I hear considerable about the value of the land, the trees which are on it, and the oil which is supposed to be under it, but, as yet I haven't brought myself to change anything. So we stand for one of the few remaining homes of first settlers in this region. Come in. You are very welcome to what we have."

Mrs. Comstock stepped forward and took the lead. She had a bowl of soft water and a pair of boots to offer for the heavy waders, for outer comfort, a glass of cold buttermilk and a bench on which to rest, in the circular arbour until dinner was ready. Philip Ammon splashed in the water. He followed to the stable and exchanged boots there. He was ravenous for the buttermilk, and when he stretched on the bench in the arbour the flickering patches of sunlight so tantalized his tired eyes, while the bees made such splendid music, he was soon sound asleep.

When Elnora and her mother came out with a table they stood a short time looking at him. It is probable Mrs. Comstock voiced a united thought when she said, "What a refined, decent looking young man! How proud his mother must be of him! We must be careful what we let him eat."

Then they returned to the kitchen where Mrs. Comstock proceeded to be careful. She broiled ham of her own sugar-curing, creamed potatoes, served asparagus on toast, and made a delicious strawberry shortcake. As she cooked dandelions with bacon, she feared to serve them to him, so she made an excuse that it took too long to prepare them, blanched some and made a salad. When everything was ready she touched Ammon's sleeve.

"Best have something to eat, lad, before you get too hungry," she said.

"Please, hurry!" he begged laughingly as he held a plate toward her to be filled. "I thought I had enough self-restraint to start out alone, but I see I was mistaken. If you would allow me, just now, I am afraid I should start a fever again. I never did smell food so good as this. It's mighty kind of you to take me in. I hope I will be man enough in a few days to do something worth while in return."

Spots of sunshine fell on the white cloth and blue china, the bees and an occasional stray butterfly came searching for food. A rose-breasted grosbeak, released from a

three hours' siege of brooding, while his independent mate took her bath and recreation, mounted the top branch of a maple in the west woods from which he serenaded the dinner party with a joyful chorus in celebration of his freedom. Ammon's eyes strayed to the beautiful cabin, to the mixture of flowers and vegetables stretching down to the road, and to the singing bird with his red-splotched breast of white and he said, "I can't realize now that I ever lay in ice packs in a hospital. How I wish all the sick folks could come here to grow strong!"

The grosbeak sang on, a big Turnus butterfly sailed through the arbour and poised over the table. Elnora held up a lump of sugar and the butterfly, clinging to her fingers, tasted daintily. With eager eyes and parted lips, the girl held steadily. When at last it wavered away, "That made a picture!" said Ammon. "Ask me some other time how I lost my illusions concerning butterflies. I always thought of them in connection with sunshine, flower pollen, and fruit nectar, until one sad day."

"I know!" laughed Elnora. "I've seen that, too, but it didn't destroy any illusion for me. I think just as much of the butterflies as ever."

Then they talked of flowers, moths, dragon flies, Indian relics, and all the natural wonders the swamp afforded, straying from those subjects to books and school work. When they cleared the table Ammon assisted, carrying several tray loads to the kitchen. He and Elnora mounted specimens while Mrs. Comstock washed the dishes. Then she came out with a ruffle she was embroidering.

"I wonder if I did not see a picture of you in Onabasha, last night," Ammon said to Elnora. "Aunt Anna took me to call on Miss Brownlee. She was showing me her crowd — of course, it was you! But it didn't half do you justice, although it looked the nearest human of any of them. Miss Brownlee is very fond of you. She said the finest things."

Then they talked of Commencement, and at last Ammon said he must go or his friends would become anxious about him.

Mrs. Comstock brought him a blue bowl of creamy milk and a plate of bread. She stopped a passing team and secured a ride to the city for him, as his exercise of the morning had been a little too violent, and he was forced to admit he was tired.

"May I come to-morrow afternoon and chase moths awhile?" he asked Mrs. Comstock as he arose. "We will 'sugar' a tree and put a light by it, if I can get stuff to make the preparation. Possibly we can take some that way. I always enjoy moth hunting, I'd like to help Miss Elnora, and it would be a charity to me. I've got to remain outdoors some place, and I'm quite sure I'd get well faster here than anywhere else. Please say I may come."

"I have no objections, if Elnora really would like help," said Mrs. Comstock.

In her heart she wished he would not. She wanted her newly found treasure all to herself, for a time, at least. But Elnora's were eager, shining eyes. She thought it would be splendid to have help, and great fun to try book methods for taking moths, so it was arranged. As Ammon rode away, Mrs. Comstock's eyes followed him. "What a nice young man!" she said.

"He seems fine," agreed Elnora.

"He comes of a good family, too. I've often heard of his father. He is a great lawyer."

"I am glad he likes it here. I need help. Possibly——"

"Possibly what?"

"We can get a great many moths."

"What did he mean about the butterflies?"

"That he always had connected them with sunshine, flowers, and fruits, and thought of them as the most exquisite of creations; then one day he found some clustering thickly over carrion."

"Come to think of it, I have seen butterflies ——"

"So had he," laughed Elnora, "and that is what he meant."

CHAPTER 14

Wherein a New Position Is Tendered Elnora, and Philip Ammon Is Shown Limberlost Violets

THE next morning Mrs. Comstock called to Elnora, "The mail carrier stopped at our box."

Elnora ran down the walk and came back carrying an official looking letter. She tore it open and read:

MY DEAR MISS COMSTOCK:

At the weekly meeting of the Onabasha School Board last night, it was decided to add the position of Lecturer on Natural History to our corps of city teachers. It will be the duty of this person to spend two hours a week in each of the grade schools exhibiting and explaining specimens of the most prominent objects in nature; animals, birds, insects, flowers, vines, shrubs, bushes, and trees. These specimens and lectures should be appropriate to the seasons and the comprehension of the grades. This position was unanimously voted to you. I think you will find the work delightful and much easier than the routine grind of the other teachers. It is my advice that you accept and begin to prepare yourself at once. Your salary will be $750 a year, and you will be allowed $200 for expenses in procuring specimens and books. Let us know at once if you want the position, as it is going to be difficult to fill satisfactorily if you do not.

Very truly yours,
DAVID THOMPSON. President, Onabasha Schools.

"I hardly understand," marvelled Mrs. Comstock.

"It is a new position. They never have had anything like it before. I suspect it arose from the help I've

been giving the grade teachers in their nature work. They are trying to teach the children something, and half the instructors don't know a blue jay from a kingfisher, a beech leaf from an elm, or a wasp from a hornet."

"Well, do you?" anxiously inquired Mrs. Comstock.

"Indeed, I do!" laughed Elnora, "and several other things beside. When Freckles bequeathed me the swamp, he gave me a bigger inheritance than he knew. While you have thought I was wandering aimlessly, I have been following a definite plan, studying hard, and storing up the stuff that will earn these seven hundred and fifty dollars. Mother, dear, I am going to accept this, of course. The work will be a delight. I'd love it most of anything in teaching. You must help me. We must find nests, eggs, leaves, queer formations in plants and rare flowers. I must have flower boxes made for each of the rooms and filled with wild things. I should begin to gather specimens this very day."

Elnora was on her feet. Her face was flushed and her eyes bright.

"Oh, what great work that will be!" she cried. "You must go with me so you can see the little faces when I tell them how the goldfinch builds its nest, and how the bees make honey."

So Elnora and her mother went into the woods behind the cabin to study nature.

"I think," said Elnora, "the idea is to begin with fall things in the fall, keeping to the seasons throughout the year."

282

"What are fall things?" inquired Mrs. Comstock.

"Oh, fringed gentians, asters, ironwort, every fall flower, leaves from every tree and vine, what makes them change colour, abandoned bird nests, winter quarters of caterpillars and insects, what becomes of the butterflies and grasshoppers — just myriads of stuff. I never can use the half there will be to show. I shall have to be very wise to select the things it will be most beneficial for the children to learn."

"Can I really help you?" Mrs. Comstock's strong face was pathetic.

"Indeed, yes!" cried Elnora. "I never can get through it alone. There will be an immense amount of work connected with securing and preparing specimens."

Mrs. Comstock lifted her head proudly and began doing business at once. Her sharp eyes ranged from earth to heaven. She investigated everything, asking innumerable questions. By noon she was as eager and interested as Elnora. The morning was filled with happiness for both of them. Near noon Mrs. Comstock took the specimens they had collected, and went to prepare dinner, while Elnora followed the woods down to Sintons' to show her letter.

She had to explain what became of her moths, and why college would have to be abandoned for that year, but Margaret and Wesley vowed not to tell. Wesley waved the letter excitedly, explaining it to Margaret as if it was a personal possession. Margaret was deeply impressed, while Billy volunteered first aid in gathering material.

"Now, anything you want in the ground, Snap can dig it out," he said. "Uncle Wesley and I found a hole three times as big as Snap, that he dug at the roots of a tree."

"We will train him to hunt pupæ cases," said Elnora.

"Are you going to the woods this afternoon?" asked Billy.

"Yes," answered Elnora. "Dr. Ammon's nephew from Chicago is visiting in Onabasha. He is going to show me how men put some sort of compound on a tree, hang a light by it, and take moths that way. It will be interesting to watch and learn."

"May I come?" asked Billy.

"Of course, you may come!" answered Elnora.

"Is this nephew of Dr. Ammon a young man?" inquired Margaret.

"About twenty-six, I should think," said Elnora. "He said he had been out of college and at work in his father's law office three years."

"Does he seem nice?" asked Margaret, and Wesley smiled.

"Finest kind of a person," said Elnora. "He can teach me so much. It is very interesting to hear him talk. He knows considerable about moths that will be a help to me. He had a fever and he has to stay outdoors until he grows strong again."

"Billy, I guess you better help me this afternoon," said Margaret. "Maybe Elnora had rather not bother with you."

"There's no reason on earth why Billy should not come!" cried Elnora, and Wesley smiled again.

"I must hurry home and get my dinner or I won't be ready," she added.

Hastening down the road with glowing face she entered the cabin.

"I thought you never would come," said Mrs. Comstock. "If you don't hurry Mr. Ammon will be here before you get dressed."

"I forgot about him until just now," said Elnora. "I am not going to dress. He's not coming to visit. We are only going to the woods for more specimens. I can't wear anything that requires care. The limbs take the most dreadful liberties with hair and clothing."

Mrs. Comstock opened her lips, looked at Elnora and closed them. In her heart she was pleased that the girl was so interested in her work that she had forgotten Philip Ammon's coming. But it did seem to her that such a pleasant young man should have been greeted by a girl in a fresh dress. "If she isn't disposed to primp at the coming of a man, heaven forbid that I should be the one to start her," thought Mrs. Comstock. So she did the primping in honour of the occasion. It consisted of a fresh gingham dress and hair coiled a little more loosely than usual.

Ammon came whistling down the walk between the cinnamon pinks, pansies, and strawberries. He carried several packages, while his face flushed with more colour than on the previous day.

"Only see what has happened to me!" cried Elnora, offering her letter.

"I'll wager I know!" answered Ammon. "Isn't it great! Everyone in Onabasha is talking about it. At last there is something new under the sun. All of them are pleased. They think you'll make a big success. This will give an incentive to work. In a few days more I'll be myself again, and we'll overturn the fields and woods around here."

He went on to congratulate Mrs. Comstock.

"Aren't you proud of her, though?" he asked. "You should hear what folks are saying! They say she created the necessity for the position, and everyone seems to feel that it is a necessity. Now, if she succeeds, and she will, all of the other city schools will have such departments, and first thing you know she will have made the whole world just a little better. Let me rest a few seconds; my feet are acting up again. Then we will cook the compound and put it to cool."

He laughed as he sat breathing shortly.

"It doesn't seem possible that a fellow could lose his strength like this. My knees are actually trembling, but I'll be all right in a minute. Uncle Doc said I could come. I told him how you took care of me, and he said I would be safe here."

Then he began unwrapping packages and explaining to Mrs. Comstock how to cook the compound to attract the moths. He followed her into the kitchen, kindled the fire, and stirred the preparation as he talked. While the mixture cooled, he and Elnora walked through the vegetable garden behind the cabin and strayed from there into the woods.

"What about college?" he asked. "Miss Brownlee said you were going."

"I had hoped to," replied Elnora, "but I had a streak of dreadful luck, so I 'll have to wait until next year. If you won't speak of it I'll tell you."

Ammon promised, and Elnora recited the history of the yellow Emperor. She was so interested in doing the Emperor justice she did not notice how many personalities went into the story. A few pertinent questions told Ammon the rest. He looked at the girl in wonder. In face and form she was as lovely as any one of her age and type he ever had seen. Her school work far surpassed that of most girls of her age he knew. She differed in other ways. This vast store of learning she had gathered from field and forest was a wealth of attraction no other girl possessed. Her frank, matter-of-fact manner was an inheritance from her mother, but there was something more. Once, as they talked he thought "sympathy" was the word to describe it and again "comprehension." She seemed to possess a large sense of brotherhood for all human and animate creatures. She spoke to him as if she had known him all her life. She talked to the grosbeak in exactly the same manner, as she laid strawberries and potato bugs on the fence for his family. She did not swerve an inch from her way when a snake slid by her, while the squirrels

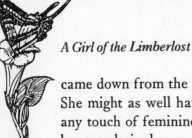

came down from the trees and took corn from her fingers.
She might as well have been a boy, so lacking was she in
any touch of feminine coquetry toward him. He studied
her wonderingly.

As they went along the path they reached a large slime-
covered pool surrounded by decaying stumps and logs
thickly covered with water hyacinths and blue flags.
Ammon stopped.

"Is that the place?" he asked.

Elnora assented.

"The doctor told you?"

"Yes. It was tragic. Is that pool really bottomless?"

"So far as we ever have been able to discover."

Ammon stood looking at the water, while the long,
sweet grasses, thickly sprinkled with blue flag bloom,
over which wild bees clambered, swayed around his
feet. Then he turned to the girl. She had worked hard.
The same lavender dress she had worn the previous day
clung to her in limp condition. But she was as evenly
coloured and of as fine grain as a wild rose petal, her
hair was really brown, but never was such hair touched
with a redder glory, while her heavy arching brows
added a look of strength to her big gray-blue eyes.

"And you were born here?"

He had not intended to voice that thought.

"Yes," she said looking into his eyes. "Just in time
to prevent my mother from saving the life of my father.
She came near never forgiving me."

"Ah, cruel!" cried Ammon.

"I find a great deal in life that is cruel, from our standpoints," said Elnora. "It takes the large wisdom of the Unfathomable, the philosophy of the Almighty, to bear some of it. But there is always right somewhere, and at last it seems to come."

"Will it come to you?" asked Ammon, who found himself suffering intensely.

"It has come," said the girl serenely. "It came a week ago. It came in fullest measure when my mother ceased to regret that I had been born. Now, work that I love has come — that should constitute happiness. A little farther along is my violet bed. I want you to see it."

As Philip Ammon followed he definitely settled upon the name of the unusual feature of Elnora's face. It should be called "experience." She had known hard experiences early in life. Suffering had been her familiar more than joy. He watched her with intense earnestness, his heart deeply moved. She led him into a swampy half-open space in the woods, stopped and stepped aside. Ammon uttered a cry of surprised delight.

A few decaying logs were scattered around, the grass grew in tufts long and fine. Blue flags waved, clusters of cowslips nodded gold heads, but the whole earth was purple with a thick blanket of violets nodding from stems a foot in length. Elnora knelt and slipping her fingers through the leaves and grasses to the roots, gathered a few violets and gave them to Philip.

"Can your city greenhouses surpass them?" she asked.

Ammon sat on a log to examine the blooms.

"They are superb!" he said. "I never saw such length of stem or such rank leaves, while the flowers are the deepest blue, the truest violet I ever saw growing wild. They are coloured exactly like the eyes of the girl I am going to marry."

Elnora handed him several others to add to those he held.

"She must have wonderful eyes," she commented.

"No other blue eyes are quite so beautiful," he said. "In fact, she is altogether lovely."

"It is customary for a man to think the girl he is going to marry lovely. I wonder if I should find her so."

"You would," said Ammon. "No one ever fails to. She is tall as you, very slender, but perfectly rounded; you know about her eyes; her hair is black and wavy — while her complexion is clear and flushed with red."

Elnora knelt among the flowers as she looked at him.

"Why, she must be the most beautiful girl in the whole world!" she cried.

Ammon laughed.

"No, indeed!" he said. "She is not a particle better looking in her way than you are in yours. She is a type of dark beauty, but you are just as perfect. She is unusual in her combination of black hair and violet eyes, although everyone thinks them black at a little distance. You are quite as unusual with your fair face, black brows and brown hair; indeed, I know many people who would prefer your bright head to her dark one. It's all a question of taste — and being engaged to the girl," he added.

"That would be likely to prejudice one," laughed Elnora.

"Edith has a birthday soon; if these last will you let me have a box of them to send her ?"

"I will help gather and pack them for you, so they will carry nicely. Does she hunt moths with you ?"

Back went Philip Ammon's head in a gale of laughter.

"No!" he cried. "She says they are 'creepy.' She would scream herself into a spasm if she were compelled to touch those young caterpillars I saw you handling yesterday."

"Why would she ?" marvelled Elnora. "Haven't you told her that they are perfectly clean, helpless, and harmless as so much animate velvet ?"

"No, I have not told her. She wouldn't care enough about caterpillars to listen."

"In what is she interested ?"

"What interests Edith Carr ? Let me think! First, I believe she takes pride in being just a little handsomer and better dressed than any girl of her set. She is interested in having a beautiful home, fine appointments about her, in being petted, praised, and the acknowledged leader of society. She likes to find new things which amuse her, and to always and in all circumstances have her own way about everything."

"Good gracious!" cried Elnora, staring at him. "But what does she do? How does she spend her time?"

"'Spend her time!'" repeated Ammon. "Well, she would call that a joke. Her days are never long enough. There is endless shopping, to find the pretty things; regular visits to the dressmakers, calls, parties, theatres, entertainments. She is always rushed. I never get to see half as much of her as I would like."

"But I mean work," persisted Elnora. "In what is she interested that is useful to the world?"

"Me!" cried Ammon promptly.

"I can understand that," laughed Elnora. "What I can't understand is how you can be in ——" She stopped short in confusion, but she saw that he had finished the sentence as she had intended. "I beg your pardon!" she cried. "I didn't mean to say that. But I cannot understand these people I hear about who live only for their own amusement. Perhaps it is very great; I'll never have a chance to know. To me, it seems the only pleasure in this world worth having is the joy we get out of living for those we love, and those we can help. I hope you are not angry with me."

Ammon sat silently looking far away, with deep thought in his eyes.

"You are angry," faltered Elnora.

His look came back to her as she knelt before him among the flowers and he gazed at her steadily.

"No doubt I should be," he said, "but the fact is I am not. I cannot understand a life purely for personal pleasure myself. But she is only a girl, and this is her playtime. When she is a woman in her own home, then she will be different, will she not?"

Elnora never resembled her mother so closely as when she answered that question.

"I would have to be well acquainted with her to know, but I should hope so. To make a real home for a tired business man is a very different kind of work from that required to be a leader of society. It demands different talent and education. Of course, she means to change, or she would not have promised to make a home for you. I suspect our dope is cool now, let's go try for some butterflies."

As they went back along the path together Elnora talked of many things but Ammon answered absently. Evidently he was thinking of something else. But the moth bait recalled him and he was ready for work as they made their way back to the woods. He wanted to try the Limberlost, but Elnora was firm about keeping on home ground. She did not tell him that lights hung in the swamp would be a signal to call up a band of men whose presence she dreaded. So they set out, Ammon carrying the dope, Elnora the net, Billy and Mrs. Comstock following with cyanide boxes and lanterns.

First they tried for butterflies and captured several fine ones with little trouble. They also called swarms of ants, beetles, bees, and flies. When it grew dusk, Mrs. Comstock and Ammon went to prepare supper. Elnora and Billy remained until the butterflies went to

bed. Then they lighted the lanterns, repainted the trees and followed the home trail.

"Do you 'spect you 'll get just a lot of moths?" asked Billy, as he walked beside Elnora.

"I am sure I hardly know," said the girl. "This is a new way for me. Perhaps they will come to the lights, but few moths eat; and I have some doubt about those which the lights attract settling on the right trees. Maybe the smell of that dope will draw them. Between us, Billy, I think I like the old way best. If I can find a hidden moth, slip up and catch it unawares, or take it in full flight, it's my captive, and I can keep it until it dies naturally. But this way you seem to get it under false pretences, it has no chance, and it will probably ruin its wings struggling for freedom before morning."

"Well, any moth ought to be proud to be taken anyway, by you," said Billy. "Just look what you do! You can make everybody love them. People even quit hating caterpillars when they see you handle them and hear you tell all about them. You just must have some to show people how they are. It's not like killing things to see if you can, or because you want to eat them, the way most men kill birds. I think it is right for you to take enough for collections, to show city people, and to illustrate the Bird Woman's books. You go on and take them! The moths don't care. They're glad to have you. They like it!"

"Billy, I see your future," said Elnora. "We will educate you and send you up to Mr. Ammon to make a great lawyer. You'd beat the world as a special pleader. You actually make me feel that I am doing the moths a kindness to take them."

"And so you are!" cried Billy. "Why, just from what you have taught them, Uncle Wesley and Aunt Margaret never think of killing a caterpillar until they look whether it's the beautiful June moth kind, or the horrid tent ones. That's what you can do. You just go ahead!"

"Billy, you are a jewel!" cried Elnora, throwing her arm across his shoulders as they came down the path.

"My, I was scared!" said Billy with a deep breath.

"Scared?" questioned Elnora.

"Yes, sir-ee! Aunt Margaret scared me. May I ask you a question?"

"Of course, you may!"

"Is that man going to be your beau?"

"Billy! No! What made you think such a thing?"

"Aunt Margaret said likely he would fall in love with you, and you wouldn't want me around any more. Oh, but I was scared! It isn't so, is it?"

"Indeed, no!"

"I am your beau, ain't I?"

"Surely you are!" said Elnora, tightening her arm.

"I do hope Aunt Kate has ginger cookies," said Billy with a little skip of delight.

her she stood on the path holding a pair of moths. Her eyes were wide with excitement, her cheeks pink, her red lips parted, and on the hand she held out to them clung a pair of delicate blue-green moths, with white bodies, and touches of lavender and straw colour. All about her lay flower-brocaded grasses, behind the deep green background of the forest, while the sun slowly sifted gold from heaven to burnish her hair. Mrs. Comstock heard a sharp breath behind her.

"Oh, what a picture!" exulted Ammon at her shoulder. "She is absolutely and altogether lovely! I'd give a small fortune for that faithfully set on canvas!"

He picked the box from Mrs. Comstock's fingers and slowly advanced with it. Elnora held down her hand and transferred the moths. Ammon closed the box carefully, but the watching mother saw that his eyes were following the girl's face. He was not making the slightest attempt to conceal what he felt.

"I wonder if a woman ever did anything lovelier than to find a pair of Luna moths on a forest path, early on a perfect June morning," he said to Mrs. Comstock, as he returned the box.

She glanced at Elnora. The girl had gone back to work, and was intently searching the bushes.

"Look here, young man," said Mrs. Comstock. "You seem to find that girl of mine about right."

"I could suggest no improvement," said Ammon. "I never saw a more attractive girl anywhere. She seems absolutely perfect to me."

"You are wiser than you ever have been before," answered Ammon. "I feel it, too."

"I also," breathed Elnora.

The moth spread its wings, shivered them tremulously, opening and closing them rapidly. Ammon handed the box to Elnora.

She shook her head.

"I can't take that one," she said. "Let her go."

"But, Elnora," protested Mrs. Comstock, "I don't want to let her go. She's mine. She's the first one I ever found this way. Can't you put her in a big box, and let her live without hurting her? I can't bear to let her go. I want to learn all about her."

"Then watch while we get these on the trees," said Elnora. "We will take her home until night and then decide what to do. She won't fly for a long time yet."

Mrs. Comstock settled on the ground, an elbow on her knee, her chin in her palm, gazing at the moth. Elnora and Ammon went to the baited trees, placing several large moths and a number of smaller ones in the cyanide jar, and searching the bushes beyond where they found several paired specimens of differing families. When they returned Elnora showed her mother how to hold her hand before the moth so that it would climb upon her fingers. Then they started back to the cabin, Elnora and Ammon leading the way; Mrs. Comstock followed slowly, stepping with great care lest she stumble and jar the moth. Her face wore a look of

comprehension, in her eyes was an exalted light. On she came to the blue-bordered pool lying beside her path.

A turtle scrambled from a log and splashed into the water, while a red-wing shouted, "O-ka-lee!" to her. Mrs. Comstock paused and looked intently at the slime-covered quagmire, framed in a flower riot and homed over by sweet-voiced birds. Then she gazed at the thing of incomparable beauty clinging to her fingers and said softy: "If you had known about wonders like these in the days of your youth, Robert Comstock, could you ever have done what you did?"

Elnora missed her mother, and turning to look for her, saw her standing beside the pool. Would the old fascination return? A panic of fear seized the girl. She went back swiftly.

"Are you afraid she is going?" Elnora asked. "If you are, cup your other hand over her for shelter. Carrying her through this air and in the hot sunshine will dry her wings and make them ready for flight very quickly. You can't trust her in such air and light as you can in the cool dark woods."

As she talked she took hold of her mother's sleeve, anxiously smiling a pitiful little smile that Mrs. Comstock understood. Ammon set his load at the back door, returning to hold open the garden gate for Elnora and Mrs. Comstock. He reached it just in time to see them standing together beside the pool. The mother bent swiftly and kissed the girl on the lips. Ammon wheeled and was busily hunting moths on the raspberry bushes when they reached the gate. And so excellent are the rewards of attending your own business, that he found a splendid Promethea on a lilac in a corner, a moth of such rare wine-coloured, velvety shades that it almost sent Mrs. Comstock to her knees again. But this one was fully developed, able to fly, and had to be taken into the cabin hurriedly. Mrs. Comstock stood in the middle of the room holding up her Regalis.

"Now what must I do?" she asked.

Elnora glanced at Philip Ammon. Their eyes met and both of them smiled; he with amusement at the tall, spare figure, with dark eyes and white crown, asking the childish question so confidingly; and Elnora with exultant pride. The girl was beginning to appreciate the greatness of her mother.

"How would you like to sit and see her finish development? I'll get dinner," proposed the girl.

After they had dined, Ammon and Elnora carried the dishes to the kitchen, brought out boxes, sheets of cork, pins, ink, paper for slips and everything necessary for mounting and classifying the moths they had taken. When the housework was finished Mrs. Comstock brought her ruffle and sat near, watching and listening. She remembered all they said that she understood, and when uncertain she asked questions. Occasionally she laid down her work to straighten some flower which needed attention or to go to the garden for a bug for the grosbeak. In one of these absences Elnora said to Ammon, "These replace quite a number of the moths I lost for

the man of India. With a week of such luck, I could almost begin to talk college again."

"There is no reason why you should not have the week and the luck," said Ammon. "I have taken moths until the middle of August, though I suspect one is more apt to find late ones in the north where it is colder than here. The next week is hay-time, but we can count on a few double-brooders and strays, and by working the exchange method for all it is worth, I think we can complete the collection again."

"You almost make me hope," said Elnora, "but I must not allow myself. I don't truly think I can replace all I lost, not even with your help. If I could, I can't see my way clear to leave mother this winter. I have found her so recently, and she is so precious, I can't risk losing her again. I am going to take the nature position in the Onabasha schools, and I shall be most happy doing the work. Only, these are a temptation."

"I wish you might go to college this fall with the other girls," said Ammon. "I feel that if you don't you never will. Isn't there some way?"

"I can't see it if there is, and I really don't want to leave mother."

"Well, mother is mighty glad to hear it," said Mrs. Comstock, entering the arbour.

Ammon noticed that her face was pale, her lips quivering, her voice cold.

"I was just saying to your daughter that she should

go to college this winter," he explained, "but she says she don't want to leave you."

"If she wants to go, I wish she could," said Mrs. Comstock, a look of relief spreading over her face.

"Oh, all girls want to go to college," said Ammon. "It's the only proper place to learn bridge and embroidery; not to mention midnight lunches of mixed pickles and fruit cake, and all the delights of the sororities."

"I have thought a great deal about going to college," said Elnora, "but I never thought of any of those things."

"That is because your education in fudge and bridge has been sadly neglected," said Ammon. "You should hear my sister Polly! This was her last year! Lunches and sororities were all I heard her mention, until Tom Levering came on deck; now he is the leading subject. I can't see from her daily conversation, that she knows half as much really worth knowing as you do, but she can beat you miles on fun."

"Oh, we had some good times in the high school," said Elnora. "Life hasn't been all work and study. Is Edith Carr a college girl?"

"No. She is the very selectest kind of a private boarding school girl."

"Who is she?" asked Mrs. Comstock.

Ammon opened his lips.

"She is a girl in Chicago, that Mr. Ammon knows very well," said Elnora. "She is beautiful and rich, and a friend of his sister's. Or, didn't you say that?"

"I don't remember, but she is," said Ammon. "This moth needs an alcohol bath to take off the dope."

"Won't the down come, too?" asked Elnora anxiously.

"No. You watch and you will see it come out, as Polly would say, 'a perfectly good' moth."

"Is your sister younger than you?" inquired Elnora.

"Yes," said Ammon, "but she is three years older than you. She is the dearest sister in all the world. I'd love to see her now."

"Why don't you send for her," suggested Elnora. "Perhaps she'd like to help us catch moths."

"Yes, I think Polly in a Virot hat, Picot embroidered frock and three-inch heels would take more moths than anyone that ever struck the Limberlost," laughed Ammon.

"Well, you get lots of them, and you are her brother."

"Yes, but that is different. Father was raised in Onabasha, and he loved the country. He trained me his way and mother took charge of Polly. I don't just understand it. Mother is a great home body herself, but she did succeed in making Polly strictly ornamental."

"Does Tom Levering need a 'strictly ornamental' girl?"

"You are too matter of fact! Too 'strictly' material! He needs a darling girl who will love him plenty, and Polly is that."

"Well, then, does the Limberlost need a 'strictly ornamental' girl?"

"No!" cried Ammon. "You are ornament enough for the Limberlost. I have changed my mind. I don't want Polly here. She would not enjoy catching moths, or anything we do."

"She might," persisted Elnora. "You are her brother, and surely you care for these things."

"The argument does not hold," said Ammon. "Polly and I do not like the same things when we are at home, but we are very fond of each other. The member of my family who would go crazy about this is my father. I wish he could come, if only for a week. I'd send for him, but he is tied up in preparing some papers for a great corporation case this summer. He likes the country. It was his vote that brought me here."

Ammon leaned back in the arbour, watching the grosbeak as it hunted food between a tomato vine and a day lily. Elnora set him to making labels, and when he finished them he asked permission to write a letter. He took no pains to conceal his page, and from where she sat opposite him, Elnora could not look his way without reading, "My dearest Edith." He wrote busily for a time and then sat staring out across the garden.

"Have you run out of material so quickly?" asked Elnora.

"That's about it," said Ammon. "I have said that I am getting well as rapidly as possible, that the air is fine, the folks at Uncle Doc's all well, and entirely too good to me; that I am spending most of my time in the country helping catch moths for a collection, which is

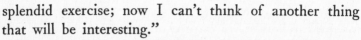

splendid exercise; now I can't think of another thing
that will be interesting."

There was a burst of exquisite notes in the maple.

"Put in the grosbeak," suggested Elnora. "Tell her
you are so friendly with him you feed him potato bugs."

Ammon dropped the pen to the sheet, bent forward,
then hesitated.

"Blest if I do!" he cried. "She'd think a grosbeak was a depraved person with a large nose. She'd
never dream that it was a black-robed lover, with a breast
of snow and a crimson heart. She don't care for hungry
babies and potato bugs. I shall write that to father.
He will find it exquisite."

Elnora deftly picked up a moth, pinned it and placed
its wings. She straightened the antennæ, drew each
leg into position and set it in perfectly lifelike manner.
As she lifted her work to see if she had it right, she glanced
at Ammon. He was still frowning and hesitating over
the paper.

"I dare you to let me dictate a couple of paragraphs,"
she said.

"Done!" cried Ammon. "Go slowly enough that I
can write it."

Elnora laughed softly.

"I am writing this," she began, "in an old grape
arbour in the country, near a log cabin where I had my
dinner. From where I sit I can see directly into the
home of the next-door neighbour on the west. His
name is R. B. Grosbeak. From all I have seen of him,

he is a gentleman of the old school; the oldest school there is, no doubt. He always wears a black suit and cap and a white vest, decorated with one large red heart, which I think must be the emblem of some ancient order. I have been here a number of times, and I never have seen him wear anything else, or his wife appear in other than a brown dress with touches of white.

"It has appeared to me at times that she was a shade neglectful of her home duties, but he does not seem to see it that way. He cheerfully stays about the sitting room, while she is away having a good time, and sings as he cares for the four small children. I must tell you about his music. I am sure he never saw inside a conservatory. I think he merely picked up what he knows by ear and without vocal training, but there is a tenderness in his tones, a depth of pure melody, that I never have heard surpassed. It may be that I think more of his music than that of some other good vocalists hereabout, because I see more of him and appreciate his devotion to his home life.

"I just had an encounter with him at the west fence, and induced him to carry a small gift to his children. When I see the perfect harmony in which he lives, and the depth of content he and the brown lady find in life, I am almost persuaded to — now this is going to be poetry," said Elnora. "Move your pen over here and begin with a quote and a cap."

Ammon's face had been an interesting study as he

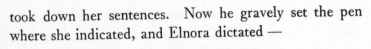

took down her sentences. Now he gravely set the pen where she indicated, and Elnora dictated —

> "Buy a nice little home in the country,
> And settle down there for life."

"That's the truth!" cried Ammon. "It's as big a temptation as I ever had. Go on!"

"That's all," said Elnora. "You can finish. The moths are done. I am going hunting for whatever I can find for the grades."

"Wait a minute," begged Ammon. "I am going, too."

"No. You stay with mother and finish your letter."

"It is done. I couldn't add anything to that."

"All right! Sign your name and come on. But I forgot to tell you all the bargain. Maybe you won't send the letter when you hear that. The rest is that you show me the reply to my part of it."

"Oh, that's easy! I wouldn't have the slightest objection to showing you the whole letter."

He signed his name, folded the sheets and slipped them into his pocket.

"Where are we going and what do we take?"

"Will you go, mother?" asked Elnora.

"I have a little work that should be done," said Mrs. Comstock. "Could you spare me? Where do you want to go?"

"We will go down to Aunt Margaret's and see her a few minutes and get Billy. We will be back in time for supper."

Mrs. Comstock smiled as she watched them down the road. What a splendid looking pair of young creatures they were! How finely proportioned, how full of vitality! Then her face grew troubled as she saw them in earnest conversation. Just as she was wishing she had not trusted her precious girl with so much of a stranger, she saw Elnora stoop to lift a branch and peer under. The mother grew content. Elnora was thinking only of her work. She was to be trusted utterly.

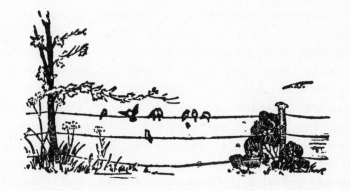

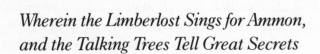

CHAPTER 16

Wherein the Limberlost Sings for Ammon,
and the Talking Trees Tell Great Secrets

A FEW days later Ammon handed Elnora a sheet of paper and she read: "In your condition I should think the moth hunting and life at that cabin would be very good for you, but for any sake keep away from that Grosbeak person, and don't come home with your head full of granger ideas. No doubt he has a remarkable voice, but I can't bear untrained singers, and don't you get the idea that a June song is perennial. You are not hearing the music he will make when the four babies get the scarlet fever and the measles, and the gadding wife leaves him at home to care for them then. Poor soul, I pity her! How she exists where rampant cows bellow at you, frogs croak, mosquitoes consume you, the butter goes to oil in summer and bricks in winter, while the pump freezes every day, and there is no earthly amusement, and no society! Poor things! Can't you influence him to move? No wonder she gads when she has a chance! I should die. If you are thinking of settling in the country, think also of a woman who is satisfied with white and brown to accompany you! Brown! Of all deadly colours! I should go mad in brown."

Elnora laughed as she read. Her face was dimpling as she handed back the sheet. "Who's ahead?" she asked.

"Who do you think?" he parried.

"She is," said Elnora. "Are you going to tell her in your next that R. B. Grosbeak is a bird, and that he probably will spend the winter in a wild plum thicket in Tennessee?"

"No," said Ammon. "I shall tell her that I understand her ideas of life perfectly, and, of course, I never shall ask her to deal with oily butter and frozen pumps —"

"— and measley babies," interpolated Elnora.

"Exactly!" said Ammon. "Just the same I find so much to counterbalance those things, that I should not object to bearing them myself, in view of the recompense. Where do we go and what do we do to-day?"

"We will have to wander along the roads and around the edge of the Limberlost to-day," said Elnora. "Mother is making strawberry preserves, and she can't come until she finishes. Suppose we go down to the swamp and I'll show you what is left of the flower-room that Terrence O'More, the big lumber man of Great Rapids, made when he was a homeless boy here. Of course, you have heard the story?"

"Yes, and I've met the O'Mores who are frequently in Chicago society. They have friends there. I think them one ideal couple."

"That sounds like they might be the only one, or close to it," said Elnora, "and, indeed, they are not.

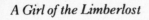

I know dozens. Aunt Margaret and Uncle Wesley are another, the Brownlees another, and my mathematics professor and his wife. The world is full of happy people, but no one ever hears of them. You have to fight and make a scandal to get into the papers. No one knows about all the happy people. I am happy myself, and just look how perfectly inconspicuous I am."

"You only need go where you will be seen," began Ammon, when he remembered and finished. "What do we take to-day?"

"Ourselves," said Elnora. "I have a vagabond streak in my blood and it's in evidence. I am going to show you where real flowers grow, real birds sing, and if I feel quite right about it, perhaps I shall raise a note or two myself."

"Oh, do you sing?" asked Ammon politely.

"At times," answered Elnora. "'As do the birds, because I must,' but don't be scared. The mood does not possess me often. Perhaps I shan't raise a note when we get there."

They went down the road to the swamp, climbed the snake fence, followed the path to the old trail and then turned south along it. Elnora indicated to Ammon the trail with remnants of sagging barbed wire.

"It was ten years ago," she said. "I was just a little school girl, but I wandered widely even then, and no one cared. I saw him often. He had been in a city institution all his life, when he took the job of keeping timber thieves out of this swamp, before many trees

316

had been cut. It was strong man's work, and he was a frail boy, but he grew hardier as he lived out of doors. This trail we are on is the path his feet first wore, in those days when he was insane with fear and eaten up with loneliness, but he stuck to his work and won out. I used to come down to the road and creep in among the bushes as far as I dared, to watch him pass. He walked mostly, sometimes he rode a wheel.

"Some days his face was dreadfully sad, some days it was so determined a little child could see the force in it, and once it was radiant. That day the Swamp Angel was with him. I can't tell you what she was like. I never saw any one who resembled her. He stopped near here to show her a bird's nest. Then they went on to a sort of flower-room he had made, and he sang for her. By the time he left, I had gotten bold enough to come out on the trail, and I met the big Scotchman Freckles lived with. He saw me catching moths and butterflies, so he took me to the flower-room and gave me everything there. I don't dare come alone often, and so I can't keep it up as he did, but you can see something of how it was."

Elnora led the way and Ammon followed. The outlines of the room were not distinct, because many of the trees were gone, but Elnora showed how it had been as nearly as she could.

"The swamp is almost ruined now," she said. "The maples, walnuts, and cherries are all gone. The talking trees are the only things left worth while."

"The 'talking trees'! I don't understand," commented Ammon.

"No wonder!" laughed Elnora. "They are my discovery. You know all trees whisper and talk during the summer, but there are two that have so much to say they keep on the whole winter, when the others are silent. The beeches and oaks so love to talk, they cling to their dead, dry leaves. In the winter the winds are stiffest and blow most, so these trees whisper, chatter, sob, laugh, and at times roar until the sound is deafening. They never cease until new leaves come out in the spring to push off the old ones. I love to stand beneath them with my ear to the great trunks, interpreting what they say to fit my moods. The beeches branch low, and their leaves are small so they only know common earthly things; but the oaks run straight above almost all other trees before they branch, their arms are mighty, their leaves large. They meet the winds that travel around the globe, and from them learn the big things."

Ammon studied the girl face. "What do the beeches tell you, Elnora?" he asked gently.

"To be patient, to be unselfish, to do unto others as I would have them do to me."

"And the oaks?"

"They say 'be true,' 'live a clean life,' 'send your soul up here and let the winds of the world teach it what honour achieves.'"

"Wonderful secrets, those!" marvelled Ammon. "Are they telling them now? Could I hear?"

"No. They are only gossipping now. This is play-time. They tell the big secrets to a white world, when the music inspires them."

"The music?"

"All other trees are harps in the winter. Their trunks are the frames, their branches the strings, the winds the musicians. When the air is cold and clear, the world very white, and the harp music swelling, then the talking trees tell the strengthening, uplifting things."

"You wonderful girl!" cried Ammon. "What a woman you will be!"

"If I am a woman at all worth while, it will be because I have had such wonderful opportunities," said Elnora. "Not every girl is driven to the forest to learn what God has to say there. Here are the remains of Freckles's room. The time the Angel came here he sang to her, and I listened. I never heard music like that. No wonder she loved him. Everyone who knew him did, and they do yet. Try that log, it makes a fairly good seat. This old store box was his treasure house, just as it's now mine. I will show you my dearest possession. I do not dare take it home because mother can't overcome her dislike for it. It was my father's, and in some ways I am like him. This is the strongest."

Elnora lifted the violin and began to play. She wore a school dress of green gingham, with the sleeves rolled to the elbows. She seemed a part of the setting all around her. Her head shone like a small dark sun, and her face never had seemed so rose-flushed and fair.

From the instant. she drew the bow, her lips parted and her eyes fastened on something far away in the swamp, and never did she give more of that impression of feeling for her notes and repeating something audible only to her. Ammon was too near to get the best effect. He arose and stepped back several yards, leaning against a large tree, looking and listening with all his soul.

As he changed positions he saw that Mrs. Comstock had followed them, and was standing on the trail, where she could not have helped hearing everything Elnora had said. So to Ammon before her and the mother watching on the trail, Elnora played the Song of the Limberlost. It seemed as if the swamp hushed all its other voices and spoke only through her dancing bow. The mother out on the trail had heard it all, once before from the girl, many times from her father. To the man it was a revelation. He stood so stunned he forgot Mrs. Comstock. He tried to realize what a great city audience would say to that music, from such a player, with a like background, and he could not imagine.

He was wondering what he dared say, how much he might express, when the last note fell and the girl laid the violin in the case, closed the door, locked it and hid the key in the rotting wood at the end of a log. Then she came to him. Ammon stood looking at her curiously.

"I wonder," he said, "what people would say to that?"

"I did it in public once," said Elnora. "I think they liked it, fairly well. I had a note yesterday offering

me the leadership of the high school orchestra in Onabasha. I can take it as well as not. None of my talks
to the grades come the first thing in the morning. I
can play a few minutes in the orchestra and reach the
rooms in plenty of time. It will be more work that I
love, and like finding the money. I would gladly play
for nothing, just to be able to express myself."

"With some people it makes a regular battlefield of
the human heart — this struggle for self-expression,"
said Ammon. "You are going to do beautiful work in
the world, and do it well. When I realize that your
violin belonged to your father, that he played it before
you were born, and it no doubt affected your mother
strongly, and then couple with that the years you have
roamed these fields and swamps finding in nature all
you had to lavish your great heart upon, I can see how
you evolved. I understand what you mean by self-
expression. I know something of what you have to express. The world never so wanted your message as it
does now. It is hungry for the things you know. I can
see easily how your position came to you. What you
have to give is taught in no college, and I am not sure
but you would spoil yourself if you tried to run your
mind through a set groove with hundreds of others. I
never thought I should say such a thing to anyone, but
I do say to you, and I honestly believe it; give up the
college idea. Your mind does not need that sort of development, it is far past it. Stick close to your work in
the woods. You are getting so infinitely greater on it,

than the best college student I ever knew, that there is no comparison. When you have money to spend, take that violin and go to one of the world's great masters and let the Limberlost sing to him; if he thinks he can improve it, very well. I have my doubts."

"Do you really mean that you would give up all idea of going to college, if you were me?"

"I really mean it," said Ammon. "If I now held the money to send you in my hands, and could give it to you in some way you would accept I would tear it up and throw it away first. I do not know why it is the lot of the world always to want something different from what life gives them. If you only could realize it, my girl, you are in college, and have been always. You are in the school of experience, and it has taught you to think, and given you a heart. God knows I envy the man who wins it! You have been in the college of the Limberlost all your life, and I never met a graduate from any other institution who could begin to compare with you in sanity, clarity, and interesting knowledge. I wouldn't even advise you to read too many books on your lines. You get your stuff first hand, and you know that you are right. What you should do is to begin early to practise self-expression. Don't wait too long to tell us about the woods as you know them."

"Follow the course of the Bird Woman, you mean?" asked Elnora.

"In your own way; with your own light. She won't live forever. You are younger, and you will be ready

to begin where she ends. The swamp has given you all
you need so far, now you give it to the world in payment.
College be confounded! Go to work and show people
what there is in you!"

Not until then did he remember that Mrs. Comstock
was somewhere very near.

"Should we go out to the trail and see if your mother
is coming?" he asked.

"Here she is now," said Elnora. "Gracious, it's
a mercy I got that violin put away in time! I didn't
expect her so soon," whispered the girl as she turned
and went toward her mother. Mrs. Comstock's face
was a study as she looked at Elnora.

"I forgot that you were making sun-preserves and
they didn't require much cooking," she said. "We
should have waited for you."

"Not at all!" answered Mrs. Comstock. "Have you
found anything yet?"

"Nothing that I can show you," said Elnora. "I
am not sure but I have found an idea that will revolu-
tionize the whole course of my work, thought, and
ambitions."

"'Ambitions!' My, what a hefty word!" laughed
Mrs. Comstock. "Now, who would suspect a little
red-haired country girl of harbouring such a deadly
germ in her body? Can you tell mother about it?"

"Not if you talk to me that way, I can't," said Elnora.

"Well, I guess we better let ambition lie. I've
always heard it was safest asleep. If you ever get a

bona fide attack, it will be time to attend it. Let's hunt specimens. It is June. Philip and I are in the grades. You have an hour to put an idea into our heads that will stick for a lifetime, and grow for good. That's the way I look at your job. Now, what are you going to give us? We don't want any old silly stuff that has been hashed over and over, we want a big new idea to plant in our hearts. Come on, Miss Teacher, what is the boiled-down, double-distilled essence of June? Give it to us strong. We are large enough to furnish it developing ground. Hurry up! Time is short and we are waiting. What is the miracle of June? What one thing epitomizes the whole month, and makes it just a little different from any other?"

"The birth of these big night moths," said Elnora promptly.

Ammon clapped his hands. The tears started to Mrs. Comstock's eyes. She took Elnora in her arms, and kissed her forehead.

"You'll do!" she said. "June is June, not because it has bloom, bird, fruit, or flower, exclusive to it alone. It's half May and half July in all of them. But as I figure it, it's just June, when it comes to these great, velvet-winged night moths which sweep its moonlit skies, consummating their scheme of creation, and dropping like a bloomed-out flower. Give them moths for June. Then make that the basis of your year's work. Find the distinctive feature of each month, the one thing which marks it a time apart, and hit them squarely between the eyes with it. Even the babies of the lowest grades can comprehend moths when they see a few emerge, and learn their history, as it can be lived before them. You should show your specimens in pairs, then their eggs, the growing caterpillars, and then the cocoons. You want to dig out the red heart of every month in the year, and hold it pulsing before them.

"I can't name all of them off-hand, but I think of one more right now. February belongs to our winter birds. It is then the great horned owl of the swamp courts his mate, the big hawks pair, and even the crows begin to take notice. These are truly our birds. Like the poor we have them always with us. You should hear the musicians of this swamp in February, Philip, on a mellow night. Oh, but they are in earnest! For twenty-one years I've listened by night to the great owls, all the smaller sizes, the foxes, coons, and every resident left in these woods, and by day to the hawks, yellow-hammers, sap-suckers, titmice, crows, and all our winter birds. Only just now it's come to me that the distinctive feature of February is not linen bleaching, nor sugar making; it's the love month of our very own birds. Give them hawks and owls for February, Elnora."

The girl looked at Ammon with flashing eyes. "How's that?" she said. "Don't you think I will make it, with such help? You should hear the concert she is talking about! It is simply indescribable when the ground is covered with snow, and the moonlight white."

"It's about the best music we have," said Mrs. Comstock. "I just wonder if you couldn't copy that alone and make a strong, original piece out of it for your violin, Elnora?"

There was one tense breath, then—"I could try," said Elnora simply.

Ammon rushed to the rescue. "We must go to work," he said, and began examining a walnut branch for Luna moth eggs. Elnora joined him while Mrs. Comstock drew her embroidery from her pocket and sat on a log. She said she was tired, they could come for her when they were ready to go. She could hear their voices all around her until she called them at supper time. When they came to her she stood waiting on the trail, the sewing in one hand, the violin in the other. Elnora became very white, but took the trail without a word. Ammon, unable to see a woman carry a heavier load than he, reached for the instrument. Mrs. Comstock shook her head. She carried the violin home, took it into her room and closed the door. Elnora turned to Ammon.

"If she destroys that, I will die!" cried the girl.

"She won't!" said Ammon. "You misunderstand her. She wouldn't have said what she did about the owls, if she had meant to. She is your mother. No one loves you as she does. Trust her! Myself — I think she's simply great!"

Mrs. Comstock returned with serene face, and all of them helped with the supper. When it was over Ammon

and Elnora sorted and classified the afternoon's specimens, and made a trip to the woods to paint and light
several trees for moths. When they came back Mrs.
Comstock sat in the arbour, and they joined her. The
moonlight was so intense, print could have been read by
it. The damp night air held odours near to earth,
making flower and tree perfume strong. A thousand
insects were serenading, and in the maple the grosbeak
occasionally said a reassuring word to his wife, while
she answered that all was well. A whip-poor-will
wailed in the swamp and back by the blue-bordered
pool a chat complained disconsolately. Mrs. Comstock
went into the cabin, but she returned almost instantly,
laying the violin and bow across Elnora's lap. "I wish
you would give us a little music," she said.

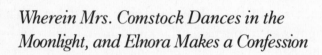

CHAPTER **17**

Wherein Mrs. Comstock Dances in the Moonlight, and Elnora Makes a Confession

BILLY was swinging in the hammock, at peace with himself and all the world, when he thought he heard something. He sat bolt upright, his eyes staring. Once he opened his lips, then thought again and closed them. The sound persisted. Billy vaulted the fence, and ran down the road with his queer sidewise hop. When he neared the Comstock cabin, he left the warm dust of the highway and stepped softly at slower pace over the rank grasses by the roadside. He had heard aright. The violin was in the grape arbour, singing like mad, singing a perfect jumble of everything, poured out in an exultant tumult. The strings were voicing the joy of a happy girl heart.

Billy climbed the fence enclosing the west woods and crept down toward the arbour. He was not a spy and not a sneak. He merely wanted to satisfy his child-heart as to whether Mrs. Comstock was at home, and Elnora at last playing her loved violin with her mother's consent. One peep sufficed. Mrs. Comstock sat in the moonlight, her head leaning against the arbour; on her face was a look of perfect peace and contentment.

As he stared at her the bow hesitated a second and Mrs. Comstock spoke.

"That's all very melodious and sweet," she said, "but I do wish you could play Money Musk and some of the tunes I danced as a girl."

Elnora had been avoiding carefully every note that might be reminiscent of her father. At the words she laughed softly and struck into "Turkey in the Straw." An instant later Mrs. Comstock was dancing like mad in the moonlight. Ammon sprang to her side, caught her in his arms, while to Elnora's laughter and the violin's impetus they danced until they dropped panting on the arbour bench.

Billy scarcely knew when he got back on the road. His light feet barely touched the soft way, so swiftly he flew. He vaulted the fence and burst into the house.

"Aunt Margaret! Uncle Wesley!" he screamed. "Listen! Listen! She's playing it! Elnora's playing her violin at home! And Aunt Kate is dancing like anything before the arbour! I saw her in the moonlight! I ran down! Oh, Aunt Margaret!"

Billy fled to his haven and sobbed on Margaret's breast.

"Why, Billy!" she chided. "Don't cry, you little dunce! That's what we've all prayed for these many years; but you must be mistaken about Kate. I can't believe it."

Billy lifted his head. "Well, you just have to!" he said. "When I say I saw anything, Uncle Wesley knows

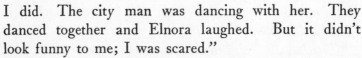

I did. The city man was dancing with her. They danced together and Elnora laughed. But it didn't look funny to me; I was scared."

"Who was it said 'wonders would never cease'?" asked Wesley. "You mark my word, once you get Kate Comstock started, you can't stop her. There's a wagon load of penned-up force in her. Dancing in the moonlight! Well, I'll be hanged!"

Billy was at his side instantly. "Well, whoever does it will have to hang me, too," he cried.

Sinton threw his arm around Billy and drew him close. "Tell us all about it, son," he said. Billy told. "And when Elnora just stopped a breath, 'Can't you play some of the old things I knew when I was a girl?' said her ma. Then Elnora began to do a thing that made you want to whirl round and round, and quicker 'an scat there was her ma a-whirling. The city man, he ups and grabs her and whirls, too, and back in the woods I was going just like they did. Elnora begins to laugh, and I ran to tell you, 'cos I knew you'd like to know. Now, all the world is right, ain't it?" ended Billy as he leaned against Sinton in supreme satisfaction.

"You just bet it is!" said Wesley.

Billy looked steadily at Margaret. "Is it, Aunt Margaret?"

Margaret Sinton smiled at him bravely.

An hour later when Billy was ready to climb the stairs to his room, he went to Margaret to say good night. He leaned against her an instant, and brought his lips close her ear. "Wish I could get your little girls back for you!" he whispered and dashed for the stairs.

Down at the Comstock cabin the violin played on until Elnora was so tired she scarcely could lift the bow. Then Ammon went home. The women walked to the gate with him, and stood watching him from sight.

"That's what I call one decent young man!" said Mrs. Comstock. "To see him fit in with us, you'd think he'd been raised in a cabin; but it's likely he's always had the very cream o' the pot."

"Yes, I think so," laughed Elnora, "but it hasn't hurt him. I've never seen anything I could criticize. He's teaching me so much, unconsciously. You know he graduated from Harvard, and has several degrees in law. He's coming in the morning, and we are going to put in a big day on Catocalæ."

"Which is —— ?"

"Those gray moths with wings that fold back like big flies, and they appear as if they had been carved from old wood. Then, when they fly, the lower wings flash out and they are red and black, or gold and black, or pink and black, or dozens of bright, beautiful colours combined with black. No one ever has classified all of them and written their complete history, unless the Bird Woman is doing it now. She wants everything she can get about them."

"I remember," said Mrs. Comstock. "They are mighty pretty things. I've started up slews of them

from the vines covering the logs, all my life. I must be cautious and catch them after this, but they seem powerful spry. I might get hold of something rare." She thought intently and added, "And wouldn't know it if I did. It would just be my luck. I've had the rarest thing on earth in reach this many a day and only had the wit to cinch it just as it was going. I'll bet I don't let anything else escape me."

Next morning Ammon came early, and he and Elnora went at once to the fields and woods. Mrs. Comstock had come to believe so implicitly in him that she now stayed at home to complete the work before she joined them, and when she did she often sat sewing, leaving them wandering hours at a time. It was noon before she finished, and then she packed a basket of lunch. She found Elnora and Philip near the violet patch, which was still in its prime. They all lunched together in the shade of a wild crab thicket, with flowers spread at their feet, and the gold orioles streaking the air with flashes of light and trailing ecstasy behind them, while the red-wings, as always, asked the most impertinent questions. Then Mrs. Comstock carried the basket back to the cabin, and Ammon and Elnora sat on a log, resting a few minutes. They had unexpected luck, and both were eager to continue the search.

"Do you remember your promise about these violets?" asked Ammon. "To-morrow is Edith's birthday, and if I'd put them special delivery on the morning train, she'd get them in the late afternoon. They ought to keep well that long. She leaves for the North next day."

"Of course, you can have them," said Elnora. "We will quit long enough before supper to gather a great bunch. They can be packed so they will carry all right. They should be perfectly fresh, especially if we gather them this evening and let them drink all night."

Then they went back to hunt Catocalæ. It was a long and a happy search. It led them into new, unexplored nooks of the woods, by a red-poll nest, and where goldfinches prospected for thistledown for the cradles they would line a little later. It led them into real forest, where deep, dark pools lay, where the hermit thrush and the wood robin extracted the essence from all other bird melody, and poured it out in their pure bell-tone notes. It seemed as if every old gray tree-trunk, slab of loose bark, and prostrate log yielded the flashing gray treasures; while of all others they seemed to take alarm most easily, and be most difficult to capture.

Ammon came to Elnora at dusk, daintily holding one by the body, its dark wings showing and its long slender legs trying to clasp his fingers and creep from his hold.

"Oh, for mercy's sake!" cried Elnora, and stared at him.

"I half believe it!" exulted Ammon.

"Did you ever see one?"

"Only in collections, and mighty seldom there."

Elnora studied the black wings intently. "I surely believe that's Sappho," she marvelled. "The Bird Woman will be overjoyed."

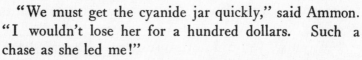

"We must get the cyanide jar quickly," said Ammon. "I wouldn't lose her for a hundred dollars. Such a chase as she led me!"

Elnora got the jar and began gathering up paraphernalia.

"When you make a find like that," she said, "it's the right time to quit and feel glorious all the rest of that day. I tell you I'm proud! We will go now. We have barely time to carry out our plans before supper. Won't mother be pleased to see that we have a rare one?"

"I'd like to see anyone more pleased than I am!" said Philip Ammon. "I feel as if I'd earned my supper to-night. Let's go."

He took the greater part of the load and stepped aside for Elnora to precede him. She went down the path, broken by the grazing cattle, toward the cabin and nearest the violet patch she stopped, laid down her net, and the things she carried. Ammon passed her and hurried straight toward the back gate.

"Aren't you going to ——?" began Elnora.

"I'm going to get this moth home in a hurry," he said. "This cyanide has lost its strength, and it's not working well. We need some fresh in the jar."

He had forgotten the violets! Elnora stood looking after him, a curious expression on her face. One second so —- then she picked up the net and followed. At the blue-bordered pool she paused and half turned back, then she closed her lips firmly and went on. It was nine o'clock when Ammon said good-bye, and started to town. His gay whistle floated to them from the farthest corner of the Limberlost. Elnora complained of being tired, so she went to her room and to bed. But sleep would not come. Thought was racing in her brain and the longer she lay the wider awake she grew. At last she softly slipped from bed, lighted her lamp and began opening boxes. Then she went to work. Two hours later a beautiful birch bark basket, strongly and artistically made stood on her table. She set a tiny alarm clock at three, returned to bed and fell asleep instantly with a smile on her lips.

She was on the floor with the first tinkle of the alarm, and hastily dressing, she picked up the basket and a box to fit it, crept down the stairs, and out to the violet patch. She was unafraid as it was so near morning, and lining the basket with damp mosses she swiftly began picking with practised hands, the youngest of the flowers. It was so dark she scarcely could tell which were freshest at times, but day soon came creeping over the Limberlost and peeped down at her. The robins awoke all their neighbours, and a babel of bird notes filled the air. The dew was dripping, and the first strong rays of light fell on a world in which Elnora worshipped. When the basket was filled to overflowing, she set it in the stout pasteboard box, packed it solid with mosses, tied it firmly and slipped under the cord a note she had written the previous night.

Then she took a short cut across the woods and walked swiftly to Onabasha. It was after six o'clock, but all

of the city she wished to avoid were asleep. She had no trouble in finding a small boy out, and she stood at a distance waiting while he rang Dr. Ammon's bell and delivered the package for Philip to a maid, with the note which was to be given him at once.

On the way home through the woods passing some baited trees she collected the captive moths. She entered the kitchen with them so naturally that Mrs. Comstock made no comment. After breakfast Elnora went to her room, cleared away all trace of the night's work and was out in the arbour mounting moths when Ammon came down the road. "I am tired sitting," she said to her mother. "I think I will walk a few rods and meet him."

"Who's a trump?" called Ammon from afar.

"Well, not you!" retorted Elnora. "Confess that you forgot!"

"Completely!" said Ammon. "But luckily it would not have been fatal. I wrote Polly last week to send Edith something appropriate and handsome to-day, with my card. But that touch from the woods will be mighty effective. Thank you more than I can say. Aunt Anna and I unpacked it to see the basket, and it was a beauty. She says you are always doing things like that."

"Well, I hope not!" laughed Elnora. "If you'd seen me sneaking out before dawn, not to waken mother and coming in with moths to make her think I'd been to the trees, you'd know it was a most especial occasion."

336

Then Ammon understood two things. Elnora's mother did not know of the early morning trip to the city, and the girl had come to meet him to tell him so.

"You were a brick to do it!" he whispered as he closed the gate behind them. "I'll never forget you for it. Thank you ever so much. You are too kind to me."

"I did not do that for you," said Elnora tersely. "I did it mostly to preserve my own self-respect. I saw you were forgetting. If I did it for anything besides that, I did it for her."

"Just look what I've brought!" said Ammon entering the arbour and greeting Mrs. Comstock. "Borrowed it of the Bird Woman. And it isn't hers. A rare edition of Catocalæ with coloured plates. I told her the best I could, and she said to try for Sappho here. I suspect the Bird Woman will be out presently. She was all excitement."

Then they bent over the book together and with the mounted moth before them determined her family. The Bird Woman did come later, and carried the moth away to put into a book and Elnora and Ammon were freshly filled with enthusiasm.

So these days were the beginning of the weeks that followed. Six of them flying on Time's wings, each filled to the brim with interest. After June, the moth hunts grew less frequent; the fields and woods were scoured for material for Elnora's grade work. The most absorbing occupation they found was in carrying

out Mrs. Comstock's suggestion to learn the vital thing for which each month was distinctive, and make that the key to the nature work.   They wrote out a list of the months, opposite each the things all of them could suggest which seemed to pertain to that month alone, and then tried to sift until they found something typical. Mrs. Comstock was a great help. Her mother had been Dutch and had brought from Holland numerous quaint sayings and superstitions easily traceable to Pliny's Natural History; and in Mrs. Comstock's early years in Ohio she had heard much Indian talk among her elders, so she knew the signs of each season, and sometimes they helped. Always her practical thought and sterling common-sense were useful. When they were afield until exhausted they came back to the cabin for food, to prepare specimens and classify them, and to talk over the day. Sometimes Ammon brought books and read while Elnora and her mother worked, and every night Mrs. Comstock asked for the violin. Her perfect hunger for music was sufficient evidence of how she had suffered without it.   So the days crept by, golden, filled with useful work and pure pleasure.

The grosbeak had led the family in the maple abroad and a second brood, in a wild grape vine clambering over the well, was almost ready for flight. The dust lay thick on the country roads, the days grew warmer; summer was just poising to slip into fall, and Ammon stayed on, coming each day as if he had belonged there always and expected to remain forever.

One warm August afternoon Mrs. Comstock looked up from the ruffle on which she was engaged to see a blue-coated messenger enter the gate.

"Is Philip Ammon here?" asked the boy.

"He is," said Mrs. Comstock.

"I have a message for him."

"He is in the woods back of the cabin. I will ring the bell, and he will come. Do you know if it is important?"

"Urgent," said the boy; "I rode hard."

Mrs. Comstock stepped to the back door and clanged the dinner bell sharply, paused a second, and rang again. In a short time Ammon and Elnora came down the path on the run.

"Are you ill, mother?" cried Elnora.

Mrs. Comstock indicated the boy. "There is an important message for Philip," she said.

Ammon muttered an excuse and tore open the telegram. His colour faded slightly. "I have to take the first train," he said. "My father is ill and I am needed."

He handed the sheet to Elnora. "I have about two hours, as I remember the trains north, but my things are all over Uncle Doc's house, so I must go at once."

"Certainly," said Elnora giving back the message. "Is there anything I can do to help? Mother, get Philip a glass of buttermilk to start on. I will gather what you have here."

"Never mind. There is nothing of importance. I

don't want to be hampered. I'll send for it if I miss
anything I need."

Ammon drank the milk, said good-bye to Mrs. Comstock, repeatedly thanked her for all her kindness, and
turned to Elnora.

"Will you walk to the edge of the Limberlost with
me?" he asked. Elnora assented. Mrs. Comstock
followed to the gate, urged him to come again soon, and
repeated her good-bye. Then she went back to the
arbour to await Elnora's return. As she watched down
the road she smiled softly.

"I had an idea he would speak to me first," she thought,
"but this may change things some. He hasn't time.
Elnora will come back a happy girl, and she has good
reason. He is a model young man. Her lot will be
mighty different from mine."

She picked up her embroidery and began setting
dainty, precise little stitches, possible only to certain
women.

On the road Elnora spoke first. "I do hope it is
nothing serious," she said. "Is he usually strong?"

"Quite strong," said Philip. "I am not at all alarmed
but I am very much ashamed. I have been well enough
for the last month to have gone home and helped him
with some critical cases that were keeping him at work
in this heat. I was enjoying myself so I wouldn't offer
to go, and he would not ask me to come, so long as he
could help it. I have allowed him to overtax himself
until he is down, and mother and Polly are north at our

340

cottage. He's never been sick before, and it's probable I am to blame that he is now."

"He intended you to stay this long when you came," urged Elnora.

"Yes, but it's hot in Chicago. I should have remembered him. He is always thinking of me. Possibly he has needed me for days. I am ashamed to go to him in splendid condition and admit that I was having such a fine time I forgot to come home."

"You have had a fine time, then?" asked Elnora.

They had reached the fence. Ammon vaulted over to take a short cut across the fields. He turned and looked at her.

"The best, the sweetest, and most wholesome time any man ever had in this world," he said. "Elnora, if I talked hours I couldn't make you understand what a girl I think you are. I never in all my life hated anything as I hate leaving you. It seems to me that I have not strength to do it."

"If you have gotten anything worth while from me," said Elnora, "that should be it. Just to have strength to go to your duty, and to go quickly."

Ammon caught the hand she held out to him in both his. "Elnora, these days we have had together, have they been sweet to you?"

"Beautiful days!" said Elnora. "Each like a perfect dream to be thought over and over all my life. Oh, they have been the only really happy days I've ever known; these days rich with mother's love, and doing

useful work with your help. Good-bye! You must
hurry!"

Ammon gazed at her. He tried to drop her hand,
and only clutched it closer. Suddenly he drew her
toward him. "Elnora," he whispered, "will you kiss
me good-bye?"

Elnora drew back and stared at him with wide eyes.
"I'd strike you sooner!" she said. "Have I ever said
or done anything in your presence that made you feel
free to ask that, Philip Ammon?"

"No!" panted Ammon. "No! I think so much of
you, I just wanted to touch your lips once before I left
you. You know Elnora ——"

"Don't distress yourself," said Elnora calmly. "I
am broad enough to judge you sanely. I know what
you mean. It would be no harm to you. It would not
matter to me, but here we will think of someone else.
Edith Carr would not want your lips to-morrow if she
knew they had touched mine to-day. I was wise to say
'Go quickly!'"

Ammon still clung to her. "Will you write me?" he
begged.

"No," said Elnora. "There is nothing to say, save
good-bye. We can do that now."

Ammon held on. "Promise that you will write me
only one letter," he urged. "I want just one message
from you to lock in my desk, and keep always. Promise
you will write once, Elnora."

Elnora looked straight into his eyes, and smiled

serenely. "If the talking trees tell me this winter, the secret of how a man may grow perfect, I will write you what it is, Philip. In all the time I have known you, I never have liked you so little. Good-bye."

She drew away her hand and swiftly turned back to the road. Philip Ammon, wordless, started toward Onabasha on a run.

Elnora crossed the road, climbed the fence and sought the shelter of their own woods. She took a diagonal course and followed it until she came to the path leading past the violet patch. She went down this hurriedly. Her hands were clenched at her sides, her eyes dry and bright, her cheeks red-flushed, and her breath coming fast. When she reached the patch she turned into it and stood looking around her.

The mosses were dry, the flowers gone, weeds a foot high covered it. She turned away and went on down the path until she was almost in sight of the cabin.

Mrs. Comstock smiled and waited in the arbour until it dawned on her that Elnora was a long time coming, so she went to the gate. The road stretched away toward the Limberlost empty and lonely. Then she knew that Elnora had gone into their own woods and would come in the back way. She could not understand why the girl did not hurry to her with what she would have to tell. She went out and wandered around the garden. Then she stepped into the path and started back along the way leading to the woods, past the pool now framed in a thick setting of yellow lilies. Then

she saw, and stopped, gasping for breath. Her hands
flew up and her lined face grew ghastly. She stared at
the sky and then at the prostrate girl figure. Over and
over she tried to speak, but only a dry breath came.
She turned and fled back to the garden.

In the familiar enclosure she gazed around her like a
caged animal seeking escape. The sun beat down on
her bare head mercilessly, and mechanically she moved
over to the shade of a half-grown hickory tree that
voluntarily had sprouted by the milk house. At her
feet lay an axe with which she made kindlings for fires.
She stooped and picked it up. That prone figure sobbing in the grass caught her with a renewed spasm.
She shut her eyes as if to close it out. That made
hearing so acute she felt certain she heard Elnora
moaning by the path. The eyes flew open. They fell
squarely on a few spindling tomato plants set too
near the tree and stunted by its shade. Mrs. Comstock whirled on the hickory and swung the axe. Her
hair shook down, her clothing became disarranged,
in the heat the perspiration streamed, but stroke fell
on stroke until the tree crashed over, grazing a corner
of the milk house and smashing the garden fence on
the east.

At the sound Elnora sprang to her feet and came running down the garden walk. "Mother!" she cried.
"Mother! What in the world are you doing?"

Mrs. Comstock wiped her ghastly face on her apron.
"I've laid out to cut that tree for years," she said. "It

shades the beets in the morning, and the tomatoes in the afternoon!"

Elnora uttered one wild little cry and fled into her mother's arms. "Oh, mother!" she sobbed. "Will you ever forgive me?"

Mrs. Comstock's arms swept together in a tight grip around Elnora.

"There isn't a thing on God's footstool from a to izzard I won't forgive you, my precious girl!" she said. "Tell mother what it is!"

Elnora lifted her wet face. "He told me," she panted, "just as soon as he decently could — that second day he told me. Almost all his life he's been engaged to a girl at home. He never cared anything about me. He was just interested in the moths and growing strong."

Mrs. Comstock's arms tightened. With a shaking hand she stroked the bright hair.

"Tell me, honey," she said. "Is he to blame for a single one of these tears?"

"Not one!" sobbed Elnora. "Oh, mother, I won't forgive you if you don't believe that. Not one! He never said, or looked, or did anything all the world might not have known. He likes me very much as a friend. He hated to go dreadfully!"

"Elnora!" the mother's head bent until the white hair mingled with the brown. "Elnora, why didn't you tell me at first?"

Elnora caught her breath in a sharp snatch. "I

know I should!" she sobbed. "I will bear any punishment for not, but I didn't feel as if I possibly could. I was afraid."

"Afraid of what?" the shaking hand was on the hair again.

"Afraid you wouldn't let him come!" panted Elnora. "And, oh, mother, I wanted him so!"

CHAPTER 18

*Wherein Mrs. Comstock Experiments
with Rejuvenation, and Elnora Teaches
Natural History*

FOR the next week Mrs. Comstock and Elnora worked so hard there was no time to talk, and they were compelled to sleep from physical exhaustion. Neither of them made any pretense of eating, for they could not swallow without a great effort, so they drank milk and worked. Elnora went on setting bait for Catacolæ and Sphinginæ, which, unlike the big moths of June, live several months. She took all the dragon flies and butterflies she could, and when she went over the list for the man of India, she found, to her amazement, that with Ammon's help she once more had it complete save a pair of Yellow Emperors.

This circumstance was so amazing she had a fleeting thought of writing Ammon and asking him to see if he could not secure her a pair. She did tell the Bird Woman, and from every source at her command she tried to complete the series with these moths, and could not find any for sale.

"I think the mills of the Gods are grinding this grist,"

said Elnora, "and we might as well wait patiently until they choose to send a Yellow Emperor."

Mrs. Comstock invented work. When she had nothing more to do, she hoed in the garden although the earth was hard and dry and there were no plants that really needed attention. Then came a notification that Elnora would be compelled to attend a week's session of the Teachers' Institute held at the county seat twenty miles north of Onabasha the following week. That gave them something of which to think and real work to do. Elnora was requested to bring her violin. As she was on the programme of one of the most important sessions for a talk on nature work in grade schools, she was driven to prepare her speech, and to select and practise some music. Her mother turned her attention to clothing.

They went to Onabasha together and purchased a simple and appropriate fall suit and hat, goods for a dainty little coloured frock, and a dress skirt and several fancy waists. Margaret Sinton came down and the sewing began. When everything was finished and packed, Elnora kissed her mother good-bye at the depot, and the train pulled out. Mrs. Comstock went into the waiting-room and dropped into a seat to rest. Her heart was so sore her whole right side felt tender. She was half starved for the food she had no appetite to take. She had worked in dogged determination until she was exhausted. For a time she simply sat and rested. Then she began to think. She was glad Elnora had gone where she would be compelled to fix her mind on other things for a few days. She remembered the girl had said she wanted to go.

School would begin the following week. She thought over what Elnora would have to do to accomplish her work successfully. She would be compelled to arise at six o'clock, walk three miles through varying weather, lead the high school orchestra, and then put in the rest of the day travelling from building to building over the city, teaching a specified length of time every week in each room. She must have her object lessons ready, and she must do a certain amount of practising with the orchestra. Then a cold lunch at noon, and a three-mile walk at night.

"Humph!" said Mrs. Comstock, "To get through that the girl would have to be made of cast-iron. I wonder how I can help her best?"

She plunged in deepest thought again.

"The less she sees of what she's been having all summer, the sooner she'll feel better about it," she muttered.

She arose, went to the bank and inquired for the cashier.

"I want to know just how I am fixed here," she said.

The cashier laughed. "Well, you haven't been in a hurry," he replied. "We have been ready for you any time these twenty years, but you didn't seem to pay much attention. Your account is rather flourishing. Interest, when it gets to compounding is quite a money breeder. Come back here to a table and I will show you your balances."

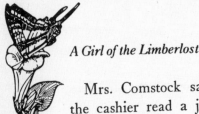

Mrs. Comstock sank into a chair and waited while the cashier read a jumble of figures to her. It meant that her deposits had exceeded her expenses from one to three hundred dollars a year, according to the cattle, sheep, hogs, poultry, butter, and eggs she had sold. The aggregate of these sums had been compounding interest throughout the years. Mrs. Comstock stared at the total with dazed and unbelieving eyes. Through her sick heart rushed the realization, that if she merely had stood before that wicket and asked one question, she would have known that all those bitter years of skimping for Elnora and herself had been unnecessary. She arose and went back to the depot.

"I want to send a message," she said. She picked up the pencil and, with rash extravagance, wrote, "Found money at bank didn't know about. If you want to go to college, come on first train and get ready." She hesitated a second and then she said to herself grimly, "Yes, I'll pay for that, too," and recklessly added, "With love, Mother." Then she sat waiting for the answer. It came in less than an hour. "Going to teach this winter. With dearest love, Elnora."

Mrs. Comstock held the message a long time. When she arose she was ravenously hungry, but the pain in her heart was a little easier. She went to a restaurant and got some food, then to a dressmaker where she ordered four dresses; two very plain every-day ones, a serviceable dark gray cloth suit, and a soft light gray silk with touches of lavender and lace. She made a heavy list of purchases at Brownlees, and the remainder of the day she did business in her direct and spirited way. At night she was so tired she scarcely could walk home, but she built a fire and cooked and ate a hearty meal.

Later she went out by the west fence and gathered an armful of tansy which she boiled to a thick green tea. Then she stirred in oatmeal until it was a stiff paste. She spread a sheet over her bed and began tearing strips of old muslin. She bandaged each hand and arm with the mixture and plastered the soggy, evil-smelling stuff in a thick poultice over her face and neck. She was so tired she had to sleep, and when she awoke she was half skinned. She bathed her face and hands, did the work and went back to town, coming home at night to go through the same process.

By the third morning she was a raw even red, the fourth she had faded to a brilliant pink under the soothing influence of a cream recommended. That day came a letter from Elnora saying that she would remain where she was until Saturday morning, and then come to Ellen Brownlee's at Onabasha and stay for the Saturday's session of teachers to arrange their year's work. Sunday was Ellen's last day at home, and she wanted Elnora very much. She had to get together the orchestra and practise them Sunday; and could not come home until after school Monday night. That suited Mrs. Comstock, and she at once answered the letter saying so.

The next day Mrs. Comstock was a pale pink, and

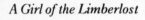
the following a delicate porcelain white. That day she went to a hairdresser and had the great rope of snowy hair which covered her scalp washed, dressed, and fastened with such pins and combs as were decided to be most becoming. She took samples of her dresses, went to a milliner, and bought a street hat to match her suit, and a gray satin with lavender orchids to wear with the silk dress. Her last investment was a loose coat of soft gray broadcloth with white lining, and touches of lavender on the embroidered collar, and gray gloves to match.

Then she went home, rested and worked by turns until Monday. When school closed on that evening, and Elnora, so tired she almost trembled, came down the long walk after a late session of teachers' meeting, a messenger boy stopped her.

"There's a lady wants to see you most important. I am to take you to the place," he said.

Elnora groaned. She could not imagine who wanted her, but there was nothing to do but go and find out, tired and anxious to see her mother as she was.

"This is the place," said the boy, and went his way whistling. Elnora was three blocks from the high school building on the same street. She was before a quaint old house, fresh with paint and covered with vines. There was a long wide lot, grass-covered, closely set with trees, and a barn and chicken park at the back that seemed to be occupied. Elnora stepped on the veranda which was furnished with straw rugs, bent-hickory chairs, hanging baskets, and a table with a work-box and magazines, and knocked at the screen door.

Inside she could see bare polished floors, walls freshly papered in low-toned harmonious colours, straw rugs and madras curtains. It seemed to be a restful, homelike place to which she had come, and a second later down an open stairway came a tall, dark-eyed woman with cheeks faintly pink and a crown of fluffy snow-white hair. She wore a lavender gingham dress with white collar and cuffs, and she called as she advanced, "That screen isn't latched! Open it and come see your brand-new mother, my girl."

Elnora stepped inside the door. "Mother!" she cried. "You my mother! I don't believe it!"

"Well, you better!" said Mrs. Comstock, "because it's true! You said you wished I were like the other girls' mothers, and I've shot as close the mark as I could without any practice. I thought that walk would be too much for you this winter, so I just rented this house and moved in, to be near you, and help more in case I'm needed. I've only lived here a day, but I like it so well I've a mortal big notion to buy the place."

"But, mother!" protested Elnora, clinging to her wonderingly. "You are perfectly beautiful, and this house is a little paradise, but how will we ever pay for it? We can't afford it!"

"Humph! Have you forgotten I telegraphed you I'd found some money I didn't know about? All I've

done is paid for, and plenty more to settle for all I propose to do."

Mrs. Comstock glanced around with supreme satisfaction.

"I may get homesick as a pup before spring," she said, "but if I do I can go back. If I don't, I'll sell some timber and put a few oil wells where they don't show much. I can have land enough cleared for a few fields and put a tenant on our farm, and we will buy this and settle here. It's for sale."

"You don't look it, but you've surely gone mad!" exclaimed Elnora.

"Just the reverse, my girl," said Mrs. Comstock, "I've gone sane. If you are going to undertake this work, you must be convenient to it. And your mother should be where she can see that you are properly dressed, fed, and cared for. This is our — let me think — reception room. How do you like it? This door leads to your workroom and study. I didn't do much there because I wasn't sure of my way. But I knew you would want a rug, curtains, table, shelves for books, and a case for your specimens, so I had a carpenter shelve and enclose that end of it. 'Looks pretty neat to me. The dining room and kitchen are back, one of the cows in the barn, and some chickens in the coop. I understand that none of the other girls' mothers milk a cow, so a neighbour boy will tend to ours for a third of the milk. There are three bedrooms, and a bath upstairs. Go take one, get in some fresh clothes, and come to supper. You can find your room because your things are in it."

Elnora kissed her mother over and over, and hurried upstairs. She identified her room by the dressing-case. There was a pretty rug, and curtains, white iron bed, plain and rocking chairs to match her case, a shirtwaist chest, and the big closet was filled with her old clothing and several new dresses. She found the bathroom, bathed, dressed in fresh linen and went down to a supper that was an evidence of Mrs. Comstock's highest art in cooking. Elnora was so hungry she ate her first real meal in two weeks. But the bites went down slowly because she forgot about them in watching her mother.

"How on earth did you do it?" she said at last. "I always thought you were naturally brown as a nut."

"Oh, that was just tan and sunburn!" explained Mrs. Comstock. "I always knew I was white underneath it. I hated to shade my face because I hadn't anything but a sunbonnet, and I couldn't stand for it to touch my ears, so I went bareheaded and took all the colour I accumulated. But when I began to think of moving you in to your work, I saw I must put up an appearance that wouldn't disgrace you, so I thought I'd best remove the crust. It took some time, and I hope I may die before I ever endure the feel and the smell of the stuff I used again, but it skinned me nicely. What you now see is my own with just a little dust of rice powder, for protection. I'm sort of tender yet."

"And your lovely, lovely hair?" breathed Elnora.

355

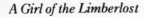

"Hair dresser did that!" said Mrs. Comstock. "It cost like smoke. But I watched her, and with a little help from you I can wash it alone next time, though it will be hard work. I let her monkey with it until she said she had found 'my style.' Then I tore it down and had her show me how to build it up again three times. I thought my arms would drop. When I paid the bill for her work, the time I'd taken, the pins, and combs she'd used, I nearly had heart failure, but I didn't turn a hair before her. I just smiled at her sweetly and said, 'How reasonable you are!' Come to think of it, she was! She might have charged me ten dollars for what she did just as well as nine seventy-five. I couldn't have helped myself. I had made no bargain to begin on."

Then Elnora leaned back in her chair and shouted, in a gust of hearty laughter, and a little of the ache ceased in her breast. There was no time to think, the remainder of that evening, she was so tired she had to sleep, and her mother did not awaken her until she barely had time to dress, breakfast and get to school. There was nothing in the new life to remind her of the old, while it seemed as if there never came a minute for retrospection, but her mother appeared on the scene with more work, or some entertaining thing to do.

Mrs. Comstock invited Elnora's friends to visit her, and proved herself a bright and interesting hostess. She digested a subject before she spoke; and when she advanced a view, her point was sure to be original and

tersely expressed. Before three months people waited
to hear what she had to say. She kept her appearance
so in mind that she made a handsome and a distinguished
figure.

Elnora never mentioned Philip Ammon, neither did
Mrs. Comstock. Early in December came a note and
a big box from him. It contained several books on nature
subjects which would be a great help in school work,
a number of conveniences Elnora could not afford, and
a pair of glass-covered plaster casts, for each large moth
she had. In these the upper and under wings of male
and female showed. Ammon explained that she would
break her specimens easily, carrying them about in boxes.
He had seen these and thought they would be of use.
Elnora was delighted with them, and at once began the
tedious process of softening the mounted moths and
fitting them to the casts moulded to receive them.
Her time was so taken in school, she progressed slowly,
so her mother undertook this work. After trying one or
two very common ones she learned to handle the most
delicate with ease. She took keen pride in relaxing
the tense moths, fitting them to the cases, polishing the
glass covers to the last degree and sealing them. The
results were beautiful to behold.

Soon after Elnora wrote Ammon:

DEAR FRIEND:

I am writing to thank you for the books, and the box of conveniences
sent me for my work. I can use everything with fine results. Hope
I am giving good satisfaction in my position. You will be interested
to learn that when the summer's work was classified and pinned, I

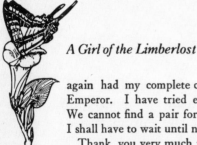

again had my complete collection for the man of India, save a Yellow Emperor. I have tried everywhere I know, so has the Bird Woman. We cannot find a pair for sale. Fate is against me, at least this season. I shall have to wait until next year and try again.

Thank you very much for helping me with my collection and for the books and things.

Sincerely yours,
ELNORA COMSTOCK.

Ammon was disappointed over that note and instead of keeping it he tore it into bits and dropped them into the waste basket.

That was precisely what Elnora hoped he would do. Christmas brought beautiful cards of greeting to Mrs. Comstock and Elnora, Easter others, and the year went rapidly toward spring. Elnora's work had been intensely absorbing, and she had gone into it with all her power. She had made it a wonderful success and won new friends. Mrs. Comstock had helped in every way she could, and she was very popular also.

Throughout the winter they had enjoyed the city thoroughly, and the change of life it afforded, but signs of spring did wonderful things to the hearts of the country-bred women. A restlessness began on bright February days, calmed during March storms and attacked full force in April. When neither could bear it any longer they were forced to discuss the matter and admit they were growing ill with pure homesickness. They decided to keep the city house during the summer, but to go back to the farm to live just as soon as school closed.

So Mrs. Comstock would prepare breakfast and lunch

and then slip away to the farm to make up beds in her ploughed garden, plant seeds, trim and tend her flowers, and prepare the cabin for occupancy. Then she would go home and make the evening as cheerful as possible for Elnora; in these days she lived only for the girl.

Both of them were glad when the last of May came and the schools closed. They packed the books and clothing they wished to take into a wagon and walked across the fields to the old cabin. As they approached it, Mrs. Comstock said to Elnora, "You are sure you won't be lonely here?"

Elnora knew what she really meant.

"Quite sure," she said. "For a time last fall I was glad to be away, but that all wore out with the winter. Spring made me homesick as I could be. I can scarcely wait until we get back again."

So they began that summer just as they had begun all others — with work. But both of them took a new joy in everything, and the violin sang by the hour in the twilight.

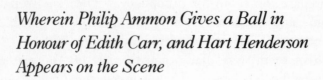

CHAPTER 19

*Wherein Philip Ammon Gives a Ball in
Honour of Edith Carr, and Hart Henderson
Appears on the Scene*

EDITH CARR stood in a vine-enclosed side veranda of
the Lake Shore Club House waiting while Philip Ammon
gave some important orders. In a few days she would
sail for Paris to select a wonderful trousseau she
had planned for her marriage in October. To-night
Philip was giving a club dance in her honour, and three
hundred of their friends were bidden to share their happiness. Philip had spent days in devising new and exquisite effects in decorations, entertainment, and supper.
Weeks before the favoured guests had been notified.
Days before they had received the invitations asking
them to participate in this entertainment by Philip
Ammon in honour of Miss Carr. They spoke of it as
'Phil's' dance for Edith!

As Edith Carr stood waiting, she smiled softly. She
could hear the rumble of carriages and the panting of
automobiles as in a steady stream they rolled to the
front entrance. She could catch glimpses of floating
draperies of gauze and lace, the flash of jewels, and the
passing of exquisite colour. Everyone was newly

arrayed in her honour in the loveliest clothing, and the most expensive jewels they could command. As she thought of it she lifted her head a trifle higher and her eyes flashed proudly.

She was robed in a French creation suggested and designed by Philip. He had said to her, "I know a competent judge who says the distinctive feature of June is her exquisite big night moths. I want you to be the very essence of June that night, as you will be the embodiment of love. Be a moth. The most beautiful of them is either the pale green Luna or the Yellow Imperialis. Be my moon lady, or my gold Empress."

He took her to the museum and showed her the moths. She instantly decided on the yellow. Secretly because she knew the shades would make her more startlingly beautiful than any other colour. To him she said, "A moon lady seems so far away and cold. I would be of earth and very near on that night. I choose the Empress."

So she matched the colours exactly, wrote out the idea and forwarded the order to Paquin. To-night when Philip Ammon came for her, he stood speechless for a minute and then silently kissed her hands.

For she stood tall, lithe, of grace inborn, her dark waving hair high piled and crossed by gold bands studded with amethyst and at one side an enamelled lavender orchid rimmed with diamonds, which flashed and sparkled. The soft yellow robe of lightest weight velvet fitted her form perfectly, while from each shoulder

fell a great velvet wing lined with lavender, and flecked with embroidery of that colour in imitation of the moth. Around her throat was a wonderful necklace and on her arms were bracelets of gold set with amethyst and rimmed with diamonds. Philip had said that her gloves, fan, and slippers must be lavender, because the feet of the moth were that colour. These accessories had been made to order and embroidered with gold. It had been arranged that her mother, Philip's, and a few best friends should receive his guests. She was to appear when she led the grand march with Philip Ammon. Miss Carr was as positive that she would be the most beautiful, and most exquisitely gowned woman present as she was of life. In her heart she thought of herself as "Imperialis Regalis," as the Yellow Empress. In a few moments she would stun her world into feeling it as Philip Ammon had done, for she had taken pains that the history of her costume should be whispered to a few who would give it circulation. She lifted her head proudly and waited, for was not Philip planning something unusual and unsurpassed in her honour? Then she smiled.

But in all the fragmentary thoughts crossing her brain the one that never came was that of Philip Ammon as the Emperor. Philip the king of her heart, and at least her equal in all things. She was the Empress — yes, but Philip was a mere man, to devise entertainments, to provide luxuries, to humour whims, to kiss hands!

"Ah, my luck!" cried a voice behind her.

Edith Carr turned and smiled exquisitely.

"I thought you were on the ocean," she said.

"I only reached the dock," replied the man. "When I had a letter that recalled me by the first limited."

"Oh! Important business?"

"The only business of any importance in all the world to me. I'm triumphant that I came. Edith, you are the most superb woman in every respect that I have ever seen. One glimpse is worth the whole journey."

"You like my dress?" she moved toward him and turned, lifting her arms. "Do you know what it is intended to represent?"

"Yes, Polly Ammon told me. I knew when I heard about it how you would look, so I started a sleuth hunt, to get the first peep. Edith, I can become intoxicated just with looking at you to-night."

He half-closed his eyes and smilingly stared straight at her. He was taller than she, a lean man, with close-cropped light hair, steel gray eyes, a square chin and "man of the world" written all over him.

Edith Carr flushed. "I thought you realized when you went away that you were to stop that, Hart Henderson," she cried.

"I did, but this letter of which I tell you called me back to start it all over again."

She came a step closer. "Who wrote that letter, and what did it contain concerning me?" she demanded.

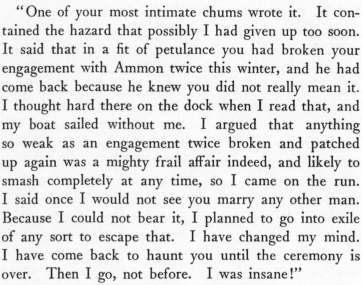

"One of your most intimate chums wrote it. It contained the hazard that possibly I had given up too soon. It said that in a fit of petulance you had broken your engagement with Ammon twice this winter, and he had come back because he knew you did not really mean it. I thought hard there on the dock when I read that, and my boat sailed without me. I argued that anything so weak as an engagement twice broken and patched up again was a mighty frail affair indeed, and likely to smash completely at any time, so I came on the run. I said once I would not see you marry any other man. Because I could not bear it, I planned to go into exile of any sort to escape that. I have changed my mind. I have come back to haunt you until the ceremony is over. Then I go, not before. I was insane!"

The girl laughed merrily. "Not half so insane as you are now, Hart!" she cried gaily. "You know that Philip Ammon has been devoted to me all my life. Well, now I'll tell you something else, because this looks serious for you. I love him with all my heart. Not while he lives shall he know it, and I will laugh at him if you tell him, but the fact remains: I intend to marry him, but no doubt I shall tease him constantly. It's good for a man to be uncertain. If you could see Ammon's face at the quarterly return of his ring, you would understand the fun of it. You had better have taken your boat."

"Possibly," said Henderson calmly. "But you are the only woman in the world for me, and while you are free, as I now see my light, I stay by you. You know the old adage."

"But I'm not 'free'!" cried Edith Carr. "I'm just telling you I am not. This night is my public acknowledgment that Phil and I are promised, as our world has surmised since we were children. That promise is an actual fact, because of what I just have told you. My little fits of temper don't count with Phil. He's been raised on them. In fact, I often invent one in a perfect calm to see him perform. He is the most amusing spectacle. But, please, please, do understand that I love him, and always will, and that we will be married."

"Just the same, I'll wait and see it an accomplished fact," said Henderson. "And, Edith, because I love you, with the sort of love it is worth a woman's while to inspire, I want your happiness before my own. So I am going to say this to you, for I never dreamed you were capable of the feeling you have displayed for Phil. If you do love him, and have loved him always, a disappointment would cut you deeper than you know. Go careful from now on! Don't strain that patched engagement of yours any further. I've known Philip all my life. I've known him through boyhood, in college, and since. All men respect him. Where the rest of us confess our sins, he stands clean. You can go to his arms with nothing to forgive. Mark this thing! I have heard him say, 'Edith is my slogan,' and I have seen him march home strong in the strength of his love for you, in the face of temptations before which every

365

other man of us fell. Before the gods! that ought to be worth something to a girl, if she really is the delicate, sensitive, refined thing she would have man believe. It would take a woman with the organism of an ostrich to endure some of the men here to-night, if she knew them as I do; but Phil is sound to the core. So this is what I would say to you. First, your instincts are right in loving him, why not let him feel it in the ways a woman knows? Second, don't break your engagement again. As men know the man, any of us would be afraid to the soul. He loves you, yes! He is long-suffering for you, yes! But men know he has a limit. When the limit is reached, he will stand fast, and all the powers can't move him. You don't seem to think it, but you can go too far!"

"Is that all?" laughed Edith Carr sarcastically.

"No, there is one thing more," said Henderson. "Here or hereafter, now and so long as I breathe, I am your slave. You can do anything you choose and know that I will kneel before you again. So carry this in the depths of your heart; now or at any time, in any place or condition, merely lift your hand, and I will come. Anything you want of me, that thing will I do. I am going to wait; if you need me, it is not necessary to speak; only give me the faintest sign. All your life I will be somewhere near you waiting for it."

"Idjit! You rave!" laughed Edith Carr. "How you would frighten me! What a bugbear you would raise! Be sensible and go find what keeps Phil. I was waiting patiently, but my patience is going. I won't look nearly so well as I do now when it is gone."

At that instant Philip Ammon entered. He was in full evening dress and exceptionally handsome. "Everything is ready," he said; "they are waiting for us to lead the march. It is formed."

Edith Carr smiled entrancingly. "Do you think I am ready?"

Philip looked what he thought, and offered his arm. Edith Carr nodded carelessly to Henderson, and moved away. Servants parted the curtains and the Yellow Empress bowing right and left, swept the length of the ballroom and took her place at the head of the formed procession. The great open dancing pavilion was draped with yellow silk caught up with lilac flowers. Every corner was filled with bloom of those colours. The music was played by harpers dressed in yellow and violet, and the ball opened.

The midnight supper was served with the same colours and the last half of the programme was well under way. Never had girl been more complimented and petted in the same length of time than Edith Carr. Every minute she seemed to grow more worthy of praise. A partners' dance was called and the floor was filled with couples waiting for the music. Ammon stood whispering delightful things to Edith facing him. From out of the night, in at the wide front entrance to the pavilion there swept in slow wavering flight a great yellow moth and fluttered toward the centre cluster of glaring electric

367

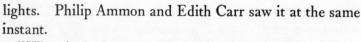

lights.   Philip Ammon and Edith Carr saw it at the same instant.

"Why, isn't that ——?" she began excitedly.

"It's a Yellow Emperor!   This is fate!" cried Ammon. "The last one Elnora needs for her collection.   I must have it! Excuse me!"

He ran toward the light.   "Hats! Handkerchiefs! Fans! Anything!" he panted.   "Everyone hold up something and stop that! It's a moth; I've got to catch it!"

"He wants it for Edith!" ran in a murmur around the hall.   The girl's face flushed, while she bit her lip in vexation.

Instantly everyone began holding up something to keep the moth from flying back into the night.   One fan held straight before it served, and the moth gently settled on it.

"Hold steady!" cried Ammon.   "Don't move for your life!" he rushed toward the moth made a quick sweep and held it up between his fingers.   "All right!" he called.   "Thanks, everyone! Excuse me a minute."

He ran to the office.

"An ounce of gasolene, quick!" he ordered.   "A cigar box, a cork, and the glue bottle."

He poured some glue into the bottom of the box, set the cork in it firmly, dashed the gasolene over the moth repeatedly, pinned it to the cork, poured the remainder of the liquid over it, closed the box, and fastened it. Then he laid a bill on the counter.

"Pack that box with cork around it, in one twice its size, tie securely and express to this address at once."

He scribbled on a sheet of paper and shoved it over.

"On your honour, will you do that faithfully as I say?" he asked the clerk.

"Certainly," was the reply.

"Then keep the change," called Ammon as he ran back to the pavilion.

Edith Carr stood where he left her, thinking rapidly. She heard the murmur that went up when Philip started to capture the exquisite golden creature she was impersonating. She saw the flash of surprise that went over unrestrained faces when he ran from the room, without even showing it to her. "The last one Elnora needs," rang in her ears. He had told her that he helped collect moths the previous summer, but she had understood that the Bird Woman, with whose work Miss Carr was familiar, wanted them to put in a book.

He had spoken of a country girl he had met who played the violin wonderfully, and at times, he had showed a disposition to exalt her as a standard of womanhood. Miss Carr had ignored what he said, and talked of something else. But that girl's name had been Elnora. It was she who was collecting moths! No doubt she was the competent judge who was responsible for the yellow costume Philip had devised. Had Edith Carr been in her room, she would have torn off the dress at the thought.

Being in a circle of her best friends, which to her

meant her keenest rivals and harshest critics, she grew rigid with anger. Her breath hurt her paining chest. No one thought to speak to the musicians and, seeing the floor filled, they began the waltz. Only half the guests could see what had happened, and at once the others formed and commenced to dance. Laughing couples came sweeping past her.

Edith Carr grew very white as she stood alone. Her lips turned pale, while her dark eyes flamed with anger. She stood perfectly still where Philip had left her, and the approaching men guided their partners around her, while the girls, looking back, could be seen making exclamations of surprise.

The idolized only daughter of the Carr family hoped that she would drop dead from mortification, but nothing happened. She was too perverse to step aside laughingly and say that she was waiting for Philip. Then came Tom Levering dancing with Polly Ammon. Being in the scales with the Ammon family, Tom scented trouble from afar, so he whispered to Polly, "Edith is standing in the middle of the floor, and she's awful mad about something."

"That won't hurt her," laughed Polly. "It's an old pose of hers. She knows she looks superb when she is angry, so she keeps herself furious half the time on purpose."

"She looks like the mischief!" answered Tom. "Hadn't we better steer over and wait with her? She's the ugliest sight I ever saw!"

"Why, Tom!" cried Polly. "Stop, quickly!"

They hurried to Edith.

"Come, dear," said Polly. "We are going to wait with you until Phil gets back. Let's go for a drink. I am so thirsty!"

"Yes, do!" begged Tom, offering his arm. "Let's get out of here until Phil comes."

There was an opportunity to laugh and walk away, but Edith Carr would not accept it. Anger only seemed to flame higher.

"My betrothed left me here," she said. "Here I shall remain until he returns for me, and then — he will be my betrothed no longer!"

Polly grasped Edith's arm.

"Oh, Edith!" she implored. "Don't make a scene here, and to-night. Edith, this has been the loveliest dance ever given at the club house. Everyone is saying so. Edith! Darling, do come! Phil will be back in a second. He can explain! It's only a breath since I saw him go out. I thought he had returned."

As Polly panted these disjointed ejaculations, Tom Levering began to grow angry on her account.

"He has been gone just long enough to show every one of his guests that he will leave me standing alone, like a neglected fool, for any passing whim of his. Explain! His explanation would sound well! Do you know for whom he caught that moth? It is being sent to a girl he flirted with all last summer. It has just

occurred to me that the dress I am wearing is her suggestion. Let him try to explain!"

Speech unloosed the fountain. She stripped off her gloves to free her hands. At that instant the dancers parted to admit Philip. Instinctively they stopped as they approached and with wondering faces walled in Edith and Philip, Polly and Tom.

"Mighty good of you to wait!" cried Ammon, his face beaming with delight over his success in capturing the Yellow Emperor. "I thought when I heard the music you were going on."

"How did you think I was going on?" demanded Edith Carr in frigid tones.

"I thought you would step aside and wait a few seconds for me, or dance with Henderson. It was most important to have that moth. It just completes a valuable collection for a person who needs the money. Come!"

He held out his arms.

"I 'step aside' for no one!" stormed Edith Carr. "I await no other girl's pleasure! You may 'complete the collection' with that!"

She drew her engagement ring from her finger and reached to place it in one of Philip's outstretched hands. Ammon saw and drew back. Instantly Edith dropped the ring. As it fell, almost instinctively Philip caught it in air. With amazed face he looked closely at Edith Carr. Her distorted features were scarcely recognizable. He held the ring toward her.

"Edith, for the love of mercy, wait until I can explain," he begged. "Put on your ring and let me tell you how it is."

"I know perfectly 'how it is,'" she answered. "I never will wear that ring again."

"You won't even hear what I have to say? You won't take back your ring?" he cried.

"Never! Your conduct is infamous!"

"Come to think of it," said Ammon deliberately, "it is infamous to cut a girl, who has danced all her life, out of a few measures of a waltz. As for asking forgiveness for so black a sin as picking up a moth, and starting it to a friend who lives by collecting them, I don't see how I could! I have not been gone three minutes by the clock, Edith. Put on your ring and finish the dance like a dear girl."

He thrust the glittering ruby into her fingers and again held out his arms. She dropped the ring, and it rolled some distance from them. Henderson followed its shining course, and caught it before it was lost.

"You really mean it?" demanded Ammon in a voice as cold as hers ever had been.

"You know I mean it!" cried Edith Carr.

"I accept your decision in the presence of these witnesses," said Philip Ammon.

"Where is my father?" he asked of those around them. The elder Ammon with a distressed face hurried to him. "Father, take my place," said Philip. "Excuse me to

my guests. Ask all my friends to forgive me. I am going out for a time."

He turned and walked from the pavilion. As he went Hart Henderson rushed to Edith Carr and forced the ring into her fingers. "Edith, quick! Come, quick!" he implored. "There's just time to catch him. If you let him go that way, he never will return in this world. Remember what I told you."

"Great prophet! aren't you, Hart?" she sneered. "Who wants him to return? If that ring is thrust upon me again I shall fling it into the lake. Signal the musicians to begin, and take this dance with me."

Henderson put the ring into his pocket, and began the dance. He could feel the muscular spasms of the girl in his arms, her face was cold and hard, but her breath burned with the scorch of fever. She finished the dance and all others, taking Phil's numbers with Henderson, who had arrived too late to arrange a programme. She left with the others, merely inclining her head as she passed Ammon's father taking his place, and entered the big touring car for which Henderson had telephoned.

She sank limply into a seat and moaned softly.

"Shall I drive awhile in the night air?" asked Henderson.

She nodded. Henderson instructed the chauffeur.

She raised her head in a few seconds. "Hart, I'm going to pieces," she said. "Won't you put your arm around me a little while?"

Henderson gathered her into his arms and her head fell on his shoulder. "Closer!" she cried.

Henderson gripped her with the strength of a practised athlete, and held her until his arms were numb, but he did not know it. The tricks of fate are cruel enough, but there scarcely could have been a worse one than that. To care for a woman as he loved Edith Carr and have her given into his arms because she was so numb with misery over her trouble with another man that she did not know or care what she did. Dawn was streaking the east when he spoke to her.

"Edith, it is growing light."

"Take me home," she said.

Henderson helped her up the steps and rang the bell. When the door was opened he went inside and guided her to her room.

"Miss Carr is ill," he said to the footman. "Rouse her maid instantly, and have her prepare something hot as quickly as possible."

"Edith," he cried, "Just a word. I have been thinking. It isn't too late yet. Take your ring and put it on. I will go find Phil at once and tell him you have, that you are expecting him, and he will come."

"Think what he said!" she cried. "He accepted my decision as final, 'in the presence of witnesses,' as if it were court. He can return it to me, if I ever wear it again."

"You think that now, but in a few days you will find that you feel very differently. Living a life of heartache

375

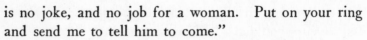

is no joke, and no job for a woman. Put on your ring and send me to tell him to come."

"No."

"Edith, there was not a soul who saw that, but sympathized with Phil. It was ridiculous for you to get so angry over a thing which was never intended for the slightest offence, and by no logical reasoning could have been so considered."

"Do you think that?" she demanded.

"I do!" said Henderson. "If you had laughed and stepped aside an instant, or laughed and stayed where you were, Phil would have been back; or, if he needed punishment in your eyes, to have found me having one of his dances would have been enough. I was waiting. You could have called me with one look. But to publicly do and say what you did, my lady — I know Phil, and I know you went too far. Put on that ring, and send him word you are sorry, before it is too late."

"I will not! He shall come to me."

"Then God help you!" said Henderson, "for you are plunging into misery whose depth you do not dream. Edith, I beg of you ——!"

She swayed where she stood. Her maid opened the door and caught her. Henderson went down the hall and out to his car.

CHAPTER 20

Wherein the Elder Ammon Offers Advice, and Edith Carr Experiences Regrets

PHILIP AMMON walked from among his friends a humiliated and a wounded man. Never before had Edith Carr appeared quite so beautiful. All evening she had treated him with unusual consideration. Never had he loved her so deeply. Then in a few seconds everything was different. Seeing the change in her face, and hearing her meaningless accusations, killed something in his heart. Warmth went out and a cold weight took its place. But even after that, he had offered the ring to her again, and asked her before others to reconsider. The answer had been further insult.

He walked straight ahead, paying no heed to where he went. He had traversed many miles when he became aware that his feet had chosen familiar streets. He was passing his home. Dawn was near, but the first floor was lighted. He staggered up the steps and was instantly admitted. The library door stood open, while his father sat with a book pretending to read. At Philip's entrance the father scarcely glanced up.

"Come on!" he called. "I have just told Banks to

377

bring me a cup of coffee before I turn in. Have one with me!"

Philip sat by the table and leaned his head on his hands, but he drank a cup of steaming coffee and felt better.

"Father," he said, "father, may I talk with you a little while?"

"Of course," answered Mr. Ammon. "I am not at all tired. I think I must have been waiting in the hope that you would come. I want no one's version of this but yours. Tell me the straight of the thing, Phil."

Philip told all he knew, while his father sat in deep thought.

"On my life I can't see any occasion for such a display of temper, Phil. It passed all bounds of reason and breeding. Can't you think of anything more?"

"I cannot!"

"Polly says everyone expected you to carry the moth you caught to Edith. Why didn't you?"

"She screams if a thing of that kind comes near her. She never has taken the slightest interest in them. I was in a big hurry. I didn't want to miss one minute of my dance with her. The moth was not so uncommon, but by a combination of bad luck it had become the rarest in America for a friend of mine, who is making a collection to pay college expenses. For an instant last June the series was completed; when a woman's uncontrolled temper ruined this specimen and the search for it began over. A few days later a pair was secured, and again the money was in sight for several hours. Then an accident wrecked one-fourth of the collection. I helped replace those last June, all but this Yellow Emperor which we could not secure, and we haven't been able to find, buy or trade for one since. So my friend was compelled to teach this past winter instead of going to college. When that moth came flying in there to-night, it seemed to me like fate. All I thought of was, that to secure it would complete the collection and get the money. So I caught the Emperor and started it to Elnora. I declare to you that I was not out of the pavilion over three minutes at a liberal estimate. If I only had thought to speak to the orchestra! I was sure I would be back before enough couples gathered and formed for the dance."

The eyes of the elder Ammon were very bright.

"The friend for whom you wanted the moth is a girl?" he asked indifferently, as he ran the book leaves through his fingers.

"The girl of whom I wrote you last summer, and told you about in the fall. I helped her all the time I was away."

"Did Edith know of her?"

"I tried many times to tell her, to interest her, but she was so indifferent that it was insulting. She would not hear me."

"We are neither one in any condition to sleep. Why don't you begin at the first and tell me about this girl? To think of other matters for a time may clear our vision for a sane solution of this. Who is she, just what is she doing, and what is she like? You know I was reared among those Limberlost people, I can understand readily. What is her name and where does she live?"

Philip gave a man's version of the previous summer, while his father played with the book industriously.

"You are very sure as to her refinement and education?" he asked.

"In almost two months' daily association, could a man be mistaken? She can far and away beat Polly, Edith, or any girl of our set on any common, high school, or supplementary branch, and you know high schools have French, German, and physics now. Besides, she is a graduate of two other institutions. All her life she has been in the school of Hard Knocks. She has the biggest, tenderest, most human heart I ever knew in a girl. She has known life in its most cruel phases, and instead of hardening her, it has set her trying to save other people suffering. Then this nature position of which I told you; she graduated in the School of the Woods, before she got that. The Bird Woman, whose work you know, helped her there. Elnora knows more interesting things in a minute than any other girl I ever met knew in an hour, provided you are a person who cares to understand plant and animal life."

The book leaves slid rapidly through his fingers as the father drawled, "What sort of looking girl is she?"

"Tall as Edith, a little heavier, pink, even complexion, wide open blue-gray eyes with heavy black brows, and lashes so long they touch her cheeks. She has a rope of waving, shining hair that makes a real crown on her head, and it appears almost red in the light. She is as handsome as any fair woman I ever saw, but she doesn't know it. Every time anyone pays her a compliment, her mother, who is a caution, discovers that, for some reason, the girl is a fright, so she has no appreciation of her looks."

"And you were in daily association two months with a girl like that! How about it, Phil?"

"If you mean, did I trifle with her, no!" cried Philip hotly. "I told her the second time I met her all about Edith. Almost every day I wrote to Edith in her presence. Elnora gathered violets and made a fancy basket to put them in for Edith's birthday. I started to err in too open admiration for Elnora, but her mother brought me up with a whirl I never forgot. Fifty times a day in the swamps and forests Elnora made a perfect picture, but I neither looked nor said anything. I never met any girl so downright noble in bearing and actions. I never hated anything as I hated leaving her, for we were dear friends, like two wholly congenial men. Her mother was almost always with us. She knew how much I admired Elnora, but so long as I concealed it from the girl, the mother did not care."

"Yet you left such a girl and came back whole-hearted to Edith Carr!"

"Surely! You know how it has been with me about Edith all my life."

"Yet the girl you picture is far her superior to an unprejudiced person, when thinking what a man would require in a wife to be happy."

"I never have thought what I would 'require' to be happy! I only thought whether I could make Edith happy. I have been an idiot! What I've borne you'll never know! To-night is only one of many outbursts like that, in varying and lesser degrees."

"Phil, I love you, when you say you have thought only of Edith! I happen to know that it is true. You are my only son, and I have had a right to watch you closely. I believe you utterly. Anyone who cares for you as I do, and has had my years of experience in this world over yours, knows that in some ways, to-night would be a blessed release, if you could take it; but you cannot! Go to bed now, and get some rest. To-morrow, go back to her and fix it up."

"You heard what I said when I left her! I said it because something in my heart died a minute before that, and I realized that it was my love for Edith Carr. Never again will I voluntarily face such a scene. If she can act like that at a ball, before hundreds, over a thing of which I thought nothing at all, she would go into actual physical fits and spasms, over some of the household crises I've seen the Mater meet with a smile. Sir, it is truth that I have thought only of her up to the present. Now, I will admit I am thinking about myself. Father, did you see her? Life is too short, and it can be too sweet, to throw away in a battle with an unrestrained woman. I am no fighter — where a girl is concerned, anyway. I respect and love her or I do nothing. Never again is either respect or love possible between me and Edith Carr. Whenever I think of her in the future, I will see her as she was to-night. But I can't face the crowd just yet. Could you spare me a few days?"

"It is only ten days until you were to go north for the summer, go now."

"I don't want to go north. I don't want to meet people I know. There, the story would precede me. I do not need pitying glances or rough condolences. I wonder if I could not hide at Uncle Ed's in Wisconsin for awhile?"

The book closed suddenly. The father leaned across the table and looked into the son's eyes.

"Phil, are you sure of what you just have said?"

"Quite sure!"

"Do you think you are in any condition to decide to-night?"

"Death cannot return to life, father. My love for Edith Carr is dead. I hope never to see her again."

"If I thought you could be certain so soon! But, come to think of it, you are very like me in many ways. I am with you in this. Public scenes and disgraces I would not endure. It would be over with me, were I in your position, that I know."

"It is done for all time," said Philip Ammon. "Let us not speak of it further."

"Then, Phil," the father leaned closer and looked

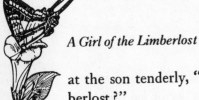

at the son tenderly, "Phil, why don't you go to the Limberlost?"

"Father!"

"Why not? No one can comfort a hurt heart like a tender woman; and, Phil, have you ever stopped to think that you may have a duty in the Limberlost, if you are free? I don't know! I only suggest it. But, for a country schoolgirl, unaccustomed to men, two months with a man like you might well awaken feelings of which you do not think. Because you were safeguarded is no sign the girl was. She might care to see you. You can soon tell. With you, she comes next to Edith, and you have made it clear to me that you appreciate her in many ways above. So I repeat it, why not go to the Limberlost?"

A long time Philip Ammon sat in deep thought. At last he raised his head.

"Well, why not!" he said. "Years could make me no surer than I am now, and life is short. Please ask Banks to get me some coffee and toast, and I will bathe and dress so I can take the early train."

"Go to your bath. I will attend to your packing and everything. And Phil, if I were you, I would leave no addresses."

"Not an address!" said Ammon. "Not even Polly."

When the train pulled out, the elder Ammon went home to find Hart Henderson waiting.

"Where is Phil?" he demanded.

"He did not feel like facing his friends at present,

and I am just back from driving him to the station. He said he might go to Siam, or Patagonia. He would leave no address."

Henderson almost staggered. "He's not gone? And left no address? You don't mean it! He'll never forgive her!"

"Never is a long time, Hart," said Mr. Ammon. "And it seems even longer to those of us who are well acquainted with Phil. Last night was not the last straw. It was the whole straw-stack. It crushed Phil so far as she is concerned. He will not see her again voluntarily, and he will not forget if he does. You can take it from him, and from me, we have accepted the lady's decision. Will you have a cup of coffee?"

Twice Henderson opened his lips to speak of Edith Carr's despair. Twice he looked into the stern, inflexible face of Mr. Ammon and could not betray her. He held out the ring.

"I have no instructions as to that," said the elder Ammon, drawing back. "Possibly Miss Carr would have it as a keepsake."

"I am sure not," said Henderson curtly.

"Then suppose you return it to Peacock. I will 'phone him. He will give you the price of it, and you might add it to the children's Fresh Air Fund. We would be obliged if you would do that. No one here cares to handle the object."

"As you choose," said Henderson. "Good morning!" Then he went to his home, but he could not think of

385

sleep. He ordered breakfast, but he could not eat. He paced the library for a time, but it was too small. Going out on the streets he walked until exhausted, then he called a hansom and was driven to his club. He had thought himself familiar with every depth of suffering; that night had taught him that what he felt for himself was not to be compared with the anguish which wrung his heart over the agony of Edith Carr. He tried to blame Philip Ammon, but being an honest man, Henderson knew that was unjust. The fault lay wholly with her, but that only made it harder for him, as he realized it would in time for her. As he sauntered into the room an attendant hurried to him.

"You are wanted most urgently at the 'phone, Mr. Henderson," he said. "You have had three calls from Main 5770."

Henderson shivered as he picked down the receiver and gave the call.

"Is that you, Hart?" came Edith's voice.

"Yes."

"Did you find Phil?"

"No."

"Did you try?"

"Yes. As soon as I left you I went straight there."

"Wasn't he home yet?"

"He has been home and gone again."

"Gone!"

The cry tore Henderson's heart.

"Shall I come and tell you, Edith?"

"No! Tell me now."

"When I got to the house Banks said Mr. Ammon and Phil were out in the motor, so I waited. Mr. Ammon came back soon. Edith, are you alone?"

"Yes. Go on!"

"Call your maid. I can't tell you until someone is with you."

"Tell me instantly!"

"Edith, he said he had been to the station. He said Phil had started to Siam or Patagonia, he didn't know which, and left no address. He said ——"

Distinctly Henderson heard her fall. He set the buzzer ringing, and in a few seconds heard voices, so he knew she had been found. Then he crept into a private den and shook with a hard, nervous chill.

The next day Edith Carr started on her trip to Europe. Henderson felt certain she hoped to meet Philip there. He was sure she would be disappointed, though he had no idea where Ammon could have gone. But after much thought he decided he would see Edith soonest by remaining at home, so he spent the summer in Chicago.

CHAPTER 21

Wherein Philip Ammon Returns to the Limberlost, and Elnora Studies the Situation

WE must be thinking about supper, mother," said Elnora, as she set the wings of a Cecropia with great care. "It seems as if I can't get enough to eat, or enough of being at home. I enjoyed that city house. I don't believe I could have gotten through my work if I had been compelled to walk back and forth. I thought at first I never wanted to come here again. Now, I feel as if I could not live anywhere else."

"Elnora," said Mrs. Comstock, "there's someone coming down the road."

"Coming here, do you think?"

"Yes, coming here, I suspect."

Elnora glanced quickly at her mother and then turned to the road as Philip Ammon reached the gate.

"Careful, mother!" the girl instantly warned. "If you change your treatment of him a hair's breadth, he will suspect. Come with me to meet him."

She dropped her work and sprang up.

"Well, of all the delightful surprises!" she cried.

She was a trifle thinner than during the previous summer. On her face there was a more mature, patient look, but the sun struck her bare head with the same ray of red gold. She wore one of the old blue gingham dresses, open at the throat and rolled to the elbows. Mrs. Comstock did not look at all the same woman, but Ammon saw only Elnora; heard only her greeting. He caught both hands where she offered but one.

"Elnora," he cried, "if you were engaged to me, and we were at a ball, among hundreds, where I offended you very much, and didn't even know I had done anything, and if I asked you before all of them to allow me to explain, to forgive me, to wait, would your face grow distorted and unfamiliar with anger? Would you drop my ring on the floor and insult me repeatedly? Oh, Elnora, would you?"

Elnora's big eyes seemed to leap, while her face grew very white. She wrenched away her hands.

"Hush, Phil! Hush!" she protested. "That fever has you again! You are dreadfully ill. You don't know what you are saying."

"I am sleepless and exhausted; I'm heartsick; but I am well as I ever was. Answer me, Elnora, would you?"

"Answer nothing!" cried Mrs. Comstock. If Wesley Sinton had been speaking to her just then he would have called her "Kate." "Answer nothing! Hang your coat there on your nail, Phil, and come split some kindling. Elnora, clean away that stuff, and set the table. Can't you see the boy is starved and tired? He's come home to rest and get a decent meal. Come on, Phil!"

Mrs. Comstock marched away, and Ammon hung his coat in its old place and followed. Out of sight and hearing she turned on him.

"Do you call yourself a man or a hound?" she flared.

"I beg your pardon ——!" stammered Philip Ammon.

"I should think you would!" she ejaculated. "I'll admit you did the square thing and was a man last summer, though I'd liked it better if you'd faced up and told me you were promised; but to come back here babying, and take hold of Elnora like that, and talk that way because you have had a fuss with your girl, I don't tolerate. Split that kindling and I'll get your supper, and then you best go. I won't have you working on Elnora's big heart, because you have quarreled with some one else. You'll have it patched up in a week and be gone again, so you can go right away."

"Mrs. Comstock, I came here to ask Elnora to marry me."

"The more fool you, then!" cried Mrs. Comstock. "This time yesterday you were engaged to another woman, no doubt. Now, for some little flare-up you come racing here to use Elnora as a tool to spite the other girl. A week of sane living, and you will be sorry and ready to go back to Chicago, or, if you really are man enough to be sure of yourself, she will come to claim you. She has her rights. An engagement of years is a serious matter, and not broken for a whim. If you don't go, she'll come. Then, when you patch up your affairs and go sailing away together, where does my girl come in?"

"I am a lawyer, Mrs. Comstock," said Ammon. "It appeals to me as beneath your ordinary sense of justice to decide a case without hearing the evidence. It is due me that you hear me first."

"Hear your side!" flashed Mrs. Comstock. "I'd a heap sight rather hear the girl!"

"I wish to my soul that you had heard and seen her last night, Mrs. Comstock," said Ammon. "Then, my way would be clear. I never even thought of coming here to-day. I'll admit I would have come in time, but not for many months. My father sent me."

"Your father sent you!" repeated Mrs. Comstock. "Why?"

"Father, mother, and Polly were present last night. They, and all my friends, saw me insulted and disgraced in the worst exhibition of uncontrolled temper any of us ever witnessed. All of them knew it was the end. Father liked what I had told him of Elnora, and he advised me to come here, so I came. If she does not want me, I can leave instantly, but, oh, I hoped she would understand!"

"You people are not splitting wood," called Elnora from the back door.

"Oh, yes, we are!" answered Mrs. Comstock. "You set out the things for biscuit, and lay the table." She turned again to Ammon. "I know considerable about your father," she said. "I have met your Uncle's family frequently this winter. I've heard your Aunt Anna say that she didn't at all like Miss Carr, and

that she and all your family secretly hoped that something would happen to prevent your marrying her. That chimes right in with your saying that your father sent you here. I guess you better speak your piece."

Ammon gave his version of the previous night.

"Do you believe me?" he finished.

"Yes," said Mrs. Comstock.

"May I stay?"

"Oh, it looks all right for you, but what about her?"

"Nothing, so far as I am concerned. Her plans were all made to start to Europe to-day. I suspect she is on the way by this time. Elnora is very sensible, Mrs. Comstock. Hadn't you better let her decide this?"

"The final decision rests with her, of course," admitted Mrs. Comstock. "But look you one thing! She's all I have. As Solomon says, 'she is the one child, the only child of her mother.' I've suffered enough in this world that I fight against any suffering which threatens her. So far as I know you've always been a man, and you may stay. But if you bring tears and heartache to her, don't have the assurance to think I'll bear it tamely. I'll get right up and fight like a catamount, if things go wrong for Elnora!"

"I have no doubt but you will," replied Ammon, "and I don't blame you in the least if you do. I have the utmost devotion to offer Elnora, a good home, fair social position, and my family will love her dearly. Think it over. I know it is sudden, but my father advised it."

"Yes, I reckon he did!" said Mrs. Comstock dryly. "I guess instead of me being the catamount, you had the genuine article up in Chicago, masquerading in peacock feathers, and posing as a fine lady, until her time came to scratch. Human nature seems to be pretty much the same the world over. But I'd give a pretty to know that secret thing you say you don't, that set her to raving over your just catching a moth for Elnora. You might get that crock of strawberries in the spring house."

They prepared and ate supper. Afterward they sat in the arbour and talked, or Elnora played until time for Ammon to go.

"Will you walk to the gate with me?" he asked Elnora as he arose.

"Not to-night," she answered lightly. "Come early in the morning if you like, and we will go over to Sleepy Snake Creek and hunt moths and gather dandelions for dinner."

Ammon leaned toward her. "May I tell you to-morrow why I came?" he asked.

"I think not," replied Elnora. "The fact is, I don't care why you came. It is enough for me that we are your very good friends, and that in trouble, you have found us a refuge. I fancy we had better live a week or two before you say anything. There is a possibility what you have to say may change in that length of time."

"It will not change one iota!" cried Ammon.

"Then it will have the grace of that much age to give

393

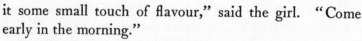

it some small touch of flavour," said the girl. "Come early in the morning."

She lifted the violin and began to play a dainty fairy dance.

"Well, bless my soul!" softly ejaculated the astounded Mrs. Comstock. "To think I was worrying for fear you couldn't take care of yourself!"

Elnora laughed as she played.

"Shall I tell you what he said?" inquired Mrs. Comstock.

"Nope! I don't want to hear it!" said Elnora. "He is only six hours from Chicago. I'll give her a week to find him and fix it up, if he stays that long. If she don't put in an appearance then, he can tell me what he wants to say, and I'll take my time to think it over. Time in plenty, too! There are three of us in this, and one has got to be left with a sore heart for life. If the decision rests with me I propose to be very sure that it is the one who deserves such hard luck. Let's go to bed."

The next morning Ammon came early, dressed in the outing clothing he had worn the previous summer, and aside from a slight paleness seemed very much the same as when he left. Elnora met him on the old footing, and for a week life went on exactly as it had the previous summer. Mrs. Comstock made mental notes and watched in silence. She could see that Elnora was on a strain, though she hoped Ammon would not. The girl grew restless as the week drew to a close. Once when the gate clicked she suddenly lost colour and moved nervously. Billy came down the walk.

Ammon leaned toward Mrs. Comstock and said, "I am expressly forbidden to speak to Elnora as I would like just now. Would you mind telling her for me that I had a letter from my father this morning saying that Miss Carr is on her way to Europe for the summer?"

"Elnora," said Mrs. Comstock promptly, "I have just heard that Carr woman is on her way to Europe, and I wish to my gracious stars she'd stay there!"

Philip Ammon shouted, but Elnora arose hastily and went to meet Billy. They came into the arbour together and after speaking to Mrs. Comstock and Ammon, Billy said, "Uncle Wesley and I found something funny, and we thought you'd like to see."

"I don't know what I should do without you and Uncle Wesley to help me," said Elnora. "What have you found now?"

"Something I couldn't bring. You have to come to it. I tried to get one and I killed it. They are a kind of insecty things, and they got a long tail that is three fine hairs. They stick those hairs right into the hard bark of trees, and if you pull, the hairs stay fast and it kills the bug."

"We will come at once," laughed Elnora. "I know what they are, and I can use some in my work."

"Billy, have you been crying?" inquired Mrs. Comstock.

Billy lifted a chastened face. "Yes, ma'am," he replied. "This has been the worst day."

"What's the matter with the day?"

"The day is all right," admitted Billy. "I mean every single thing has gone wrong with me."

"Now, that is too bad!" sympathized Mrs. Comstock. "Tell me about it."

"Began early this morning," said Billy. "All Snap's fault, too."

"Now, what has poor Snap been doing?" demanded Mrs. Comstock, her eyes beginning to twinkle.

"Digging for woodchucks, just like he always does. He gets up at two o'clock to dig for them. He was coming in from the woods all tired and covered thick with dirt. I was going to the barn with the pail of water for Uncle Wesley to use in milking. I had to set down the pail to shut the gate so the chickens wouldn't get into the flower beds, and old Snap stuck his dirty nose into the water and began to lap it down. I knew Uncle Wesley wouldn't use that, so I had to go 'way back to the cistern for more, and it pumps awful hard. Made me mad, so I threw the water on Snap."

"Well, what of it?"

"Nothing, if he'd stood still. But it scared him awful, and when he's afraid he just goes a-humping for Aunt Margaret. When he got right up against her he stiffened out and gave a big shake. You oughter seen the nice blue dress she had put on to go to Onabasha!"

Mrs. Comstock and Ammon laughed, but Elnora put

her arms around the boy. "Oh, Billy!" she cried. "That was too bad!"

"She got up early and ironed that dress to wear because it was cool. Then, when it was all dirty, she wouldn't go, and she wanted to real bad." Billy wiped his eyes. "That ain't all, either," he added.

"We'd like to know about it, Billy," suggested Mrs. Comstock, struggling with her face.

"'Cos she couldn't go to the city, she's most worked herself to death, to-day. She's done all the dirty, old hard jobs she could find. She's fixing her grape juice now."

"Sure!" cried Mrs. Comstock. "When a woman is disappointed she always works like a dog to gain sympathy!"

"Well, Uncle Wesley and I are sympathizing all we know how, without her working so. I've squeezed until I almost busted to get the juice out from the seeds and skins. That's the hard part. Now, she has to strain it through white flannel and seal it in bottles, and it's good for sick folks. Most wish I'd get sick myself, so I could have a glass. It's so good!"

Elnora glanced swiftly at her mother.

"I worked so hard," continued Billy, "that she said if I would throw the leavings in the woods, then I could come for you to see about the bugs. Do you want to go?"

"We will all go," said Mrs. Comstock. "I am mightily interested in those bugs myself."

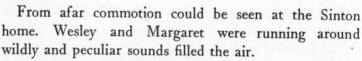

From afar commotion could be seen at the Sinton home. Wesley and Margaret were running around wildly and peculiar sounds filled the air.

"What's the trouble?" asked Ammon, hurrying to Wesley.

"Cholera!" groaned Sinton. "My hogs are dying like flies."

Margaret was softly crying. "Wesley, can't I fix something hot? Can't we do anything? It means several hundred dollars and our winter meat."

"I never saw stock taken so suddenly and so hard," said Wesley. "I have 'phoned for the veterinary to come as soon as he can get here."

All of them hurried to the feeding pen into which the pigs seemed to be gathering from the woods. Among the common stock were big white beasts of pedigree which were Wesley's pride at county fairs. Several of these rolled on their backs, pawing the air feebly and emitting little squeaks. A huge Berkshire sat on his haunches, slowly shaking his head, the water dropping from his eyes, until he, too, rolled over with faint grunts. A pair crossing the yard on wavering legs collided, and attacked each other in anger, only to fall, so weak they scarcely could squeal. A fine snowy Plymouth Rock rooster after several attempts, flew to the fence, balanced with great effort, wildly flapped his wings and started to emit a guttural crow, but broke off and fell sprawling among the pigs, too helpless to stand.

"Did you ever see such a dreadful sight?" sobbed Margaret.

Billy climbed on the fence, took one long look and turned an astounded face to Wesley.

"Why them pigs is drunk!" he cried. "They act just like my pa!"

Wesley turned on Margaret.

"Where did you put the leavings from that grape juice?" he demanded.

"I sent Billy to throw it in the woods."

"Billy ——" began Wesley.

"Threw it just where she told me to," cried Billy. "But some of the pigs came by there coming into the pen, and some were close in the fence corners."

"Did they eat it?" demanded Wesley.

"They just chanked into it," replied Billy graphically. "They pushed, and squealed, and fought over it. You couldn't blame 'em! It was the best stuff I ever tasted!"

Faint squealing, punctuated by feeble crows filled the long pause which ensued.

"Margaret," said Wesley, "run, 'phone that doctor he won't be needed. Billy, take Elnora and Mr. Ammon to see the bugs. Katharine, suppose you help me a little."

Wesley took the clothes basket from the back porch and started in the direction of the cellar. Margaret returned from the telephone.

"I just caught him," she said. "There's that much saved. Why, Wesley, what are you going to do?"

"You go sit on the front porch a little while," said Wesley. "You will feel better if you don't see this."

"Wesley," cried Margaret aghast. "Some of that wine is ten years old. There's days and days of hard work in it, and I couldn't say how much sugar. Dr. Ammon keeps people alive with it when nothing else will stay on their stomachs."

"Let 'em die, then!" said Wesley. "You heard the boy, didn't you?"

"It's a cold process. There's not a particle of fermentation about it!"

"Not a particle of fermentation! Great day, Margaret! Look at those pigs!"

Margaret took a long look. "Leave me a few bottles for mince-meat," she wavered.

"Not a smell for any cause on this earth! You heard the boy! He shan't say, when he grows to manhood that he learned to like it here!"

Wesley made a clean sweep, Mrs. Comstock cheerfully assisting. Then they all went to the woods to see and learn about the wonderful insects. The day ended with a big supper at Sintons', and then they went down to the Comstock cabin for a concert. Elnora played beautifully that night. When the Sintons left she kissed Billy with particular tenderness. She was so moved that she was kinder to Ammon than she had intended to be, and Elnora as an antidote to a disappointed lover, was a decided success in any mood.

However strong the attractions of Edith Carr had

been, once the bond was finally broken, Philip Ammon
could not help realizing that Elnora was the superior
woman, and that he was fortunate to have escaped,
just when he regarded his ties strongest. Every day,
while working with Elnora, he saw more to admire.
He grew very thankful that he was free to try to win
her, and impatient to justify himself to her.

Elnora did not evince the slightest haste to hear what
he had to say, but waited the week she had set, in spite
of Philip's hourly manifest impatience. When she did
consent to listen, Philip realized before he had talked
five minutes, that she was putting herself in Edith Carr's
place, and judging him from what the other girl's stand-
point would be. That was so disconcerting, he did not
plead his cause nearly so well as he had hoped, for when
he ceased Elnora sat in silence.

"You are my judge," he said at last. "What is your
verdict?"

"If I could hear her speak from her heart as I
just have heard you, then I could decide," answered
Elnora.

"She is on the ocean," said Philip. "She went
because she knew she was wholly in the wrong. She
had nothing to say, or she would have remained."

"That sounds plausible," reasoned Elnora, "but it
is pretty hard to find a woman in an affair that
involves her heart, with nothing at all to say. I
fancy if I could meet her just now she would say
several things. I should love to hear them. If I could

talk with her three minutes, I could tell what answer to make you."

"Don't you believe me, Elnora?"

"Unquestioningly," answered Elnora. "But I would believe her also. If only I could meet her I soon would know."

"I don't see how that is to be accomplished," said Ammon, "but I am perfectly willing. There is no reason why you should not meet her, except that she probably would lose her temper and insult you."

"Not to any extent," said Elnora calmly. "I have a tongue of my own, while I am not without some small sense of personal values."

Ammon glanced into her face and began to laugh. Very different of facial formation and colouring, Elnora at times, closely resembled her mother. She joined in Ammon's laugh a little ruefully.

"The point is this," she said. "Someone is going to get hurt, most dreadfully. If the decision as to who it shall be rests with me, I must know it is the right one. Of course, no one ever hinted it to you, but you are a very attractive man, Philip. You are mighty good to look at, and you have a trained, refined mind, that makes you most interesting. For years Edith Carr has felt that you were hers. She has lived expecting to assume the closest relations of life with you. She has thought of you as hers, and you were hers. Now, how is she going to change? I have been thinking — thinking deep and long, Phil. If I were in her place, I simply could not give you up, unless you had made yourself unworthy of love. Undoubtedly, you never seemed so desirable to her as just now, when she is told she can't have you. What I think is that she will come to claim you yet."

"You overlook the fact that it is not in a woman's power to throw away a man and pick him up at leisure," said Ammon with some warmth. "She publicly and repeatedly cast me off. I accepted her decision as publicly as it was made. You have done all your thinking from a wrong viewpoint. You seem to have an idea that it lies with you to decide what I shall do, that if you say the word, I shall return to Edith. Get that thought out of your head! Now, and for all time to come, she is a matter of indifference to me. She killed all feeling in my heart for her so completely, that I do not even dread meeting her. I could see her coming down the walk now without the quickening of a heartbeat. I can meet her as casually as any woman I ever met, and liked least of all women.

"If I hated her, or was angry with her, I could not be sure the feeling would not die. As it is, she has deadened me into a creature of indifference. So you just revise your viewpoint a little, Elnora. Cease thinking it is for you to decide what I shall do, and that I will obey you. I make my own decisions in reference to any woman, save you. The question you are to decide is whether I may remain here, associating with you as I did last summer; but with the difference that it is understood that I am free; that it is my intention to care for

you all I please, to make you return my feeling for you if I can. There is just one question for you to decide, and it is not triangular. It is between us. May I remain? May I love you? Will you give me the chance to prove what I think of you?"

"You speak very plainly," said Elnora.

"This is the time to speak plainly," said Philip Ammon. "There is no use in allowing you to go on threshing out a problem which does not exist. If you do not want me here, say so and I will go. Of course, I warn you before I start, that I will come back. I won't yield without the stiffest fight it is in me to make. I will have all you have to give any man if I can get it. But drop thinking it lies in your power to send me back to Edith Carr. If she were the last woman in the world, and I the last man, I'd jump off the planet before I would give her further opportunity to exercise her temper on me. Narrow this to us, Elnora. Will you take the place she vacated? Will you take the heart she threw away? I'd give my right hand and not flinch, if I could offer you my life, free from any contact with hers, but that is not possible. I can't undo things which are done. I can only profit by experience and build better in the future."

"I don't see how you can be sure of yourself," said Elnora. "I don't see how I could be sure of you. You loved her first, you never can care for me anything like that. Always I'd have to be afraid you were thinking of her and regretting."

"Folly!" cried Ammon. "Regretting what? That I was not married to a woman who was liable to rave at me any time or place, without my being conscious of having given offence? A man does relish that! I am likely to pine for more!"

"You'd be thinking she'd learned a lesson. You would think it wouldn't happen again."

"No, I wouldn't be 'thinking,'" said Ammon. "I'd be everlastingly sure! I wouldn't risk what I went through that night again, not to save my life! Just you and me, Elnora. Decide for us."

"I can't !" cried Elnora. "I am afraid!"

"Very well," said Ammon. "We will wait until you feel that you can. Wait until fear vanishes. Just decide now whether you would rather have me go for a few months, or remain with you. Which shall it be, Elnora?"

"You can never love me as you did her," wailed Elnora.

"I am happy to say I cannot," replied Ammon. "I've cut my matrimonial teeth. I'm cured of wanting to swell in society. I've gotten over being proud of a woman for her looks alone. I have no further use for lavishing myself on a beautiful, elegantly dressed creature, who thinks only of self. I have come to the surface. I have learned that I am just a common man. I admire beauty and beautiful clothing just as much as I ever did; but, first, I want an understanding, deep as the lowest recess of my soul, with the woman I marry. I

405

want to work for you, to plan for you, to build you a
home with every comfort, to give you all good things I
can, to shield you from every evil. I want to interpose
my body between yours and fire, flood, or famine.
I want to give you everything; but I hate the idea of getting nothing at all on which I can depend in return.
Edith Carr had only good looks to offer, and when anger
overtook her, beauty went out like a snuffed candle.

"I want you to love me. I want some consideration.
I even crave respect. I've kept myself clean. So far
as I know how to be, I am honest and scrupulous. It
wouldn't hurt me to feel that you took some interest in
these things. Pretty fierce temptations strike a man,
every few days, in this world. I can keep decent, for a
woman who cares for decency, but when I do, I'd like
to have the fact recognized, by just enough of a show of
appreciation that I could see it. I am tired of this
one-sided business. It has made me selfish. After this,
I want to get a little in return for what I give. Elnora,
you have love, tenderness, and honest appreciation of
the finest in life. Take what I offer, and give what
I ask."

"You do not ask much," said Elnora.

"As for not loving you as I did Edith," continued
Ammon, "as I said before, I hope not! I have a newer
and a better idea of loving. The feeling I offer you was
inspired by you. It is a Limberlost product. It is as much
bigger, cleaner, and more wholesome than any feeling
I ever had for Edith Carr, as you are bigger than she,

when you stand before your classes and in calm dignity explain the marvels of the Almighty, while she stands on a ballroom floor, and gives way to uncontrolled temper. Ye gods, Elnora, if you could look into my soul, you would see it leap and rejoice over my escape! Perhaps it isn't decent, but it's human, and I'm only a common human being. I'm the gladdest thing alive that I'm free! I would turn somersaults and yell if I dared. What an escape! Just snatched out of it with a clean conscience, when I was most besotted. Stop straining after Edith Carr's viewpoint and take a look from mine. Put yourself in my place and try to study out how I feel.

"I am so happy I get religious over it. Fifty times a day I catch myself whispering, 'My soul is escaped!' As for you, take all the time you want. If you had rather be alone, I'll take the next train and stay away as long as I can bear it, but I'll come back. You can be most sure of that. Straight as your pigeons to their loft, I'll come back to you, Elnora. Shall I go?"

"Oh, what's the use to be extravagant?" murmured Elnora.

CHAPTER 22

Wherein Philip Ammon Kneels to the Queen of Love, and Chicago Comes to the Limberlost

THE month which followed was a reproduction of the previous June. There were long moth hunts, days of specimen gathering, wonderful hours with great books, big dinners all of them helped to prepare, and perfect nights filled with music. Everything was as it had been, with the difference that Philip was now an avowed suitor. He missed no opportunity to advance himself in Elnora's graces. At the end of the month he was no nearer any sort of understanding with her than he had been at the beginning. He revelled in the privilege of loving her, but he got no response. Elnora believed in his love, yet she hesitated to accept him, because she could not forget Edith Carr.

One afternoon early in July, Ammon came across the fields, through the Comstock woods, and entered the garden. He inquired for Elnora at the back door and was told that she was reading under the willow. He went around the west end of the cabin to her. She sat on a rustic bench they had made and placed beneath a drooping branch. Ammon had not seen her before in the dress she was wearing. It was clinging mull of pale green, trimmed with narrow ruffles and touched with knots of black velvet; a simple dress, but vastly becoming. Every tint of her bright hair, her luminous eyes, her red lips, and her rose-flushed face, neck, and arms grew a little more vivid with the delicate green setting.

Ammon stopped short. She was so near, so temptingly sweet, he lost control. He went to her with a half-smothered cry after that first long look, dropped on one knee beside her and reached an arm behind her to the bench back, so that he was very near. He caught her hands.

"Elnora!" he cried tensely, "end it now! Say this strain is over. I pledge you that you will be happy. You don't know! If you only would say the word, you would awake to new life and great joy! Won't you promise me now, Elnora?"

The girl sat staring into the west woods, while strong in her eyes was her father's look of seeing something invisible to others. Ammon's arm slipped from the bench around her. His fingers closed firmly over hers, his face came very near.

"Elnora," he pleaded, "you know me well enough. You have had time in plenty. End it now. Say you will be mine!"

He gathered her closer, pressing his face against hers, his breath on her cheek.

"Can't you quite promise yet, my girl of the Limber-lost?"

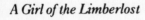

Elnora shook her head. Instantly he released her.

"Forgive me," he begged. "I had no intention of thrusting myself upon you, but, Elnora, you are the veriest Queen of Love, this afternoon. From the tips of your toes to your shining crown, I worship you. All my life I will. I want no woman save you. You are so wonderful this afternoon, I couldn't help urging. Forgive me. Perhaps it was something that came this morning for you. I wrote Polly to send it. May we just try if it fits? Will you tell me if you like it?"

He drew a little white velvet box from his pocket and showed her a splendid emerald ring.

"It may not be right," he said. "The inside of a glove finger is not very accurate for a measure, but it was the best I could do. I wrote Polly to get it, because she and mother are home from the East this week, but next they will go on to our cottage in the north, and no one knows what is right quite so well as Polly."

He laid the ring in Elnora's hand.

"Dearest," he said, "don't slip that on your finger; put your arms around my neck and promise me, all at once and abruptly, or I'll keel over and die of sheer joy."

Elnora smiled.

"I won't! Not all those venturesome things at once; but, Phil, I'm ashamed to confess that ring simply fascinates me. It is the most beautiful one I ever saw, and do you know that I never owned a ring of any kind in my life? Would you think me unwomanly if I slip it on just a second, before I can say for sure. Phil, you know I care! I care very much! You know I will tell you the instant I feel right about it."

"Certainly you will," agreed Ammon promptly. "It is your right to take all the time you choose. I can't put that ring on you until it means a bond between us. I'll shut my eyes and you try it on, so we can see if it fits and looks well."

Philip turned his face toward the west woods and tightly closed his eyes. It was a boyish thing to do, and it caught the hesitating girl in the depths of her heart as the boy element in a man ever appeals to a motherly woman. Before she quite realized what she was doing, the ring slid on her finger. With both arms she caught Ammon and drew him to her breast, holding him closely. Her head drooped over his, her lips were on his hair. So an instant, then her arms dropped. Ammon lifted a convulsed, white face.

"Dear Lord!" he whispered. "You — you didn't mean that, Elnora! You —— What made you do it?"

"You — you looked so boyish!" panted Elnora. "I didn't mean it! I — I forgot that you were older than Billy. Look — look at the ring!"

She thrust her hand before him to distract his attention.

"'The Queen can do no wrong,'" quoted Ammon between his set teeth. "But don't you do that again, Elnora, unless you do mean it. Kings are not so good as queens, and there is a limit with all men. As you say, we will look at your ring. It seems very lovely to me.

Suppose you leave it on until time for me to go. Please do! I have heard of mute appeals; perhaps it will plead for me. I am wild for your lips this afternoon. I am going to take your hands."

He caught both of them and covered them with kisses. He lifted his face.

"Elnora," he said, "will you be my wife?"

"I must have a little more time," she whispered. "I must be absolutely certain, for when I say yes, and give myself to you, only death shall part us. I would not give you up. So I want just a little more time — but, I think I will."

"Thank you," said Ammon. "If at any time you feel that you have reached a decision, will you tell me? I don't feel as if I could lose a second waiting to stumble on that fact. Will you promise me to tell me instantly, or shall I keep asking you until the time comes?"

"You make it difficult," said Elnora. "But I will promise you that. Whenever the last doubt vanishes, I will let you know instantly — if I can."

"Would it be hard for you?" whispered Ammon.

"I — I don't know," faltered Elnora.

"It seems as if I can't be man enough to put this thought aside and give up this afternoon," said Ammon. "I am ashamed of myself, but I can't help it. I am going to ask God to make that last doubt vanish before I go this night. I am going to believe that ring will plead for me. I am going to hope that doubt will disappear suddenly. I will be watching. Every second I will be watching. If it happens and you can't speak, give me your hand. Just the least movement toward me, I will understand. Would it help you to talk it over with your mother? Shall I call her? Shall I ——?"

Honk! Honk! Honk! Hart Henderson set the alarm of the big automobile going as it shot from behind the trees lining the Brushwood road. The picture of a vine-covered cabin, a great drooping tree, a green-clad girl, and a man bending over her very closely flashed into view. Edith Carr caught her breath with a snap. Polly Ammon gave Tom Levering a quick touch and wickedly winked at him.

Several days before, Edith had returned from Europe suddenly. She and Henderson had called at the Ammon residence saying that they were going to motor down to the Limberlost to see Philip a few hours, and urged that Polly and Tom accompany them. Mrs. Ammon knew that her husband would disapprove of the trip, but it was easy to see that Edith Carr had determined on going. So the mother thought it better to have Polly along to support Philip than to allow him to confront Edith unexpectedly and alone. Polly was full of spirit. She did not relish the thought of Edith as a sister. Always they had been in the same set, always Edith, because of greater beauty and wealth, had patronized Polly. Although it had rankled, she had borne it sweetly. But two days before, her father had extracted a promise of secrecy, given her Philip's address and told her to send him the finest emerald ring she could select. Polly

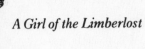

knew how that ring would be used. What she did not know was that the girl who accompanied her went back to the store afterward, made an excuse to the clerk that she had been sent to be absolutely sure that the address was right, and so secured it for Edith Carr.

Two days later Edith had induced Hart Henderson to take her to Onabasha. By the aid of maps they located the Comstock land and passed it, merely to see the place. Henderson hated that trip, and implored Edith not to take it, but she made no effort to conceal from him what she suffered, and it was more than he could endure. He pointed out that Philip had gone away without leaving an address, because he did not wish to see her, or any of them. But Edith was so sure of her power, she felt certain Philip needed only to see her to succumb to her beauty as he always had done, while now she was ready to plead for forgiveness. So they came down the Brushwood road, and Henderson had just said to Edith beside him, "This should be the Comstock land on our left."

A minute later the wood ended, while the sunlight, as always pitiless, etched with distinctness the scene at the west end of the cabin. Instinctively, to save Edith, Henderson set the whistle blowing. He had thought to go on to the city, but Polly Ammon stood, crying, "Phil! Phil!" Tom Levering was on his feet shouting and waving, while Edith in her most imperial manner ordered him to turn into the lane leading through the woods beside the cabin.

"Fix it some way that I get a minute alone with her," she commanded as he stopped the car.

"That is my sister Polly, her fiancé Tom Levering, a friend of mine named Henderson, and ——" began Ammon.

"— and Edith Carr," volunteered Elnora.

"And Edith Carr," repeated Philip Ammon. "Elnora, be brave, for my sake. Their coming can make no difference in any way. I won't let them stay but a few minutes. Come with me!"

"Do I look scared?" inquired Elnora serenely. "This is why you haven't had your answer. I have been waiting just six weeks for that motor. You may bring them to me at the arbour."

Ammon glanced at her and broke into a laugh. She had not lost colour. Her self-possession was perfect. She deliberately turned and walked toward the grape arbour, while he sprang over the west fence and ran to the car.

Elnora standing in the arbour entrance made a perfect picture, framed in green leaves and tendrils. No matter how her heart ached, it was good to her, for it pumped steadily, and kept her cheeks and lips suffused with colour. She saw Philip reach the car and gather his sister into his arms. Past her he reached a hand to Levering, then to Edith Carr and Henderson. He lifted his sister to the ground, and assisted Edith to alight. Instantly, she stepped beside him, and Elnora's heart played its first trick.

She could see that Miss Carr was splendidly beautiful, while she moved with the hauteur and grace supposed to be the prerogatives of royalty. And she had instantly taken possession of Philip Ammon. But Ammon also had a brain which was working with rapidity. He knew Elnora was watching so he swung around to the others.

"Give her up, Tom!" he cried. "I didn't know I wanted to see the little nuisance so badly, but I do. How are father and mother? Polly, didn't the mater send me something?"

"She did!" said Polly Ammon, stopping on the path and lifting her chin as a little child, while she drew away her veil.

Philip caught her in his arms and stooped for his mother's kiss.

"Be good to Elnora!" he whispered.

"Umhu!" assented Polly. And aloud — "Look at that ripping green and gold symphony! I never saw such a beauty! Thomas Asquith Levering, you come straight here and take my hand!"

Edith's move to compel Ammon to approach Elnora beside her had been easy to see; also its failure. Henderson stepped into Ammon's place as he turned to his sister. Instead of taking Polly's hand Levering ran to open the gate. Edith passed through first, but Polly darted in front of her on the run, with Phil holding her arm, and swept up to Elnora. Polly looked for the ring and saw it. That settled matters with her.

"You lovely, lovely, darling girl!" she cried, throwing her arms around Elnora and kissing her. With her lips near Elnora's ear, Polly whispered, "Sister! Dear, dear sister!"

Elnora drew back, staring at Polly in confused amazement. She was a beautiful girl, dressed in some wonderful way, her eyes were sparkling and dancing, and as she turned to make way for the others, she kept one of Elnora's hands in hers. Polly would have dropped very dead in that instant if Edith Carr could have killed with a look, for not until then did she realize that Polly would even many a slight, and that it had been a great mistake to bring her.

Edith bowed low, muttered something and touched Elnora's fingers. Tom Levering took his cue from Polly.

"I always follow a good example," he said, and before anyone could divine his intention he kissed Elnora as he gripped her hand and cried, "Mighty glad to meet you! Like to meet you a dozen times a day, you know!"

Elnora laughed and her heart pumped smoothly. They had accomplished their purpose. They had let her know they were there through compulsion, but on her side. In that instant only pity was in Elnora's breast for the flashing dark beauty, standing with smiling face while her heart must have been filled with exceeding bitterness. Elnora stepped back from the entrance.

"Come into the shade," she urged. "You must have found it warm on these country roads. Won't you lay

aside your dust-coats and have a cool drink? Philip,
would you ask mother to come, and bring that pitcher
in the spring house?"

They entered the arbour exclaiming at the dim, green
coolness. There was plenty of room and wide seats
around the sides, a table in the centre, on which lay a
piece of embroidery, magazines, books, the moth apparatus, and the cyanide jar containing several specimens.
Polly rejoiced in the cooling shade, slipped off her duster,
removed her hat, rumpled her pretty hair and seated
herself to indulge in the delightful occupation of paying
off old scores. Tom Levering followed her example.
Edith took a seat, but refused to remove her hat and
coat, while Henderson stood in the entrance.

"There goes something with wings! Should you have
that?" cried Levering.

He seized a net from the table and raced across the
garden after a butterfly. He caught it and came back
mightily pleased with himself. As the creature struggled
in the net, Elnora noted a repulsed look on Edith Carr's
face. Levering helped the situation beautifully.

"Now what have I got?" he demanded. "Is it just
a common one that everyone knows and you don't keep,
or is it the rarest bird off the perch?"

"You must have had practice, you took that so perfectly," said Elnora. "I am sorry, but it is quite common
and not of a kind I keep. Suppose all of you see how
beautiful it is and then it may go nectar hunting again."

She held the butterfly where all of them could see,

showed its upper and under wing colours, answered Polly's questions as to what it ate, how long it lived, and how it died. Then she put it into Polly's hand saying, "Stand there in the light and loosen your hold slowly and easily."

Elnora caught a brush from the table and began softly stroking the creature's sides and wings. Delighted with the sensation the butterfly slowly opened and closed its wings, clinging to Polly's soft little fingers, while everyone cried out in surprise. Elnora laid aside the brush, and the butterfly sailed away.

"Why, you are a wizard! You charm them!" marvelled Levering.

"I learned that from the Bird Woman," said Elnora. "She takes soft brushes and coaxes butterflies and moths into the positions she wants for the illustrations of a book she is writing. I have helped her often. Most of the rare ones I get go to her."

"Then you don't keep all you take?" questioned Levering.

"Oh, dear, no!" cried Elnora. "Not a tenth! For myself, a pair of each kind to use in illustrating the lectures I give in the city schools in the winter, and one pair for each collection I make. One might just as well keep the big night moths of June, for they only live four or five days anyway. For the Bird Woman, I only save rare ones she has not yet secured. Sometimes I think it is cruel to take such creatures from freedom, even for an hour, but it is the only way to teach the masses

of people how to distinguish the pests they should destroy, from the harmless ones of great beauty, and secure propagation privileges for them. Here comes mother with something cool to drink."

Mrs. Comstock came deliberately, talking to Ammon as she approached. Elnora gave her one searching look, but could discover only an extreme brightness of eye to denote any unusual feeling. She wore one of her lavender dresses, while her snowy hair was high piled. She had taken care of her complexion, and her face had grown fuller during the winter. She might have been anyone's mother with pride, and she was perfectly at ease.

Polly instantly went to her and held up her face to be kissed. Mrs. Comstock's eyes twinkled and she made the greeting hearty.

The drink was compounded of the juices of oranges and berries from the garden. It was cool enough to frost glasses and pitcher and delicious to dusty tired travellers. Soon the pitcher was empty, and Elnora picked it up and went to refill it. While she was gone Henderson asked Philip about some trouble he was having with his car. They went to the woods and began a minute examination to find a defect which did not exist. Polly and Levering were having an animated conversation with Mrs. Comstock. Henderson saw Edith arise, follow the garden path next the woods and stand waiting under the willow which Elnora would pass on her return. It was for that meeting he had made the trip. He got down on the ground, tore up the car, worked, asked for help, and kept Philip busy screwing bolts and applying the oil can. All the time Henderson kept an eye on Edith and Elnora under the willow. But he took pains to lay the work he asked Philip to do where that scene would be out of his sight. When Elnora came around the corner with the pitcher, she found herself facing Edith Carr.

"I want a minute with you," said Miss Carr.

"Very well," replied Elnora, walking on.

"Set the pitcher on the bench there," commanded Edith Carr, as if speaking to a servant.

"I prefer not to offer my guests a warm drink," said Elnora. "I'll come back if you really wish to speak with me."

"I came solely for that," said Edith Carr.

"It would be a pity to travel so far in this dust and heat for nothing. I'll only be gone a second."

Elnora set the pitcher before her mother. "Please serve this," she said. "Miss Carr wishes to speak with me."

"Well, don't you pay the least attention to anything she says," cried Polly. "Tom and I didn't come here because we wanted to. We just came to checkmate her. I hoped I'd get the opportunity to say a word to you, and now she has given it to me. I just want to tell you that she threw Phil over in perfectly horrid style. All of us detest her for it, as much as he does. She hasn't any right to lay the ghost of a claim to him, has she, Tom?"

"Nary a claim," said Tom Levering earnestly. "Why,

421

even you, Polly, couldn't serve me as she did Phil, and ever get me back again. If I were you, Miss Comstock, I'd send my mother to talk with her and I'd stay here."

Tom had gauged Mrs. Comstock rightly. Polly put her arms around Elnora. "Let me go with you, dear," she begged.

"I promised I would speak with her alone," said Elnora, "and she has to be considered. But thank you, very much."

"How I shall love you!" exulted Polly, giving Elnora a parting hug.

The girl slowly and gravely walked back to the willow. She could not imagine just what was coming, but she was promising herself that she would be very patient and control her temper.

"Will you be seated?" she asked politely.

Edith Carr glanced at the bench, while a shudder shook her.

"No. I prefer to stand," she said. "Did Mr. Ammon give you the ring you are wearing, and do you consider yourself engaged to him?"

"By what right do you ask such personal questions as those?" inquired Elnora.

"By the right of a betrothed wife. I have been promised to Philip Ammon ever since I wore short skirts. All our lives we have expected to marry. An agreement of years cannot be broken in one insane moment. Always he has loved me devotedly. Give me ten minutes with him and he will be mine for all time."

"I seriously doubt that," said Elnora. "But I am perfectly willing that you should make the test. I will call him."

"Stop!" commanded Edith Carr. "I told you that it was you I came to see."

"I remember," said Elnora.

"Mr. Ammon is my betrothed," continued Edith Carr. "I expect to take him back to Chicago with me."

"You expect considerable," murmured Elnora. "I will raise no objection to your taking him, if you can — but, I tell you frankly, I don't think it possible."

"You are so sure of yourself as that," scoffed Edith Carr. "One hour in my presence will bring back the old spell, full force. We belong to each other. I will not give him up."

"Then it is untrue that you twice rejected his ring, repeatedly insulted him, and publicly renounced him?"

"That was through you!" cried Edith Carr. "Phil and I never had been so near and so happy as we were on that night. It was your clinging to him for things that caused him to desert me among his guests, while he tried to make me await your pleasure. I realize the spell of this place, for a summer season. I understand what you and your mother have done to inveigle him. I know that your hold on him is quite real. I can see just how you have worked to ensnare him!"

"Men would call that lying," said Elnora calmly. "The second time I met Philip Ammon he told me of his engagement to you, and I respected it. I did by you

as I would want you to do by me. He was here parts
of each day, almost daily last summer. The Almighty
is my witness that never once, by word or look did I
ever make the slightest attempt to interest him in my
person or personality. He wrote you frequently in my
presence. He forgot the violets for which he asked to
send you. I gathered them and carried them to him.
I sent him back to you in unswerving devotion, and the
Almighty is also my witness that I *could* have changed
his heart last summer, if I had tried. I wisely left that
work for you. All my life I shall be glad that I lived
and worked on the square. That he ever would come
back to me free, by your act, I never dreamed. When
he left me I did not hope or expect to see him again,"
Elnora's voice fell soft and low, "and, behold! You
sent him — and free!"

"You exult in that!" cried Edith Carr. "Let me tell
you he is not free! We have belonged for years. We
always will. If you cling to him, and hold him to rash
things he has said and done, because he thought me
still angry and unforgiving with him, you will ruin all
our lives. If he married you, before a month you
would read heart-hunger for me, in his eyes. He could
not love me as he has done, and give me up for a little
scene like that!"

"There is a great poem," said Elnora, "one line of
which reads, 'For each man kills the thing he loves.'
Let me tell you that a woman can do that also. He did
love you — that I concede. But you killed his love

424

everlastingly, when you disgraced him in public. Killed it so completely he does not even feel resentment toward you. To-day, he would do you a favour, if he could; but love you, no! That is over!"

Edith Carr stood truly regal and filled with scorn. "You are mistaken! Nothing on earth could kill that!" she cried, and Elnora saw that the girl really believed what she said.

"You are very sure of yourself!" said Elnora.

"I have reason to be sure," answered Edith Carr. "We have lived and loved too long. I have had years with him to match against your days. He is mine! His work, his ambitions, his friends, his place in society are with me. You may have a summer charm for a sick man in the country; if he tried placing you in society, he soon would see you as others will. It takes birth to position, schooling, and endless practice to meet social demands gracefully. You would put him to shame in a week."

"I hardly think I should follow your example so far," said Elnora dryly. "I have a feeling for Philip that would prevent my hurting him purposely, either in public of private. As for managing a social career for him he never mentioned that he desired such a thing. What he asked of me was that I should be his wife. I understood that to mean that he desired me to keep him a clean house, serve him digestible food, mother his children, and give him loving sympathy and tenderness."

"Shameless!" cried Edith Carr.

"To which of us do you intend that adjective to apply?" inquired Elnora. "I never was less ashamed in all my life. Please remember I am in my own home, and your presence here is not on my invitation."

Miss Carr lifted her head and struggled with her veil. She was very pale and trembling violently, while Elnora stood serene, a faint smile on her lips.

"Such vulgarity!" panted Edith Carr. "How can a man like Ammon endure it?"

"Why don't you ask him?" inquired Elnora. "I can call him with one breath; but, if he judged us as we stand, I should not be the one to tremble at his decision. Miss Carr, you have been quite plain. You have told me in carefully selected words just what you think of me. You insult my birth, education, appearance, and home. I assure you I am legitimate. I will pass a test examination with you on any high school or supplementary branch, or French or German. I will take a physical examination beside you. I will face any social emergency you can mention with you. I am acquainted with a whole world in which Philip Ammon is keenly interested, that you scarcely know exists. I am not afraid to face any audience you can get together anywhere with my violin. I am not repulsive to look at, and I have a wholesome regard for the proprieties and civilities of life. Philip Ammon never asked anything more of me, why should you?"

"It is plain to see," cried Edith Carr, "that you took him when he was hurt and angry and kept his wound wide open. Oh, what have you not done against me?"

"I did not promise to marry him when an hour ago he asked me the last time, and offered me this ring, because there was so much feeling in my heart for you, that I knew I never could be happy, if I felt that in any way I had failed in doing justice to your interests. I did slip on this ring, which he had just brought, because I never owned one, and it is very beautiful, but I made him no promise, nor shall I make any, until I am quite, quite sure, that you fully realize he never would marry you if I sent him away this hour."

"You know perfectly that if your puny hold on him were broken, if he were back in his home, among his friends, and where he was meeting me, in one little week, he would be mine again, as he always has been. In your heart you don't believe what you say. You don't dare trust him in my presence. You are afraid to allow him out of your sight, because you realize what the results would be. Right or wrong, you have made up your mind to ruin him and me, and you are going to be selfish enough to do it. But ——"

"That will do!" said Elnora. "Spare me the enumeration of how I will regret it. I shall regret nothing. I shall not act until I know there will be nothing to regret. I have decided on my course. You may return to your friends."

"What do you mean?" demanded Edith Carr.

"That is my affair," replied Elnora. "Only this!

When your opportunity comes, seize it! Any time you
are in Philip Ammon's presence, exert the charms of
which you boast, and take him. I grant you are justified in doing it if you can. I want nothing more than
I want to see you marry Philip, if he wants you. He is
just across the fence under that automobile. Go spread
your meshes and exert your wiles. I won't stir to stop
you. Take him to Onabasha, and to Chicago with you.
Use every art you possess. If the old charm can be
revived I will be the first to wish both of you well. Now,
I must return to my guests. Kindly excuse me."

Elnora turned and went back to the arbour. Edith
Carr followed the fence and passed through the gate
into the west woods where she asked Henderson if the
car was ready. As she stood near him she whispered,
"Take Phil back to Onabasha with us."

"I say, Ammon, can't you go to the city with us and
help me find a shop where I can get this pinion fixed?"
asked Henderson. "We want to lunch and start back
by five. That will get us home by midnight. Why
don't you bring your automobile here?"

"I am a working man," said Philip. "I have no
time to be out motoring. I can't see anything the matter
with your car, myself; but, of course, you don't want to
break down in the night, on strange roads, with women
on your hands. I'll see."

Philip went into the arbour, where Polly took possession of his lap, fingered his hair, and kissed his forehead
and lips.

"When are you coming to the cottage, Phil?" she asked. "Come soon, and bring Miss Comstock for a visit. All of us would be so glad to have her."

Philip beamed on Polly. "I'll see about that," he said. "Sounds pretty good. Elnora, Henderson is in trouble with his automobile. He wants me to go to Onabasha with him to show him where the doctor lives and help him get fixed so he can start back this evening. It will take about two hours. May I go?"

"Of course, you must go," she said, laughing lightly. "You can't leave your sister. Why don't you go back to Chicago with them? There is plenty of room, and you could have a fine visit."

"I'll be back in just two hours," said Ammon. "While I am gone, you be thinking over what we were talking of when the folks came."

"Miss Comstock can go with us just as well as not," said Polly. "That back seat was made for three, and I can sit on your lap."

"Come on! Do come!" urged Ammon instantly, and Tom Levering joined him, but Henderson and Edith silently waited at the gate.

"No, thank you," laughed Elnora. "That would crowd you, and it's warm and dusty. We will say good-bye here."

She offered her hand to all of them, and when she came to Ammon she gave him one long steady look in the eyes, then shook hands with him also.

429

CHAPTER 23

Wherein Elnora Reaches a Decision, and Freckles and the Angel Appear

"WELL, she came, didn't she?" remarked Mrs. Comstock to Elnora as they watched the automobile speed down the road. As it turned the Limberlost corner, Ammon arose and waved to them.

"She hasn't got him yet, anyway," said Mrs. Comstock, taking heart. "What's that on your finger, and what did she say to you?"

Elnora explained about the ring as she drew it off.

"I have several letters to write, then I am going to change my dress and walk down toward Aunt Margaret's for a little exercise. I may meet some of them, and I don't want them to see this ring. You keep it until Philip comes," said Elnora. "As for what Miss Carr said to me, many things, two of importance. One, that I lacked every social requirement necessary for the happiness of Philip Ammon, and that if I married him I would see inside a month that he was ashamed of me ——"

"Aw, shockins!" scorned Mrs. Comstock. "Go on!"

"The other was that she has been engaged to him for years, that he belongs to her, and she refuses to give

him up. She said that if he were in her presence one
hour, she would have him under a mysterious thing she
calls 'her spell' again; if he were where she could see
him for one week, everything would be made up. It
is her opinion that he is suffering from wounded pride,
and that the slightest concession on her part will bring
him to his knees before her."

Mrs. Comstock giggled. "I do hope the boy isn't
weak-kneed," she said. "I just happened to be passing
the west window this afternoon ——"

Elnora laughed. "Nothing save actual knowledge
ever would have made me believe there was a girl in all
this world so infatuated with herself. She speaks
casually of her power over men, and boasts of 'bringing
a man to his knees' as complacently as I would pick
up a net and say, 'I am going to take a butterfly.' She
actually and honestly believes that if Philip were with
her a little while she could re-kindle his love for her
and awaken in him every particle of the old devotion.
Mother, the girl is honest! She is absolutely sincere!
She so believes in herself and the strength of Phil's love
for her, that all her life she will believe in and brood
over that thought, unless she is taught differently. So
long as she thinks that, she will nurse wrong ideas and
pine over her blighted life. She must be taught that
Phil is absolutely free, and yet he will not go to her."

"But how on earth are you proposing to teach her
that?"

"The way will open."

"Lookey here, Elnora!" cried Mrs. Comstock. "That Carr girl is the handsomest dark woman I ever saw. She's got to the place where she won't stop at anything. Her coming here proves that. I don't believe there was a thing the matter with that automobile. I think that was a scheme she fixed up to get Phil where she could see him alone, as she worked to see you. If you are going deliberately to put Philip under her influence again, you've got to brace yourself for the possibility that she may win. A man is a weak mortal, where a lovely woman is concerned, and he never denied that he loved her once. You may make yourself downright miserable."

"But, mother, if she won, it wouldn't make me half so miserable as to marry Phil myself, and then read hunger for her in his eyes! Someone has got to suffer over this. If it proves to be me, I'll bear it, and you'll never hear a whisper of complaint from me. I know the real Philip Ammon better in our months of work in the fields, than she knows him in all her years of society engagements. So she shall have the hour she asked, many, many of them, enough to make her acknowledge that she is wrong. Now, I am going to write my letters and take my walk."

Elnora threw her arms around her mother and kissed her repeatedly. "Don't you worry about me," she said. "I will get along all right, and whatever happens, I always will be your girl and you my darling mother."

She left two sealed notes on her desk. Then she changed her dress, packed a small bundle which she dropped with her hat from the window by the willow, and softly went downstairs. Mrs. Comstock was in the garden. Elnora picked up the hat and bundle, hurried down the road a few rods, then climbed the fence and entered the woods. She took a diagonal course, and after a long walk reached a road two miles west and one south. There she straightened her clothing, put on her hat and a thin dark veil and waited the passing of the next trolley. She left it at the first town and took a train for Fort Wayne. She made that point just in time to climb on the evening train north, as it pulled from the station. It was after midnight when she left the car at Grand Rapids, and went into the depot to await the coming of day.

Tired out, she laid her head on her bundle and fell asleep on a seat in the women's waiting-room. Long after light she was awakened by the roar and rattle of trains. She washed, re-arranged her hair and clothing, and went into the general waiting-room to find her way to the street. She saw him as he entered the door. There was no mistaking the tall, lithe figure, the bright hair, the lean, brown-splotched face, the steady gray eyes. He was dressed for travelling, and carried a light overcoat and a bag. Straight to him Elnora went speeding.

"Oh, I was just starting to find you!" she cried.

"Thank you!" he said.

"You are going away?" she panted.

433

"Not if I am needed. I have a few minutes. Can you be telling me briefly?"

"I am the Limberlost girl to whom your wife gave the dress for Commencement last spring, and both of you sent lovely gifts. There is a reason, a very good reason, why I must be hidden for a time, and I came straight to you — as if I had a right."

"You have!" answered Freckles. "Any boy or girl who ever suffered one pang in the Limberlost, has a claim to the best drop of blood in my heart. You needn't be telling me anything more. The Angel is at our cottage on Mackinac. You shall tell her and play with the babies while you want shelter. This way!"

They breakfasted in a luxurious car, talked over the swamp, the work of the Bird Woman; Elnora told of her nature lectures in the schools, and soon they were great friends. In the evening they left the train at Mackinaw City and crossed the Straits by boat. Sheets of white moonlight flooded the water and paved a molten path across the breast of it straight to the face of the moon.

The island lay a dark spot on the silver surface, its tall trees sharply outlined on the summit, and a million lights blinked around the shore. The night guns boomed from the white fort and a dark sentinel paced the ramparts above the little city tucked down close to the water. A great tenor summering in the north came out on the upper deck of the big boat, and, baring his head, faced the moon and sang, "Oh, the moon shines bright on my old Kentucky home!" Elnora thought of the Limberlost, of Philip, and her mother, and almost choked with the sobs that would rise in her throat. On the dock a woman of exquisite beauty swept into the arms of Terrence O'More.

"Oh, Freckles!" she cried. "You've been gone a month!"

"Four days, Angel, just four days by the clock," remonstrated Freckles. "Where are the children?"

"Asleep! Thank goodness! I'm worn to a thread. I never saw such inventive, active children. I can't keep track of them!"

"I have brought you help," said Freckles. "Here is the Limberlost girl in whom the Bird Woman is interested. Miss Comstock needs a rest before beginning her school work for next year, so she came to us."

"You dear thing! How good of you!" cried the Angel. "We shall be so happy to have you!"

In her room that night, in a beautiful cottage furnished with every luxury, Elnora lifted a tired face to the Angel.

"Of course, you understand there is something back of this?" she said. "I must tell you."

"Yes," agreed the Angel. "Tell me! If you get it out of your system, you will stand a better chance of sleeping."

Elnora stood brushing the copper-bright masses of her hair as she talked. When she finished the Angel was almost hysterical.

435

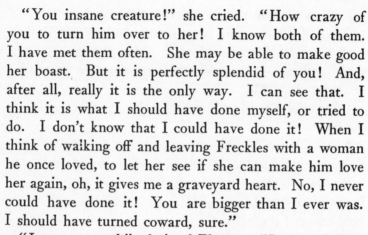

"You insane creature!" she cried. "How crazy of you to turn him over to her! I know both of them. I have met them often. She may be able to make good her boast. But it is perfectly splendid of you! And, after all, really it is the only way. I can see that. I think it is what I should have done myself, or tried to do. I don't know that I could have done it! When I think of walking off and leaving Freckles with a woman he once loved, to let her see if she can make him love her again, oh, it gives me a graveyard heart. No, I never could have done it! You are bigger than I ever was. I should have turned coward, sure."

"I am a coward," admitted Elnora. "I am soul-sick! I am afraid I shall lose my senses before this is over. I didn't want to come! I wanted to stay, to go straight into his arms, to bind myself with his ring, to love him with all my heart. It wasn't my fault that I came. There was something inside that just pushed me. She is beautiful ——"

"I quite agree with you!"

"You can imagine how fascinating she can be. She used no arts on me. Her purpose was to cower me. She found she could not do that, but she did a thing which helped her more. She proved that she was honest, perfectly sincere in what she thought. She believes that if she merely beckons to Philip, he will go to her. So I am giving her the opportunity to learn from him what he will do. She never will believe it from anyone else. When she is satisfied, I shall be also."

"But, child! Suppose she wins him back!"

"That is the supposition with which I shall eat and sleep for the next few weeks. Would one dare ask for a peep at the babies before going to bed?"

"Now, you are perfect!" announced the Angel. "I never should have liked you all I can if you had been content to go to sleep in this house without asking to see the babies. Come this way. We named the first boy for his father, of course, and the girl for Aunt Alice. The next boy is named for my father, and the baby for the Bird Woman. After this we are going to branch out."

Elnora began to laugh.

"Oh, I suspect there will be quite a number of them," said the Angel serenely. "I am told the more there are the less trouble they make. The big ones take care of the little ones. We want a large family. This is our start."

She entered a dark room and held aloft a candle. She went to the side of a small white iron bed in which lay a boy of eight and another of three. They were perfectly formed, rosy children, the elder a replica of his mother, the other very like. Then they came to a cradle where a baby girl of almost two slept soundly, and looked a picture.

"But just see here!" said the Angel. She threw the light on a sleeping girl of six. A mass of red curls swept the pillow. Line and feature the face was that of Freckles. Without asking, Elnora knew the colour and expression of the closed eyes. The Angel handed

437

Elnora the candle, and, stooping, straightened the child's body. She ran her fingers through the bright curls, and lightly touched the aristocratic little nose.

"The supply of freckles holds out in my family, you see!" she said. "Both of the girls will have them, and the second boy a few."

She stood an instant longer, then, bending, ran her hand caressingly down a rosy bare leg, while she kissed the babyish red mouth. There had been some reason for touching all of them, the kiss fell on the lips which were like Freckles's.

To Elnora she said a tender good night, whispering brave words of encouragement and making plans to fill the days to come. Then she went away. An hour later there was a light tap on the girl's door.

"Come!" she called as she lay staring into the dark.

The Angel felt her way to the bedside, sat down and took Elnora's hands.

"I just had to come back to you," she said. "I have been telling Freckles, and he is almost hurting himself with laughing. I didn't think it was funny, but he does. He thinks it's the funniest thing that ever happened. He says that to run away from Mr. Ammon, when you had made him no promise at all, when he wasn't sure of you, won't send him home to her; it will set him hunting you! He says if you had combined the wisdom of Solomon, Socrates, and all the rest of the wise men, you couldn't have chosen any course that would have sealed him to you so surely. He feels that now Ammon will perfectly hate her for coming down there and driving you away. And you went to give her the chance she wanted. Oh, Elnora! It is getting funny! I see it, too!"

The Angel rocked on the bedside. Elnora faced the dark in silence.

"Forgive me," gulped the Angel. "I didn't mean to laugh. I didn't think it was funny, until all at once it came to me. Oh, dear! Elnora, it *is* funny! I've got to laugh!"

"Maybe it is," admitted Elnora, "to others; but it isn't very funny to me. And it won't be to Philip, or to mother."

That was very true. Mrs. Comstock had been slightly prepared for stringent action of some kind, by what Elnora had said. The mother instantly had guessed where the girl would go, but nothing was said to Philip. That would have been to invalidate Elnora's test in the beginning, and Mrs. Comstock knew her child well enough to know that she never would marry Ammon, unless she felt it right that she should. The only way to know was to find out, and Elnora had gone to seek the information. There was nothing to do but wait until she came back, and her mother was not in the least uneasy but that the girl would return brave and self-reliant, as always.

Philip Ammon hurried back to the Limberlost, strong in the hope that now he might take Elnora into his arms and receive her promise to become his wife. His first shock of disappointment came when he found her gone.

In talking with Mrs. Comstock he learned that Edith Carr had made an opportunity to speak with Elnora alone. He hastened down the road to meet her, coming back an agitated man. Then search revealed the notes. His read:

DEAR PHILIP:

I find that I am never going to be able to answer your question of this afternoon fairly to all of us, when you are with me. So I am going away a few weeks to think over matters alone. I shall not tell you, or even mother, where I am going, but I shall be safe, well cared for, and happy. Please go back home and live among your friends, just as you always have done, and on or before the first of September, I will write you where I am, and what I have decided. Please do not blame Edith Carr for this, and do not avoid her. I hope you will call on her and be friends. I think she is very sorry, and covets your friendship at least. Until September, then, as ever,

ELNORA.

Mrs. Comstock's note was much the same. Ammon was ill with disappointment. In the arbour he laid his head on the table, among the implements of Elnora's loved work, and gulped down dry sobs he could not restrain. Mrs. Comstock never had liked him so well. Her hand involuntarily crept toward his dark head, then she drew back. Elnora would not want her to do anything whatever to influence him.

"What am I going to do to convince Edith Carr that I do not love her, and Elnora that I am hers?" he demanded.

"I guess you have to figure that out yourself," said Mrs. Comstock. "I'd be glad to help you if I could, but it seems to be up to you."

Ammon sat a long time in silence. "Well, I have decided!" he said abruptly. "Are you perfectly sure Elnora had plenty of money and a safe place to go?"

"Absolutely!" answered Mrs. Comstock. "She has been taking care of herself ever since she was born, and she always has come out all right, so far; I'll stake all I'm worth on it, that she always will. I don't know where she is, but I'm not going to worry about her safety."

"I can't help worrying!" cried Philip. "I can think of fifty things that may happen to her when she thinks she is safe. This is distracting! First, I am going to run up to see my father. Then, I'll let you know what we have decided. Is there anything I can do for you?"

"Nothing!" said Mrs. Comstock.

But the desire to do something for him was so strong with her she scarcely could keep her lips closed or her hands quiet. She longed to tell him what Edith Carr had said, how it had affected Elnora, and to comfort him as she felt she could. But loyalty to the girl held her. If Elnora truly felt that she could not decide until Edith Carr was convinced, then Edith Carr would have to yield or triumph. It rested with Philip. So Mrs. Comstock kept silent, while Philip took the night limited, a bitterly disappointed man.

By noon the next day he was in his father's offices. They had a long conference, but did not arrive at much until the elder Ammon suggested sending for Polly. Anything that might have happened could be explained

after Polly had told of the private conference between Edith and Elnora.

"Talk about lovely woman!" cried Philip Ammon bitterly. "One would think that after such a dose as Edith gave me, she would be satisfied to let me go my way, but no! Not caring for me enough herself to save me from public disgrace, she must now pursue me to keep any other woman from loving me. I call that too much! I am going to see her, and I want you to go with me, father."

"Very well," said Mr. Ammon, "I will go."

When Edith Carr came into her reception room that afternoon, gowned for conquest, she expected only Philip, and him penitent. She came hurrying toward him, smiling, radiant, ready to use every allurement she possessed, and paused in dismay when she saw his cold face and his father.

"Why, Phil!" she cried. "When did you come home?"

"I am not at home," answered Philip. "I merely ran up to see my father on business, and to inquire of you what it was you said to Miss Comstock yesterday that caused her to disappear before I could get back to the Limberlost."

"Miss Comstock disappear! Impossible!" cried Edith Carr. "Where could she go?"

"I thought perhaps you could answer that, since it was through you that she went."

"Phil, I haven't the faintest idea where she is," said the girl gently.

"But you know perfectly why she went! Kindly tell me that."

"Let me see you alone, and I will."

"Here and now, or not at all."

"Phil!"

"What did you say to the girl I love?"

Then Edith Carr stretched out her arms.

"Phil, I am the girl you love!" she cried. "All your life you have loved me. Surely it cannot be all gone in a few weeks of misunderstanding. I was jealous of her! I did not want you to leave me an instant that night for any other girl living. That was the moth I was representing. Everyone knew it! I wanted you to bring it to me. When you did not, I knew instantly it had been for her that you worked last summer, she who suggested my dress, she who had power to take you from me, when I wanted you most. The thought drove me mad, and I said and did those insane things. Phil, I beg your pardon! I ask your forgiveness. Yesterday she said that you had told her of me at once. She vowed both of you had been true to me — and, Phil, I couldn't look into her eyes and not see that it was the truth. Oh, Phil, if you understood how I have suffered you would forgive me. Phil, I never knew how much I cared for you! I will do anything — anything!"

"Then tell me what you said to Elnora yesterday that drove her, alone and friendless, into the night, heaven knows where!"

"You have no thought for anyone save her?"

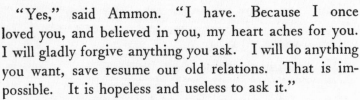

"Yes," said Ammon. "I have. Because I once loved you, and believed in you, my heart aches for you. I will gladly forgive anything you ask. I will do anything you want, save resume our old relations. That is impossible. It is hopeless and useless to ask it."

"You truly mean that!"

"Yes."

"Then find out from her what I said!"

"Come, father," said Philip rising.

"You were going to show Edith Miss Comstock's letter," suggested Mr. Ammon.

"I have not the slightest interest in Miss Comstock's letter," said Edith Carr.

"You are not even interested in the fact that she says you are not responsible for her going, and that I am to call on you and be friends with you ?"

"That is interesting, indeed!" sneered Miss Carr.

She took the letter, read and returned it.

"She has done what she could for my cause, it seems," she said coldly. "How very generous of her! Do you propose calling out Pinkertons and instituting a general search ?"

"No," replied Ammon. "I simply propose to go back to the Limberlost and live with her mother, until Elnora becomes convinced that I am not courting you, and never will be. Then, perhaps, she will come home to us. Good-bye. Good luck to you always!"

CHAPTER 24

Wherein Edith Carr Wages a Battle, and Hart Henderson Stands Guard

MANY people looked, a few followed, as Edith Carr slowly came down the main street of Mackinac, pausing here and there to note the glow of colour in one small booth after another, overflowing with gay curios. That street of packed white sand, winding with the curves of the shore, outlined with brilliant shops, and thronged with laughing, bare-headed people in outing costumes was a picturesque and fascinating sight. Thousands annually made long journeys and paid exorbitant prices to take part in that pageant.

As Edith Carr slowly progressed, she was the most distinguished figure of the old street. Her clinging black gown was sufficiently elaborate for a dinner dress. On her head was a large, wide, drooping-brimmed black hat, with immense floating black plumes, while on the brim, and among the laces on her breast, glowed velvety, deep red roses. Some way these made up for the lack of colour in her cheeks and lips, and while her eyes seemed unnaturally bright, to a close observer they looked weary. Despite the effort she made to move lightly she was very tired, and dragged her heavy feet with an effort.

She turned at the little street leading down to the dock, and went out to meet the big lake steamer ploughing up the Straits from Chicago. Past the landing place, on to the very end of the pier she went, then sat down, leaned against a dock support and closed her tired eyes. When the steamer came very near she languidly watched the people lining the railing. Instantly she marked one lean anxious face turned toward hers, and with a throb of pity she lifted a hand and waved to Hart Henderson. He was the first man off the boat, coming to her instantly. She spread her trailing skirts and motioned him to sit beside her. Silently they looked across the softly lapping water. At last she forced herself to speak to him.

"Did you have a successful trip?"

"I accomplished my purpose."

"You didn't lose any time getting back."

"I never do when I am coming to you."

"Do you want to go to the cottage for anything?"

"No."

"Then let us sit here and wait until the Petosky steamer comes in. I like to watch the boats. Sometimes I study the faces, if I am not too tired."

"Have you seen any new types to-day?"

She shook her head. "This has not been an easy day, Hart."

"And it's going to be worse," said Henderson bitterly. "There's no use putting it off. Edith, I saw someone to-day."

"You should have seen thousands," she said lightly.

"I did. But of them all, only one will be of interest to you."

"Man or woman?"

"Man."

"Where?"

"Lake Shore private hospital."

"An accident?"

"No. Nervous and physical breakdown."

"Phil said he was going back to the Limberlost."

"He went. He was there three weeks, but the strain broke him. He has an old letter in his hands that he has handled until it is ragged. He held it up to me and said, 'You can see for yourself that she says she will be well and happy, but we can't know until we see her again, and that may never be. She may have gone too near that place her father went down, some of that Limberlost gang may have found her in the forest, she may lie dead in some city morgue this instant, waiting for me to find her body."

"Hart! For pity sake stop!"

"I can't," cried Henderson desperately. "I am forced to tell you. They are fighting brain fever. He did go back to the swamp and he prowled it night and day. The days down there are hot now, and the nights wet with dew and cold. He paid no attention and forgot his food. A fever started and his uncle brought him home. They've never had a word from her, or found a trace of her. Mrs. Comstock thought she had gone to O'More's at Grand Rapids, so when Phil got sick

447

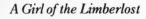

she telegraphed there. They had been gone all summer, so her mother is as anxious as Phil."

"The O'Mores are here," said Edith. "I haven't seen any of them, because I haven't gone out much in the few days since we came, but this is their summer home."

"Edith, they say at the hospital that it will take careful nursing to save Phil. He is surrounded by stacks of maps and railroad guides. He is trying to frame up a plan to set the entire detective agency of the country to work. He says he will stay there just two days longer. The doctors say he will kill himself when he goes. He is a sick man, Edith. His hands are burning and shaky and his breath was hot against my face."

"Why are you telling me?" It was a cry of acute anguish.

"He thinks you know where she is."

"I do not! I haven't an idea! I never dreamed she would go away when she had him in her hand! I should not have done it!"

"He said it was something you said to her that made her go."

"That may be, but it don't prove that I know where she went."

Henderson looked across the water and suffered keenly. At last he turned to Edith and laid a firm, strong hand over hers.

"Edith," he said, "do you realize how serious this is?"

"I suppose I do."

"Do you want as fine a fellow as Phil driven any

further? If he leaves that hospital now, and goes out to the exposure and anxiety of a search for her, there will be a tragedy that no after regrets can avert. Edith, what did you say to Miss Comstock that made her run away from Phil?"

The girl turned her face from him and sat still, but the man gripping her hands and waiting in agony could see that she was shaken by the jolting of the heart in her breast.

"Edith, what did you say?"

"What difference can it make?"

"It might furnish some clue to her action."

"It could not possibly."

"Phil thinks so. He has thought so until his brain is worn enough to give way. Tell me, Edith!"

"I told her Phil was mine! That if he were away from her an hour and back in my presence, he would be to me as he always had been."

"Edith, did you believe that?"

"I would have staked my life, my soul on it!"

"Do you believe it now?"

There was no answer. Henderson took her other hand and gripping both of them firmly he said softly, "Don't mind me, dear. I don't count! I'm just old Hart! You can tell me anything. Do you still believe that?"

The beautiful head barely moved in negation. Henderson gathered both her hands in one of his and stretched an arm across her shoulders to the post to support her.

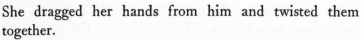

She dragged her hands from him and twisted them together.

"Oh, Hart!" she cried. "It isn't fair! There is a limit! I have suffered my share. Can't you see? Can't you understand?"

"Yes," he panted. "Yes, my girl! Tell me just this one thing yet, and I'll cheerfully kill anyone who annoys you further. Tell me, Edith!"

Then she lifted her great, dull, pain-filled eyes to his and cried, "No! I do not believe it now! I know it is not true! I killed his love for me. It is dead and gone forever. Nothing will revive it! Nothing in all this world. And that is not all. I did not know how to touch the depths of his nature. I never developed in him those things he was made to enjoy. He admired me. He was proud to be with me. He thought, and I thought, that he worshipped me; but I know now that he never did care for me as he cares for her. Never! I can see it! I planned to lead society, to make his home a place sought for my beauty and popularity. She plans to further his political ambitions, to make him comfortable physically, to stimulate his intellect, to bear him a brood of red-faced children. He likes her and her plans as he never did me and mine. Oh, my soul! Now, are you satisfied?"

She dropped back against his arm exhausted. Henderson held her and learned what suffering truly means. He fanned her with his hat, rubbed her cold hands and murmured broken, incoherent things. By and by great slow tears slipped from under her closed lids, but when she opened them her eyes were dull and hard.

"What a rag one is when the last secret of the soul is torn out and laid bare!" she cried.

Henderson thrust his handkerchief into her fingers and whispered, "Edith, the boat has been creeping up. It's very near. Maybe some of our crowd are on it. Hadn't we better get away from here before it lands?"

"If I can walk," she said. "Oh, I am so dead tired, Hart!"

"Yes, dear," said Henderson soothingly. "Just try to get past the landing before the boat anchors. If I only dared carry you!"

They struggled through the waiting masses, but directly opposite the landing there was a backward movement in the happy, laughing crowd, the gang-plank came down with a slam, and people began hurrying from the boat. Crowded against the fish house on the dock, Henderson could only advance a few steps at a time. He was straining every nerve to protect and assist Edith. He saw no one he recognized near them, so he slipped his arm across her back to help support her. He felt her stiffen against him and catch her breath. At the same instant, the clearest, sweetest male voice he ever had heard called, "Be careful there, little men!"

Henderson shot a swift glance toward the boat. Terrence O'More just had stepped from the gang-plank, escorting a little daughter, so like him, it was comical. There followed a picture not easy to describe. The Angel

in the full flower of her beauty, richly dressed, a laugh
on her cameo face, the setting sun glinting on her gold
hair, escorted by her eldest son, who held her hand
tightly and carefully watched her steps. Next came
Elnora, dressed with equal richness, a trifle taller and
slenderer, almost the same type of colouring, but with
different eyes and hair, facial lines and expression. She
was led by the second O'More boy who convulsed the
crowd by crying, "Tareful, Elnora! Don't 'oo be
'teppin' in de water!"

People surged around them, purposely closing them in.

"What lovely women! Who are they? It's the
O'Mores. The lightest one is his wife. Is that her
sister? No, it is his! They say he has a title in Eng-
land."

Whispers ran fast and audible. As the crowd pressed
around the party an opening was left beside the fish sheds.
Edith ran down the dock. Henderson sprang after her,
catching her arm and assisting her to the street.

"Up the shore! This way!" she panted. "Everyone
will go to dinner the first thing they do."

They left the street and started around the beach,
but Edith was breathless from running, while the yielding
sand made hard walking.

"Help me!" she cried clinging to Henderson. He
put his arm around her, almost carrying her out of sight
into a little cove walled by high rocks at the back, while
there was a clean floor of white sand, and logs washed
from the lake for seats. He found one of these with

a back rest, and hurrying down to the water he soaked his handkerchief and carried it to her. She passed it across her lips, over her eyes, and then pressed the palms of her hands upon it. Henderson removed the heavy hat, fanned her with his, and wet the handkerchief again.

"Hart, what makes you?" she said wearily. "My mother doesn't care. She says this is good for me. Do you think this is good for me, Hart?"

"Edith, you know I would give my life if I could save you this," he said, and could not speak further.

She leaned against him, closed her eyes and lay silent so long the man fell into panic.

"Edith, you are not unconscious?" he whispered, touching her.

"No. Just resting. Please don't leave me."

He held her carefully, softly fanning her. She was suffering almost more than either of them could bear.

"I wish your boat was here," she said at last. "I want to sail fast with the wind in my face."

"There is no wind. I can get my motor around in a few minutes."

"Then get it."

"Lie on the sand. I can 'phone from the first booth. It won't take but a little while."

Edith lay on the white sand, and Henderson covered her face with her hat. Then he ran to the nearest booth and talked imperatively. Presently he was back bringing a hot drink that was stimulating. Shortly the motor

453

ran close to the beach and stopped. Henderson's servant brought a row-boat ashore and took them to the launch. It was filled with cushions and wraps. Henderson made a couch and soon, warmly covered, Edith sped out over the water in search of peace.

Hour after hour the boat ran up and down the shore. The moon arose and the night air grew very chilly. Henderson put on an overcoat and piled more covers on Edith.

"You must take me home," she said at last. "The folks will be uneasy."

He was compelled to take her to the cottage with the battle still raging. He went back early the next morning, but already she had wandered out over the island. Instinctively Henderson felt that the shore would attract her. There was something in the tumult of rough little Huron's waves that called to him. It was there he found her, crouching so close the water the foam was dampening her skirts.

"May I stay?" he asked.

"I have been hoping you would come," she answered. "It's bad enough when you are here, but it is a little easier than bearing it alone."

"Thank God for that!" said Henderson sitting beside her. "Shall I talk to you?"

She shook her head. So they sat by the hour. At last she spoke.

"Of course, you know there is something I have got to do, Hart!"

"You have not!" cried Henderson violently. "That's all nonsense! Give me just one word of permission. That is all that is required of you."

"'Required'? You grant, then, that there is something 'required'?"

"One word. Nothing more."

".Did you ever know one word could be so big, so black, so desperately bitter? Oh, Hart!"

"No."

"But you know it now, Hart!"

"Yes."

"And still you say that it is 'required'?"

Henderson suffered unspeakably. He twisted and fumed impotently. At last he said, "If you had seen and heard him, Edith, you, too, would feel that it is 'required.' Remember ——"

"No! No! No!" she cried. "Don't ask me to remember even the least of my pride and folly. Let me forget!"

She sat silent a long time.

"Will you go with me?" she whispered.

"Of course."

At last she arose.

"I might as well give up and get it over," she faltered.

That was the first time in her life that Edith Carr ever had proposed to give up anything she wanted.

"Help me, Hart!"

Henderson started around the beach assisting her all he could. Finally he stopped.

"Edith, there is no sense in this! You are too tired to go. You know you can trust me. You wait in any of these lovely places and send me. You will be safe, and I'll run. One word is all that is necessary."

"But I've got to say that word myself, Hart!"

"Then write it, and let me carry it. The message is not going to prove who went to the office and sent it."

"That is quite true," she said dropping wearily, but she made no movement to take the pen and paper he offered.

"Hart, you write it," she said at last.

Henderson turned away his face. He gripped the pen, while his breath sucked between his dry teeth.

"Certainly!" he said when he could speak. "Mackinac, August 27, 1908. Philip Ammon, Lake Shore Hospital, Chicago." He paused with suspended pen and glanced at Edith. Her white lips were working, but no sound came. "Miss Comstock is at Terrence O'More's, on Mackinac Island," prompted Henderson.

Edith nodded.

"Signed, Henderson," continued the big man.

Edith shook her head.

"Say, 'She is well and happy,' and sign, Edith Carr!" she panted.

"Not on your life!" flashed Henderson.

"For the love of mercy, Hart, don't make this any harder! It is the least I can do, and it takes every ounce of strength in me to do it."

"Will you wait for me here?" he asked.

She nodded, and, pulling his hat lower over his eyes, Henderson ran around the shore. In less than an hour he was back. He helped her a little farther to where the Devil's Kitchen lay cut into the rocks; it furnished places to rest, and cool water. Before long his man came with the boat. From it they spread blankets on the sand for her, and made chafing-dish tea. She tried to refuse it, but the fragrance overcame her and she drank ravenously. Then Henderson cooked several dishes and spread an appetizing lunch. She was young, strong, and almost famished for food. She was forced to eat. That made her feel a world better. Then Henderson helped her into the boat and ran it through shady coves of the shore, where there were refreshing breezes. When she fell asleep the girl did not know, but the man did. Sadly in need of rest himself, he ran that boat for five hours through quiet bays, away from noisy parties, and where the shade was cool and deep. When she woke he took her home, and as they went she knew that she had been mistaken. She would not die. Her heart was not even broken. She had suffered horribly; she would suffer more; but eventually the pain must wear out. Into her head crept a few lines of an old opera —

> "Hearts do not break, they sting and ache,
> For old love's sake, but do not die,
> As witnesseth the living I."

That evening they were sailing down the Straits before a stiff breeze and Henderson was busy with the

tiller when she said to him, "Hart, I want you to do something more for me."

"You have only to tell me," he said.

"Have I only to tell you Hart?" she asked softly.

"Haven't you learned that yet, Edith?"

"I want you to go away."

"Very well," he said quietly, but his face whitened visibly.

"You say that as if you had been expecting it."

"I have. I knew from the beginning that when this was over you would dislike me for having seen you suffer. I have grown my Gethsemane in a full realization of what was coming, but I could not leave you, Edith, so long as it seemed to me that I was serving you. Does it make any difference to you where I go?"

"I want you where you will be loved, and good care taken of you."

"Thank you!" said Henderson, smiling grimly. "Have you any idea where such a spot might be found?"

'It should be with your sister at Los Angeles. She always has seemed very fond of you."

"That is quite true," said Henderson, his eyes brightening a little. "I will go to her. When shall I start?"

"At once."

Henderson began to tack for the landing, but his hands shook until he scarcely could manage the boat. Edith Carr sat watching him indifferently, but her heart was throbbing painfully. "Why is there so much suffering in the world?" she kept whispering to herself.

Inside her door Henderson took her by the shoulders almost roughly.

"For how long is this, Edith, and how are you going to say good-bye to me?"

She raised tired, pain-filled eyes to his.

"I don't know for how long it is," she said. "It seems now as if it had been a slow eternity. I wish to my soul that God would be merciful to me and make something 'snap' in my heart, as there did in Phil's, that would give me rest. I don't know for how long, but I'm perfectly shameless with you, Hart. If peace ever comes and I want you, I won't wait for you to find it out yourself, I'll cable, Marconigraph, anything. As for how I say good-bye; any way you please. I don't care in the least what happens to me."

Henderson studied her intently.

"In that case, we will shake hands," he said. "Good-bye, Edith. Don't forget that every hour I am thinking of you and hoping all good things will come to you soon."

CHAPTER 25

*Wherein Philip Finds Elnora, and
Edith Carr Offers a Yellow Emperor*

"OH, I need my own violin," cried Elnora. "This one may be a thousand times more expensive, and much older than mine; but it wasn't inspired and taught to sing by a man who knew how. It don't know 'beans,' as mother would say, about the Limberlost."

The guests in the O'More music room laughed appreciatively.

"Why don't you write your mother to come for a visit and bring yours?" suggested Freckles.

"I did that three days ago," acknowledged Elnora. "I am half expecting her on the noon boat. That is one reason why this violin gets worse every minute. There is nothing at all the matter with me."

"Splendid!" cried the Angel. "I've begged and begged her to do it. I know how anxious these mothers become. When did you send? What made you? Why didn't you tell me?"

"'When?' Three days ago. 'What made me?' You. 'Why didn't I tell you?' Because I can't be sure in the least that she will come. Mother is the most individual person. She never does what everyone expects

460

she will. She may not come, and I didn't want you to
be disappointed."

"How did I make you?" asked the Angel.

"Loving Alice. It made me realize that if you cared
for your girl like that, with Mr. O'More and three other
children, possibly my mother, with no one, might like
to see me. I know good and plenty I want to see her,
and you had told me to so often, I just sent for her. Oh,
I do hope she comes! I want her to see this lovely
place."

"I have been wondering what you thought of Mackinac," said Freckles.

"Oh, it is a perfect picture, all of it! I should like
to hang it on the wall, so I could see it whenever I wanted
to; but it isn't real, of course; it's nothing but a picture."

"These people won't agree with you," smiled Freckles.

"That isn't necessary," retorted Elnora. "They know
this, and they love it; but you and I are acquainted
with something different. The Limberlost is life. Here
it is a carefully kept park. You motor, sail, and golf,
all so secure and fine. But what I like is the excitement
of choosing a path carefully, in the fear that the quagmire may reach out and suck me down; to go into the
swamp naked-handed and wrest from it treasures that
bring me books and clothing, and I like enough of a
fight for things that I always remember how I got them.
I even enjoy seeing a canny old vulture eyeing me as
if it were saying, 'Ware the sting of the rattler, lest I
pick your bones as I did old Limber's.' I like sufficient

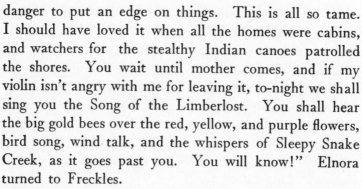

danger to put an edge on things. This is all so tame. I should have loved it when all the homes were cabins, and watchers for the stealthy Indian canoes patrolled the shores. You wait until mother comes, and if my violin isn't angry with me for leaving it, to-night we shall sing you the Song of the Limberlost. You shall hear the big gold bees over the red, yellow, and purple flowers, bird song, wind talk, and the whispers of Sleepy Snake Creek, as it goes past you. You will know!" Elnora turned to Freckles.

He nodded. "Who better?" he asked. "This is secure while the children are so small, but when they get larger, we are going farther north, into real forest, where they can learn self-reliance and develop backbone."

Elnora laid away the violin. "Come along, children," she said. "We must get at that backbone business at once. Let's race to the playhouse."

With the brood at her heels Elnora ran, and for an hour lively sounds stole from the remaining spot of forest on the Island, which lay beside the O'More cottage. Then Terry went to the playroom to bring Alice her doll. He came racing back, dragging it by one leg, and crying, "There's company! Someone has come that mamma and papa are just tearing down the house over. I saw through the window."

"It could not be my mother, yet," mused Elnora. "Her boat is not due until twelve. Terry, give Alice that doll ——"

"It's a man-person, and I don't know him, but my
father is shaking his hand right straight along, and my
mother is running for a hot drink and a cushion. It's
a kind of a sick person, but they are going to make
him well right away, anyone can see that! This is the
best place. I'll go tell him to come lie on the pine
needles in the sun and watch the sails go by. That will
fix him!"

"Watch sails go by," chanted Little Brother. "'At
fix him! Elnora fix him, won't you?"

"I don't know about that," answered Elnora. "What
sort of a looking person is he, Terry?"

"A beautiful white person; but my father is going to
'colour him up,' I heard him say so. He's just out of the
hospital, and he is a bad person, 'cause he ran away from
the doctors and made them awful angry. But father
and mother are going to doctor him better. I didn't
know they could make sick people well."

"'Ey do anyfing!" boasted Little Brother.

Before Elnora missed her, Alice, who had gone to
investigate, came flying across the shadows and through
the sunshine waving a paper. She thrust it into Elnora's
hand.

"There is a man-person — a stranger-person!" she
shouted. "But he knows you! He sent you that!
You are to be the doctor! He said so! Oh, do hurry!
I like him heaps!"

Elnora read Edith Carr's telegram to Philip Ammon
and understood that he had been ill, that she had been

463

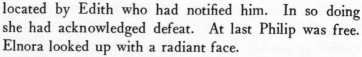

located by Edith who had notified him. In so doing
she had acknowledged defeat. At last Philip was free.
Elnora looked up with a radiant face.

"I like him 'heaps' myself!" she cried. "Come on,
children, we will go tell him so."

Terry and Alice ran, but Elnora had to suit her steps
to Little Brother, who was her loyal esquire, and would
have been heartbroken over desertion and insulted
at being carried. He was rather dragged, but he was
arriving, and the emergency was great, he could see that.

"She's coming!" shouted Alice.

"She's going to be the doctor!" cried Terry.

"She looked just like she'd seen angels when she
read the letter," explained Alice.

"She likes you 'heaps'! She said so!" danced Terry.
"Be waiting! Here she is!"

Elnora helped Little Brother up the steps, then deserted him and came at a rush. The stranger-person
stood holding out trembling arms.

"Are you sure, at last, runaway?" asked Philip
Ammon.

"Perfectly sure!" cried Elnora.

"Will you marry me now?"

"This instant! That is, any time after the noon
boat comes in."

"Why such unnecessary delay?" demanded Ammon.

"It is almost September," explained Elnora. "I
sent for mother three days ago. We must wait until
she comes, and we either have to send for Uncle Wesley

and Aunt Margaret, or go to them. I couldn't possibly be married properly without those dear people."

"We will send," decided Ammon. "The trip will be a treat for them. O'More, would you get off a message at once?"

Everyone met the noon boat. They went in the motor because Ammon was too weak to walk so far. As soon as people could be distinguished at all Elnora and Philip sighted an erect figure, with a head like a snowdrift. When the gang-plank fell the first person across it was a lean, red-haired boy of eleven, carrying a violin in one hand and an enormous bouquet of yellow marigolds and purple asters in the other. He was beaming with broad smiles until he saw Ammon. Then his expression changed.

"Aw, say!" he exclaimed reproachfully. "I bet you Aunt Margaret is right. He is going to be your beau!"

Elnora stooped to kiss Billy as she caught her mother.

"There, there!" cried Mrs. Comstock. "Don't knock my headgear into my eye. I'm not sure I've got either hat or hair. The wind blew like bizzem coming up the river."

She shook out her skirts, straightened her hat, and came forward to meet Philip, who took her into his arms and kissed her repeatedly. Then he passed her along to Freckles and the Angel to whom her greetings were mingled with scolding and laughter over her wind-blown hair.

"No doubt I'm a precious spectacle!" she said to the

Angel. "I saw your pa a little before I started, and he sent you a note. It's in my satchel. He said he was coming up next week. What a lot of people there are in this world! And what on earth are all of them laughing about? Did none of them ever hear of sickness, or sorrow, or death? Billy, don't you go to playing Indian or chasing woodchucks until you get out of those clothes. I promised Margaret I'd bring back that suit good as new."

Then the O'More children came crowding to meet Elnora's mother.

"Merry Christmas!" cried Mrs. Comstock, gathering them in. "Got everything right here but the tree, and there seems to be plenty of them a little higher up. If this wind would stiffen just enough more to blow away the people, so one could see this place, I believe it would be right decent looking."

"See here," whispered Elnora to Ammon. "You must fix this with Billy. I can't have his trip spoiled."

"Now, here is where I dust the rest of 'em!" complacently remarked Mrs. Comstock, as she climbed into the motor car for her first ride, in company with Ammon and Little Brother. "I have been the one to trudge the roads and hop out of the way of these things for quite a spell."

She sat very erect as the car rolled into the broad main avenue, where only stray couples were walking. Her eyes began to twinkle and gleam. Suddenly she leaned forward and touched the driver on the shoulder.

"Young man," she said, "just you toot that whistle suddenly and shave close enough a few of those people, so that I can see how I look when I leap for ragweed and snake fences."

The amazed chauffeur glanced questioningly at Ammon, who slightly nodded. A second later there was a quick "honk!" and a swerve at a corner. A man engrossed in conversation grabbed the woman to whom he was talking and dashed for the safety of a lawn. The woman tripped in her skirts, and as she fell the man caught and dragged her. Both of them turned red faces to the car and berated the driver. Mrs. Comstock laughed in unrestrained enjoyment. Then she touched the chauffeur again.

"That's enough," she said. "It seems a mite risky." A minute later she added to Ammon, "If only they had been carrying six pounds of butter and ten dozen eggs apiece, wouldn't that have been just perfect?"

Billy had wavered between Elnora and the motor, but his loyal little soul had been true to her, so the walk to the cottage began with him at her side. Long before they arrived the little O'Mores had crowded around and captured Billy, and he was giving them an expurgated version of Mrs. Comstock's tales of Big Foot and Adam Poe, boasting that Uncle Wesley had been in the camps of Me-shin-go-me-sia and knew Wa-ca-co-nah before he got religion and dressed like white men; while the mighty prowess of Snap as a woodchuck hunter was done full justice. When they reached the cottage

467

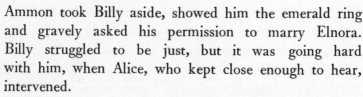

Ammon took Billy aside, showed him the emerald ring and gravely asked his permission to marry Elnora. Billy struggled to be just, but it was going hard with him, when Alice, who kept close enough to hear, intervened.

"Why don't you let them get married?" she asked. "You are much too small for her. You wait for me!"

Billy studied her intently. At last he turned to Ammon. "Aw, well! Go on, then!" he said gruffly. "I'll marry Alice!"

Alice reached her hand. "If you got that settled let's put on our Indian clothes, get the boys, and go to the playhouse."

"I haven't got any Indian clothes," said Billy ruefully.

"Yes, you have," explained Alice. "Father got you some coming from the dock. You can put them on in the playhouse. The boys do."

Billy examined the playhouse with gleaming eyes. Never had he encountered such possibilities. He could see a hundred amusing things to try, and he could not decide which to do first. The most immediate attraction seemed to be a dead pine, held perpendicularly by its fellows, while its bark had decayed and fallen, leaving a bare, smooth trunk.

"If we just had some grease that would make the dandiest pole to play Fourth of July with!" he shouted.

The children remembered the Fourth. It had been great fun.

"Butter is grease. There is plenty in the 'frigerator,'" suggested Alice speeding away.

Billy caught the cold roll and began to rub it against the tree excitedly.

"How are you going to get it greased to the top?" inquired Terry.

Billy's face lengthened. "That's so!" he said. "The thing is to begin at the top and grease down. I'll show you!"

Billy put the butter in his handkerchief and took the corners between his teeth. He climbed the pole, greasing it as he slid down.

"Now, I got to try first," he said, "because I'm the biggest and so I have the best chance; only the one that goes first hasn't hardly any chance at all, because he has to wipe off the grease on himself, so the others can get up at last. See?"

"All right!" said Terry. "You go first and then I will, and then Alice. Phew! It's slick. He'll never get up."

Billy wrestled manfully, and when he was exhausted he boosted Terry, and then both of them helped Alice, to whom they awarded a prize of her own doll. As they rested Billy remembered.

"Do your folks keep cows?" he asked.

"No, we buy milk," said Terry.

"Gee! Then what about the butter? Maybe your ma needs it for dinner!"

"No, she don't!" cried Alice. "There's stacks of it! I can have all the butter I want."

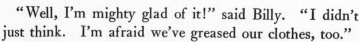

"Well, I'm mighty glad of it!" said Billy. "I didn't just think. I'm afraid we've greased our clothes, too."

"That's no difference," said Terry. "We can play what we please in these things."

"Well, we ought to be all dirty, and bloody, and have feathers on us to be real Indians," said Billy.

Alice tried a handful of dirt on her sleeve and it streaked beautifully. Instantly all of them began smearing themselves.

"If we only had feathers," lamented Billy.

Terry disappeared and shortly returned from the garage with a feather duster. Billy fell on it with a shriek. Around each one's head he firmly tied a twisted handkerchief, and stuck inside it a row of stiffly upstanding feathers.

"Now, if we just only had some pokeberries to paint us red, we'd be real, for sure enough Indians, and we could go on the war path and fight all the other tribes and burn a lot of them at the stake."

Alice sidled up to him. "Would huckleberries do?" she asked softly.

"Yes!" shouted Terry, wild with excitement. "Anything that's a colour!"

Alice made another trip to the refrigerator. Billy crushed the berries in his hands and smeared and streaked all their faces liberally.

"Now are we ready?" asked Alice.

Billy collapsed. "I forgot the ponies! You got to ride ponies to go on the war path!"

"You ain't neither!" contradicted Terry. "It's the very latest style to go on the warpath in a motor. Everybody does! They go everywhere in them. They are much faster and better than any old ponies."

Billy gave one genuine whoop. "Can we take your motor?"

Terry hesitated.

"I suppose you are too little to run it?" said Billy.

"I am not!" flashed Terry. "I know how to start and stop it, and I drive lots for Stephens. It is hard to turn over the engine when you start."

"I'll turn it," volunteered Billy. "I'm strong as anything."

"Maybe it will start without. If Stephens has just been running it, sometimes it will. Come on, let's try."

Billy straightened up, lifted his chin and cried, "Houpe! Houpe! Houpe!"

The little O'Mores stared in amazement.

"Why don't you come on and whoop?" demanded Billy. "Don't you know how? You are great Indians! You got to whoop before you go on the warpath. You ought to kill a bat, too, and see if the wind is right. But maybe the engine won't run if we wait to do that. You can whoop, anyway. All together now!"

They did whoop, and after several efforts the cry satisfied Billy, so he led the way to the big motor, and took the front seat with Terry. Alice and Little Brother took the back.

"Will it go?" asked Billy, "or do we have to turn it?"

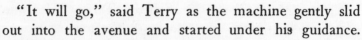

"It will go," said Terry as the machine gently slid out into the avenue and started under his guidance.

"This is no warpath!" scoffed Billy. "We got to go a lot faster than this, and we got to whoop. Alice, why don't you whoop?"

Alice arose, took hold of the seat in front and whooped.

"If I open the throttle, I can't squeeze the bulb to scare people out of our way," said Terry. "I can't steer and squeeze, too."

"We'll whoop enough to get them out of the way. Go faster!" urged Billy.

Billy also stood, lifted his chin and whooped like the wildest little savage that ever came out of the West. Alice and Little Brother added their voices, and when he was not absorbed with the steering gear, Terry joined in.

"Faster!" shouted Billy.

Intoxicated with the speed and excitement, Terry threw the throttle wider and the big car leaped forward and shot down the avenue. In it four black, feather-bedecked children whooped in wild glee until suddenly Terry's war cry changed to a scream of panic.

"The lake is coming!"

"Stop!" cried Billy. "Stop! Why don't you stop?"

Paralyzed with fear Terry clung to the steering gear and the car sped onward.

"You little fool! Why don't you stop?" screamed Billy catching Terry's arm. "Tell me how to stop!"

A bicycle shot along beside them and Freckles standing

on the pedals shouted, "Pull out the pin in that little circle at your feet!"

Billy fell on his knees and tugged and the pin yielded at last. Just as the wheels struck the white sand the bicycle sheered close, Freckles caught the lever and with one strong shove set the brake. The water flew as the car struck Huron, but luckily it was shallow and the beach smooth. Hub deep the big motor stood quivering as Freckles climbed in and backed it to dry sand.

Then he drew a deep breath and stared at his brood.

"Terrence, would you kindly be explaining?" he said at last.

Billy looked at the panting little figure of Terry.

"I guess I better," he said. "We were playing Indians on the warpath, and we hadn't any ponies, and Terry said it was all the style to go in automobiles now, so we ——"

Freckles's head went back, and he did some whooping himself.

"I wonder if you realize how nearly you came to being four drowned children?" he said gravely, after a time.

"Oh, I think I could swim enough to get most of us out," said Billy. "Anyway, we need washing."

"You do indeed," said Freckles. "I will head this procession to the garage, and there we will remove the first coat." For the remainder of Billy's visit the nurse, chauffeur, and every servant of the O'More household had something of importance on their minds, and Billy's every step was shadowed.

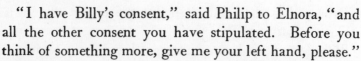

"I have Billy's consent," said Philip to Elnora, "and all the other consent you have stipulated. Before you think of something more, give me your left hand, please."

Elnora gave it gladly, and the emerald slipped on her finger. Then they went together into the forest to tell each other all about it, and talk it over.

"Have you seen Edith?" asked Ammon.

"No," answered Elnora, "but she must be here, or she may have seen me when we went to Petosky a few days ago. Her people have a cottage over on the bluff, but the Angel never told me until to-day. I didn't want to make that trip, but the folks were so anxious to entertain me, and it was only a few days until I intended to let you know myself where I was."

"And I was going to wait just that long, and if I didn't hear then I was getting ready to turn over the country. I can scarcely realize yet that Edith sent me that telegram."

"No wonder! It's a difficult thing to believe. I can't express how I feel for her."

"Let us never again speak of it," said Ammon. "I came nearer feeling sorry for her last night than I have yet. I couldn't sleep on that boat coming over, and I couldn't put away the thought of what sending that message cost her. I never would have believed it possible that she would do it. But it is done. We will forget it."

"I scarcely think I shall," said Elnora. "It is the sort of thing I like to remember. How suffering must

474

have changed her! I would give a great deal to bring her peace."

"Henderson came to see me at the hospital a few days ago. He's gone a pretty wild pace, but if he had been held from youth by the love of a good woman he might have lived differently. There are things about him one cannot help admiring."

"I think he loves her," said Elnora softly.

"He does! He always has! He never made any secret of it. He will cut in now and do his level best, but he told me that he thought she would send him away. He understands her thoroughly."

Edith Carr did not understand herself. She went to her room after her good-bye to Henderson, lay on her bed and tried to think why she was suffering as she was.

"It is all my selfishness, my unrestrained temper, my pride in my looks, my ambition to be first," she said. "That is what has caused this trouble."

Then she went deeper.

"How does it happen that I am so selfish, that I never controlled my temper, that I thought beauty and social position the vital things of life?" she muttered. "I think that goes a little past me. I think a mother who allows a child to grow up as I did, who educates it only for the frivolities of life, has a share in that child's ending. I think my mother has some responsibility in this," Edith Carr whispered to the night. "But she will recognize none. She would laugh at me if I tried to tell her what I have suffered and the bitter, bitter lesson I have learned.

No one really cares, but Hart. I've sent him away, so there is no one! No one!"

Edith pressed her fingers across her burning eyes and lay still.

"He is gone!" she whispered at last. "He would go at once. He would not see me again. I should think he never would want to see me any more. But I will want to see him! My soul! I want him now! I want him every minute! He is all I have. And I've sent him away. Oh, these dreadful days to come, alone! I can't bear it. Hart! Hart!" she cried aloud. "I want you! No one cares but you. No one understands but you. Oh, I want you!"

She sprang from her bed and felt her way to her desk.

"Get me someone at the Henderson cottage," she said to Central, and waited shivering.

"They don't answer."

"They are there! You must get them. Turn on the buzzer."

After a time the sleepy voice of Mrs. Henderson answered.

"Has Hart gone?" panted Edith Carr.

"No! He came in late and began to talk about starting to California. He hasn't slept in weeks to amount to anything. I put him to bed. There is time enough to start to California when he wakens. Edith, what are you planning to do next with that boy of mine?"

"Will you tell him I want to see him before he goes?"

"Yes, but I won't wake him."

"I don't want you to.   Just tell him in the morning."

"Very well."

"You will be sure?"

"Sure!"

Hart was not gone.   Edith fell asleep.   She arose at noon the next day, took a cold bath, ate her breakfast, dressed carefully, and leaving word that she had gone to the forest, she walked slowly across the leaves.   It was cool and quiet there, so she sat where she could see him coming, and waited.   She was thinking hard and fast.

Henderson came swiftly down the path.   A long sleep, food, and Edith's message had done him good.   He had dressed in new light flannels that were becoming.   Edith arose and went to meet him.

"Let us walk in the forest," she said.

They passed the old Catholic graveyard, and went back into the deepest wood of the Island.   Back where all shadows were green, all voices of humanity ceased, and there was no sound save the whispering of the trees, a few bird notes and squirrel rustle.   There Edith seated herself on a mossy old log, and Henderson studied her.   He could detect a change.   She was still pale and her eyes tired, but the dull, strained look was gone.   He wanted to hope, but he did not dare.   Any other man would have forced her to speak.   The mighty tenderness in Henderson's heart shielded her in every way.

"What have you thought of that you wanted yet,

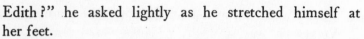

Edith?" he asked lightly as he stretched himself at her feet.

"You!"

Henderson lay tense and very still.

"Well, I am here!"

"Thank Heaven for that!"

Henderson sat up suddenly, leaning toward her with questioning eyes. Not knowing what he dared say, afraid of the hope which found birth in his heart, he tried to shield her and at the same time to feel his way.

"I am more thankful than I can express that you feel so," he said. "I would be of use, of comfort, to you if I knew how, Edith."

"You are my only comfort," she said. "I tried to send you away. I thought I didn't want you. I thought I couldn't bear the sight of you, because of what you have seen me suffer. But I went to the root of this thing last night, Hart, and with self in mind, as usual, I found that I could not live without you."

Henderson began breathing lightly. He was afraid to speak or move.

"I faced the fact that all this is my own fault," continued Edith, "and came through my own selfishness. Then I went further back and realized that I am as I was reared. I don't want to blame my parents, but I was carefully trained into what I am. If Elnora Comstock had been like me, Phil would have come back to me. I can see how selfish I look to him, and how I appear to you, if you would admit it."

"Edith," said Henderson desperately, "there is no use to try to deceive you. You have known from the first that I found you wrong in this. But it's the first time in your life I ever thought you wrong about anything — and it's the only time I ever will. Understand, I think you the bravest, most beautiful woman on earth, the one most worth loving."

"I'm not to be considered in the same class with her."

"I don't grant that, but if I did, you must remember how I compare with Phil. He's my superior at every point. There's no use in discussing that. You wanted to see me, Edith. What did you want?"

"I didn't want you to go away."

"Not at all?"

"Not at all! Not ever! Not unless you take me with you, Hart."

She slightly extended one hand to him. Henderson took that hand, kissing it again and again.

"Anything you want, Edith," he said brokenly. "Just as you wish it. Do you want me to stay here, and go on as we have been?"

"Yes, only with a difference."

"Can you tell me, Edith?"

"First, I want you to know that you are the dearest thing on earth to me, right now. I would give up everything else, before I would you. I can't honestly say that I love you with the love you deserve. My heart is too sore. It's too soon to know. But I love you some way. You are necessary to me. You are my comfort,

479

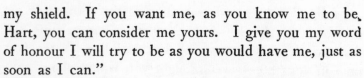

my shield. If you want me, as you know me to be, Hart, you can consider me yours. I give you my word of honour I will try to be as you would have me, just as soon as I can."

Henderson kissed her hand passionately. "Don't, Edith," he begged. "Don't say those things. I can't bear it. I understand. Everything will come right in time. Love like mine must bring a reward. You will love me some day. I can wait. I am the most patient fellow."

"But I must say it," cried Edith. "I — I think, Hart, that I have been on the wrong road to find happiness. I planned to finish life as I started it with Phil; and you see how glad he was to change. He wanted the other sort of girl far more than he ever wanted me. And you, Hart, honest, now — I'll know if you don't tell me the truth! Would you rather have a wife as I planned to live life with Phil, or would you rather have her as Elnora Comstock intends to live with him?"

"Edith!" cried the man, "Edith!"

"Of course, you can't say it in plain English," said the girl. "You are far too chivalrous for that. You needn't say anything. I am answered. If you could have your choice you wouldn't have a society wife, either. In your heart you'd like the smaller home of comfort, the furtherance of your ambitions, the palatable meals regularly served, and little children around you. I am sick of all we have grown up to, Hart. When your hour of trouble comes, there is no comfort for you. I am tired to death. You find out what you want to do, and be, that is a man's work in the world, and I will plan our home, with no thought save your comfort. I'll be the other kind of a girl, as fast as I can learn. I can't correct all my faults in one day, but I'll change as rapidly as I can."

"God knows, I will be different, too, Edith. You shall not be the only generous one. I will make all the rest of life worthy of you. I will change, too!"

"Don't you dare!" said Edith Carr, taking his head between her hands and holding it against her knees, while the tears slid down her cheeks. "Don't you dare change, you big-hearted, splendid lover! I am little and selfish. You are the very finest, just as you are!"

Henderson was not talking then, so they sat through a long silence. At last he heard Edith draw a quick breath, and lifting his head he looked where she pointed. Up a fern stalk climbed a curious looking object. They watched breathlessly. By lavender feet clung a big, pursy, lavender-splotched, yellow body. Yellow and lavender wings began to expand and take on colour. Every instant great beauty became more apparent. It was one of those double-brooded freaks, which do occur on rare occasions, or merely an Eacles Imperialis moth that in the cool damp northern forest had failed to emerge in June. Edith Carr drew back with a long, shivering breath. Henderson caught her hands and gripped them firmly. Steadily she looked the thought of her heart into his eyes.

"By all the powers, you shall not!" swore the man. "You have done enough. I will smash that thing!"

"Oh, no, you won't!" cried the girl, clinging to his hands. "I am not big enough yet, Hart, but before I leave this forest I shall have grown to breadth and strength to carry that to her. She needs two of each kind. Phil only got her one!"

"Edith I can't bear it! That's not demanded! Let me take it!"

"You may go with me. I know where the O'Mores' cottage is. I have been there often."

"I'll say you sent it!"

"You may watch me deliver it!"

"Phil may be there by now."

"I hope he is! I should like him to see me do one decent thing by which to remember me."

"I tell you that is not necessary!"

"'Not necessary!'" cried the girl, her great eyes shining. "Not necessary? Then what on earth is the thing doing here? I just have boasted that I would change, that I would be like her, that I would grow bigger and broader. As the words are spoken God gives me the opportunity to prove whether I am sincere. This is my test, Hart! Don't you see it? If I am big enough to carry that to her, you will believe that there is some good in me. You will not be loving me in vain. This is an especial Providence, man! Be my strength! Help me, as you always have done!"

Henderson arose and shook the leaves from his clothing.

He drew Edith Carr to her feet and carefully picked the mosses from her skirts.   He went down to the water and moistened his handkerchief to bathe her face.

"Now a dust of powder," he said when the tears were washed away.

From a tiny book Edith tore leaves that she passed over her face.

"All gone!" cried Henderson, critically eyeing her. "You look almost half as lovely as you really are!"

Edith Carr drew a wavering breath.   She stretched one hand to him.

"Hold tight, Hart!" she said.   "I know they handle these things, but I would quite as soon touch a snake."

Henderson clenched his teeth and held steadily.   The moth had emerged too recently to be troublesome.   It climbed on her fingers quietly and obligingly clung there without moving.   So hand in hand they went down the dark forest path.   But when they came to the avenue, the first person they met paused with an ejaculation of wonder.   The next stopped also, and everyone following. They could make little progress on account of marvelling, interested people.   A strange excitement took possession of Edith.   She began to feel proud of the creature.

"Do you know," she said to Henderson, "this is growing easier every step.   Its clinging is not disagreeable, as I thought it would be.   I feel as if I were saving it, protecting it.   I am proud that we are taking it to be put into a collection or a book.   It seems like doing a thing worth while.   Oh, Hart, I wish we could work together

at something for which people would care as they seem
to for this. Hear what they say! See them lift their
little children to look at it!"

"Edith, if you don't stop," said Henderson, "I will
take you in my arms and kiss the face half off you, here
on the avenue. You are adorable!"

"Don't you dare!" laughed Edith Carr. The colour
rushed to her cheeks and a new light leaped in her eyes.

"Oh, Hart!" she cried. "Let's work! Let's do
something! That's the way she makes people love her
so. There's the place, and, thank goodness, there is a
crowd."

"You darling!" whispered Henderson as they passed
up the walk. Her face was rose-flushed with excitement
and her eyes shone.

"Hello, everyone!" she cried as she came on the wide
veranda. "Only see what we found up in the forest!
We thought you might like to have it for some of your
collections."

She held out the moth as she walked straight to Elnora,
who arose to meet her, crying, "How perfectly splendid!
I don't even know how to begin to thank you."

Elnora took the moth. Edith shook hands with all
of them and asked Philip if he were improving. She
said a few polite words to Freckles and the Angel, declined to remain on account of an engagement, and went
away, gracefully.

"Well, bully for her!" said Mrs. Comstock. "She's
a little thoroughbred after all!"

"That was a mighty big thing for her to be doing," said Freckles in a hushed voice.

"If you knew her as well as I do," said Philip Ammon, "you would have a better conception of what that cost."

"It was a terror!" cried the Angel. "I never could have done it."

"'Never could have done it!'" echoed Freckles. "Why, Angel, dear, that is the one thing of all the world you would have done!"

"I have to take care of this," faltered Elnora, hurrying for the door to hide the tears which were rolling down her cheeks.

"I must help," said Ammon disappearing also. "Elnora," he called, catching up with her, "take me where I can cry, too. Wasn't she great?"

"Superb!" exclaimed Elnora. "I have no words. I feel so humbled!"

"So do I," said Ammon. "I think a great deed like that always makes one feel so. Now are you happy?"

"Unspeakably happy!" answered Elnora.